Love in Carson Falls

PAISLEIGH AUMACK

April,

Always trust in the magic of new beginnings.
thanks for the support
and hope you enjoy!.

xoxo

Darby
Auk
or
Kari Nappi

First Edition:

Ebook ISBN-13: 978-0-9991411-0-6

Print ISBN-13: 978-0-9991411-1-3

Editor Joanne Thompson

Proofreader Karen Hrdlicka

Formatting: CP Smith

Cover Design: Cassy Roop with Pink Ink DesignsCover Photographs: Shutterstock.com, depositphotos.com

Information address: authorpaisleighaumack@gmail.com

ACKNOWLEDGEMENTS

I would like to start this off by giving thanks to my mom, Lynn. Without her constant and consistent unconditional love, guidance, and support, I never would have realized exactly what it meant to follow your dreams. Thank you will never be enough for being a double parent for most of my life. I love you.

To the very best man I know, Matt. Your love has made me come alive. You saved me when I had lost all hope in love and life and helped me to hear the music again. Throughout every up and down we have had, your support and encouragement will always be a driving force to finish everything I start in life. You are the River to my Arianna. I love you so much more than I could ever write. Thank you for all you give me.

Les. My Lesssy. This would never have happened without you. I couldn't have asked for a better friend, partner, and assistant. You always knew what I needed and what to say to whip me into shape. Writing is a piece of your soul and sometimes you doubt what you do but you never doubted me for a second. You were always able to let me sink just enough under the surface of the water so that I could feel that, vent it out to you, and grab your hand to be pulled back up. I need you by my side for as long as and wherever this journey is going. You are stuck with me and my crazy no matter how much you want to strangle me sometimes. I have loved this adventure with you and I love you so much!

To my betas. Les Crane, Kristi Lynn, Crystal Solis, Shanna Blanton, TD Ross, Angel Gallentine Lee, Jaye Mae, Di Anne Sandvik, Lee Ann Kanowsky, Stephanie Renae Evans, and Delaney Foster. Your insight and contributions to make this story the best it can be were so incredible. Your messages made me laugh, while some made me cry. I could not have had a better team. Thank you so much.

Noey, Jami, Delaney, CP, and every single author friend who has helped me, mentored in some way, let me sound off, or even just shared a teaser, the bond and admiration I have for each of you is never-ending. Thank you so much for being in my life and all your words of wisdom. This ride has been a lot less bumpy with you by my side.

Thank you to my amazing cover designer, Cassy Roop. She took what I envisioned and brought it to life. I love your work and can't say enough about how much I love this cover.

Thank you to my editing team for taking my words and polishing them. Without you, it's just a jumbled mess.

Thank you to my friend and formatter, Teeny. You are amazing and I adore you so much! Thank you for making my book baby beautiful. You went above what anyone should have had to to help me and I will never ever forget it.

To every reader and blogger who takes the time to read my words, THANK YOU! Without you, people like me would not be able to do what we love and crave. There isn't enough space or time to list every single one of you, but please know, I see you and thank you from the bottom of my heart.

Chickens4Life. You were there before I officially even set any idea down on paper. My life is not the same since we met and I couldn't have picked better friends or support system. You girls allow me to be myself no matter what form that comes in. There is just no better way to be. Thank you for your persistent support and your unwavering honesty. It is truly immeasurable what you girls mean to me.

Last but certainly not least, to my dad in heaven. The short time we had together on this earth, left me with some of the most important life lessons. I know you wanted me to chase every dream I had, but really go after the ones I could catch. You wanted the best for your little girl and for me to be as happy as I can be no matter what life throws at me. You were the example set forth for the father River was. You and Mom showed me what real, unconditional love is. Thank you for always being the wind beneath my wings allowing me to fly.

To two Chickens and a Panda.
My life is incomplete without you.
I could not ask for better friends.
I love you girls so much.

Love in Carson Falls

with the phone in hand, I dialed 911.

"911. What's your emergency?" the dispatcher asked.

"I need an ambulance. Please hurry. I'm pregnant." Those were the final words I remember speaking before I passed out.

Three days later…

I woke up to blinding, bright lights flooding through the slits of my swollen and bruised eyes. I could vaguely comprehend that I was in a hospital by the beeping from the machines and the tube in my nose. Still groggy, confusion clouded my mind. I felt like I needed to move. I attempted to pull the covers off me, but a nurse rushed in at that moment and stopped me.

"Sweetheart, you shouldn't be moving like that. You need to stay still so you don't injure yourself further and can heal," the nurse said to me with knowing eyes.

"What happened to my baby?" I asked her in a raspy voice, throat dry to the point of pain, completely desperate for the information. But I knew. I could feel the hollowness from the loss already, and the way the nurse was looking at me confirmed that empty feeling.

"You'll need to wait for the doctor, honey. He should be in shortly to see you, now that you're awake. You've been in and out of consciousness for three days, so he needs to check you over," she told me as she squeezed my hand before shuffling out the door.

I lay back and stared at the ceiling. My mind consumed with thoughts of what my little boy would have looked like. I was almost five months along, but no one would have known that. I barely had a noticeable bump, or at least that was what I kept telling myself when my clothes started to no longer fit. And I'd just found out the baby's gender the week before this nightmare occurred. As much as I didn't want to think it, I wondered if losing this baby was the best thing in this situation. It didn't matter. Nothing mattered now.

The doctor came in, startling me from my thoughts. He was a middle-aged, tall man with dark hair and kind, light brown eyes. He approached me, and I knew what was coming.

"Ms. Morgan, my name is Doctor Shaw. How are you feeling today?" he asked as he flipped through the chart in his hands. He looked at me as I started to speak.

"My body feels like it's been through a cheese grater. Every time I take a breath, I feel like I'm being stabbed in my sides. But I'm more worried about my baby. Can you please tell me about my baby?" I pleaded. I didn't want to accept that this nightmare was real.

"I'm so sorry, Ms. Morgan. We were not able to save your baby. We did an ultrasound to confirm and were not able to locate a heartbeat. Your baby was stillborn upon arrival. We had to do a dilation and evacuation procedure, or what is more commonly known as a D&E, due to the amount of bleeding you presented with when you got here," he answered. As he continued to go over the extent of my injuries, I just lay there completely and utterly numb. I whispered back a question because I needed to know if this was it for me.

"My injuries…will I ever be able to have children after this?" I asked as sobs wrenched from my chest.

"Ms. Morgan. If there is any good news or a silver lining in this nightmare that I can give you, I am happy to say that yes, you can. The scarring post-procedure seems to be minimal and shouldn't hinder your efforts at becoming a mom later on down the road should you choose to conceive. He took a lot from you, but not that."

Shortly after the doctor left, two uniformed officers entered the room. After a series of questions and paperwork, they assured me that Andrew would be caught and brought to justice for this. They explained to me that while they would do everything in their power to find him, I needed to find a safe place to go. Were they kidding? There was no place here where Andrew couldn't find me. I needed to leave Seattle. Even if they arrested him, he had more than enough money to post bail. It would only be a matter of time before he was out and he would stop at nothing to find me. By the time the police left, I realized that the life I knew, was over.

Seven days later…

4

After being released from the hospital, I received a police escort to the house. I couldn't risk being alone and Andrew being at the house when I got there. I couldn't work up the nerve to call our friends to tell them what had happened or that I was leaving because they would never believe Andrew had done something like this. The worst part was, I felt like this was partially my fault because I had been covering up the abuse all these years. Maybe it was sheer blind weakness, but I stayed with him even after the first time he raised a hand to me. This was the result of that weakness. The cops say I'm one of the lucky ones because he didn't succeed in killing me. Right now, I wished he had. There were teams of policemen still looking for Andrew but, by all accounts, they were almost positive that he had fled the state or was in some type of safe house somewhere.

On the ride home, I felt the anxiety building inside of me. I had no idea what I would do if I came face-to-face with Andrew; I felt nauseous, and my mind was racing through various scenarios. All I wanted to do was get my things and get out. I pulled out my cell phone and made the call that would hopefully save my life. I needed to get as far away from here as possible, and I knew that I would have to go somewhere he couldn't find me. I would have been naïve to think that he would let me walk away and live. He would find me if I stayed here, and he would kill me.

As the police cruiser pulled up in front of the house that had now become my living hell, I was relieved to see that Andrew was nowhere in sight. In the back of my mind, I guess I thought he would show up even if the cops hadn't found him and there were no leads yet. I knew this was my only window of opportunity to finally escape him before it was too late.

Rushing into the house the best I could without wincing in pain, I surveyed the damage from our fight that night. The glass coffee table in the living room was shattered where Andrew had tossed me onto it, my body still baring the cuts from the jagged pieces. All of our picture frames that once lined the walls, categorizing a much happier time, now lay in disarray on the floor. We had been together for just about seven years. We never married, but we did live together, so most of the furnishings and memories that were here, were shared between us. Although, most of the memories I could do without. Andrew had been my first serious relationship after college. I was performing at a concert sponsored by his office; I had been a part of the Seattle Philharmonic Orchestra for about three years. Once Andrew became a part of my life, music had no place in it anymore and, little by little, I lost all sense of who I once was.

With the police officers standing guard by the front door, I made my way to the bedroom and froze when I saw the blood stains covering the floor. My chest began to heave, my heart began to race, and I had to steady myself with a hand against the wall. The trail leading over to the nightstand brought back the horror I experienced ten nights ago. Collecting myself enough to get this done, I moved to the closet, grabbed my luggage set, and rushed to collect what I could of my belongings. When I stepped into the bathroom to get what I needed from there, I caught my reflection in the mirror. Stunned by the marks left behind from the brutal assault, I stood there staring at someone completely unrecognizable. How did I let it get this far? Why wasn't I strong enough to leave?

Making my last trek through this hellhole, I stopped at the doorway and took one last look around before I walked out of that house, leaving the only life I had ever known. I pulled up the handle on my suitcase and rolled it out to the police cruiser that was waiting by the curb, ready to take me to the bus station to begin my journey to my safe haven.

Chapter 1

Carson Falls
Arianna

The bus smelled like old moth balls, mildew, and sweat. The interior was stained from years of caked-on foot traffic and spills. It was evident that many secrets had passed through the seats of the old Greyhound. It would be keeping my secrets, too.

From Seattle, the trip wound up taking just over two days. The driver took the Northern route with the fewest drop-off stops along the way. The first state we pulled into was Montana. I had read that Montana housed the largest grizzly bear population in the United States, so I wasn't shocked at the 'Beware of the Bears' warnings attached to all the fences surrounding the station. We only stayed at that stop for twenty minutes which was not enough time to even catch a glimpse of one grizzly in the woods behind the terminal. The driver headed back out to the bus and announced that we wouldn't be stopping again for another seven hours or so.

I spent the next six-and-a-half hours trying to coordinate with Penny on where she was picking me up. Once I was finally able to get a stable cell signal on my pay-as-you-go phone through the mountains and solidify the plans with her, the bus arrived at the next stop in Wisconsin. When I stepped outside, I took in my surroundings and noticed the sign that boasted 'Home of the Ice Cream Sundae' right across the road. I knew that Wisconsin was home to the Mustard Museum, but had no idea the state could claim the ice cream sundae as well. I was one of those people that knew random facts about even more random things, so it interested me. After wandering away from the other passengers who also got off the bus to move around, I snapped a picture of the sign with my camera. When we were ready to board, and hit the road again, it was announced that this time we were driving straight through to the final stop.

It had only been ten days and I was exhausted trying to smile at the folks on the bus and make small talk. I tried to stare out the window for most of the trip, but sooner or later I needed to interact. I couldn't hide the bruises and didn't try. No one had asked any questions, and I was grateful for that.

When the Greyhound pulled into the bus station in Carson Falls, Tennessee, around eight a.m. Thursday, I stared in shock out the window. What I saw, couldn't have been real. The Greyhound terminal looked like it had magically jumped off a Hallmark card. Benches lined the front of the brown brick building and gas street lamps were lit along the pathway leading to the parking lot. I stood but almost lost my balance. Sitting in a cramped seat for that long, wreaked havoc on my battered and sore body, but I was just too exhausted to register the pain. I painstakingly reached into the packed overhead compartment, pulled my suitcase down, since I didn't put it with the rest of the other passengers' luggage, and picked up my carry-on bag. The only possessions I had were in there, and I wasn't willing to chance losing all I had left. The driver understood, and I am assuming wouldn't have argued anyway because of my face. I popped up the handle and headed toward the exit.

As I stepped down onto the cobblestone sidewalk, I caught sight of Penny at the far corner of the lot standing outside her car, searching for me. I lifted my arm as far as it would go so she could see that I saw her; the left over aches and pains hindering my full range of motion.

She pushed off the white Nissan Altima and headed my way to meet me. When she got to me, I stopped, brought my black roller suitcase up next to me, and set my purse on top of it so my arms were free to wrap around the friend I hadn't seen in what felt like forever. I warned her to be gentle because I still had pain, and she immediately let go. Penny stepped back and looked me over from top to toe, and as she took in the remnants of that night, tears welled up in her gorgeous blue eyes. My tears were already streaming down my face before her first one fell over the curve of her cheek. I grabbed her and hugged her again. We stood there and sobbed on each other's shoulders for what seemed like an eternity. Once the tears were spent, Penny grabbed my bags, loaded my stuff in the trunk, and drove us to her apartment.

Penelope Sloane was my best friend, but I have always called her Penny. We met at The Juilliard School in New York City. Penny was briefly a drama major, and I was a music major. My concentration was in classical piano composition. I wanted to compose and perform an overture for the New York Philharmonic. Penny wanted to go to Hollywood and be a famous actress or director when we first started school. She had a flare for the dramatic since the first day I met her, so I was shocked when she decided to become a teacher after the first year of college.

We met on Move-in Day, my Aunt Claire and I had rented a van to transport all my stuff to my dorm. Before you could actually move into the dorm, you had to stop at a table to check yourself in. I had just placed the pen down after signing in and was bumped from behind. I turned and saw this girl dressed in jeans torn at the knees, a t-shirt that said 'When You Kiss Your Boyfriend…Let Me Know How I Taste', brown cowboy boots, chocolate brown hair with flecks of copper that reached her mid-back, and the bluest eyes I had ever seen. She smiled at me and said in a twang, "Sorry for bumpin' ya, Darlin'. I'm Penny. Hope this isn't the last I see that face, ya hear?" Then she winked at me, yes winked, then turned and walked to her stuff that she had stacked by the curb. I just giggled to myself because her accent was sweet, and she had that shirt on. It all told me that she might be a little crazy, but exactly what I needed.

I walked back to my aunt to see her eyes wide, staring at Penny's shirt as Penny walked by her. I giggled again because seriously, that shirt was awesome and totally in your face. I should have known that day what I was in for with Penny. But her personality was something I don't think I ever saw coming. I was shy and not very outgoing, while Penny could approach anyone and ask for anything. When I looked in the direction my Aunt Claire was still staring, I saw Penny looking back at us, and she smiled. That was the day I found my best friend, and I am so beyond lucky that she's still in my life.

From that day forward, we were inseparable. We roomed together in the dorms, partied together or, more accurately, I watched from the corner as Penny partied, and we even performed together occasionally before she changed majors. I don't think I really thought about it being fate or some other cosmic force bringing us together at the time, but now, I unequivocally believed it. She has never let me down and, even in my current circumstance, there were no questions asked. Penny was always there for me, so it was no surprise when she agreed to pick me up at the bus station and let me stay with her until I figured out what I was going to do. She told me it would be like us rooming together in the dorms all over again. I didn't have the heart to tell her I wasn't that person anymore. Her excitement to live with me again was sweet, and I didn't want her to think I was ungrateful.

Penny clued into what had been happening with Andrew when she came to visit once and saw the bruises I tried to cover up on my neck, but clearly failed at doing. I explained that it wasn't as bad as it seemed and lied to her that it was the first time Andrew had put his hands on me. I told her that he apologized and said it would never happen again. Penny begged me to leave. She hadn't liked Andrew since the first time she met him and said there was something off in his eyes. I, on the other hand, was in love and couldn't see what she was talking about. That was the first of many similar conversations Penny and I had about the abuse.

I stayed for three more years after that visit Penny made. Needless to say, she didn't visit again after that, but we talked on the phone any time I could sneak it. She always told me during those calls that she would help me, that she would get me out of there and make me safe. I explained to her there were months at a time when Andrew and I had good times, and there was no abuse. She knew that, when it happened, it was always when we talked about children or our future. Penny figured out first why Andrew didn't like these conversations. She knew that he was selfish and didn't want to share me with a child. A child would take my time and attention away from him. I always told him I would love a child and him equally, but he wouldn't listen and would just become the monster who hurt me instead of the man who should have loved me. Penny told me he would never give me children and that I should move on to someone who would. I loved kids and knew from an early age that I had always wanted them, but had no idea what me actually becoming pregnant would do to him. In my heart, I really had hoped our child would change him. I couldn't have been more wrong.

We made a right turn out of the parking lot of the bus station and headed straight down Main Street. I stared out the window and watched as the main strip of Carson Falls came into view. It was unlike anything I had ever seen before. This town looked like it belonged on the set of a movie. At least, that was the only time I had ever seen anything like this. I was used to city life.

As we approached, there were shops that lined both sides of the street, each with its own awning depicting the store name on them. There were parking spaces all diagonally lined in front of the shops. Along the sidewalks, there were trees placed at every other storefront, and benches placed where there were no trees. Each tree housed a mini garden of bright flowers around its base. Finishing off the look, there were beautifully ornate outdoor post lanterns lining the cobblestone sidewalks, giving it that old-timey, small-town feel.

Among the stores were a bakery, a coffee shop, a hardware store, and post office. My eyes were immediately drawn to a little antique shop, that was nestled on the corner of the opposite side of the street. Through the windows, I saw a baby grand piano. It was black from years of use, and had lost some of its shine. The ivory of the keys was just the slightest bit off-white. Even from this vantage point, one could tell it had seen many fingers dance across it. I saw an older lady spraying down the front window and wiping it clean. I assumed she must be the owner because of the pride she took in her work. She was squeezing in between two gorgeous, mahogany rocking chairs, just to make it shine.

At the end of the strip, Penny made a left turn onto First Street, and the town square immediately came into view. Settled in the center was an oversized gazebo with four sets of stairs jutting out from it. The concrete walkways came off the cobblestone and led up to the stairs. They were adorned with beautiful benches, surrounded by barrels used as flowerpots. The grass was a shade of green I was not used to seeing. On the grass, there were picnic tables, an outdoor play area for kids, and tents set up for some sort of event.

After the town square, we made the first right onto Jefferson Place. There was a hidden driveway, a little less than a block down the street, into which Penny turned. I looked ahead and saw the big brick apartment complex come into view. As she pulled into her parking spot outside the building, I sighed and tried to call up any feelings of unease I might have had. Except, they were nowhere to be found. I felt a sense of home here in Carson Falls, even if it was all new to me. It was a strange feeling, but one that I welcomed with opened arms. I turned to look at Penny and gave her a small smile so that she knew I was fine. I owed Penny so much for letting me crash with her. I hoped that she knew how grateful I was for her friendship and the sense of peace she was giving me.

"I hope you'll be comfortable on the sleeper sofa. I wish I had more room." Penny said to me as she helped me unload my stuff from her car.

"Penny…please stop worrying. I am fine with whatever. As long as I'm here and not in Seattle, it doesn't make a difference to me. I would sleep on the floor if I had to." I looked at her and smiled. She was so worried about her space being too small. It really wasn't a big deal. I had a roof over my head, food, and my best friend. Anything else was a bonus.

"Look, Ari. I know you need time, and I want you to take as much as you need. Go out and explore the town once you get settled. I know it's not a big city or remotely close to what you're used to, but I know that you'll find some things to do. Once you feel better and are healed up, we can hit the night scene over in Gifford. They have this amazing dance club called Reckless," she said with a mischievous gleam in her eyes.

"You must be crazy if you think I'm going dancing." I shook my head and started to walk away from her car and up the stairs to her apartment. "Besides, as soon as I can, I'm getting a job. I don't want to burden you more than I have already."

"Ari, shut the hell up. You're not a burden. You're my best friend, and I would do anything for you. I am just so sorry that it's under these circumstances that you finally got your ass out here." Penny never was one to mince her words. Straight to the point and completely unfiltered. That was my Penny.

We reached the top of the stairs, and I stepped to the side so Penny could unlock the door. She pushed it open and motioned for me to go on ahead of her. I walked into her apartment and stopped dead in my tracks.

"What the hell?!" I yelled as I jumped back outside the door, almost knocking Penny to the floor of the concrete walkway. My heart raced a mile a minute, and I felt like I was about to hyperventilate until Penny burst into a fit of laughter. With my hand to my chest to try to calm my heart from beating out of my chest, I glared at her.

"Oh, sorry. I guess I forgot to mention the dolls," she wheezed out between laughs.

"Dolls? Those are not dolls. They're terrifying as hell. Why in God's name do you still have these things?" I choked out.

"They're Living Dead Dolls. Just because you don't like them, doesn't mean I stopped collecting over the years. Look, Beetlejuice is here. He isn't scary, is he?" she asked as she stepped into the apartment and picked up Beetlejuice.

"Penny, I can't believe you never grew out of this. I was not expecting this when I walked through the door. Geez, didn't you start collecting them in college?" I had forgotten she loved these hideous things and guessed a part of me was hoping against all hope she had long outgrown them. How could I bring myself to tell her that I was scared to death to sleep in a dark room with these things? All it would take would be me getting up in the middle of the night and running into one of these little monsters, and I would have a heart attack.

"Yeah, I actually kept up with it. I have every collection to date. Well, except the newest one that just released a couple of weeks ago. Look, if they make you too nervous, I can box them up and put them in storage while you're here. I don't mind, and besides, I remember how big of a scaredy cat you've always been. Some things never change," she laughed as she placed Beetlejuice back in the window beside a mock graveyard featuring another ridiculously ugly doll sporting a gouged-out eye. I felt my skin begin to crawl.

"Please do that. I won't be able to sleep at all if you don't," I said to her back as she walked into the kitchen. I made my way over to the couch, put down my suitcase, and opened it to retrieve the envelope I placed on top of the clothes when I packed. Penny was standing at the counter, so I walked to her and slid the envelope to her.

"Penny, I need you to take this. It isn't much, but it's all I could get from the safe in the time I had before I left." Penny backed away shaking her head.

"Ari, you know better than that. I won't accept that money. Keep it and use it for yourself. I have no use for it. I am fine and didn't bring you here for your money." I huffed out a huge sigh and crossed my arms.

"Penny. I don't want to be in your way, and I know you didn't bring me here for my money. But you need to know that I don't have any other way of saying thank you except for this. So please, just take it." I took the few steps toward her and held it out for her to grab.

"Ari, it's just not going to happen. And babe, you just said all I need. Thank you *is* enough. Now, no more money talk. Let's get you unpacked, settled, and then I have to head to work. I can drop you off at the square on my way in if you want."

"Sounds good. Besides, I got a second wind."

I started unpacking, hung up the clothes I needed to in the hall closet, and put the rest into the chest sitting at the base of the window under

Beetlejuice's graveyard.

"You are going to put these things up the minute you get home, right?" I glanced over at Penny and back at the hideous creatures as she belly laughed and said yes.

"Penny, have I told you lately how much I love you?" I asked with a big smile on my face, the first genuine one that had crossed my face in over twelve days.

"No babe, you haven't. But you can butter me up on our way out the door. I have to get to work before my boss goes ape-shit. She let me take first period off, but if I'm not there by the second, those hellions will trash my classroom."

"Fine. Let's go, but can you drop me off on the main strip instead of the square?" I asked, devising a plan in my head of what to see first.

"Sure. Whatever tickles your pickle," Penny said with a giggle.

Before I knew it, we were back in the car and on our way. You would think that I would be totally tired of sitting in a moving vehicle, but I figured I'd walk around a while and really uncover the small gems this town had to offer. I hadn't felt this excited in a while, so I was eager to go.

Penny pulled up in front of the busy coffee shop, called Carla's Coffee Clutch, and parked the car. I glanced up to see people filling the seats inside. She pulled the keys out of the ignition, slid a spare key off, and handed it to me.

"Here, babe. If you get ready to head back to the apartment before I get off of work, just head into the post office and ask for George. He lives out at the apartments and can give you a ride back. Don't worry; he's about sixty and as harmless as a fly." She winked at me as I took the key out of her hand.

"Thanks Penny. For everything." I closed the car door, glanced around, and spotted the antique shop from where I stood. It was already open, but I needed coffee first. I knew myself, and once I got inside that shop, I'd be lost in there for hours. Penny took off with a honk of her horn, waving her hand wildly out her open window.

I headed inside the coffee shop, and a few heads turned to look at me. I knew my bruises were still visible and I became self-conscious with the stares. I hung my head down and tried not to look at anyone. Thankfully, there was no line at the counter, and I placed my order for a non-fat caramel macchiato.

"Excuse me, ma'am? What was that you wanted?" I looked up at the barista, and my brows drew together.

"What do you mean what was that I wanted? A non-fat caramel macchiato, please," I said, confused.

"Um, ma'am. We have coffee. Not fancy coffee, just plain coffee. Caffeinated, or not. Small, medium, and large. I don't think I can even pronounce what you asked for. These are your choices. What will it be?" he asked, bored. He must hate when out of town folk stop in here.

"Oh. I'm so sorry. I didn't realize you didn't do fancy coffee. I'll take a medium coffee with milk and sugar. Thank you." I'd been scoping out a spot to sit down and glanced back at him to see him shake his head and walk away. Great impression I must have made. Joe, the barista, must have thought I was a complete snob.

Two minutes later, my coffee was ready. I paid Joe and headed to a little table by the window. On the ledge sat today's newspaper. Some other patron must have left it, so I grabbed the paper and unfolded it to the front page. I skimmed the headlines, turned the page, and found a Want Ad for Thelma's Treasures and Trinkets. Glancing out the window, I looked across the street. On top of the storefront windows, where I'd seen the older woman cleaning, was an awning boasting the same name. I refolded the newspaper, placed it back on the window sill, and continued to sip on my coffee while I stared across the street at the antique shop.

"Miss, are you new to town?" a deep voice asked from the direction of the table across from mine.

"Yes, sir. I'm staying with my friend Penny." I smiled at the older gentleman who was smiling at me.

"I see. Well, welcome to Carson Falls. I'm Harry. I own the hardware store, Harry's Hardware House, but I'm retired now. My son Harry Jr. runs it for me. What's your name, Sugar?" he asked me with a curious look in his eye.

"My name is Arianna, but everyone calls me Ari. Nice to meet you,

Harry. I will be sure to check out your store if I'm ever in need of any hardware," I said back as politely as possible. He meant well, and I knew that, but I also knew that he wanted to ask if I was all right. He saw what I'd seen every day for the past two weeks. The yellowing marks from the fading bruises. I could just tell everyone that I was in a bad wreck or I fell down the stairs, but that is too cliché. I won't allow him to control me anymore and I won't lie for him anymore.

"It is lovely to meet you, Arianna. What a beautiful name! How long are you staying with us here in the Falls?" Harry was very talkative, but I didn't want to give him a bad impression of me, so I continued the conversation.

"Well, I'm hoping to stay here for a while. Once I get my feet on the ground and get a job, I plan on getting a place somewhere in Carson Falls or Gifford. I'm excited just to get out and explore the town today. It's my first day here, and I'm getting the lay of the land," I yammered on.

"Well, Darlin', I hope you find whatever it is you set out to look for. Carson Falls is small, country living. We are close knit, but we always accept strays. Don't be a stranger. Come and chat with me anytime you need to, Sugar. Have fun discovering the town. Make sure you stop into Barb's Blissful Bites. Don't pay no mind to the name now. Barb don't really bite but makes a mean treat. Cookies are to die for, but the pies are otherworldly," Harry mused.

"Thanks, Harry. I will make sure to do that. It was so nice to meet you. Hope I see you again soon." I stood, rounding the table to the exit and paused before leaving to look back at Harry, offering him a little wave over my shoulder. Once outside, I walked straight up to the corner and waited for the cars to pass so I could cross.

I opened the door and entered Thelma's Treasures and Trinkets to the overhead bell tinkling. I inhaled the smell of the old wood that was all over the store. I began to browse through the first aisle. Among the many trinkets, snow globes, Precious Moments statues, and old-style picture frames lined the shelves. I picked up the Precious Moment of a little boy in what looked like angel wings. I flipped it over, and on the bottom, it said, 'My Guardian Angel' in small print. I immediately gasped for air as the tears started to well in my eyes. I placed the knick-knack back on the shelf and wiped under my eyes. When I looked up, I saw the lady that was cleaning the window staring at me. Her head tilted to the side, she had a look of curiosity and concern on her face.

"Are you okay dear?" she asked with a shaky voice.

"Yes, ma'am. I just found a trinket that hit home for me," I answered back.

"I saw your tears, sweetheart. Come to the front with me, and let Miss Thelma get you a Kleenex. You can have a seat on the piano bench while I grab them from the bathroom." The woman, who I now knew was Miss Thelma, slowly teetered away. She disappeared in the back, and I turned to look at the piano. It was the same one I saw when Penny and I drove by. I ran my fingers along the keys. It had been years since I'd played. I wondered to myself if this beautiful instrument was in tune. I wasn't allowed to even breathe near the one Andrew bought and had on display in our foyer. My fingers itched to play.

"Go ahead and play dear. I have it tuned once a month in case a customer wants to test-drive the merchandise before buying. Do you know how to play?" Thelma asked me.

"Yes, ma'am, I do," I muttered.

"Who is this ma'am person? Call me Thelma, or Miss Thelma. That's what everyone calls me. Ma'am is my mother, and she's dead. Now, go on. Play me something." Miss Thelma shuffled to the stool behind the cash register counter. I stared at her; wasn't sure if I could do this. I lay my fingers flat against the keys and closed my eyes as I allowed my fingertips to feel the cool, slick, familiar ivory. I allowed my hands to take their natural curve as I began to feel the memories of the notes filter through my body. Just as it always did, the music ignited inside me and released through the flow of my fingers. I began to play "Keyboard Concerto in D Minor," by Johann Sebastian Bach.

Miss Thelma was staring at me with her mouth open as I peeked up at her. She must have thought I would have played something more modern. The pedals were a bit tough to press down, but a little oil and they would be as good as new. I continued the concerto, and after the four minutes it took to play, I let the last note linger as I looked at Miss

Thelma. She seemed to be crying.

I immediately got up and charged toward her. "I'm so sorry Miss Thelma. I didn't mean to upset you." I hung my head and sighed. I wasn't really making things easy on the people of Carson Falls today.

"Don't you dare apologize for the beauty you just gave me, Sweetheart. I'm crying because I've never heard anything like that in all my years. Not only that, but I have never seen anyone captured by the instrument like you were, or how your body reacted to it. It exuded from you. Where on earth did you learn to play like that?" She asked me, still wiping away the tears.

"I attended The Juilliard School in New York City for four years and studied piano composition. I've been classically trained for as long as I can remember. Music is something I've always migrated to. It heals the heart and makes the soul dance. At least that's what my music teachers always said," I answered, feeling an excitement I haven't felt in what seemed like forever.

"What's your name, honey?" Miss Thelma finally asked me.

"I'm Arianna. Everyone calls me Ari though. It's nice to meet you, Miss Thelma." I extended my hand to shake hers.

"The pleasure is certainly all mine, dear. I haven't seen you in these parts before. I do know your friend Penny though. She talks about you a bunch. She told me yesterday that her friend Arianna was staying with her for a while. Don't know any other Ariannas, so that must be you," she stated, matter-of-factly.

"Yes, that's me. Penny and I met in college. She's the very best friend a girl could ask for. I needed a place to crash while I get on my feet, and she's letting me stay with her. Speaking of which, do you have the time?" I asked in a semi-panic, not sure how long I'd been chatting or playing.

"It's only about eleven thirty in the morning dear. You got somewhere you need to be? If so, I can see if I can get you to where that is. We don't have them fancy Ubers here in the Falls, but we do have taxis." Thelma reached for her cordless phone and her Rolodex. YES! Rolodex.

"No, I just lost track of time. Penny isn't out of work until three, so I have some time still." I stood up and walked toward the rocking chairs

19

by the windows.

"Darlin,' can I ask you a question?" Miss Thelma waited for me to look at her and give the go-ahead before continuing, "Why were you crying over that trinket?"

A little taken aback by the personal nature of her question, I held my composure and answered, "I recently lost my baby. It was a sign to me that I'm doing the right thing, and he's guiding me to where I need to be."

"Oh, honey, I am so sorry to hear this. Come here and give Miss Thelma a squeeze." She began to round the counter toward me. Thinking what the hell, I hugged her. And, as she petted my hair, she told me she was going to help me. I pulled away out of her arms and looked at her confused. How in the world was she going to help me? Better yet, why did she want to help me?

"What do you mean you're going to help me?" I asked as I wiped the tears away again from under my eyes.

"You are going to work here with Miss Thelma until something better comes along, and you can get settled. I see what lies behind your eyes child, and demons need slaying. You can't work on slaying them if you're worried about a job. So, you got a job. Now let's get the paperwork together to fill out." Miss Thelma shuffled her way to the storeroom to grab what, I could only assume, was an application for employment.

I walked out of Thelma's Treasures and Trinkets feeling like I knew what lay ahead for the first time in years. No longer was I worried about any decisions I had made, people I had spoken to, or most importantly, playing music again. Carson Falls was definitely not what I had expected, but it might have been exactly what I needed.

Chapter 2

Frozen
River

"Cady! Come on baby girl. Turn the movie off. You have to eat breakfast and get to school," I yelled from the kitchen at my daughter for the fourth time. Seriously, if I never had to watch *Frozen* again, it would be too soon. I loved my daughter, but why did all five-year-old girls have to obsess over that God-awful movie. The song "Let It Go," is enough to drive any man to the edge. This was our routine every morning before Cady went to school. I ran around like a lunatic trying to get her lunch packed, her outfit on her, and her appearance presentable for school, so folks didn't think I was a bad dad. All my girl liked to do was plant her ass in front of the big screen and perform every word, song, and move to this ridiculous movie. It was very entertaining to watch, but only when we had time. And right then, if she didn't haul her little ass in here to eat, she'd be late again. I really didn't want Penelope Sloane on my case. She could be a bigger pain in my ass than this movie.

I had always wanted kids, but I never thought I would have to be a single dad. My baby girl, Cadence, or Cady as we called her, was a gorgeous five-year-old girl with blue-gray eyes, long, curly brown hair, and a smile that melted my heart every single time it was thrown my way, which was probably why she got away with torturing me with shit like *Frozen*. She had my eyes, but everything else was her mom's. It used to be hard to look at that smile and her hair and not think of her mom. Now, I'm just sadly reminded of all that Cady's mom, Emma, was before she wasn't.

Emma was beautiful. She had the longest brown hair I'd ever seen with curls you wanted to wrap your fingers around. It wasn't very often she wore it down, most of the time it was braided and covered with a cowboy hat, but it was down the day I met her. Emma's eyes were as green as a lily pad. I knew I was attracted to her in a way that wasn't just physical when she opened that mouth, started talking in that twang, and then laughed for the very first time. After that, we were inseparable. I assumed that she was it for me. You know what they say about assumptions.

We'd dated for a year before she became pregnant. When she told me she was carrying my baby, I saw something flash in Emma's eyes that should have been a red flag, but I was too in love with her and too ecstatic to see any warning signs of what was to come. That was the only time I ever saw that look cloud her eyes. She acted like the happy, glowing, pregnant woman every day after and never gave more indication that something was off. Emma and I talked about marriage and decided it was the best thing for the baby. We were married less than three months later in a ceremony in the town square. There were big white tents that housed a makeshift dance floor, tables and chairs covered in white linens, and a DJ booth that butted up to the food tables. It was a bit cramped and thrown together, but to me, it was perfect. Everyone I cared about was there, and my beautiful girl was giving me a baby.

Emma had a difficult pregnancy. The first few months, all she did was throw up. It didn't matter what time of the day it was, she still wretched all the time. After the first five months, things eased up a bit. Emma wasn't as sick, but she was exhausted. I knew that with pregnancy came certain changes, but all I could do to help her was get whatever she needed, whenever she needed it. She slept most of the time and had very few cravings. She also cried all the time. She blamed it on hormones, but I could just sense that there was more to it than she would say.

Cadence Allegra Bradshaw was born almost four months later on August 13th, 2011. She was a big baby at eight pounds, eight ounces, and nineteen inches long. Emma did great throughout the labor and delivery. It was when we got home that things changed for the worse. Emma was very distant, and I urged her to go talk to someone. I tried but couldn't get through to her. Her parents and her sister tried, but no luck. I knew she needed professional help going by what I read about postpartum depression. Emma was exuding all the signs. I wanted to help her, but we had a newborn to care for, too. Cady was my first priority. It sounds cold-hearted and mean, but babies need constant care, and Emma was in no shape to help.

Eventually, after three weeks, the depression grew into something that I could only assume was too much for Emma to handle, so she left us with a note that read:

River,

I am not good enough for you. I will never be a good enough mother for Cady. I should have told you early on in the pregnancy that it was not what I wanted. I am so sorry. I don't want to be tied down to this life. Marriage and kids were never in my plan. Please don't look for me, because I am not coming back.

Emma

I couldn't believe that a mother could leave her newborn baby like that and not fight with everything she had to beat back whatever demons were chasing her. Then again, I saw the look that day when she told me she was pregnant. She held true to her letter and never came back. Emma sent me divorce papers about two months later. She also signed away all her parental rights. It was a relief but at the same time, broke my heart for my baby girl. I just hoped when the time came, I could ease the hurt that would inevitably settle in my daughter's soul.

Emma never made contact with us again, but that didn't mean I didn't find out about everything she got mixed up in. When Cady was two years old, I saw Emma in Gifford, the town over from Carson Falls, when I was called in as backup on a four-alarm fire. She had track marks on both arms, was extremely thin, and had visible bruises all over her body. She was walking curled into the side of some guy who didn't look much better than she did.

Two weeks after that sighting, I received a 'courtesy' call from a buddy at the local sheriff's office, because she was Cadence's mom, to let me know that she had been beaten to death by her drug dealer boyfriend. My world screeched to a jarring halt. I wasn't in love with Emma anymore, but she was the mother of my child, and I took it pretty hard. How was I supposed to tell my daughter that her mom gave up on her and died at the hands of a man that also filled her body with poison?

So, for the last five years, I've raised my daughter with help from some really great friends I've made. The more Cady grows, the more I see of Emma in her. It's not a hardship loving Cady because she is such a smart, lively, beautiful girl. But sometimes, the reality of her growing up and being anything like Emma, scares me to death. I know I can guide her on the right path, but will it be enough without a female influence in her life?

"Okay, Cady! I'm not going to ask you again. If you don't come eat and you're late for school again, you can forget about piano lessons all together." I turned to the stove and switched the burner off as I slid out the eggs I scrambled for my girl. I turned just in time to see her little self-scurry across the room, grab her plate and fork, sit in her chair at the table, and start shoveling in the eggs.

"Cadence Allegra, what did Daddy say about that movie?" I looked at her with raised eyebrows.

"No more movie before school. Sorry, Daddy." She pouted and gave me puppy-dog eyes. I hated when she gave me those eyes. Even at five, she knew how to get her way.

"We will talk about *Frozen* again when I get home from work tonight. Finish your eggs. We have to leave in five minutes. Do you have your backpack by the door?" I asked.

"Yes, Daddy. I put it there before I turned on *Frozen*," she said as she hopped down from her chair and put her dish and fork in the sink. She really was a good girl and used to the routine.

"Ok, baby girl. Let's hit the road!" I said as I grabbed my fire radio, Cady's hand, and headed to the front door.

Cady was so independent and had been since she realized she could do things on her own. She'd climb into her booster seat and buckle in without my help. This didn't bode well for my future, especially when she hits her teenage years. Still, it gave me a feeling that I was doing something right.

As we drove to the school, I looked in my rearview mirror and saw Cady pretending to play the 'air piano' with her tiny little fingers going a mile a minute like she was having her own concert back there. She'd been going on and on about wanting to play the piano. I'd been wanting to get her lessons, but just hadn't found anyone who gave private lessons, and with whom I would allow my baby girl to be around for any length of time, comfortably. I really needed to do more research because it would really be good for Cady.

We pulled up to the drop-off section of the school, and Cady immediately undid her seatbelt and reached for the door.

"Cady wait for me to come around and get you. It's very busy here today, and I want you to hold my hand while I walk you to Miss Penny," I told her.

"Daddy, hurry! I see Bryce, and I want to see him before Miss Penny takes us inside," she pushed. Bryce. The little five-year-old boy with whom my daughter was already smitten and had wrapped around her little finger was a father's worst nightmare. He was already a cute kid, and if they stayed friends growing up, I was definitely not seeing good things for my future as Cady's dad.

I came around the side and grabbed Cady's hand as she hopped down from the truck. We made our way over to where I saw Penny standing. When the coast was clear, I squatted down and looked into my daughter's eyes. "Have a good day baby girl. I love you. Don't forget that Megan is picking you up after school today and will stay with you until I get home from work. Make sure you listen to her. Homework done, bath, and no *Frozen* tonight until we can talk about what happened this morning. Okay?" She started to open her little mouth to backtalk, but she knew what was at stake, and if she wanted those lessons, she wouldn't say a word.

Instead, she turned those eyes to mine, smiled bright, and said. "I love you too, Daddy. No *Frozen*, I promise. And I will listen to Meggie. Can I go see Bryce now?" She was so attached to that kid. A quick kiss to the top of her head and a quick nod in the affirmative, and she darted away, yelling for Bryce. I headed over to talk to Penny.

"Hey River. Good to see you made it on time. How is everything?" Penny immediately started busting my balls. I have known this woman most of my life. The only time we didn't really talk was when she was away at Juilliard for school.

"Hey, Penny. Things are good, smart-ass. It's too early for you to be giving me shit, woman. Now, before I forget, do you think you can help me find a piano instructor who doesn't creep me out and would give private lessons to my girl?" I watched as a ridiculous smile spread across her face; Penny knew I caved into my daughter's wants. It was not my fault and couldn't be avoided when you look into those blue-gray eyes of Cady's.

"Sure, River. Let me ask around, and I will get back to you. You know, you really should get out there again. You're too hot not to share that with a woman, River. You're all dark hair, great eyes, amazingly built body, and all kinds of broody when Cady isn't around. You soak panties everywhere you go, but you never…" Penny stopped talking as my fire radio chirped and alerted me to a call.

"Thanks for your scrutiny and description of me, Pen, but I'm just fine. I've got to go to this call. Let me know what you find out about the lessons. See ya." I turned and started jogging to my truck to get my ass to this call.

I got to the firehouse, geared up, and the boys and I headed out to the call. From Cady's school to the firehouse, and then to the scene, it took all of ten minutes. When we arrived, I quickly assessed the area to see if it was safe to approach the car that was engulfed in flames. The old Pontiac Fiero's owner was safely perched on the back of an ambulance with an oxygen mask. He took in some smoke, so they were just taking precautions, but he was fine. We put the flames out fairly quickly and were just thankful that no injuries occurred and the owner knew the telling signs since this wasn't his first go-round with a car fire.

We ended up back at the firehouse an hour later. As we backed up to the first bay of the red brick building, I appreciated the small town charm. The retractable doors were up as usual and the bays were wide open adding to the old-fashioned charm. There was a handmade sign that hung dead center of the four bay doors that read 'Carson Falls Firehouse Ladder 1' in big red text over a white background. Simple and to the point. Large bells on each side of the sign were used to alert residents that trucks were exiting for a call. The open bay doors were white when pulled down. The windows upstairs all had red shutters on them that matched the red in the sign.

Hopping down out of the truck, I made my way inside to change out of my gear in the back of the bays next to the pole. Yes, the firehouse had a pole and sometimes, we still slid down it like in the movies, but mostly we kept it for the kids that came to the firehouse on field trips. It was the highlight of the trip for most kids. I hung my gear on my hook and made my way upstairs to the office.

The upstairs of the firehouse held an office and small kitchenette. In the office, there was a single desk in front of the window that held an older computer that still worked, just slowly. The walls and carpet were a plain cream color. It wasn't set up for decor, but rather efficiency. It did what it is set up to do. The kitchenette across the hall was a bit livelier, likely because it was used more. Stainless steel appliances, sage green walls, and black and white checkered linoleum floors made it more inviting. The refrigerator was usually stocked with water and food donated by the people of the Falls. I grabbed a bottle of water, chugged it down, grabbed another, and headed across the hall.

It was my job to write up the reports after every call, so I set out to get that done. Doing this was tedious and really not what I wanted to do, but it wouldn't take long. The rest of the guys were downstairs getting ready to hose down the trucks since it was such a beautiful day. Hose downs were fun because they usually drew out some of the town folk, and it was always nice when we get to interact with them.

Twenty minutes later, I had finished typing up the report, and headed downstairs. I checked my phone for the time and saw it was almost noon. Lunchtime. The guys should start bellyaching about how starved they were shortly, but I just made my way over to the hoses, grabbed one, and started spraying the truck. All of Carson Falls Fire Department's trucks were the traditional red and white. As I made my way to the front of the truck, Harry Sr. approached the driveway, walked right up to me, and said, "River Bradshaw. We need to talk, boy."

"Harry. Good to see you. What's on your mind old man?" I dropped the hose and turned to face him. Harry owned Harry's Hardware House for years and his son Harry Jr., had just recently taken it over, so the old man had a ton of time on his hands to meddle. And, I got the feeling he was about to prove me right.

"Watch your manners boy. I got some news for you. Not sure you're aware or not," he said, somewhat mysteriously. My chin went up as if to say, go on, and he proceeded, "There's a new young lady in town and," I raised my hand, effectively cutting him off.

"No way Harry. We aren't doing this. Between you and Penny, I don't know who's worse with this shit." Walking back to the hose, I grabbed it and finished what I was doing. Harry stood there staring at me with his arms crossed, shaking his head back and forth.

He finally turned and walked away but called out loud for the town to hear, "River Bradshaw, the world as you know it is about to throw you for a loop. Don't say I didn't try to warn you. When you're ready to listen, come find me." And, Harry would prove to me, once again, that he was right the next day.

Brushing that whole scene off, I turned to walk back into the firehouse to eat lunch with the rest of the guys. Harry meant well and all, but I got enough from Penny. There just wasn't anyone who'd caught my eye. I was not against relationships, but I was cautious. It would be amazing if I found the person I could spend my life with and maybe give Cady a good role model. I was just a man, and I did the best I could, but I didn't know about glitter, dresses, dolls, or any of that other girlie shit my baby girl liked. Any help received in that area would be a blessing in disguise.

As I parked my truck in the driveway, my gaze landed on the home I built for my daughter and me. It was not a modern structure, but a more classic log cabin with the structural beams visible from the inside. The windows were large to allow as much natural light inside as possible. There were ledges on each of the lower floor windows with long pots and flowers planted in each. It was something Cady and I did together in the spring. She loved it, so we made it a fun tradition. The porch was my absolute favorite part of the entire house. Three steps led up to it, where we kept a swing to the left, and a log couch to the right. It was made of the same style of logs as the house was but had this great big cushion on which you could sit or lie. There were also two Adirondack chairs with a tree trunk table in the middle.

The land surrounding the house boasted a pond with a great little waterfall built into it with huge, heavy rocks. The pond was full of freshwater fish for the catch and release fishing Cady and I sometimes did. There are some rock steps that led to the pond in case anyone wanted to get their feet wet or swim. Various kinds of trees surrounded the property, providing us with a kaleidoscope of colors in the fall when their leaves changed. A few benches were placed on the land, but one in particular was under the weeping willow, tucked almost at the property line.

Sighing at all that beauty, I jumped out of my truck and headed into the house. I knew Meggie was most likely exhausted from my baby girl chatting her ear off and just going non-stop since school. As I opened the door, I was greeted by the sound of little feet running right for me. Meg followed behind and proved that Cady was a handful.

"DADDY!!!" My girl shouted like it was the first time I had ever walked through the door. She was always so happy to see me.

"Meg, thanks for watching her. I can already tell she was a handful. What do I owe you?" I asked her knowing I was doubling anything she said.

"Just the usual Mr. Bradshaw. Cady was fine. She had a good day at school. Bryce drew her a picture, so she was excited, that's all," she said, and I handed her a fifty.

"Keep it. I appreciate your help more than you know. Go have fun with your friends this weekend, and we will see you Tuesday."

I watched as Meg collected her stuff and walked to her parents' car that was parked at the curb, idling while they waited. Meg was only sixteen years old so I watched her go, and once she was safely inside, my baby girl and I went to get ready for her bedtime routine where we talked about our day, and then read a story together. We have done it every night since she was a baby.

Closing the door, we turned, Cady holding tight to my pinky, and headed into the living room. I saw that her toys were put away, but the picture that Bryce drew her was still on the coffee table. I walked over, picked it up, and turned to my daughter who was now standing and looking at me with a very cute, very adult smile on her face. Christ, she was five. Bryce was already in her sights, and he seemed to adore her back, but that look made me feel like she was growing too fast, which of course she was.

"Ok baby girl, upstairs and in bed. We can talk about this drawing there. And then story time, yeah?"

"Ok Daddy," Cady turned and dashed all the way to her room on the second floor. When I made it upstairs, she was already snuggled under the covers with her choice of books to read, *The Snow Queen*, which is what *Frozen* was based on. Big shock there. It was everywhere in her room.

Cady had always been very girly. When she was old enough to choose, she wanted her walls in alternating purple and pink, with white furniture. Her dresser and desk were all white, but one wall was covered in *Frozen* stickers to go with her *Frozen* sheets, posters, and curtains. A huge pink and purple swirled throw rug dotted the center of the room. Her bookcase was across from her bed, next to her closet. Her bookshelves were full but *The Snow Queen* won out every night for the last four months. Maybe one day I'd get a reprieve.

"Okay, Cady, scoot your little self over baby, so I can sit with you. Before we get into the drawing, we need to discuss what happened this morning," I heard her sigh as I tried to fit my big body on her little bed.

"Daddy, I'm sorry. I don't know what comes over me when I start watching. I just want to sing and dance all day," she looked at me with those eyes.

"Cady, baby, I know you do. But, in the mornings during the week, you know the drill. No *Frozen* before school. You get too distracted and make us late. I love that you enjoy the singing and dancing so much baby girl, but if we are late to school, they yell at Daddy. You don't want Daddy to get into trouble do you?" I stuck out my lip and pouted. Although Cady needed to listen, I didn't want her to ever lose her spirit. I wanted our talk to be gentle so she knew she could always come to me without fear, but I also needed her to know that it was not okay for her not to listen. She was a good kid and always had been, but her school was pretty strict about attendance.

"No Daddy. I don't want you in trouble. No more *Frozen* before school. Am I grounded?" she looked up at me with unshed tears in her eyes and sniffled a little bit.

"No baby girl. I just really need you to listen to me okay? We're a team remember? We have to help each other out. Don't cry. Nothing to cry over. Give your dad a hug and tell me about the picture." She jumped into my arms, and we chatted about Bryce, the picture, and then read the story together until she fell asleep.

Heading downstairs to grab a beer from the kitchen, I stopped in the living room to put the game on the big screen. In the kitchen, I hung the picture Bryce drew for Cady on the refrigerator and shook my head at how much swagger Bryce had for his mere five years of age. Beer in hand, it was now time for me to sit and relax a bit.

The next morning, after Cady had breakfast and watched *Frozen* (Lord, help me), we headed into town so that we could spend time at the park. We parked on Main Street, in front of Barb's Blissful Bites. As I reached up to grab Cady's hand, I heard the bells to Thelma's Treasures and Trinkets go off. I looked up and saw a tall, blonde, curvy woman with the faintest hint of bruises all over her face.

"Daddy, can we get some cookies now?" Cady startled me out of my stare, and I looked down to her.

"Of course, baby. Let's get you some cookies, then we can go to the park," I grabbed Cady's hand, and we made our way inside the bakery only to find Penny standing at the entrance with her arms crossed and a Cheshire cat smirk on her face. Then, she full-on smiled, looked at Thelma, and gave a wave to the woman who I had just seen walk in earlier, standing near the front window.

Turning to Penny, I asked, "Do you know her?"

"I do. She is my best friend from college. And, I have a feeling she will be turning more than your head big guy," Penny said.

"What does that even mean?" I retorted.

"Give it time, and you will see," she said as she started to walk away. "And just so you know, I think I may know someone who can give those lessons," Penny threw over her shoulder with a shit-eating grin on her face.

Shit. Penelope Sloane. She is up to no good. Pain in my ass.

Chapter 3
Piano Lessons
Arianna

No one ever really starts a new job on a Saturday, but I'm not like everyone else. At least my situation doesn't seem to be. Waking up for my first day was not the hard part, but getting ready was. I wanted to be able to focus on what Miss Thelma needed me to do for the day and not be self-conscious about the remnants my ex left on my face, so I took some extra time and effort doing my hair and makeup. Penny had been up for a while, had a run already under her belt, and was ready to face the day. She asked me to go into town early with her so we could grab coffee and stop at the bakery.

Penny drove us in and parked between Carla's Coffee Clutch and Barb's Blissful Bites. We got out and headed inside Carla's to get our coffees first. As we entered, I saw Harry and gave him a small smile and head nod. He tipped his head down and said, "Mornin' darlin' girls."

"Hey, Harry. Good to see ya," Penny responded. She didn't really chitchat with the man but instead was laser-focused on getting to the counter to place her order.

I yanked on her hand to pull her closer to me just before we made it to the counter so I could mutter low, "Why are all these local town folks so nice? It's like they don't have an unpleasant bone in their bodies."

"They don't. It's small-town Tennessee, Ari. We're a close-knit community. We're friendly, and we like small talk. Now, what would you like to order?"

"Yeesh. Friending much? I'll take a medium coffee with milk and sugar."

Penny placed our order and once done, we slid down the counter to wait for it to be prepared. As we waited, I glanced around the Carla's Coffee Clutch and saw that it was quite busy for a Saturday morning. It seemed that the people of Carson Falls didn't like to waste a perfectly good Saturday sleeping in or lounging at home.

Coffees in hand, we headed next door to Barb's. There was a crowd, and we had to wait a while to get up to the glass counter to place our muffin order. There were all types of flavors of muffins. More than I even knew existed. But, my favorite was always blueberry, and Penny's was banana nut. So that's what we ordered. We grabbed a table and dove in. The first bite was like an out-of- body experience. Every bite after, my eyes rolled back, I moaned out loud, and made a scene. It was just warm enough, with the perfect amount of blueberries throughout. I couldn't contain myself. Just a small slice of heaven on the other side of the hell I had been living.

"Ari, what the hell? Are you fucking kidding me right now? Tell me you didn't just have an orgasm in the middle of Barb's after a few bites of a blueberry muffin?"

"Shut it, Penelope Gertrude. It was good. I haven't had much good, and I enjoyed it. Is that all right with you?" I snapped at her.

"Geez. Fine. No need for the full name. Just don't want people thinking I gave you that little mini "O" in the middle of the damn bakery. But I am glad you liked it so much," she said as she winked at me.

"Sorry. I really did like it though. So, what are your plans today?"

"I may go into Gifford and hit the shops. I need to get some outfits. I saw what you unpacked. I won't accompany you anywhere until I have clothes as kickass as yours."

"Penny, you can borrow or have whatever you want. They are just clothes." *Clothes bought as hush presents. Clothes that came with the warning that I would get it even worse if I opened my mouth.*

"No way chick. It was payday yesterday, and I am all paid up on bills. The shops are calling out to me. If I see something I think will look killer on you, I will be getting it. And don't argue with me," she glared at me as she said that last bit.

"Whatever, Penny. I have to go. It's almost nine," I stated as I got up from the table.

"Okay, well just call me when you are ready to be picked up."

Making my way toward the door, I turned my head to look back at Penny; she was collecting all the garbage from our muffins to throw away. I smiled again at the thought of Penelope Gertrude Sloane. Just knowing her made me a better person.

Walking to the corner, I waited patiently for the cars to pass, when this pretty sweet pickup truck pulled into a parking spot. The traffic cleared, and I crossed but glanced quickly back at the truck. It was so sleek and well maintained. Too much so to go unnoticed. A tall, built, dark haired, beautiful man exited the driver's side and rounded the front of the hood to the passenger side door. Not waiting to see who he was gentlemanly opening the door for, I walked up to Thelma's Treasures and Trinkets, opened the door, and walked through. The damn bells Miss Thelma had to alert her that someone entered the store chimed loudly. I turned left and headed to the big window. Penny stood in the entrance of Barb's and smiled like a loon at the beautiful man who had a little girl by the hand.

Staring at the backs of the man and little girl walking up to the bakery door, I watched in awe at the little girl's brunette pigtails bouncing back and forth as she shifted from foot to foot with excitement. She must be a student of Penny's out with her dad to enjoy a Saturday morning and stopped for a treat first. I glanced at Penny, and she gave me a small wave but had a very mischievous smirk on her face. She looked back at the beautiful man, who looked to me and back to Penny again, said something and full-on smiled. They exchanged more words, and then Penny walked toward me at Thelma's. One last look over her shoulder and something else was spoken. Penny's face had an 'up to no good' look written all over it as she headed my way. Shit.

Releasing a sigh, I turned and looked for Miss Thelma. I really just wanted to be busy when Penny came through the door because whatever it was she had up her sleeve, was more like a disaster hiding under the guise of a good idea. Miss Thelma shuffled out from the back room, and I met her at the counter. The chimes from the loudest bells in creation sounded off, and I already knew Penny had walked through the door.

"Hey, Miss Thelma! How you doin' today?" Penny asked.

"Oh, you know darlin' girl. One day at a time for these old bones. What brings you into my store today, Penelope?"

"I was wondering if I could have a word with Ari. I know she is supposed to start working, but I need to speak to her. It's kind of important," Penny almost begged Miss Thelma.

"Sure thing darlin' girl. No rush. Nothin' is going anywhere. It never does, unless you count my looks. Those you may find back in 1989," she laughed at herself and scurried off to the back room again.

"Penny, what the hell are you up to? I saw you talking to that guy. You forget that I know you. My knowledge of your shenanigans is classified as expert. Don't lie to me either, Pen."

"Arianna, the guy I was talking to is River Bradshaw, father to Cady. Cady is tormenting her father for piano lessons. You are a classically trained piano player. Do you see where I am going with this?"

"Penny. Seriously? I haven't played piano in years."

I wasn't allowed to indulge in frivolous activities that didn't contribute to the household.

"And I wouldn't know the first thing about giving lessons to a little girl. Also, having, say, a piano, may be useful in giving lessons," I spat back.

"You can give the lessons here in the storeroom, and use the piano you played on the other day, darlin'," Miss Thelma chimed in from behind us. That woman was pretty quiet when she wanted to be.

"Miss Thelma, thank you for the offer, but there is no way I can give lessons to this little girl. Making a fool out of myself is just not something I'm willing to do right now. I'm still healing and in no shape to be around a child. What exactly is in it for you, Penny? I mean, I

36

don't know this River guy from a hole in the wall. You think I'm ready to be around a man and his little girl with the way I still look or the loss she will remind me of? How will I answer the questions that, babe, we both know, will inevitably come? I haven't even landed firmly on my feet. I'm getting there but Penny, I need some time. I love you Pen, but no."

"Ari, I…I'm so sorry. I didn't think," Penny said as she came over and embraced me in a hug.

"Pen, it's fine."

"If I may say something," Miss Thelma started, "and please hear me out, girl. Many moons ago I had me a handsome young fella. He was the fella all the other girls wanted. He walked on water in my eyes, until one day, he didn't anymore. And, the reason he didn't was because I wasn't ready to go to Parks Pointe and make it in his daddy's car, so he backhanded me. He landed it right on my cheek below my eye. Needless to say, the next day I woke up with a black eye. It lasted a week, but it was my reminder. I didn't let it mark my spirit. Instead, I used it to remember to notice the signs of an abusive man. I know your story is very different, and much more recent, but Arianna, the loss you're experiencing will ease in time, and not every man will put his hands to a woman. You also have the experience to pinpoint the signs now. River Bradshaw is a man that would never do that and his daughter looks at that piano with a twinkle in her eye and nearly faints every time she passes the window. The way you played the other day for me when I asked, you should have no problems. Give that dream to a little girl who lost her mom and let the music mend you."

"Holy crap, Miss Thelma," Penny breathed out. She looked at me. The tears just streamed down my face, and I let out a sob. I covered my mouth and ran to the bathroom in the back.

Staring at my reflection in the mirror after slamming the door closed, I watched myself take a deep breath in and then let it out. Deep inside, I knew I was not the only person to ever be hit by a man who was supposed to love me. But, my baby boy died at his hands less than two weeks ago. Being around that beautiful little girl would be too much. Right? Or, would it be a good way to make money and get on my feet while helping my heart heal a bit? The people in this town were definitely not shy about putting in their two cents and making it count. Miss Thelma was right about one thing though. I knew the signs, and it would be a cold day in hell before a man ever lay a hand on me again.

Cold water splashed on my face, thoughts collected, and decision made, I headed back out to Penny and Miss Thelma.

"Okay, Penny. Tell River I will do it. One hundred dollars a week for the lessons, three o'clock every afternoon. If I see that Cady is not taking to the lessons, I will let him know at that juncture, and we can discontinue them. Only this girl though. That is the deal. No spreading this around. And not one word about my history to anyone, especially this River guy. If I want to share, I will." I lay down the way it had to be. I couldn't say no after what Miss Thelma said. That little girl with a dream used to be me.

Shaking her head up and down, Penny said, "Of course. You have my word that I won't share or offer your services to anyone else. This will definitely be good for everyone involved." She hugged me again and whispered, "Promise."

"Ok, Penelope. Get on with your day. Arianna and I have some cleaning to do to get the back room ready for her to be able to teach Cady."

"Yes, Miss Thelma. Don't forget to call me when you're ready to be picked up, Ari. Have fun and thank you."

I raised my head, let out a deep breath, and caught Miss Thelma's eyes watching me intently. I held her stare because I wanted her to know that things were fine. She looked my face over and saw exactly what I was trying to give off. Miss Thelma nodded once, turned, and said, "Well, let's get to it girl. You can take a break around one o'clock. I have to run some errands during that hour so we can close up shop and both take that time. But right now, we have a ton of clearing out to do."

"Yes, ma'am."

Three and a half hours later, it was break time, and we had put a huge dent in what needed to be cleared, cleaned, or thrown away. Miss Thelma dug in her bag for the keys to the door; the woman's bag was big enough to be carry-on. It's no wonder it took her ten minutes to find them. We walked out together, and she turned to lock the door. We heard the click of the deadbolt, which was the all clear for us to go our separate ways for the next hour.

Turning right, I made my way to the corner, crossed back, and went to Barb's. My mouth was watering for another muffin, so that would be my lunch today. I wanted to eat at the square by the gazebo. Not really trying to draw attention, I walked with my head down. It wasn't that I couldn't see my surroundings or wasn't being vigilant, because I was. The fear that Andrew would pop out from somewhere lingered. My head was just bent enough so that my hair was curtaining my face, shielding me from passersby and the knowing looks they would give.

Barb's had slim pickings as far as the muffins went, so I settled on a croissant and a sweet tea to go. All paid, I made my way back outside and headed left toward the town square. The gazebo was packed so I made my way toward the bench at the park. Hair still hiding my face, I went to sip on my sweet tea and slammed right into something. Something so hard I thought it was a tree or light post. I looked up, and froze solid. River Bradshaw had grabbed my upper arms to stop me from falling back. The tension in my body and fear from feeling a man touch me made me start shaking. I dropped my bag with my croissant and my drink to the concrete path.

"You may want to watch where you are going, darlin'," River said to me, and I shook even harder. He tightened his grip on my arms so I wouldn't fall backward, and I just stared, numb. I couldn't respond.

"Jesus, you're like a scared little bird. If I let go of your arms are you going to be able to stay upright?"

No response had formed or left my lips. Beginning to calm down a bit and the shakes subsiding, I nodded in the affirmative and he let go. Immediately I stepped back, out of fear and self-preservation.

"Oh my goodness, Daddy!!! She looks just like Elsa from *Frozen*. Are you Elsa?" The cute little girl that I watched earlier asked, jumping up and down with excitement.

"Cady, baby, that is not Elsa. Elsa is a character, and this woman is real," he winked at me.

"Hope you're okay, darlin'. My name is River, and this is my daughter,

Cadence. You seem to be better but still got the shakes. Should I call someone for you? I'm not sure you should be alone. Why don't you..." He trailed off as his eyes raked over my face. His jaw tightened, and I could tell he was clenching his teeth. Shit. My bruises. Please don't ask me anything. Please.

"I'm fine. Thank you," I finally found my voice while bending to pick up my cup and bag I had dropped, "and no honey. I'm not Elsa. My name is Arianna."

"Oh," Cady said, looking completely disappointed.

"Sorry, Arianna. My girl here is a tad bit *Frozen*-crazed. Well, we need to be on our way. If there is no one I can call for you, we will leave you to it," River rushed out.

"Everything is good. Thank you though." Walking back the way I came, I hung my head completely down and watched my feet as I walked. No longer able to eat, I made my way to Carla's to grab another coffee. I didn't look at anyone except the guy taking my order. Once paid, and order prepared, I made my way back to the table that I sat at the first time I was there and looked out the big window. River and Cady reversed out of the parking space and were about to drive off when River turned and locked eyes with me. My skin prickled, and my hair stood on end. Something about my reaction to him seemed off, but I couldn't put my finger on it.

At three o'clock that afternoon, Penny picked me up. I had made the call ten minutes ago to her so that Miss Thelma had some time to dig her keys out of her bag again. Once in Penny's car, we headed to the apartment.

"Ari, I need to apologize to you again, babe."

"No, you don't. I need to move forward. You know I ran into him and his daughter on my break?"

"Really?"

"Yes. I ran into him on my walk. Like, actually walked right into him. I almost fell backward, but he reached out and grabbed me to hold me steady. It was a complete train wreck. My whole reaction was basically to become a mute and shake uncontrollably under his hold. And to top it off, that beautiful little girl of his was so disappointed when she found out I wasn't some Disney character."

"Ari, it is understandable that you had that reaction. It is going to take a while before you are comfortable with people touching you. Especially strangers and especially men."

"Maybe. I don't want that though. Andrew took enough from me Penny. I need to move on."

"Are you still going to give Cady lessons?" She asked me with a hopeful glance over to where I sat in the passenger side.

"This River guy made his displeasure at the sight of me completely known. He couldn't get away from me fast enough either, Penny. He was nice enough to ask if I needed him to call someone for me but then it was like his mission was to get away as quickly as possible," I explained to her.

We pulled into the apartment complex and into the spot designated to Penny's apartment. She put the car in park and shut down the engine. Turning to look my way, she spoke in a tone so serious, it shocked me. Her expression matched the seriousness of her tone as she schooled me on the subject that is River Bradshaw.

"River is a single dad, Ari. He didn't ask to be, but it's his reality. He was married to Cady's mom. They were the quintessential couple, at least from outward appearances. Ari, this is going to be tough to hear. But you need to know, to understand why River looked at you the way he did."

"It's bad, isn't it?"

"There aren't always happy endings to every story, babe. This is one of the ones that doesn't end well."

"Okay, tell me." Breathing in through my nose, and slowly blowing out the breath, I focused on Penny.

My face paled as she recounted the horrible story, my heart racing as if I could feel each punch Emma received until her heart stopped beating. I could feel my nails digging into the palm of my hand, and I shuddered as she finished this ugly story. I started crying. Steady streams fell over my cheeks and dripped off my chin onto my shirt. That poor baby girl. Poor River. Now it all made sense. The way his jaw clenched as his eyes took in my entire face, and his quick retreat. That little girl deserves to have everything. And if piano lessons are what she wants, I can give that to her.

"Piano lessons are still on, Penny. We just need to have the piano moved into the back room at Miss Thelma's, but we pretty much finished up today. Let River know. We can start as soon as that happens. If he doesn't want me to do it, I understand."

"Arianna Morgan, you, my best friend, are one of the bravest people I know. When the time is right, and you let people in on your story, the kindness you are extending to this little girl will be returned tenfold." I looked at her and pulled her into a hug.

"Thank you, Penny. It is going to be different teaching someone else, but I will let the music guide me."

"You always had a deeper connection with music than I did. Love you, Ari. Now, let's go have some wine, and I can show you what I bought you at the shops in Gifford!"

Shit. This is not good. Penelope Sloane. A pain in my ass.

Chapter 4
Let The Games Begin
River

You don't just bump into someone and lose the ability to speak. Nor do you tremble like that when someone tries to steady you, so you don't fall. I saw them. And my blood instantly started to burn. Bruises. Faintly there, but there all the same. I had to get away from her. It was so easy to see how beautiful she was with her long, blonde, wavy hair that fell midway down her back that you wanted to tangle your fingers in. Her eyes were a blue-green color that you were positive would change when she was happy, sad, or about to go wild for a man. Her body had so many curves in all the right places, you wanted to take your time to travel each one. All of this made it hard to lock down my emotions long enough to make sure she was going to be okay and get my awe-stricken daughter back to the truck. It took all the willpower I had. If I had stayed in her space any longer, I would have started making demands I had no right to make. So, Cady and I got out of there as fast as we could. That feeling that washed over me as our eyes locked when I pulled my truck out of the parking spot, told me that my world had just changed.

Monday morning, before Cady was due up to get ready for school, I still hadn't been able to shake the feeling I got when those eyes looked into mine. I only knew this woman's name. It didn't make any sense why I felt that way. It had been two days, and I didn't have any idea what it meant or what to do with it, but I couldn't focus on deeper meanings right now. My daughter needed to get to school. So, I went about waking her up.

As I entered her room, I saw her peaceful form lying on her girly-ass bed, and it hit me that she was growing up way too fast. Seemed like yesterday when her tiny newborn body fit right in my hand. Now she was growing more every day, and her features were constantly changing. Moving to the bed, I sat down and brushed her hair away from her face. *Emma.* Since running into that woman, Emma has popped into my thoughts quite a bit the past two days. My baby girl started to move, and I knew she was about to wake up.

"Cady, baby, you have to get up. Time to get ready for school and get breakfast in you." She opened her beautiful eyes and looked at me, still sleepy.

"Daddy, why can't I just sleep? I had a dream we met Elsa at the square. And she danced with me and sang with me. We played on the swings and everything!" My girl dove right in telling me about her dream. Guess she was thinking about the encounter, too. Cady was in shock when she saw Penny's friend, who I refer to as Bird. She immediately thought it was Elsa from *Frozen*. The minute she told Cady she wasn't the character from my girl's favorite movie, Cady's face showed the disappointment, and I hated it. I needed to make up for that.

"Wow! That is one super awesome dream! But we've got to get you fed and ready for school. Up, up, up! Let's go! We can have a cereal race this morning, but you have to get downstairs now!" I was not above manipulation to get my kid to school on time.

Before I could get up off the bed, little feet stomped across the room to the closet; she pulled out today's dress and ripped off her pajamas (*Frozen*, of course) to get changed. Cady loved our cereal races, but she never moved this fast in the mornings. I was very suspicious.

"Cady, why are you in such a rush this morning?"

"Because Daddy. The sooner I get to school, the sooner I get to tell

Bryce that I had the bestest most awesomest dream ever!" I laughed at her excitement.

"Okay, baby girl. Let's get to the cereal races," I said as she zipped by me again and rushed down the stairs. She grabbed her backpack and put it next to the door, and then headed right into the kitchen. I followed her.

Once the cereal was in the mismatched bowls, I placed them on the table and grabbed the milk out of the fridge. Cady got her spoon and sat up on her knees, ready to race. Once the milk was poured, she dug her spoon in, piled the Lucky Charms onto it, and shoved it into her little mouth. It was way too much for her, and I laughed as I saw her little cheeks puffed out with cereal.

"Don't choke baby. Smaller scoops, yeah?" She tried to answer me, but her mouth was still too full, so she shook her head. We didn't do this often, but Cady always won. I usually let her.

Twenty minutes later, teeth were brushed, hair was up in pigtails, and my girl and I were on our way out the door. She didn't even look at the television today, and I was thankful. Cady waited for me on the porch while I locked up the house, and then we headed to the rear passenger door of my truck. Holding it open for her, Cady hopped up onto the step bar and climbed into her seat. I closed the door and rounded the hood into the driver's seat and off we went to the school drop off.

Glancing in my rearview mirror, I saw my daughter looking out the window with a disturbingly sad look on her face.

"Cadence, what's going on baby? Why do you look like you're about to cry?"

She looked forward but not directly at me when she replied, "I just really was sad the other day after the park. I know it wasn't Elsa, but she still looked like a princess. She seemed so scared. I am just wondering if her daddy keeps her safe like you keep me safe. I don't want her to be scared anymore." Jesus. My daughter. Wise beyond her five years and a heart bigger than most adults.

"Cadence, you are such an amazing little girl. Do you know that? I love you, baby. I am sure that the woman has friends and family looking after her. I am so proud of you for caring so much about another person,"

I commended her because she deserved to hear it.

"I love you too, Daddy."

We pulled up to the school, and of course, Penelope was outside. I swear that woman waits for me to be late. Today, though, she started walking to me before I even had my truck turned off. She was at Cady's side of the truck helping her down by the time I rounded the hood.

"River! Just the guy I wanted to see," she smiled that I-am-up-to-no-good-smile at me as she got my daughter planted on the ground. Shit. This can't be good. Penelope Sloane. Pain in my ass.

"Before you start in on me, can I give my daughter a hug and kiss and wish her a good day in school?"

"Sure. No need to be a grump, River."

"Cady, give me a hug and kiss. I have to talk to Penny, and I see your buddy Bryce waiting for you by the tree over there," I pointed to Bryce as she came to hug me. She pecked me quickly on my cheek and then turned. I yelled, "I love you Cadence Allegra!"

She stopped, turned to me, and with her little hands on her hips she said, "Daddy! I love you too. Why you using my big name? I didn't misbehave yet or anything?"

I turned to Penny and watched as the sides of her mouth quirked up as she tried to hold in her laugh.

"You notice how she said yet?" Penny asked me, then lost her battle and burst out laughing.

"Yeah, Pen. I heard. Can't imagine where my five-year-old is learning her smart-ass tendencies from. But my money is on school." I deadpan. She just continued to laugh. I turned to Cady.

"No, Cady, honey. I just wanted to tell you I love you. Go on. Bryce is waiting for you. And please be a good girl today," I told her. She was too much sometimes. I turned back to Penny with a huge ass smile on my face and my shoulders were shaking because now that Cady was gone, I could laugh.

"That child has so much of her father's attitude, it isn't even funny. You better start preparing for her teenage years now, River. The shotgun collection could always use a few more pieces. Anyway. I wanted to talk to you about the piano lessons."

"What about them, Penny? I can't afford some big shot piano teacher. And I need to be comfortable with the person. So please don't waste my time."

"Well, Mr. Moody, I wanted to tell you I found someone to give the lessons. My best friend is working for Miss Thelma at the shop, and the old broad said Arianna could give Cady the lessons in the back storeroom. They worked all day Saturday to get it ready. All that is left to do is move the piano in there. Arianna is a classically trained pianist, and she went to school with me at Juilliard. She knows what she's doing. She says she can do one hundred dollars a week, every afternoon at three o'clock. That is a great deal, and you would be helping her too," Penny looked at me with big eyes and what I thought was hope.

"You do know that I ran into your friend two days ago, right? I mean she must have told you. I don't know, Penny. She had bruises. Not sure if I can have my daughter around whatever she is mixed up in."

"River, she isn't mixed up in anything. And Ari did tell me she ran into you. Like actually ran into you. She has had a rough go at things. I can't say any more than that because it isn't mine to give you, but trust me. I promise she is good. Cady can get her lessons, you can give her dream roots to grow, and Ari can make some extra money to get on her feet. It's a win-win for everyone involved. I would never put Cady in jeopardy, or I wouldn't have suggested it otherwise," Penny pleaded as she stuck out her lip and pouted at me. Why am I surrounded by all these women that can pull shit over on me? Jesus. I needed to go out with the guys. And soon. I mentally added a call to Braxton on my to-do list.

"Fine. What day do we start?"

"Today. Arianna and Miss Thelma are having Harry Sr. move the piano into the storeroom. They will be ready to go for three."

"I will be here to pick Cady up then today, so if you see Meggie, can you tell her about the change of schedule for now? I really have to go get these errands done. And Penny, tell Bird, Arianna, Ari, or whatever you call her, that she will have to deal with me hanging out during the lessons, yeah?" I raised a brow at her.

"Yes, macho man. I will tell her. What is with the Bird thing though?"

she looked at me for a reply.

"She was as scared as a bird when I touched her. I am pretty sure I clued into her circumstances just by that, but that is how I remember her."

"Well, okay then. But River, her name is Arianna. I call her Ari for short. Not sure she will like the Bird thing."

"I'll keep that in mind, Penny. Are we done now? Got shit to do."

"Yeah. Talk to you later, River. Stay safe out there today," she winked at me and walked away. Penelope Sloane. Pain in my fucking ass.

After the ordeal at the school, and since I had the day off, I went into town to get a coffee and do some grocery shopping. It was well past the morning rush in the Clutch, so I found a parking spot right out front. Moving in the direction of the door, I heard those infamous bells from Thelma's and turned to watch Mickey and Harry Jr. going in. What the fuck is Mickey doing there? Shit. He'd better not be there for any other reason than to help. Scrapping the idea of coffee, for now, I jogged across the empty street to Thelma's. At the door, I could see everyone except Mickey and Bird around the piano.

When I looked toward the counter the cash register was on, Mickey was standing with his hip against it, talking to Bird. *My Bird.* Shit. Where did that come from? I grabbed the door handle and continued to stare in that direction. As the door opened, all heads and eyes swung to me. My focus was on Mickey. My blood started to burn again. This time it wasn't because Bird's beautiful eyes were locked on mine. It was because this fuckwad was bad news and a piece of shit. We went to school together, and even back in high school, he didn't know how to treat girls. And, Junior knew better than to bring him around. So, it didn't shock anyone when I started in on Mickey.

"What the fuck are you doing here, Mick? You know these parts aren't opening arms to welcome you in," I turned and pointed my words at Harry Jr., "and you know better than to bring his ass here."

"Fuck you River. What are you, the goddamn mayor now? You have no authority over who comes in and out of The Falls," Mickey shot back at me.

"Well, Gifford has plenty of places for you to spend your time. There is no reason for you to be here, wasting ours. Seriously Junior. Why is he here?" I asked Harry Jr., or Junior as I call him along with most everybody else.

"Look River, cut me some slack here. Mickey and I were at the stables in Gifford, and my dad called. His arthritis is acting up, and he was supposed to help Miss Thelma move this piano to the back storeroom. He asked us to come and do it for him. That's all. We'll move it and be gone," Junior told me but looked at Mick as if to warn him against being an asshole.

"I'll do it, Junior. Take Mick and get the hell out of Carson Falls." I don't know why that old bastard didn't call me anyway. He bothers me about everything else. "Seriously, go," I barked out. I saw Bird flinch. Fuck.

Junior made his way to the door while Mick stared me down a minute more before curling his lip up at me and shaking his head. I turned, crossed my arms, and watched as they walked out the door, making sure that dick didn't get any ideas outside by the cars or my truck parked across the street. Once they pulled out of their space and drove away, I turned back to the general area of the piano. Miss Thelma and Arianna were there. Miss Thelma was trying to quell her smile, and Ari was wide-eyed with her brows practically hitting her hairline.

"Miss Thelma. Sorry about that ma'am," I tipped my head down to show my sincerity. Then, my eyes found Arianna's.

"I hope I didn't scare you, Bird. Trust me. You're better off without the likes of Mick around here. Nothing but bad news that one."

"River, sugar, that was just about the best timing you could have had. Mick was settling into his position to bein' all that is Mickey around a pretty face. In about another minute or so, he was going to pull out the whole tour guide malarkey since Arianna here told him she was new to town. I didn't have time to warn her about him. They pulled up and came in as I was coming out of the bathroom," Miss Thelma informed me, and my blood that had cooled a smidgen rocketed back to burning.

"Did you call me Bird?" Arianna cut in to ask.

"I did. We met the other day. I'm River. Cady is my daughter. She's the one who's getting the lessons from you," I stated, in case she'd forgotten us.

"I remember. But my name is Arianna. Why did you call me Bird?"

She seemed to be full of attitude today and not at all that scared little bird from the park. Wonder why today was different.

"The day we met you were shaking scared. Like a bird does when it's hurt and a human has to hold it to patch it up." *I wanted to help fix you.* The thought overwhelmed me.

"Oh. Well if you don't mind, my name, again, is Arianna. Most of my friends call me Ari, so I will answer to that, too, if you feel the need to use a nickname," she totally sassed me.

"Well, it's a good thing I don't want to be your friend then, right Bird?" I asked as I winked at Miss Thelma. She laughed low, but I could still hear her. Arianna huffed out a breath. She took the few steps from her spot between the piano and the counter to grab hold of the old wood connected to the piano leg and tried to move it. She was determined and cute as hell. I watched her with my arms crossed over my chest and a grin on my face. A few more failed attempts at pulling the piano to the back and she stood up and again huffed out another breath.

"Big man. Do you think you can use those muscles you got there and get this piano to the back? Otherwise, your girl isn't getting her lessons." Damn. What the hell happened in the last two days? Fuck me, but I will find out.

"What happened to you in the last two days? You were scared to death of me Saturday in the square; now you're being an uppity bitch."

"Excuse me? Did you just call me a bitch?" *Let me kiss the bitch out of you.* What the hell? Where did that come from?

"Indeed I did darlin'. If the shoe fits and all that."

"Penny didn't say anything about you being an asshole. Maybe I should rethink this whole thing. I've had enough asshole to last me the rest of my life."

"Bird, calm down. I'm just givin' it back as good as I'm gettin' it. So, if you're done givin' it, I'll get on with moving the piano. Are you done?"

She looked down and whispered low, "I suppose." That move and her whisper told me more of her story. Pieces started fitting together.

I walked over to the piano and tested out the weight. It was heavy as hell. I inspected the legs and saw that I needed to handle them delicately, or else they would crack off.

"I am going to need to get a dolly to move it, Miss Thelma. It is too old to not crack off the legs in the process. I will come back after lunch with one and grab Braxton to help out," I advised Miss Thelma. Arianna was staring out the window. I moved to her and stood right in front of her. She just continued to act as if I wasn't there.

I grabbed her chin firmly, but gently, and turned her head to look at me. "Bird, I'm sorry for what I said. But darlin' you can't give a man like me attitude and expect me not to react in kind. I meant it when I said I was sorry. Do you accept my apology?" This was a bold move especially considering what happened the last time I touched her. I knew this, but my body needed to connect to hers, touch her, and it was pissing me off that she wouldn't look at me.

"Yes, River. I do. I'm sorry, too. I'm not sure what came over me. I shouldn't have been a bitch. Can you please let go of my face now?" she asked sweetly to cover the sass still at the surface.

"Yeah darlin', but hear me first. I'll be here after lunch to move the piano, then again later with my Cady girl and stayin' for the entire lesson. She's going to be so excited about these lessons since she's been asking for them for near on six months now. So, I'm askin' you to please curb the attitude and join her in that excitement. And Arianna, let her think you are a princess or a queen or a dragon for all I fucking care if that is what she wants. Like I said the other day, she's obsessed with that damn movie and thinks every pretty blonde is Elsa. She's also five, so just go with it if she calls you that, yeah?" Making my point, I let go of her chin. Getting her nod of approval, I turned and walked out the door.

I jogged back across the street and hopped into my truck. Once inside, I tightened my grip on the steering wheel, trying to calm my heaving breaths and that fucking feeling that still overwhelmed me. What the hell just happened in there? There was no reason I should have touched her. Not after all she had been through. She flinched when I yelled at Mick but nothing when I made her look at me. *Get it under control, man.* It has been a really long time since I craved the attention of any woman, but to want that, *no need that*, from *this* woman, is a shit storm in the making. Fuck.

It was just coming up on one in the afternoon. Braxton was in my passenger seat, and I was already regretting my decision to have him help me. I told him everything about Bird, and he hasn't shut the fuck up about it. Braxton 'Jenks' Jenkinson has been my best friend since high school. We played football together since freshman year, and he was well versed in pussy. He was my opposite in every sense of the word. I settled early in life with a wife and baby, or at least I thought I had settled down with a wife. Jenks still liked to get his dick wet in whatever willing female he could find. He owned the club, Reckless, in Gifford, so his search wasn't exactly exhaustive.

Funny thing about Brax, which was what most people called him, except for Penelope since he had this odd thing with her, is he was pretty oblivious to most shit. It was an ongoing disaster with those two. He made it seem like it was Penelope who wasn't interested, but Penny tells a different story. Never one to meddle in anyone's business because I know how much of an annoyance it is, I've kept my opinions and questions to myself. But I know Brax still thinks about Penny because he asks about her every time I see him. So, I used this to my advantage.

"Braxton, have you seen Penny recently? She dyed her hair, let it grow out so she doesn't have those bangs covering those blue as fuck eyes anymore, and she's been running every mornin'. She is looking good, dude."

"You're an asshole, River. Why the fuck would I care about that? Besides, don't change the damn subject. It's been a long time since you've shown any interest in a woman, so I'm allowed to give you shit about it." Braxton Jenkinson. Another pain in my ass.

"We're here," I said as I backed into the spot right in front of Thelma's Treasures and Trinkets. "So, how about you shut your mouth. You'll see what I mean about her when we get inside."

"Whatever man. She really has you twisted up inside huh?"

"Jenks, what the fuck did I just say?" Using his nickname must have clued him in to how serious I was because he snapped his mouth shut, sighed, and hopped out of the truck.

Trying to stay calm, because I knew I would be seeing Bird again in a few minutes, seemed a fruitless endeavor. That feeling I got when it came to Arianna had shifted and taken over my system. My heart was racing. Sweat formed on my forehead, and I just wanted to be in her space. It's like I was twelve again and crushin' on the prettiest girl in school. Pulling down the handle on the rear gate to the bed of my truck, Braxton hopped up first to push the dolly forward to me so I could lift it down. He held open the door to Miss Thelma's so I could easily maneuver the damn thing inside. When I saw his jaw drop, I knew he had spotted my Bird. *My Bird.* She isn't mine...yet.

"Brax. Pick your jaw up, asshole and get a move on. I have to get my girl from school in an hour, so I want to get this done, yeah?"

"Fuck me, River."

That was all he said as I walked by him going straight to the piano. Following his line of sight, I turned and saw Arianna and Penny at the counter talking. *Well, at least I knew he wasn't staring at my girl.* Fuck. I needed to cut that shit out. I didn't know Penny would be here but look at my best friend. Drool and all.

Shaking my head, I growled, "Braxton!" That got his fucking attention.

"Right. Piano," he said coming out of his (what better fucking be) Penny-trance to help me.

Nodding my chin up, I gave a quick, "Hey Bird. Penelope."

"River," Penny said, then looked to Braxton and gave him, "Asshole."

I couldn't contain myself and barked out a laugh. Arianna whispered a low, "Penny!" as if to scold her friend.

"Penelope. Sugar sweet as always, I see. Lookin' good though," he tried to act like he hadn't just come in his pants at the sight of her.

"All right asshole, let's get this done."

"You got it, boss," the fucker saluted me.

Carefully, we lifted the piano onto the dolly and wheeled it into the storeroom. Much easier having help lifting this thing. Miss Thelma was already back there and pointed to the corner where she wanted it. Brax and I took the same care in placing it where she wanted. She gave her approval, and we all headed back out front.

Penny and Ari were still talking, pretending neither Brax nor I were in the same space they were. I guess my Bird still didn't get it. She would though. It was only a matter of time. Besides, she will see me every day at three o'clock, and I couldn't give a fuck if she wanted me there or not. As for Penny, it looked like Braxton may have reached his breaking point. Maybe now he will get his head out of his ass and do what he needed to do to get Penny where he so obviously wanted her.

"Be back in a bit, Bird. Remember what we talked about, yeah?" I warned over my shoulder to her as I headed to the door. Penny looked at me, and her mouth was curved up in a smile, like she knew. She most likely did. Whatever. Pain in my ass.

It was time to drop Braxton off, get my girl, then Bird watch.

Let the games begin.

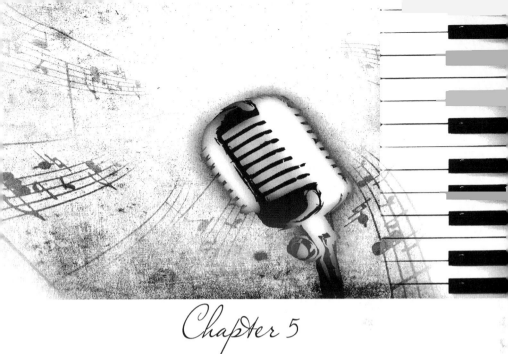

Chapter 5

Do You Want to Be My Friend?
Arianna

I had no idea what happened to me. It was like a switch flipped and I just went into bitch mode. And he had the audacity to grab my chin. Yet, at the exact instant he touched me, the anger at his silly nickname for me, and any other attitude toward him I had left, evaporated. His words were fair, and he was right. Cady would be excited, and I knew that just from the way she was when she thought I was Elsa. I needed to make sure that everything went well. The money was really going to help me get on my feet again, so I had no room to mess this up.

It was a quarter to three. River and Cady would be here any minute. Being nervous was an understatement. With our interactions thus far, it was fair to say that River freaked me out. He scared me so much, and now I was stuck playing nice and dealing with him watching my every move during the lessons. Maybe if I could get the fact that he thought of me as being anything close to gorgeous out of my mind, and throw a brown sack over his body, my sanity would restore itself. It was time to pull up my big girl panties and be an adult again. I had only been in Carson Falls for five days, but somehow it felt like so much had happened already, and things were changing so fast.

I walked to the front of the shop to wait for River and Cady to arrive and had wandered over to the Precious Moments trinket I spied the first time I was in here. It made me think how almost three weeks ago, I was carrying a life. Then I wasn't. *Andrew.* The sonofabitch had been caught. He fled the scene and carried on like he hadn't done anything wrong but they found him at some fancy-ass restaurant in Seattle with some woman who claimed to be his new girlfriend. There was not an ounce of remorse in his being. At least that was what the cop that called me, right after River had left to get the dolly this morning, had said. I was relieved they got him, but still unsure of who that man was. He wasn't the man I once knew.

I had called Penny at work after speaking to the police from Seattle about Andrew and answering more questions. Penny came to Miss Thelma's as soon as she could. It would explain my reaction to River but not entirely. I was on edge but more so because River was beautiful. His daughter was beautiful. And I knew I was damaged enough not to be worthy of either of them. I needed to get through these lessons and not think about anything but the music. The majesty of creating sound that blossomed into songs. That was my focus.

A throat cleared behind me and I startled. The Precious Moments trinket I had been holding, slipped out of my hand and almost hit the floor. My reflexes were still pretty good, so I was able to grab it before it did.

"Sorry darlin'. I didn't mean to scare you," River said.

"It's fine. I was just…"

"Cryin'?" River asked as he looked at the tears slowly falling down my cheeks.

He began to move closer to me. My heart started to race. I raised my hand to stop his progress, palm out to him.

"Stop, River. Please don't. I'm all right. Just been a long day so far. Where is Cady?" I asked him while searching the area for her.

"Cady is in the storeroom. Which she now calls the princess music room. I told her to go on back when I saw you over here. Do you want to tell me what's going on? You've been all over the map with your moods toward me today and darlin', I don't even know you all that well, so that's sayin' something."

"I really am fine, and I don't want to talk about it. I appreciate you looking out for me, but you said it yourself; we don't know each other. Now, if you will excuse me," I tried to maneuver around him, but he halted my progress by stepping in front of me with both his hands outstretched as if he were directing traffic. I think he understood that I was too emotional right now, so he didn't touch me again like this morning. But, I could tell he had something to say so I took a step back, crossed my arms over my belly in a protective move, and waited for him to start.

"Bird. My girl is in that room waiting for you to teach her how to play piano. When I told her she was getting these lessons and you were giving them to her, she about lost her little girl mind. I am currently her favorite person in the world. And I know when we walk through the door, my reign will end and you will be all she will talk about. So, darlin' please dry the tears. My baby girl is waiting for you. You don't wanna talk to me, that's fine by me. You will sooner or later. But she will want to talk, and she will ask questions. If you don't want to have to make up lies to a five-year-old girl and feel completely uncomfortable by those questions, then I suggest you get your shit together. I can stall her for a few minutes if you want to go fix yourself up in the bathroom."

"What do you mean I will talk to you sooner or later?" I asked, semi-bitchy.

"Darlin' just what I said. Now, bathroom. Go," he bossed me.

"Whatever," I whispered as I moved around him this time, and made it to the bathroom.

Who was this guy? And why hadn't his bossiness made me uncomfortable?

Five minutes later, I made my way to the storeroom and stopped at the door that was cracked open just a bit. I knew better than to eavesdrop but I couldn't help myself when I heard River interacting with Cady.

Wedging my ear into the opening in between the door and the jam, I heard Cady say, "But Daddy, she has to be some sort of princess, right? She makes pretty songs, and she looks like a princess."

"I know baby. She is very pretty. And, she is going to help you make pretty songs now, too. Cady, sugar. She isn't a princess though."

I walked through the door at that, and both of them turned their heads my way. Slowly, I looked at Cady and took her in. She was dressed in a gorgeous purple dress with cap sleeves, a lilac sash tied around the waist, tulle that put the poof in poofy, and the cutest little purple patent leather shoes that buckled on the side. A smile must have crept onto my face because she leaned over to her dad and not so quietly whispered, "See Daddy. I told you she would love my dress."

River burst out laughing and said through it, "You were right my girl. You definitely told me."

I made my way over to her and knelt down, so I was at her level. I stuck out my hand for her to shake, but she just looked up at me with these big, beautiful, blue-gray eyes.

"Cady, shake Arianna's hand. Tell her your name."

"Hi. I'm Cady and you're Bird," she said with a twinkle in her eye.

"My name is Arianna, Cady," I turned my glare to her father, "not Bird. Don't you look just beautiful today. I'm so glad I'll be making music with a princess like you, Cady."

Cady gasped and turned to her father, "Daddy! She thinks I'm a princess!"

I giggled, and it caught River's attention because he smirked at me. I shook my head at him and brought my attention back to Cady.

"Princess Cady, are you ready for your very first piano lesson? All princesses must know how to play the piano. After all, your name itself is musical, so it must be destiny."

"It is?" she asked in complete awe.

"It absolutely is. Come on let's get you started."

"Okay, Birdie."

I sighed and looked at River who was silently laughing. His broad shoulders shook up and down, giving him away. Shit, but he looked so much more beautiful when he laughed. Giving up the fight against the name Bird, I grabbed Cady's hand and helped her up on the piano bench.

The next hour and a half consisted of me teaching Cady how to properly curve her little hands, how to locate the 'C' key, and how to play the C Major scale. Every so often, I chanced a glance over to the corner opposite the piano where River sat. He watched me with his daughter so closely it made my skin tingle. There was absolutely no shame in his staring. When I caught him, he didn't even turn away like most people would. His mouth just gave that stupid sexy grin, and his eyes twinkled.

If I am honest about the whole thing, I felt safe while he was there. It had been an extremely long time since I was able to freely talk about music or even play freely and having Cady and him there made it easier. Comfortable. And, if I was honest with myself, I knew he was focused on me most of the lesson because I could feel his eyes roaming over me.

It was coming up on the end of the first lesson, and I wanted to discuss my first impressions of Cady with River. River needed to be sure to get her a keyboard or a used piano somewhere so that she could practice at home. Learning the piano required practice every day.

"Okay Princess Cady, I think we did enough for today. What did you think of your first lesson?" I watched a smile stretch so huge across her face; it almost looked painful.

"Birdie, I LOVED it! I'm so excited to scale!" she said excitedly.

"Cady, sweetie," I started through a giggle, "you play scales. YOU don't scale. The scale was C Major. I want you to practice curving your hands for me tonight and tomorrow, and we'll work on the C Major scale some more, okay?"

"Yes, Birdie!" She yelled as she hopped down and ran over to the corner where her dad was.

"Daddy! I scaled! Did you hear me?" she asked, so proud of herself.

"Baby girl, I heard you. You did so great. I am so proud of you," he said while kneeling down to give Cady a hug and kiss on her cheek. He really was good with her. Natural. I heard him whisper to Cady something about heading out to Miss Thelma. She agreed and raced out of the storeroom to the front of the shop.

"River, I wanted to just discuss a few things before you leave."

"Yeah, me too. You go on first darlin'."

"Well, I think Cady did extremely well today. She has a natural curve to her fingers, even at five. Plus, she caught on very quickly. This is all good news for me, but I am not sure it is great news for you," I said as I gazed at his face that had taken on a very confused look.

"Why do you say that?"

"Because River, I wasn't kidding. Learning piano and being good at it comes from practice. She will need to practice every day. Do you have a piano at home?"

"No, Bird. But if you say my girl needs one, I'll do whatever I can to get her one. Is that what you're saying?" River asked me.

"Yes. At the very least, she needs a keyboard. That will do until she gets older or you can save up to get her a piano."

Looking at me intensely, he muttered something under his breath and nodded his head.

"Are we done here, Bird?" He asked in a sort of clipped tone. It was almost like I did or said something to piss him off.

"Yes, River. I will see you and Cady tomorrow." Making my way quickly to the door and through it, I heard Cady and Miss Thelma chatting as I approached the counter. Well, Cady was chatting, and Miss Thelma was just smiling away at the adorable little girl.

"Come on baby girl. We've got to get going. Miss Thelma and Arianna need to close up the store," he said as he held his hand out for his daughter to grab.

"Ok, Daddy. Can I give Birdie a hug goodbye?"

"You have to ask her sweet girl."

"Birdie, can I give you a hug goodbye?" She hit me with the little girl puppy-dog eyes. Damn. How could I say no to that? I walked over to her and nodded my head in the affirmative.

She hugged me around my waist before I could even bend down. Not quite sure what was going on, I asked her if she is all right.

"Cady, sweetheart, are you okay?" Cady let go of my waist and looked up at me. She motioned with her little hand for me to come closer, so I bent down to her.

"I know you were scared the other day at the square when me and Daddy first met you. But I will be your friend, so you won't be scared anymore. Do you want to be my friend Birdie?" she asked with those gorgeous damn eyes aimed my way, again. I inhaled sharply to keep myself from crying. As I looked up to get some sort of guidance from River, he had a small, almost sad smile on his face as he watched me interact with his daughter.

"Cady, of course I'll be your friend, beautiful girl. I know that with you by my side, I won't be scared of anything," I told her as I went in to hug her again. We broke the moment when River cleared his throat. Glancing his way, I watched the emotion clear from his eyes, and they became lazy as he looked at me.

"Let's go Cadence. It's time to leave." River walked over to where Cady and I were standing, grabbed her hand, and then so low that only I could hear him, he said, "You just gave my girl one of the greatest gifts you could have. Know with that, though, comes responsibility to guard her heart. Don't hurt her, Bird. She won't be able to take it. I think you get what I'm sayin' so remember that, yeah?" I think he just reprimanded me.

"See you later, River," I said shaking my head at his forthrightness. But, if he was like that with his daughter, he was probably the same way with his women. Women. Plural. A guy as beautiful, as built, as tall, with blue-gray eyes that change with each mood, had to have lots of experience. *Don't go there, Arianna.*

Standing next to Miss Thelma, we watched the two of them make their way to the truck parked in front of the shop. She was laughing, so I turned to look at her.

"Sugar, if you didn't think you were on River Bradshaw's radar before, you should be as sure as the sky is blue that you are now. You are helping that little one in more ways than you can imagine. She needs a good woman like you in her life. Keep moving forward, and eventually, you'll see what the rest of us already do," she dropped her observation on me and shuffled away to collect her things to go home. While she did that, I called Penny to come get me.

When Penny arrived to pick me up, I was so hungry my stomach growled louder than the engine of her car. We decided to go out to grab a bite for dinner in Gifford. According to her, Gifford Diner had some of the best 'comfort' food in three counties. Honestly, I didn't care if they served rocks. I was so hungry at that point I would've eaten anything.

Eating lunch today at the store was not an option because my stomach had been in knots after hearing Andrew was found. He had money, so he would be out fairly quickly on bail. I knew this, and in my heart, I knew he would look for me. But the lesson, and Cady's embrace calmed the fear and anxiety that had started to ratchet up throughout the day.

As we pulled up to the diner, I started to laugh and just shook my head. I shouldn't have been surprised anymore by the way everything in the country looked like it jumped off a greeting card, but there it was, right in front of us. Gifford Diner was situated on the corner of two intersecting streets. It was made out of logs, like a cabin. It had these two wooden doors, the top half was open, and the bottom half was closed, like those in an old western saloon that swung open to enter and exit. The windows along the street side of the building were large, open panes with wood sills. The enormous rectangular sign above the doors read, 'Gifford Diner: Good Eatin', Good People' in very bright orange and green. We parked and made our way inside. I was still giggling.

"What's so funny?" Penny asked as she approached the door and held it open for me.

I walked in and burst out laughing. I couldn't contain my hilarity. Maybe it had been my body releasing the day's emotions but this just could not be believed. In direct view was this counter that spread the length of the dining area and curved into a half circle with a flip-up top so the wait staff could enter and exit from behind it. The seating along the front was made up of metal stools, topped with cushions the same bright orange as the sign and the expansive counter top. The wall behind the counter held the soda, coffee, and ice cream machines as well as glasses, mugs and the dessert display. The dining room walls had fun old-timey pictures and artifacts nailed to the logs. The floor was a very polished wood that matched the tables, chairs, and the church pew style benches that were evenly spaced throughout the room.

"I'm sorry. I just can't seem to get over how much these towns out here look like something from a movie set. They're so old fashioned and perfect."

"Yeah well, you get used to it. It beats the stuffy air and buildings piled on top of each other in most cities. My biggest problem when we were in New York at school, was the modernized cluster that it was. I missed the small town, country life. Plus, folks here are far nicer."

"I will agree with you about the people. Even in Seattle, the hustle and bustle of the city made people less civilized."

"Do you want to sit at the counter or a table?" Penny asked once I had calmed down and was able to act like a normal human being with some grace again.

"How about that table in the corner near the big window, away from everyone so we can talk?"

"Sounds good to me," Penny shrugged and led us to that exact table.

Once we got comfortable and placed our order with a waitress unlike any other I had seen before, I clamped my hands together in a ball, leaned forward a bit, and let out a long-suffering sigh. As I stared out the window, my thoughts roamed to the past couple of days and how quickly my life had changed. I never imagined myself not playing music. But it happened. I never thought I would ever allow a man to put a hand on me. But it happened. Now, I was in this town, regaining some of the life I had originally planned out for myself, at least where music was concerned.

I was startled out of my thoughts when our waitress, in her very fifties-style light yellow skirt uniform with white collar, cuffs, and matching white apron, whose name tag read Deb, somewhat forcefully plopped our sodas down onto the table spilling some of the liquid onto it.

"Sorry, ladies. I can wipe it up, but y'all got your own napkins right there to do it yourselves, so go ahead. I'll wait," Waitress Deb said with a small smile and a ton of sarcasm. I reached for the napkins, but Penny beat me to it.

"Now that we've established that I'm a waitress and not your maid, there's no more mashed potatoes, so you are gettin' fries. And, there's no more catfish or chicken, so burgers it is. It's your lucky night, though. The mac and cheese is still available, and you're getting two helpings of that. If you have any complaints about the changes to your meal, please fill out the form that is shoved between the salt and pepper shakers, and drop it in the comments and suggestions box on your way out. Before I go grab your food, is there anything you have to say or ask?"

I looked at Penny. She was laughing her ass off, and I just sat there stunned at the manner in which Waitress Deb went about things.

"I'll take that as a no then. Penelope, always a pleasure. Lady who looks like she just swallowed something sour, nice to meet you. Enjoy the food," Waitress Deb finished then turned and walked away.

Penny was still laughing when I looked at her. My stunned expression must not have diminished any because she at least had the good grace to get herself under control.

"Penny. What the hell was that?"

"That was Deb. She's extremely ornery and sassy. She's been doing this a long time. And just so you know, the mac and cheese is why we're here. I come in here every so often and order it. It's to die for. She knows what I like, and since you're with me, she'll give you what I get. The kitchen never runs out of anything, but she tagged you as soon as we ordered. Anyway, talk to me, Ari. You have to be feeling something after all that happened today."

"I'm feeling lots of things, Pen. Terror that he is going to figure out where I am. Loss because I will never know my child. But, most of all Penny, I feel like I'm living someone else's life. Like this is all just a crazy movie I'm playing a part in. So many things have changed so fast, I can't keep up. The only thing that soothed me today was when River and Cady were there for the piano lesson. Do you know what that beautiful little creature asked me today?"

"No babe. Tell me."

"She asked me if I would be her friend because she didn't want me to be scared anymore. She looked so cute staring up at me with her big eyes. I had no choice but to say yes. But Penny, she scares me. What River whispered to me after she asked that, scared me too. But, when we were near each other, it was the safest I have felt for as long as I can remember."

"Oh my goodness. Cadence. She is a special little girl. Smarter than the average five-year-old. But, the rest of that, Ari, will work itself out. You've been through more than most people experience in a lifetime in a little over two weeks. You're allowed to feel whatever you need to, but don't let it grab hold and drag you down. Don't allow him to harden that beautiful heart of yours that deserves happiness." Poor Penny. She must be so tired of fluffing my confidence.

"Speaking of your dick of an ex, we can go to the sheriff's office and just talk to Sheriff Gaynor. He'll tell us what precautions we can take. I'll go with you if you want me to," my best friend offered.

"I think that sounds like an excellent idea. Can we go tomorrow during my lunch hour?" I asked her, hopeful and eager to get peace of mind for the time being.

"Sure. Just text me tomorrow when you are ready to go, and I will tell my boss that I have a family emergency to attend to."

I smiled at my friend. She gave me her own smile back. I reached over the table and squeezed her hands just as Waitress Deb came back to our table with our food. She gave us and our plates the same treatment as before by plopping them down, ripping off the check from her pad, and then walking away. Before she reached the flip-up part of the counter, she looked back at me, winked, and then continued on behind the counter. Hmm. She was an odd one.

Penny and I dug into our food. And, she was so right. This food was the best I had eaten thus far in Tennessee. The burger was cooked to perfection and the bun toasted to a light golden brown. And, the cheddar jack cheese added between the lettuce and tomato blended it together better, according to Penny. The fries were crispy and had this seasoning on them that was mouthwatering. But, the mac and cheese made me happiest. The noodles were cooked to impeccable al dente status, and the four cheese blend had me salivating.

"Arianna. Act like a lady for fuck's sake. You look like you haven't eaten in weeks. And I could do without the repeat muffin orgasm performance."

"I'm sorry. This food is incredible though. And, smart-ass, I didn't eat lunch today because I was too stressed out."

"Ok. But seriously. Calm down. Waitress Deb may come back and harass you if you keep it up."

"Shut up. You can be really annoying sometimes," I said, halfheartedly.

I did calm myself down and finished my meal like a civilized person instead of some barbarian. Penny cracked jokes and made me laugh. It felt like our college days when we would stay up all night in the city diners studying or just talking about which guy we were crushing on. It was good to not think about my feelings or my situation and just be. I really did have the best friend anyone could ask for. She was my constant in this ever-changing life of mine.

We paid the bill and were on our way out the swinging half door when a big hand caught it and held it open for us to walk through. I looked up as I heard Penny mutter something under her breath that I couldn't hear. It was River's friend Braxton...or Brax. Whatever. I smiled and started to say thank you when Braxton, who I must say was pretty damn hot himself, but more a bad boy than cowboy, stood frozen in place glaring at Penny.

Finally, after a few intense moments, he came unstuck. He ushered, into the diner, a very busty redhead that had just bounced up to him and clung to his very muscular arm. As they passed us, he dipped his chin in greeting and said, "Penelope. Arianna. Good evening."

Penny just snarled at their backs and headed to the car. I tried to catch up to her, but her annoyance forced her strides to be longer and quicker than usual. She was in the car and had it started before I was even at the passenger side door. I got in and buckled up, prepared for an angry drive home. Just as my mouth opened to ask her if she was all right, she turned the stereo on, and the volume up. Loud. So loud, I knew she didn't want to talk.

By the time we pulled into the apartment complex, Penny seemed to have calmed down a bit. I took my chances.

"So maybe you want to tell me the whole story about you and Braxton, now?" I asked her as we made our way inside the apartment. Penny kept her word and put those freaky-ass dolls away, so the living room was overtaken by my stuff. Technically, it was my bedroom, right?

"Braxton Jenkinson is a man-whoring jackass. He owns Reckless, and we had a thing once, a long time ago, then again a while before you came out here. We danced, drank, and got along great. We went back to my place, and things started to happen. I should've known I wasn't anything other than just pussy for him. But, I've had a thing for him since I got back from college. I told him how I felt that night. I was drunk but not enough to not understand or remember what I was saying or doing. He said he couldn't risk hooking up with me and then he was gone. River saw me a few days later and asked me what was going on. Gave me some bullshit story about how Braxton had told him what went down. Said Braxton left me a note to call him later on that day and that he knew Braxton wouldn't just walk away from me without good reason. There was no note, Ari. I looked everywhere in my apartment after River told me that. So, Braxton Jenkinson can very much go fuck himself."

My heart hurt for my friend. I had never seen Penny so into a guy before.

"Penny. I'm so sorry honey. Maybe you should talk to Braxton yourself and not take anyone's word for it. It could be a misunderstanding."

"That ship has sailed, Arianna."

"If it has, then why do you still go to his club and why do you look like your puppy was just kidnapped?" I asked her.

She didn't answer me. She walked into her bedroom, slammed the door, and turned the stereo to loud, unhealthy volumes and didn't come out for the rest of the night. Seemed like Penny may not be as over this guy as she said. I sighed and got ready for bed.

My thoughts were of blue-gray eyes, pigtails, and melodies as my body relaxed and sleep took me under to dream.

Chapter 6

Sweetest Torture There Was
River

I had been trying to keep my cool and calm disposition around Arianna the best I could. But, to be honest, the past few weeks of sitting in a room watching her give my daughter piano lessons had come to be some of the sweetest torture there was. We had, of course, bumped into each other in town. Cady's favorite place was the park in the square, so we spent a lot of time there on the weekends, especially since the weather was so nice. Arianna seemed to have taken to eating her lunch on the benches right outside the gazebo. Whether she was doing this on purpose or not, I had no clue.

It was mid-April, so spring was in full swing. Springtime in The Falls was always magical. The county fair, chili festivals, cookouts, and the pure wonder of all the flowers blooming and people out and about. It was always the best and my absolute favorite season. It meant me and my baby girl could start fishing out back at the lake again. Cady took after me in that if we could be outside, we were.

Cady's first piano lesson was mesmerizing to me. She was absolutely a natural at it. I knew not one damn thing about the piano, but Cady was so entranced and paid such close attention to most of what Bird said. Arianna was beautiful normally, but with Cady, her light shined brightly around her and intensified that natural beauty to blinding proportions. The type of man I was, I knew what a lucky bastard I was to have a second chance at beauty like that and I sure as fuck was not going to let that chance pass me by. I just needed to proceed with caution.

I did what Bird had asked and got an old piano from a school over in Gifford that was going to auction it off. Instead, I had Braxton see if I could buy it and the school could use the money to donate directly to the cause for which they were raising the funds. The piano needed to be tuned according to Bird. She had looked at it before I purchased it one day after Cady's lessons last week. That was when it happened. A breakthrough of sorts. I learned something new about Ari. She could sing. I walked into Thelma's and into the back where the storeroom was now transformed into a music room. Bird sat on the piano bench, fingers flying across the keys, and she was singing her own version of "Fix You" by Coldplay. I stood at the door, leaned up against the jamb, and just listened. The lyrics that spoke of losing something that you couldn't replace, mixed with her record-worthy voice, told me there were more layers that I would need to peel back to get my Bird to fly free.

When she finished, I pushed off the door jamb and walked over to her.

"That was pretty fantastic, darlin'. You should be in Nashville recording music. Not sitting in an old musty room teaching piano. Can I ask you something, Bird? Why that song?" I looked straight into her eyes as I asked while approaching her. She only allowed me to touch her that one time I grabbed her chin, and even then, she tensed. But since then, she still flinched or has gone rigid any and every time I have made an attempt to get close to her. We really needed to talk about this.

"River, how long have you been watching me? Seriously, it's like you're everywhere all the time and I never know it."

"Arianna. Are we going there with the attitude again? I just gave you a compliment. Darlin', you should say thank you, not bust my balls about watchin' and listenin' to you when that is exactly what people should be doin' since you play like that and sing like that. Although, I do find it amusing that you think any attitude you give me does anything but make you even cuter. So, my little *Song Bird*, please stop deflecting my question and tell me why that song?" I placed my forearms onto the lid of the piano and leaned into her space so she knew I wanted to have an actual conversation.

She had dropped her head again and looked down to her lap. She did that the last time I called her out on her mood. The need to push her to get past this constant fear she had overwhelmed me. My gut clenched because I knew that her putting her trust in me and pushing her fear aside wouldn't happen overnight.

"Arianna, look at me." She raised her head and did as I asked. The look in her eyes, combined with her rock-solid body language told me she was scared of me. Me. Like I would ever hurt a hair on her head. It was enough to make me want to find her piece of shit ex and show him how it felt to be left beaten, broken, and scared. She wasn't able to see what anyone else may be able to give her because of him, but she would in time.

"I can see you locking up from here, and I know a little about your past to get why. But darlin', I promise, you are safe with me. I don't point your attitude out to you so you hang your head in shame. Your attitude is one of the many things about you that gets my blood pumping. Makes me want to know what buttons to push so you give it to me. The last few weeks, you sat with my daughter and showed her beauty. Anything you say to me usually has to do with Cady or the lessons. Nothing we have discussed outside of those two things has had meaning or given me any kind of glimpse into who you are. So, Bird, why don't you talk to me?" She sighed long and loud.

"River, I…I just don't understand why you care so much. We don't ever talk about anything other than your daughter because I'm here to teach her. That's it. I have nothing to offer you. Trust me. I don't say anything about myself because, River, I have no idea who I am. My life. My identity. The music. All of it was taken from me, piece by piece. I constantly feel like I'm doing something wrong, even now. I learned the difficult way that anything I did or said was wrong and that will take me time to get past. And yes, when you give it to me straight like that, it confuses and scares the dickens out of me. No one has ever been that forthcoming with me. Also, just to say, I never know what you're going to do, so I tense up. The song was just a song that I know how to play and like to sing. What is the big damn deal?"

"The big damn deal is you are lyin' right to my face. There is meaning in that song. Now, darlin', I am happy you finally said something worth a damn, but I think you're wrong. You know who you are and you're getting back to being that person. The one before him. The one you will be again. You just took a time-out. You'll learn that I don't judge you because of your past. Now, that wasn't so hard to give me, was it?"

"GOD!! You are so pushy. Look. I know you mean well, but I really should go."

I inched closer to her.

"My instincts are to keep you here any way I know how, but I know you aren't there yet, so I'll give you some time to adjust. But Bird, start talking yourself around to being in my space more and liking it." I winked at her, turned around, and walked out to my truck before she could argue or give me any more bullshit excuses about how she has nothing to offer. She has more to offer than she will ever know.

For the last week or so, I called her my Song Bird. Ari's eyes narrowed and grew the slightest bit darker every time I called her that. I wish I could say that I didn't purposely want to rile her up, but I'd be lying if I did. Every time those gorgeous eyes hit me with that pissed off look, I grinned at her. It was the only response I got out of her. Any type of friendly interactions seemed like they were out of obligation or for show in front of my daughter. I never got the truth about why that song was the one she chose. There was definitely more to it than her just knowing how to play and sing it.

Seeing Arianna uninhibited and not suppressing her talent, but unleashing her emotions and flying high on the music, made something in my chest start to burn, and it made my dick hard. She could let go. There was a wildness to her. A wild I wanted to reap the benefits of. *FUCK.* She was consuming every single thought I had since I met her. To say that my patience was wearing thin, was the understatement of the century but I knew I needed to bide my time. I really needed to just go out with Braxton and the guys this weekend.

Now, it was Monday, and I was outside waiting for Cady to get out of school so we could head into town for her lesson. My phone buzzed, and I didn't even have to look down. I knew it was Bird because I set her ringtone to the very same Coldplay song I caught her performing. We exchanged phone numbers a few days after we started in case something came up, or we couldn't make it. I could have called Miss Thelma's store, but then I wouldn't have Arianna's number. It was my way of being sneaky yet rational and still getting something I wanted. I swiped my thumb across the arrow on the screen and greeted her with, "Bird."

"Hey, River. I was just calling to see if we can possibly reschedule today's lesson or perhaps I could give Cady her lesson at your house. Miss Thelma had something important come up and has to close up the store early."

She would be in my space now.

"I don't think rescheduling will go over well with my girl, so I'll pick you up from the store once Cady gets out of school. She should be out in about five minutes or so. And, as long as your friend doesn't start busting my balls like she usually does, we should be there to get you in about fifteen minutes or so, yeah?"

"Okay, River. Thank you and sorry it is so last minute. I hope this isn't putting you out at all. I would hate to disturb things at home or interfere with any routine Cady may be on," Arianna said with concern laced in her voice.

"Arianna, if it were a problem, I would have said so. See you in fifteen minutes, Bird," I said then hung up.

My heart picked up its pace again, my chest tightened, and my mind raced at the thought of seeing her again. It had only been two days, but I was becoming more and more addicted to just the sight of her. Her smell, her talent, and her kind nature were all icing on my sweet fantasy cake.

"Daddy!!" Cady pulled on my hand to get my attention and snapped me right out of the daydream I was having of Bird.

"Hey, baby girl! How was school today?" I bent down and scooped her up so I could get a hug. My daughter will never go a day with me not showing her affection or telling her how much she is loved. She started to fill me in on her day while she had my face in both of her little hands.

"Daddy, I made a picture for Birdie. I can't wait to give it to her at Miss Thelma's today!" Cady started wiggling for me to put her down. But before I did, we needed to talk about today's lesson.

"Baby girl, that is so fantastic that you drew Bird a picture. And you'll definitely be able to give it to her, but today, we're going to pick up Arianna and take her back to our house so…" A throat clearing stopped my conversation with Cady. My daughter and I both looked to see where the noise came from. Penny. Of course. Who else would it be? No chance of me not getting my balls busted.

"So…did I just hear that Arianna was being picked up by you and being taken to your residence?" Penny quirked an eyebrow, crossed her arms over her chest, and waited for me to elaborate. She shouldn't hold her breath. If Arianna wanted to explain in detail to her meddling friend, then that was on her to do so.

"You did. Seeing as you did and I have my very excited girl in my arms, I need to go. That is all you get from me. If Bird wants to fill you in, she can. I don't even have the full story. Only that she needed to do the lesson at our house today. Gotta run. Later Pen."

"River," Penny called to me as I walked to my truck.

"Yes?" I turned back to face her, still holding Cady.

"Fragile. Remember. Handle with care, but handle it all the same," she winked at me. Yes. Winked. Penelope Sloane. Pain in my ass.

I got Cady situated in the truck, and we headed to town to pick up Bird. On the way, I filled Cady in that this visit was for her lesson, and not a time to play dolls or dress up. She had to get her lesson done first. If Ari wanted to interact on a friendlier level afterward, then that was her choice. I wouldn't force anything on her. She'd had enough of being forced to do things she didn't want to do.

I looked in the rearview at Cady to see her looking deep in thought but confused.

"What are you thinkin' about baby girl?"

"Well, Penny said fragile. What does that mean?" My kid. She didn't miss a damn thing. It was always amazing to see her curiosity and intelligence at only five years old.

"Fragile means somethin' kind of like easily broken. Like glass. So, it needs to be touched gently and loved a whole bunch." Please let that be enough of an explanation for now.

"Oh. Like my Elsa statue or something?"

"Yes, baby. Just like that."

"Ok," she said and turned to stare out the window.

Cady was quiet for a few minutes, so I thought we were in the safe zone for now. I didn't think it was appropriate for me to discuss with her the reasons why Bird was so fragile. She may understand to a point, but maybe when she was older, or even if Bird was still around, they could have that to share between them.

We pulled up out front of Miss Thelma's ten minutes later, and I saw Arianna sitting on the bench just staring out into the square where there was a man and a woman walking, holding hands with their little boy. Ari watched intently as the parents each held one of the little guy's hands and swung him in the air and back down again. I watched as she wiped under her eyes, cleared her throat, and turned away from the family. Her reaction to anything involving little boys always seemed to bring tears to her eyes. At that moment, watching her, the realization hit me. Breaking down her walls so that I could figure out if I was right about her demons needed to become a priority.

I looked in my mirror and saw that Cady was still staring out the window and was being quiet. My gaze landed on Bird as she got up from the bench and started walking over to the truck. She had on this white, short, dress and her gorgeous, wavy, blonde hair was pulled back on both sides and fastened at the back of her head with these sparkling clips that were some sort of music symbol, which I had no idea the official name of. My eyes trailed lower and landed on her choice of shoes. My dick jumped in my jeans, and I swallowed hard. She was trying to kill me. Cowboy boots. If Bird only knew what those boots did to me. She was the epitome of sexy, and she didn't even know it. At least one wet dream every teenage boy had, starred a woman the likes of Arianna. And every grown man's fantasy was to bury himself inside a woman with this amount of beauty for the rest of his life.

"DADDY!" My daughter broke through my perusal of the goddess that was, at that moment, giving me the worst case of bulge I'd ever had, by screaming and pointing Arianna's way. Even when I first saw her, Emma never made my dick get this hard.

"Yes, Cady. I see her baby girl. I'm just going to help her into the truck all right?" I said and then opened my door to meet Arianna at the passenger side door.

"Hey, River. Thanks again so much for this. It should just be for today," Arianna said as she walked up to me with her head down again, looking at her feet.

"Hey, Song Bird. What did I say about that head down shit?"

Her head popped up, and she glared at me. There it was. That heat in her eyes. It was angry heat right now, but soon it would be a heat that we could channel into something creative.

"For Pete's sake, River. Enough with the song bird stuff. Can we please just go? I really don't want to go toe to toe with you today about this. I accepted Bird. Can't that be enough for now?" Ari stepped around me and reached her hand out to open the door to the truck. I beat her to it and rested my hand on top of hers on the handle.

"Not so fast darlin'. I don't know what you were used to prior to being in The Falls, but here, we act like gentlemen when escorting a lady somewhere and that includes opening doors. Whether they're vehicle doors or building doors. So, if you would, please step back so I can open the truck door and help you up into the seat, it would be appreciated."

"You don't need to do that. I can get up into the truck just fine," she shot back. Arianna was obviously not grasping how things were here. It was going to be so much fun teaching her though.

"I know I don't need to do anything sugar, but I'm not a man who's forgotten how to treat a lady. So, stop sassin' me," I leaned into her so our faces were just inches apart and I felt her short, shallow breaths on my face, "and step back."

My dick jumped in my pants yet again when she swallowed hard, and I watched up close as her tongue darted out and ran along her full bottom lip. If I didn't have my daughter in the backseat of that damn truck, and I was sure she wouldn't knee me in my balls and run for her life, my Bird would have given me my first taste of her after that. She really was torturing me in the best way possible. We needed to get to the house so Cady could get her lesson, and so I could put some distance between us to maybe relieve myself in a cold shower because, at this point, I needed both.

She stepped back, and as I opened the door for her, she took my other outstretched hand and allowed me to help her up into the passenger seat. Before I closed the door, I pressed into her side. She stiffened in her spot but relaxed quickly; I would've missed it if I wasn't Bird watchin'. I leaned into her even closer yet and inhaled the scent that she wore. Then, before I moved away, I brushed my nose over her ear and whispered when my mouth got there, "Don't be afraid of me. That wasn't too bad, was it?"

Ari shook her head in the negative and replied, "No."

"If you let me, I will show you what a proper gentleman does other than opening doors." I blew out my breath on her ear like a teenager from some cheesy 80's movie. But it got to her. Not only did I see her shiver from it, I felt it too. At that, I shut the door, walked around the front, and hopped in to hear my daughter chatting away with her Birdie.

Making our way to the house, I kept glancing over at Arianna. She kept a small smile in place as she listened to Cady yammer on about whatever she felt was pertinent for Bird to know. I was only semi-listening at best, too distracted by the beauty next to me. Every minute spent with her made me burn. It was a constant feeling that my blood and skin were being set on fire. It hurt so good, like a pleasurable pain, that made my chest ache, my heart race, and of course my jeans get tighter the more I stared at her profile. I had picked up speed and was going faster than I normally would with Cadence in the truck with me because I was daydreaming. I had to get control, so I eased up on the gas, rested my left arm on the window frame, with the right holding the steering wheel, and focused straight ahead. Five more minutes and we would be home. *We would be home.* Fuck me. Talk about getting way ahead of yourself.

As we turned down our street, Cady had gotten quiet and so had Bird, so I asked inside the truck, "Are you two girls okay? You both got very quiet." I glanced in my rearview to see Cady looking back at me, squinting her eyes. Oh shit. I knew that look.

"Baby girl, I know that look. Ask what you want to ask."

"Well...I want to ask Birdie something. Can I Daddy?"

"I am sure you can. Can't she, Bird?" A quick glance her way and I was hit with a full smile. She must like when Cady calls her Birdie. Yet, she gave me attitude about Song Bird.

"Go ahead and ask me anything you want, Princess," Arianna answered me but directed her permission to Cady. She turned around in her seat to face my girl, and gave her undivided attention to her.

"Well...I was wondering two things. The first is, during lessons today, can we play "Twinkle Twinkle"? I practiced with Daddy, and want to show you how good I got! And then maybe, if Daddy says it's okay, would you watch *Frozen* with me? It's my favorite, and everyone should watch it." Cady had ratcheted up the puppy-dog eyes on Bird. She didn't stand a chance. It was hysterical watching Arianna shift with her uneasiness at being put on the spot and not being able to say no to my daughter. My laughter got the best of me.

"Sure sweetie. As long as your dad says it's all right," Ari finally said.

"YIPPEE!!"

"Cadence remember what we talked about?"

"Yes. I said if it was okay with you," she mouthed off.

"Watch your tone little lady. You know better."

"But..." Cady started but stopped when she took in my raised brows and face in the mirror.

"Sorry, Daddy. And sorry, Birdie. I didn't mean to ask you that," Cady's voice trembled as tears started to fall across her cheeks.

"River. She is crying. Did you have to make her feel bad? She was just excited," Arianna reprimanded me in a hushed tone.

I pulled into the driveway as I heard Arianna's seatbelt click from being released. I threw the truck in park, heard the sniffles from the back seat, and watched as Arianna climbed over the front seat, the center console, and landed in the back next to Cady. Then I watched as Bird unlatched Cady's car seat, pulled her out, and held her in her lap while rocking and shushing her. I knew I had to let Arianna do that, but my chest got tighter by the second watching her with my daughter. I overreacted, and I'll make it right with Cady. My emotions were all over the place and that was something new to me.

After about ten minutes of Bird calming Cady down in the back of my truck, I'd had enough and spoke up.

"Bird. We got to get her inside, yeah?"

Arianna looked up from my daughter's still sniffling form and directed her narrowed, gorgeous, eyes on me to reply shortly, "Fine."

"Cady, darlin', Daddy needs you to climb up here so we can talk a minute." My daughter was everything to me. I needed to make this right with her so she could learn the lesson of admitting when she was wrong and she knew that I loved her.

"Okay, Daddy." Cady's defeated little voice filled the truck, and my heart skipped. I didn't want her to ever sound like that again.

Cady wiggled free from Bird's lap and tried to climb over the center console, but her little legs wouldn't let her up and over. So, I grabbed her under her arms, lifted her over, and planted her in my lap. She tilted her head down to look at her lap. That reaction was not what I wanted my daughter to have ingrained in her. *This is what HE did to MY BIRD.* Cady must have gotten this from watching Bird and I interact. That was ending right now.

I grabbed her little chin and began my apology to my daughter.

"Cadence Allegra, look at Daddy please," directing her face so that when she opened her eyes, she was looking into mine.

"Okay, Daddy," her eyes opened, and my breath caught at the incredible amount of hurt I saw in them.

"I am so sorry baby girl. I lost my temper with you and overreacted. It wouldn't be right for me to say it won't happen again because it more than likely will, but I will try not to let it. Cady, I love you so much. You were just excited to show Birdie your favorite movie, and that's okay darlin'. After piano, you can watch your movie with Bird. That is if Bird can hang around after the lesson." My gaze found Arianna's and she had this mysterious smirk on her face while shaking her head up and down like a lunatic.

"YAY! Thank you, Daddy. I knew you weren't mean! Just crabby. Are you tired, Daddy? Maybe you should nap. You always tell me when I'm crabby that I'm tired and need to nap. You should try it," Cadence sassed me. Her turnaround time from being sad to sassy was extraordinary. Giggles sounded from the back and again I turned to watch Arianna's beauty come to life as her giggles turned into full, head thrown back, belly laughs. Apparently, it was amusing to see my five-year-old sass me as if she were a fucking teenager. Not one ounce of me was looking forward to those years.

"All right funny girls, let's get inside. We have piano lessons to take and movies to watch." Releasing a sigh, I opened the door and hopped down with Cady in my arms. I put her down and moved to open the back door. I was shocked when I saw it was still closed. Opening it, Bird looked at me, hands folded in her lap, with a shit-eating grin on her face.

"Contrary to what you think, I would never want you to feel as though you lack in the gentleman department, so I waited for you to open my door. I really could get used to the chivalry, I suppose." More sass from yet another woman in my life. Fan-fucking-tastic. Just what I needed. And no doubt my daughter will eat up every second of it and spit it back out at me. I extended my hand for her to take, and without a flinch or hesitation, she did. Progress, I thought, as I led them both inside the house to an evening I was sure I wouldn't forget.

Chapter 7

Cowboy Boots and Kisses
Arianna

After River had helped me down from the truck, I stood and stared in awe at the real-life log cabin sitting in front of me on a huge property. There was a pond that had the best man-made rock waterfall, gorgeous white cherry blossoms blooming, a kick-ass weeping willow, and the most relaxing looking porch I had ever seen in my life. It was difficult to wrap my mind around the fact that River owned all this. I wasn't sure how much firefighters made, but I was sure that salary on top of having a small child to care for wasn't enough to settle in a place like this. If my experience with Andrew was anything to go by, I would say River comes from old money. But it wasn't really any of my business. I was here to teach that sweet girl piano.

"Bird, you okay, darlin'?" River snapped me out of my gawking.

"Um..." I cleared my throat and continued, "Yes. My goodness, River. This place is gorgeous."

"Thank you, sweetheart. It was my parents' place before they passed. They left it to me in their will, since I needed a decent place to raise Cady. It needed some TLC and over the years and little by little, I gave it that. It's almost where I need it to be."

"I can't imagine it any better. This is the perfect place to just…be."

I started moving forward toward the three steps that led to a magnificent oasis of a porch. Cady and River walked by me as I started to daydream about lazy days spent on this porch. With the both of them. Shit. Why was I thinking these things? He's been so nice to me. Bossy but nice, all the same. I understood he was attracted to me, but I just didn't think I was good enough for his daughter or for him. River was a man who needed a woman who could offer him stability and a good life.

"Come on Birdie!" Cady yelled at me. She grabbed my hand and pulled me toward the front door.

"Okay, Princess. Let's get this piano thing done and then we can watch *Frozen*." We headed into the house together, her little hand clamped tightly on mine. I knew she was excited.

The inside of the house was even better than the outside. Wood floors were present throughout the entire lower level of the house. They were accented by runners with a masculine, yet modern print of deep reds, creams, and grays. The logs from the outside came through to the inside, too, which made it even more authentic and rustic. It was a mostly open plan once you made it into the main part of the house.

Through the arch to the right, after the foyer, you stepped down into a sunken living room. Huge, deep red throw pillows accentuated a deep gray sectional; the red in the pillows matched the red in the throw rug under the coffee table and the runners throughout the space. It was no ordinary coffee table either. It matched the custom log oversized couch on the front porch in style by using the same logs. The top was a slab of oval glass on the log-legs instead of a cushion.

There was a fireplace on the far wall; the mantle held framed pictures of Cady, River and Cady together, and drawings that Cady made which River framed. To the left of the fireplace nestled under a window, was the piano that River had gotten from the school in Gifford. It was perfect for Cady to learn and practice on. To the right of the fireplace, was the dining table and chairs. The table matched the coffee table, and the chairs matched the log framework found pretty much everywhere throughout the house.

Cady brought me right to the piano and pulled out the bench. She used this little step stool to help her hop up onto it. I sat down next to her while she opened the lid that slid over the keys to keep them protected. I felt his presence before I heard him clear his throat.

"Bird, since this is a bit of a different situation today, do you mind if I leave you two to it and hop in the shower?"

"Sure. Do whatever you need to do. We'll be fine."

"Darlin', it isn't what I really need to do, but it'll have to suffice. Trust me when I say I would much rather be *doing* other things. But I digress. When y'all are done, we can order some food. Any preferences?"

"That is very thoughtful of you, but I will just grab something when I get back to the apartment," I answered him and turned back to the piano to start the lesson but he interrupted once again.

"I don't doubt that you are capable of that. But if you are going to hang with my daughter and me while we watch this Godforsaken movie, I will feed you. So, again, any preferences?"

"I want pizza, Daddy! With the dots!" Cady chimed in with her order. I could only gather that dots meant pepperoni. I smiled at her.

"All right baby girl. You good with pizza?" River was clearly going to give his daughter what she wanted. My heart started to speed up a little bit at that thought. Turning to him, again, still smiling I said, sounding husky, "Sounds perfect." He smiled at me with only his eyes. That look woke up the lady parts I had almost forgotten existed with an intense tingle which led to a shiver that rippled over my entire body. Shit. That felt good. That was the moment I knew I was in serious trouble.

He disappeared to take a shower. I turned back to the piano and instructed Cady to start with her scales. I should have been listening to her, but at that moment, I couldn't keep my mind focused on anything other than what River looked like naked and wet. All it took was a look from him. Just a look. Who was I really trying to fool here though? He was beautiful. His body was such that you knew he worked out. Nice broad shoulders. Arms clearly defined by the workouts and the efforts he put into his home. He had the most beautiful blue-gray eyes set in a perfect face, chiseled jaw covered in a few days' worth of stubble, and an absolutely perfect nose. My first thoughts about his hair being dark were proven wrong upon later inspection. His dirty blonde hair was cut close to his head that made it look darker than it was but came up to the slightest point in the front. He was every girl's dream come true.

I snapped myself out of my fantasy and mental perusal of him and caught the end of Cady's scales.

"Very good, Princess. You have definitely been practicing. Are you ready to try "Twinkle, Twinkle" now?"

"YES!!!!" She was the most adorable little girl. Everyone was right when they said she was wise beyond her five years of life and a very quick learner.

Cady played the song through with a few stuttered beats. She had really practiced hard over the weekend, and I was extremely proud of her. She would have this song down by the end of the week. I instructed her just to keep playing it. Repetition would help her hand placement, and it would help her memorize the notes. Mostly listening, I did guide her at the parts she stumbled over so that she knew the place in the song that had corrections.

I imagined that my son would have played, had he been able to make it to this earth. How we could have shared that together, just like I was sharing it with Cadence. Deep down I knew there was no way any son of Andrew's would play piano. It was too feminine to him. Then again, maybe he just hated it because he hated me so much, and I loved music. With a ton of time over the last few weeks since the call came in that they had arrested him, I couldn't come up with any other reason for what he did to my boy and me.

Wrapping up the lessons, I assigned Cady a new song to practice, on top of "Twinkle, Twinkle". At her age, she was really excelling. In a year, she would be closer to my level at the pace she was taking it all in. It made me wonder if River or Cady's mom had any type of musical background. Penny explained about Cady's mom being gone, but River would be the only one to be able to answer that question. Just as Cady was closing the lid to the keys, River walked in on the phone ordering a pepperoni pizza.

Hanging up and sliding the phone into his pocket, River asked, "Are you two girls all done with the lesson? Pizza is on its way. If you're finished, Cady can go change into her pajamas, and we'll set up the movie, Bird."

"Yes, we're finished. Princess, you did fantastic today. I'm so proud of you! You will have learned and mastered two songs by the weekend!" We squeezed each other in a hug but she was first to let go.

She looked up and shouted at me, "Thank you Birdie!!! I'll be back in a few minutes. I need to get comfy so we can snuggle up!"

"Okay, baby," I smiled huge at her as she zipped past me and her dad and then stomped her tiny feet up the stairs. I was still smiling in that direction when my vision was filled with all that was River. His body wash or aftershave, not sure which, filled the air around me and his scent was permanently locked into my memory bank.

"You want to get rid of those cowboy boots and settle into the couch while I get drinks and set up the movie or…," he grabbed my hand and pulled me up off the piano bench right into his hard, delicious smelling body, "give me my first taste of you since the very cold shower I just took didn't satisfy me, and we have about four-and-a-half minutes before my girl comes back down?"

I shivered, and that tingle that was simmering low in my belly which never really disappeared from earlier, traveled down to my vagina, giving me the slightest of mini-orgasms. No one had ever spoken to me like that. Not Andrew. Not any of the guys before Andrew. It was kind of hot. Scary as all hell, but hot nonetheless. I looked up at him. Right into his eyes. They were darker than normal and almost a gun metal in color. Was I ready for this? River was not the type of guy to play around. What would one kiss hurt? His grip got a little tighter on my hand which was now laying palm down on his chest, his covering mine there, while his other arm went around my waist to keep me firmly where he wanted me.

I closed my eyes and inhaled him again. My head started to drop down, but he caught my chin with the hand that was covering mine. He forced my eyes back up and gripped me tighter to him. His uncanny ability to read exactly the moment I started to shut down was starting to piss me off. I tried to jerk out of his hold, but he held tighter.

"You're squeezing me too tight, River." My voice came out strangled.

I was starting to panic. My breathing picked up, and the tremors started. He immediately released my chin, but wrapped his arms around me and pulled me back in, closer to his heat. Fighting off my panic by taking deep breaths in through my nose and out through my mouth, I relaxed and rested my head on his shoulder. His mouth was centimeters from my ear as he started speaking in a soothing, hushed tone. Kind of like the tone he used with Cady.

"I will never hurt you. Darlin', I promise you this with every ounce of my being. Raising a hand to a woman is wrong in every conceivable way." My head came up, and I concentrated on his face and what he was saying as he went on, "He took from you, Arianna. Little pieces of your heart and your soul that I want to help give back to you the best way I know how. First and foremost is by making you feel safe. Stop fighting me and give in so I can do that, yeah? I promise I'll make things easy for you. You deserve that after what you've been through."

While he spoke the most beautiful words I had ever heard in my life thus far, the tears built up, and when he said the words "you deserve", a single tear slid out of my right eye, almost making it to my jaw. But River caught it with his thumb and swiped it away. He just stared into my eyes, giving me time to collect my thoughts.

Finally, I was able to force out the words, "I'm not any good at this. And I'm terrified that if I let you in, you may be the one to heal me."

"Isn't that a good thing, Bird?" He looked totally confused as he asked me that. He needed to know that I didn't deserve to be healed.

"No, River. It isn't. I'm not ready to explain yet. But you just need to know that I don't deserve any bandages on my soul or my heart. They aren't wounds that can or should be healed. They are gaping reminders of what I don't deserve." Trying to pull out of his arms was fruitless. He clamped down tighter again.

"Bird, you're really pissin' me the fuck off with all this you don't deserve this, and you have nothin' to offer garbage. There's more than a small chance that I get you. And you probably get that I know more than you have said," he finished just as little footsteps drew closer.

"Fuck me. This isn't over. But not in front of Cady," River muttered under his breath and pulled away from me.

I just shook my head in agreement. There was no chance in the world he would let it go. He would find a way to talk to me about it. So, I did what I could do. I walked over to the couch, unzipped my extremely worn, but favorite, cowboy boots, and toed them off. As I sat down, I tucked my knees under my ass and got comfortable. Cady dove headfirst into the couch, rolled over, rested her head in my lap, and curled the doll she had in her hands into her chest.

"You comfortable, Princess?" I asked her on a small giggle and started unknowingly playing with her hair.

"Yes, Birdie. And that feels nice," she answered me. Realizing what I was doing, I smiled again. If she liked it, I would keep doing it. This wasn't something she probably had a lot of.

River was bent at the contraption that contained his big screen and movie system, putting *Frozen* into the Blu-Ray player. He pressed play and froze in place when he saw his daughter laying in my lap. His eyes smiled again. That look was the thing that was going to make me give him his first taste of me. Shaking off the daze, he made his way over to us.

"Cady, baby, slide down a bit. You too, Bird. I get the corner."

"Okay, Daddy!" Cadence happily agreed. Me on the other hand, narrowed my eyes at him and said, "I'm comfortable where I am."

"Darlin' you can be comfortable against my side. My girl likes what you're doing to her and you can keep doin' it. Just slide down so you are doing it against me, yeah?"

"Whatever."

Yes. That is exactly what I huffed out. Like I was a child. River maneuvered me exactly where he wanted me, and he put his arm behind me along the back of the couch. But, not before he grabbed a strand of my hair and proceeded to play with it consistently throughout the movie. As much as I hated to admit it, it felt nice. Cady was onto something. Thankfully, at this point, the movie began, and Cady was in her own little *Frozen* world. She sang, muttered the dialogue in between telling me what was coming, and wiggled a little to the songs she really liked. It was all very sweet. It felt nice to be snuggled up with the both of them. It had to be the first and only time I let myself have that type of peace and comfort. It was only two hours. I could give myself two hours.

At my darker thoughts, River jostled me and got up saying, "Food is here darlin'. Gotta get the door."

"Ok."

He smirked and just shook his head like he didn't believe I was scared of him at all. Something else that was annoying.

"Can I help you with anything, River?" I shouted at his back.

He shouted back, "No." Well, all right then. Guess he took pizza preparations seriously, too. He was starting to make my head hurt.

Cady and I got up, paused the movie, and walked to the kitchen. The gasp I made was not as quiet as I had thought. Looking around, it was too much to take in. This kitchen, which was on the other side of the only wall in the mostly open lower level of the house, was straight out of one of those houses you see on the shows with all the housewives.

The logs were only visible on the ceiling in this room. The crown molding and cabinets were made of cedar wood with a heavy walnut glaze coating the front panels of the doors and what looked like stones as the knobs. The grooved design that was carved into the front panel on the cabinets was stained dark, and it added an interesting, deceiving depth to them. The backsplash underneath was made up of tiles that matched the color of the stones used on the cabinetry. The countertops were made of glossy marble with beiges, browns, blacks, and the same red of the cedar intertwined. The exhaust hood to the oven was stainless steel over the range but with an exhaust that had a hammered stainless steel which became more polished closer to the vent snaking into the ceiling.

A big bullion-framed window sat above the sink, aiming out to the rear of the property. There was a ledge under the window that held more pictures, a vase with a single tiger lily in it, and what looked like a plate with a tiny hand imprinted in the center. At the center of the room stood a gorgeous island, made completely of all kinds of different sized stones. There was storage in the island, and the doors matched the cabinets exactly. It was covered in the same countertop and spanned the length of the kitchen. Light colored pine wood stools were tucked under for extra seating. There was a set of French double doors at the end of the kitchen, off to the back left, which led to the back patio.

"Bird, you can close your mouth. Wouldn't want you to catch flies." He laughed audibly as he started digging out plates and napkins.

"This is like something out of a magazine, River. Did you do this yourself too?" I asked him, completely stunned.

"Yeah, Darlin', I did. It took a long time to get it this way. I finished it a few months ago," he responded, nonchalantly, as he handed me my plate with three huge pepperoni slices on it.

"River, I can't eat all this. One slice is plenty."

"Eat what you can. Cady will only eat one slice. What you don't finish, I will or we'll chuck it." He winked and moved into the dining area. Cady and I followed.

"Your home is really beautiful," I said as I sat down to his left. "I am completely impressed that you built this for yourself. You must be really proud of it."

He smiled and just shrugged. Hmm. River not a fan of compliments. Interesting and good to know.

After I consumed all three slices of pizza, because it was the best damn pizza I had ever tasted, and we finished watching *Frozen*, it was just about eight o'clock. I needed to get home, and Cady's bedtime had to be approaching. But, here we were, all back on the couch watching another movie. I was playing with Cady's hair, and River twirled a strand of mine mindlessly while I was snuggled up to his side, head on his shoulder. Once I realized what was happening, I straightened myself on the couch and gently moved my leg so Cady would lift up. She did and sat up on the couch, but kept watching whatever Disney flick was on now.

Scooting my ass to the edge of the couch, I bent for a boot and asked over my shoulder, "Would you be able to take me to Penny's now? I'm really tired and need to be up early tomorrow."

"Of course, Darlin'. Cady, baby. Go get your shoes on. We have to take Bird back home now." He got up, walked over to the piano bench, and grabbed my bag that I had left there earlier. I didn't even remember having it. River was making my mind cloudy, and I was losing track of the simplest things being around him, his daughter, and the beauty that was his home.

"Here ya go," he handed me the bag and continued, "and why don't you let me help with those boots." It wasn't a question. He grabbed the left one and gently lifted my leg, slid on the boot, and started pulling up the zipper on the side while he deliberately skated a finger up my leg with it. I shivered again. Shit.

"You cold Arianna?" His question came at me through a shit-eating grin. He knew exactly what he was doing.

"Nope. And, don't be an ass. You know what that was."

"Not sure I know what you're talking about, Darlin'. But I do know I like when you turn on that sass. Keep it up. You won't be going anywhere because you'll have to watch my girl while I take another cold shower since we both know nothing can happen tonight."

"For Pete's sake, River. You needed to run your finger up my leg? I may be terrified of you, but I'm still a woman. My body can have reactions to touches."

"Mmmm. Bet it can."

"ARGH! You're impossible!" I pushed his hands away from my legs and stomped over to the piano bench to put my other boot on. Last thing I needed was another reason for making him hard.

Cady came bouncing back in and was ready to go. I was more than eager to get out of this situation. I knew this was going to be trouble. More than I ever knew before. River was purposely making me uncomfortable. He didn't do it in a mean way. And it had felt amazing to feel a gentle touch from a man. That was something I had gone the better part of seven years without. I just knew that I couldn't allow it to happen again.

"Ladies, after you." Ever the gentleman, he held the front door for us, locked it, then led us to the truck. Cady was first to get situated in her seat while I waited for River to come to my door. I didn't want another scene, so I gave him his way. He helped me up, but this time stood back and waited for me to buckle my seatbelt. He didn't intrude on my space, whisper in my ear, or touch me in any way. He'd gone out of his way to do one or the other all night. Maybe he was finally getting my point. *Why did I miss that from him then?*

The drive back to the apartment was quiet. Cady was tired and fell asleep five minutes into the fifteen-minute trek. I was on my phone, the new one Penny said I needed so it had no chance of being tracked, texting her that I would be home in ten minutes.

Me: Hey Pen. Be home in 10. You gonna be there?
Penny: Yeah. I'm just making some ginger tea. Not feeling great.
Me: Oh no. :-(Ok. River is driving me back. Be there soon.
Penny: Yeah right. LMAO. Just come up when you can.
Me: What does that even mean?
Penny: You'll see. ;-)

Cady seemed to be the only person in my life at that moment who didn't wink at me. Even through text messages, I got the winky face. I had no response for her, so I slid my phone back into my bag and realized we were almost at the apartment. This needed to not be awkward, and I was the likely cause of that feeling, so I decided to speak.

"River, I can't begin to thank you enough for today. Can I give you some money for the food?" I knew before I finished speaking the words that it was not a smart question to ask because I felt the air in the truck change. He parked the truck and turned to me, nostrils flaring.

"No, Arianna. I don't want fuckin' money for the food," he bit out angrily, but quietly, so Cady didn't hear and wake up.

"Ok. Well, thanks again. I'll just…"

"Wait right where you are until I come let you out. Christ. You are somethin' else."

He exited and walked around the front of the truck to open my door, jaw clenched the whole time. He stood there with his hand outstretched, so I took it and hopped down. Gently, he closed the door. I could see in his face that he would've preferred to slam it, but again, he didn't want to wake his daughter. And I saw this up close because he had forced me back into the closed truck door.

River had me pinned with his body, hot and firm, against mine. His hands came up to rest on both sides of my neck, and he used his thumbs to gently tip my face up to his. Before I could protest, or attempt freedom from his trap, his lips crashed down on mine. My mind blanked. Nothing existed. I kissed him back. His lips were full, soft, and he took his time coaxing my mouth open. Before I knew what was happening, it turned hot, hard, and terrifyingly life altering. My body didn't tense up at the contact. It melted. That was how I knew, yet again, the trouble I had just gotten myself into was more than cowboy boots and kisses.

Chapter 8

I Am Not Him
River

I released her mouth but kept my hands where they were, pressed to either side of her neck. I couldn't move them at that moment, or my control would snap, and Arianna was not quite there yet. My first taste of her wasn't anything like how it had played out in my fantasies. It exceeded every preconceived idea I had of how it would go. She tasted like lemonade and mint. It was uniquely her, and it made me an instant connoisseur. The way she melted into me and didn't tense up at my touch told me everything I needed to know. My Bird. She was ready for more than she thought she was.

She looked fucking beautiful. She still had her eyes closed and her lips were kiss-swollen but slightly parted when I broke free from her. Slowly, she blinked her eyes open. They were hooded, and she was still dazed a bit. The color of her eyes formed this deep aquamarine that told me she enjoyed it and it turned her on. I studied her as she started to come back to reality. I needed to move away and get her inside Penny's. I did have my daughter asleep in the truck. But, it was time to begin the steps in taking what I wanted. My claim to her happened the moment our lips met. She was mine. No one else would ever have her taste on their tongue again if this went the way I hoped.

She had grabbed onto the gray Henley I had on, and when I moved away, she stumbled on her feet trying to get her balance, startled out of her daze by the sudden movements. I reached out and steadied her with my hands at her waist. Once I knew she was good to stand on her own, I let go. She just stared at me. I saw something working behind her eyes, and I knew what was coming. My only option was to shut it down before she could talk herself in to pulling away again.

"Bird. We need to talk and not while my girl is asleep in the backseat of my truck. There are things we have to hash out. Especially that kiss and what it meant." It was something she already knew but she stared at me like I had just grown another head.

"River. There is nothing to talk about. That kiss was a mistake. It shouldn't have happened. I never meant..."

"To kiss me back?" I needed to cut her off and make her see her part in it.

I moved back into her space. I needed to say this quickly and get my daughter home to her bed.

"That's right, Arianna. You kissed me back. Those gorgeous, full, soft lips parted for me the second my tongue slid across them, begging me to come inside. And Bird, once I was in, you let go. And Darlin'," I pushed my hips into her stomach so she could *feel me* and I brought my mouth to her ear, "I liked it a fuck of a lot. Evidence is clear."

"Step back, River," she demanded.

"Ari, I won't let..." I tried. She started shaking uncontrollably and the last thing I wanted to do, what went against every one of my instincts, was to step back. I needed to hold her. To show her that I wasn't going to hurt her.

"STEP BACK NOW!" She cut me off with an ear-piercing scream.

"Okay, Darlin'. Just calm down. I'm going to step back. You have your balance so I can do that?" That scream was a scream of pure fear. Something triggered her. I moved, but not too far back, so she was able to stand without falling. I heard footsteps behind me and turned to see Penelope running toward me.

"Arianna?!? Are you okay? What the fuck is going on, River? Why is she shaking like that? Oh no. Shit. River, she's having a panic attack." Penny told me what I had already figured out.

"Fuck, Penny. I kissed her and then I was trying to make sure she didn't start talking all that bullshit about her not deserving good in her life or continue to tell me that her kissing me back was a mistake. I leaned into her. Then she demanded that I step back. I didn't know that I would trigger her," I started to pace and rub the back of my neck while Penny approached Arianna.

"Ari, sugar, you're safe. River is over there. I need you take a deep breath in through your nose and let it out through your mouth. It will help to calm you down," Penny instructed Arianna. Fuck. But, I am not that asshole that hurt her. I am proving this shit to Arianna. Even if I have to keep doing it over and over again.

"Penny, please let me try. She needs to know that I'll never hurt a hair on her head. Can you just grab Cady from her seat in the back and let her crash upstairs for a bit? Once I get her calm, we need to talk."

"River, I don't think this..." Penny stopped mid-sentence when Arianna finally speaks.

"Penny. Take Cady and go up. It's time he knows the whole story." Arianna's tone was cold, empty, and I knew that whatever it was that she was going to tell me was bad.

"Fine. But Ari, maybe this isn't the best place to have this talk. I will crash on the couch and put Cadence in my bed. You two need to go somewhere private. And River," Penelope came over to me, placed her hand on my arm, and told me, "let her talk. I know you are all alpha badass and want her to see things your way, but she needs to tell you everything. Listen to what she's saying," she finished as she walked around the bed of the truck to the rear door on the driver's side of the truck to get Cady since we were blocking the easier door to her.

"Penny, I'll text you when I have a better understanding as to what the fuck is going on. Text me if Cady gives you a hard time, and I'll come right back." Penny had my girl and was heading to the apartment. Arianna and I needed to find somewhere to talk. It was nine o'clock at night, but there's an all-night coffee house in Gifford.

Arianna had already started to open the door, but stopped. She looked over her shoulder at Cady's sleeping form in Penny's arms. The only way to describe her eyes when they hit my daughter was haunted. Fuck. This was bad. I tentatively approached her at the door, but she gave her head the slightest shake to indicate that now was definitely not the time to come into her space. She needed it, so I gave it to her. After letting her climb up and in the truck by herself, making sure she was able to hop up due to the height of my truck, I made my way to the driver's side again.

"There's a coffee house that is open all night in Gifford. We can go there if that's all right with you." I knew it came out angry. But, fuck if I wasn't pissed. However, scaring her even more in this situation would totally not bode well for this conversation.

"That's fine." Cold. Empty. Cracked. Her voice and spirit matched each other perfectly. I put the truck in gear, and we drove in silence.

We made it to The Percolator. Parking spaces were only available behind the building, away from the street, and we snagged one in the far corner. I turned the truck off but didn't move. Neither did Arianna. The silence was crushing me. I remembered being shut out when the woman I gave everything to and who carried my baby, turned her back on me. And her daughter. That was cruel. But this felt so much worse. It was brutally savage to see something in someone that you never thought you would see again. Have it dangled in front of you like the sweetest chocolate, then put back in the box, never to be thoroughly enjoyed. Fucking savage.

"You can't be mad at me. You aren't allowed to be that." It came at me in such a low voice, I almost didn't catch what she said.

"Arianna. I am trying to hold on to my sanity here. I'm not mad at you. I'm mad that you reacted like that to me. To be honest, I want to kill your fucking ex," I told her, so she understood I knew the conversation we were about to have pertained to him.

"I don't want to go inside. I can't be around people right now and would like to tell you in privacy how the last seven years of my life have been spent. But I know you drove all the way here, so we can go in if you prefer that."

"For fuck's sake, Arianna. I don't give a fuck where we are. Just talk to me. I'm trying to be patient and understand that this is a delicate situation." Exhaling harshly, I grabbed the steering wheel until my knuckles went white. Then, that savage feeling I had, it began to weigh down every bone in my body as Arianna started.

"Seven years ago, I met a man I thought would love me forever, protect me, and never put a hand on me. He made me promises that he didn't keep. I endured being smacked around, kicked, and punched in every conceivable place on my body. He never stopped. Not when I screamed at the top of my lungs in pain from a steel-tipped booted foot to the temple and," she had been looking down and wringing her hands while she spoke some of the ugliest words a woman of Ari's beauty and light should ever have to say, but looked me straight in the eyes and continued with, "not even when he knew I was pregnant with our son." She dropped her head again. I hated that fucking position on her. My thoughts flashed like a movie reel in fast forward with images of my daughter, the bruises on Arianna's face when I first met her, and of some sick and twisted motherfucker beating his pregnant woman. My breaths were coming fast, but I checked my emotions. I needed her to trust me and telling me this was a part of that process.

When she didn't continue, I murmured, "Please keep goin', Ari. Give it all to me."

A small nod of her head and she went on.

"Andrew didn't want children so when I wound up pregnant, I kept it from him at first. I thought things would work out. We had good times, and had been having a longer than normal run of those good times, so why would I be stupid enough to think anything different you know?" Ari shook her head in what looked like disbelief at her own words. His name falling from those beautiful, soft lips, made it clear to me. I would do everything in my power to keep her safe and fulfill every single promise that fucker didn't.

"Anyway, we had gone to dinner one night. I was about five months along and had the slightest beginnings of a baby bump. Some of the approved clothing was starting to not fit anymore. And just to be clear, yes, I had a prescribed list of what was deemed appropriate attire for the woman on the arm of a Kelly man." She knew it as soon as she said it. Motherfucker's last name was locked in my memory bank. Her right eye twitched, and she whispered out, "Fuck."

"Yeah. Fuck. I have some other choice words, but keep goin', Arianna."

"Fine. Well, at that dinner, it was time to tell him I was pregnant. He needed to know. As adamant as he was that he wouldn't have children, the idea that this baby could have been a new beginning had me hopeful. Things were still in a calm state in our relationship, and very, very naively, I thought maybe it was over. The abuse I mean. But I was so very, very wrong." Her voice broke on that last sentence. Dammit, I needed to comfort her.

"Arianna, baby. You have to let me hold you. I don't know how much more I can take with you so far away from me," I pleaded.

"Ri..ii.ver. I a..a..am not do..one." Uncontrolled tears pour from her eyes, and she struggled to breathe between her quivering words.

"Shit. You need to give me your permission to help you up and put you in my lap. You can finish there. With my arms wrapped around you in a safe place."

Her tear-stained face and eyes, still so haunted, turned my way. Looking at me under her wet lashes, still letting the tears flow freely, she gave her permission with a sniffle and a nod. Her trust. She trusted me enough to hold her so she could relive a nightmare. I turned slightly to her and held my hand out so she could climb over the console in the middle and situate herself in my lap. Once she stopped moving and found a comfortable position, very slowly my arms snaked around her. Arianna looked up at me and gave me a half-smile. But, fuck, if that didn't make my heart race.

"You need another minute, Darlin'?" I squeezed my arms the slightest bit on the question. She shook her head no, sniffled some more, and with my arms around her, keeping her protected, Arianna's demons were let out. She didn't know it at that moment, but we started slaying those fuckers together the very second they flew free.

"Ten days before I left to come to Carson Falls, Andrew..." No fucking way. That is the last time she says his name in front of me, so I informed her, "Listen. He doesn't deserve those lips speakin' his name.

So, do us both that favor, and stop saying it, yeah?"

"Okay, River. I can do that."

"Good, baby." Shiver. She shivered under my hold. I let it go and she spoke more.

"So yeah. I thought things were actually going to work out. He had taken the news fairly calmly. But like I said, I was very mistaken. Days prior to my arrival in Carson Falls, my unborn son, lost his life before it even had a chance to begin. Andr…I mean, *he* came home completely shit-faced and was yelling at me because I was doing all the things a new mom should have been doing. I was buying baby clothes, a crib, strollers, diapers, and just stuff that any baby needed. I'm sure you understand. He claimed I was too busy for him. I wasn't paying him enough attention. So, he went out and fucked some twenty-something that works in his office. He told me in one of his tirades that I drove him to it, and I had no one to thank but my fat, useless self. Well, my hormones were all over the place. His heartless actions made me sick, so I told him to go to hell when he came home late that night and I smelled her on him. I couldn't believe he cheated on me because he was jealous of our baby. He didn't like me talking back to him." Rapid deep breathing and shaking again; I gave her the reassurance she needed to go on.

"He will not hurt you again. But more, Bird, he can't get to you while you are in my arms," I said with all the conviction I had. It worked and she continued.

"His response to my anger was to come back at me with his fists, his head, and his feet. Each and every inch of my body was beaten and bruised, including my stomach. In short, he wanted to kill me. I started bleeding on the floor after he dragged me up the stairs by my hair to our bedroom where he kept kicking my stomach. I tried. I tried so hard to protect my stomach. My son. I rolled over so he could only get to my back, but it was too late. I felt the wet and the warmth coming from between my legs. Then suddenly, I didn't feel anything. Just numbness. I looked at him standing over me through the corner of my eye. Then he ran, and I dragged my bleeding, battered body on my forearms to the nightstand, to call 9-1-1. No one heard my screams. And River, I screamed."

"Baby, this is not your fault. Not. One. Single. Part. Cady is my world. I just don't even know what words to give you to truly convey how sorry I am that he took your boy. Fuck, Arianna. I swear to Christ, right here and now, that if I ever see this motherfucker, he's going to learn what it's like to have bruises."

"That is not what I want or why I told you, River. You needed to know because you have this idea of us in your head. An idea that can't come to fruition."

The air in the truck got heavier. Here we fucking go again.

"And do you care to tell me why the fuck not?"

"Are you seriously getting mad at me after all I've just told you?" She asked me like I hadn't just heard that fucking horror. Of course, I did.

"I'm just a little confused. You're sitting in my lap, which you gave permission for, might I add, after telling me all you've been through. But still, you deny even just the idea of me being in your future. Not actually me because, if we're being honest, once my lips hit yours, you wouldn't deny me. Just like earlier." It was a dick thing to say at that moment, but it was still the fucking truth.

Arianna started to wiggle out of my arms and my lap to return to her side of the truck. Fine. She wanted to be there, she could. I picked her up and plopped her in the passenger seat. I couldn't wait to hear what she had to say now.

"Nice. Can you take me back now?" She said in the same bitchy-ass tone she used at Thelma's store.

"I can and I will as soon as you tell me the last two things I need to know."

"Didn't know I was obligated to tell you anything. But please, by all means, take a little bit more tonight. What the hell?"

"Jesus. I won't tell you this again. I. AM. NOT. HIM. I appreciate you telling me all you did so watch that attitude. I won't throw that in your face. Ever. But what exactly is holding you back from me? And what did I do tonight that triggered that episode?" I felt my jaw tighten up from all the clenching I was doing to try and put a lid on my caveman instincts.

"I've explained this already somewhat at your house, but I could have left, River. It would have been a different outcome. If I would have left, my son would still be safely growing inside my belly. But I made a choice to stay. That choice ended a life. Not saying that you aren't great from what little I do know, but I seem to be too quick to hang my star on a guy that shows me attention. Before him, I had dreams. I had a life that was filled with music. He took everything. I'm really just starting to get back to myself again."

"That's all well and good. But it still doesn't answer my question."

"You scare me," she said quickly and honestly. She'd told me this before but I still didn't get it.

"But how? Why?"

"Because you're the kind of man I used to dream about. Just like he was in the beginning. I'm scared that the stains and scars I have will damage everyone around me. And when you pressed into me, and the fog from your kiss had cleared, it was obvious that I could easily lose myself again with you."

"Arianna," I growled out. "I'm fucking begging you to hear me. You are not damaged, baby. You had a dickhead of a man in your life who raised his hand to you. You didn't do anything wrong. That's his burden to bear. Not yours."

"I'm a disaster. I couldn't possibly be what you or your daughter need. What about her, River? My life isn't exactly the stuff role models are made of." Bird had no idea how wrong she was.

"You're wrong about that. You are on the other side of your nightmare and rediscovering your music and yourself. You traveled damn near across the country to start a new life in a place where you only knew one person. And you're great with Cady. The patience, the encouragement, and the love of music that you're nestling into her soul is beauty in a form so pure, it will lock itself deep and be a part of her the rest of her life. That, above anything else, is a courage and strength I would be proud to have surrounding my daughter." That needed to sink in. She was all those things.

"Will I ever be able to change your mind?"

"No, Darlin'. You won't. You don't see what I see, but you will. Give me a chance to really show you how a *man* treats a woman. That's all I am askin'."

"Do you think maybe we can just sleep on it? It was a very emotionally draining and overwhelming night. Especially for me." Her eyes looked tired. Most likely from all the crying. I would take her home, but my mind was most definitely made up.

"You can keep telling yourself you need to sleep on it. Whatever helps you get your head together. I'm not going anywhere or backing down. You kissed me, and that sealed your fate. You're mine." Again, it was probably a dick thing to say and scared her even more, but I was done talking in circles about this. So, with that, I started the truck, and we headed back to Penny's.

In the midst of experiencing déjà vu as I parked outside Penny's apartment, I remembered the fair. It would be a good way to have some fun, get some more time with my Bird, and show her a proper date. Meggie was usually available weekends, but I would definitely be putting a call in to her to see if Friday or Saturday worked better for her. And I needed to inform Arianna of the plans.

"I'll come around and let you out. But before I do that, Darlin', I want you to go to the county fair with me. It starts this weekend, and I think it would be good to take you out. I need to make sure what day is good for my babysitter. What do you say?"

"A fair? Like with rides, games, and really bad yet delicious junk food?" The excitement and almost childlike reaction made me smile. It felt so good after all the heavy of the night.

I smiled at her and said, "Yes, just like that. They usually have some cook-offs in the square we can hit before we go. Parking is usually a pain in the ass, but we can use the firehouse and just walk from there."

"Gosh. I haven't been to a fair in years but," she looked up at me to watch my reaction, "if I agree to this, no expectations. Promise me that,

River."

"The only expectation I have is that you relax and enjoy yourself for a change. You are always on alert and tense. And, baby, I get it now. I do. But you need to start *livin'*." Ari smiled this tiny, shy smile, and shook her head yes.

"Dammit. The first time you smile at me like that and I can't take those lips the way I want to. But, Bird, help me out here just a little. Give me a small peck to tide me over." Leaning toward her, I pointed to my lips and watched her, up close, roll her eyes at me. But she leaned in and gave me what I wanted.

"Happy?" And the cheekiness returned.

"Not even fucking close to being happy with just a taste of you. But I can be patient, now that I have more information, and can strategize."

"What am I, some covert operation?" Hmm.

"No, Darlin'. But in order to get you to trust me, I need to be cognizant of what, where, and how we do things. And that takes planning."

She didn't say anything to that but looked up to the apartment, where I saw Penny spying out of the window like an anxious parent waiting up for us. Now that her ridiculous Living Dead Dolls were packed away so Bird had a place to crash, she had found yet another way to be annoying. It was time to get my baby girl and get her to her own bed.

I got Bird from her side of the truck, and we walked side by side, shoulders touching, up the stairs to the apartment. A smirking Penny greeted us. Here we go. Every time she was around me, she had to say something. It was like her smart-ass comments were a knee-jerk reaction to seeing me.

"Don't even say anything, Penelope Gertrude." Whoa. I was shocked at Arianna's feistiness. "I don't need your shit tonight."

"I didn't say a word." Her smirk turned into a grin, and she shrugged her shoulders.

"You don't have to. That face says it all. Now, let River get Cady so they can get home." Penny moved out of the way so I could go grab my girl.

Waking her up killed me, but I had to put her in her own bed. She was groggy, but I picked her up and headed back out to the living room where the two of them were going back and forth. I cleared my throat.

"Thanks for keeping an eye on her, Pen. I appreciate you giving Ari and I some time to talk," I said as I walked to Penny, kissed her cheek, and gave a quick, 'Later, Bird' to Arianna. I almost made it.

Then, in true Penny fashion, she said, "River and Arianna. It has a pretty kick-ass ring to it; wouldn't you guys say?"

I had no response except to walk out and ignore her. Penelope Sloane. Pain in my ass.

Chapter 9

Reckless

Arianna

Looking in the mirror, I made sure that my hair was still holding the loose curls I spent hours adding in, and that my makeup was still in place. Managing to perfect a dark, smoky eye that turned up the turquoise of my iris, I topped my face off with my pink (Personal Statement MAC) liquid lip color. The little, yellow cocktail dress I was wearing, gathered in the bodice and the four-inch silver, fuck-me heels topped off my outfit.

Really, the dress was too short and clung to curves that I didn't even know I had. It was not the typical outfit I would choose for myself or one that I was ever allowed to wear. The clothes in my possession were clothes that were purchased with *his* money and approval. Penny had a shopping problem, an affinity for what I call slut-wear, and knew my measurements, so I should have known this is what I would end up in. She frequently went into Gifford to peruse the racks in the boutiques. Apparently, they had the best of the designers, but at the prices of a department store.

On Tuesday, when I got home from work and after I had given Cady her lesson at River's again, Penny and I cuddled on her bed like we used to do in college. She was still sporting a sore throat, but still, annoyingly, able to get me talking. I told her everything about Monday night in the truck. She wanted to know how I felt about him, and the fact that he wanted more, even after I laid all the ugliness out for him.

I told her *my* truth.

"I don't really know him. River is stupid-sexy with this bossiness he has and all that he gives his daughter. But he also wants something that I've proven, time and again, to be bad at. That terrifies me."

Penny responded with the *actual* truth.

"You're right, babe. You don't have the best track record with guys, but part of your trepidation is because you know down to your fingertips that he's what you want. The other part, the reason you're so guarded and scared, is because he's already everything that all the other guys before him weren't. And you haven't even banged him yet."

Shaking my head at the latter part of her statement, I looked at her smiling hugely. I thought it had been long enough. The bruises were healed, and I felt freer than I had in almost a decade. Penny's mission was about to be a success.

"Okay, Pen. You can do it."

"Do what? And why the hell are you looking at me like you're surprised at my astute insight into your love life? I'm more observant than you give me credit for," Penny said through her swollen throat.

"Take me dancing." She perked up at my giving in to her. So easy to please.

"Seriously?" Penny asked, skeptically.

"Yes. It's time to start peppering some of the old me into this me."

Penny clapped excitedly, and that must have tired her out because she plopped back down onto the bed. I hoped she felt better come the weekend. Her mission, since I'd arrived here had been to get me to Reckless. It still confused me as to why she continued to go there after the whole Braxton situation. I mean, he was guaranteed to be there. He owned it. There was more to the story that my friend was keeping to herself. I was intrigued by it all. But what really had me so curious was why tonight, a school night of all nights, she wanted to go dancing.

I could only assume that she needed to get out of the apartment since she'd been sick since the night River kissed me. Every single time I have asked why we couldn't go on Friday, she just changed the subject.

So there we were, on a Thursday night, getting ready to go clubbing. Never imagined at thirty-two years old I would still be saying that. It was two days before River and I were to go to the fair, and I was nervous to be out in this club. I'd been to clubs before, but it was B-A (Before Andrew). That was the term my best friend and I decided was to be used to describe the years before I met him. There was also D-A (During Andrew), A-A (After Andrew), and her most recent gem and my personal favorite, F-A (Fuck Andrew). We giggled ourselves to tears the other night coming up with those after our talk about River. Turning from the mirror, I went in search of my friend.

I found her in the kitchen shaking up a drink. The color of it gave away what it was. When we were in college, Penny and I would pre-game at the dorms before we went out because we wanted to start our good time as soon as possible. Plus, everyone knew that the bars and clubs in NYC never put enough liquor in their overpriced drinks. That was how we came up with our own version of what some called a Grapetini. We called ours TAG (The Anti-G-BOMB). This was because the term G-BOMB usually referred to healthy foods, and our concoction held zero health value. Not unless you counted the lemons and maraschino cherries we would occasionally adorn our glasses with, if we were feeling fancy. I could never remember the recipe, but Penny perfected it and could make it in her sleep.

"You can't be serious. We aren't in the dorms anymore, Pen. Couldn't you have cracked open some wine?" I asked her.

"Ari. Babe. Are we going out to have a good time or not?"

"Yes. I mean, I sure as hell hope so since I just spent the last three hours getting ready. I still can't believe I allowed you to dress me tonight."

"Well, you did, and you look hot. Get over here and drink. We always pre-gamed, and I missed this for a long time, so stop your bitchin' and let's do this."

My best friend had a very subtle way of making me feel bad, even

106

if she spoke the truth and had no idea she landed a blow. Penny knew of the hell I'd lived through, but she would never truly get it. And I prayed to all that was holy in this world she never found out first hand. It was just that sometimes, her words hurt. I knew I needed to get a thicker skin, and not everyone had the same intentions he did, and I was working on it.

The last three days had been the best I'd had since being in The Falls. River and I had been talking more during Cady's lessons and doing it on a more personal level. After my drama and telling him everything, he'd been attentive, generous, and gracious. He'd held the lessons at his house all week because Miss Thelma hadn't been at the shop since Monday. Not one to pry into other's business, I was waiting for her to tell me what was going on. I had an idea since we did work together, and I sometimes overheard her on the phone talking to what could only be doctors or family. Miss Thelma was older and should have probably retired twenty years ago, but she was also as stubborn as an ox. The only drawback to the lessons being held at River's house was that I couldn't play. At Thelma's store, I would play whenever I could in downtime. It was my therapy. Always had been and I was missing it terribly again.

"Earth to Arianna!" Penny, the lunatic that she was, waved me out of my thoughts.

"What? Oh. Yeah. Sorry. Let's do this!" Grabbing the drink, I raised it to my mouth and took my first sip. Immediately, I spat it out and put the cocktail glass on the counter.

"Jesus, Arianna. You almost spit all over my dress. What the hell? Grape anything stains," Penny chided me.

"I don't know what that is, but it isn't what we used to drink in college. That was terrible," I told her while I made a face like I had tasted something sour. It wasn't too far from accurate.

"Okay. So, I may have added a bit too much vodka; I should have added more lemonade. Who cares? You will get your buzz on faster. I can put more grape soda in if it's really that bad."

"Penny, did you even taste this?" I asked, suspiciously.

"Yes, Sugar. I did. This is the second batch I made. The first three glasses I drank while you were perfecting your already perfect face. I needed something to do." See, this is why I couldn't stay annoyed at her. She had always told me that she thought I was beautiful. I felt the same about her.

"Whatever. Just pass me my glass so I can get this over with." My snarky 'whatever' seemed to be funny, and she giggled. I finished that one and quickly poured another TAG into the glass. I threw it back while Penny watched, still laughing at the ridiculous face I made, thanks to her heavy hand with alcohol. Penelope Sloane was a serious pain in my ass.

Once I put my glass in the sink, we both grabbed our clutches, our phones, and headed down to the town car that Penny splurged on to take us to Reckless. This was all very suspect to me, and I wanted to ask, but I didn't. Tonight was about letting loose and having fun, not spoiling it by talking about the men that may or may not be in our lives.

The town car pulled up to the front of Reckless, which was in the center of a busy, packed street. Boutiques, restaurants, and what appeared to be warehouses surrounded the building on both sides. Across the street was The Percolator coffee house, where I poured my heart out to a man who was kind of into me, while parked in his pickup truck.

There was a line of people down to the corner, all behind polished, gunmetal-based stanchions with red velvet rope attachments. The women in line had on even less than me. Some dresses that barely covered their asses and some in tube tops and mini-skirts, denim minis included, with heels higher than anyone should have on or been able to walk in. The men were dressed in button-down shirts, dress pants, or dark washed jeans, and blazers with the occasional cowboy hat thrown on a head here and there. I noticed some had cowboy boots, while others went with the standard black dress shoe.

The driver came to let us out after parking, and as I stepped out, my heart picked up its pace as the fear of being in a crowded club started to dawn on me. I was definitely feeling the buzz from the drinks at the apartment too, so maybe it was just that. I waited for Penny to climb out of the back and took a deep breath to calm myself. It seemed to work, and we headed to the huge, delicious man standing in front of the jet-black door.

As we approached, the man looked at Penny and started smiling and shaking his head at her in disbelief. She had on a very tight, red halter dress and black cowgirl boots with solid three-inch heels. Penny styled her hair teased and sprayed out wild with curls that were secured away from her face by a red satin headband. Going for the dramatic vixen look, she did sexy black-lined eyes that made her blue eyes seem so blue they glowed in the dark, light blush, and completed the look with vibrant red lips. As we got up close to him, I could see he was actually laughing.

"Hey, Tink," Penny very strangely said to the overly-large man, who now looked at her with narrowed eyes.

"For fuck's sake, Penelope. Don't call me that shit while I'm at work."

"Oh. Sorry. Wouldn't want the ladies to get wind of your nickname now, would we? But remember that the next time you want to laugh at me before saying hello to me." The sass that Penny threw at this man made me realize they knew each other.

I didn't say anything as he stated, "He is here tonight, Pen. And he has company. But you knew that already, didn't you? Showing up looking like you stepped off a magazine page. So, I'm asking you as a friend, check your shit at the door and just have fun tonight. No drama, yeah?"

"Listen, Tin . . . sorry. I mean, Reggie. I'm here to show my girl, Arianna, a good time and to dance. Keep the lectures for your boss. He's the one that needs them."

"Girl, come on in. But you're playing with fire, Penelope. You know he's going to go apeshit if he sees you in there, dressed like that, drunk and dancing with random men in his club," Reggie a.k.a. Tink said with a raised brow.

He opened the door, and we stepped inside. We made our way down a black hallway, lit only by turquoise colored rope lights that ran along the sides where the ceiling met the walls and where the walls met the floor. It was all very mysterious until you turned a corner and walked through an opening that led into the main area.

Through the opening, which was actually two, huge double-mirrored doors, that were left open to entice the crowd walking in, you could see the club in its entirety. It's what I could only describe as a nightclub and a honky-tonk mashed into one fantastically elegant place.

After you walked through the opened doors, you had to take two steps down into the main bar area. To the right, was the bar. It was striking with its deep, glossy, cherry-colored maple wood that matched the dance floor. It created an 'L' shape and ran to the midway point of the far wall. The stools lined up in front of the bar were made of a polished silver base with white cushions. The walls behind the bar, and throughout, were a cream color with mirrors and liquor bottles lined up in front. There were four stations for draft beer spread down the long portion of the bar.

There were the same turquoise-colored lights like in the hallway, except in this space, they were recessed, part of an intricate chandelier-like fixture, and backlights down the side walls. The seating was all along the opposite wall from the bar. There were some black and cream half-circle booths, love seats, and ottomans mismatched down along it. The far left corner was where the restrooms were located. Opposite the bathrooms was what must have been the VIP section since it was roped off.

The amount of people already inside was insane. Penny grabbed my hand and pulled me deeper toward the VIP area. I had on heels and had a little buzz going, so I bumped into random people as she pulled me. One of the guys I knocked into looked me over like a meal and smiled at me. It was totally creepy and made me nervous. He watched me go the rest of the distance to VIP. I still felt his eyes on me, so I looked in the direction we came from, and he wasn't there. That was strange.

We made our way to the corner section. As we approached more velvet stanchions, a sign hung on one near another gigantic gentleman that read 'Reserved for VIP Members.' Penny dug through her clutch and pulled out some type of card; it was enough to get us inside the ropes. There was one long, black couch, a private, much smaller version of the long bar, and two cream Marilyn high-back chairs. There was no one else in here, so we got comfortable on the couch after we placed our orders for professionally-made Grapetinis.

"I really want to dance. The crowd is decent tonight and full of hot guys," Penny nonchalantly said, as she scanned the crowd.

"Can we finish our drinks first? I'll go with you because I don't want to be left back here. Some guy ogled me before, and it creeped me out. It feels like he's watching me." I shivered but not like a River shiver. It was in disgust.

"Yeah, we can. But Ari, if you feel that again, tell me. I will have Reggie keep an extra eye on us."

"Sounds good to me. Now," I swigged back the remainder of my drink and stood up, "let's DANCE!"

Just as we made it to the dance floor, the song faded out, and a new one started to pump through the speakers. The selections here were either something in the wide rock, rhythm and blues, or country variety. No hip-hop. Only booty-shakin' music. The beginning of Luke Bryan's "Country Girl (Shake It for Me)" started, and Penny and I looked at each other, smiled huge, and then started to shake it for our guy Luke. The country line dance moves I learned in college came back like they never left, and we were having the time of our lives.

A few more songs, including Blake Shelton's "Footloose" reboot and Trisha Yearwood's "She's In Love With The Boy" played, and then things slowed down with Chris Stapleton's "Tennessee Whiskey". Penny and I were no strangers to dancing with each other and we were letting go tonight, so we started doing our thing.

A guy came up behind me, and he seemed familiar, but my buzz wouldn't allow me to place him. I felt hands hit my waist as I was swinging my hips to the beat. Those hands didn't incite the same shiver or tingle that River's hands did, but what the hell. I was here to have fun and dance, so I turned in his hands and saw Mick. Shit. Slowly moving to the bluesy country song, my hands rested on his shoulders, and his landed on my hips, his fingers digging in slightly, right above my ass. Too caught up in the melody, I caught my rhythm and took Mickey with me. My mind slipped into every note of the song. I didn't think anything of it and just kept in time to the music, letting it move through my blood.

When I heard the final notes to the song, my eyes opened, and I saw Penny looking at me with huge, wide eyes. I also no longer felt hands on me. Slowly, I turned around to see Mickey being escorted to the door by Reggie, Braxton weaving through people to get to our spot on the dance floor, and River. A very pissed, ready to kill, River.

I only knew this after I was done eye-fucking the deliciousness that he was. It might have been the alcohol, but at that point, I didn't care. I took my time and started at his cowboy boots. Then made my way to his dark blue-washed jeans that fit his perfect ass in such a way it should not be allowed loose on the female population. Finally, up a little more to the pink button-down shirt he had on with the two top buttons opened. No blazer. No smile. Just his hands on his hips and his eyes narrowed and full of fury.

"Riv…" I attempted, but he shut me down *fast* and cut his narrowed eyes to me.

"Darlin' the best thing for you to do right now is not say anything. Not until we have privacy and I've controlled my need to commit murder against a man who, Bird, get me when I say this, is a total dick. Mick is about one step up from your ex. I thought you got the message that day at Thelma's store. But it seems you're forgettin' a bunch of messages the past few days." I felt like I was just scolded like a child, and that started to sink in and pissed me right the heck off. Who did he think he was?

"Listen here, River Bradshaw. You are not the boss of me. Had one of those, remember? I was out having fun with my best friend, and some guy started dancing with me. So what? It's not a big deal." I wobbled on my heels, really feeling my buzz now.

"Fuck me. You can't be serious. Let's fucking go." River grabbed my elbow and started to escort me back to the VIP section. I winced slightly at his grip on an old injury, but he didn't notice it. He wasn't really hurting me, but I was being manhandled all the same, and I started to panic.

"River. Please let go. I will walk."

"You can barely stand up in those fucking shoes."

"I had some drinks, but I'm fine. If you must drag me around, can you please hold my hand instead of gripping me there?" I asked in a pained voice, looking at my elbow.

"Shit, Bird. Did I hurt you? Fuck. I'm sorry. I just wanted…"

"You didn't hurt me. I have an old injury that didn't heal right. That's all. You just grabbed it the wrong way." We went right to the barstools at the private VIP bar, and he picked me up and set me down on one, facing him, my back to the bar.

He leaned to the side and told the bartender, whose name happened to be Rafael but River called him Rafe, to get me a water. I looked that way and said to the traitorous bartender, who I also saw check me out, "I would prefer another Grapetini, Rafael."

"Rafe, if you bring her a drink that is anything but the water I asked for, we'll have problems," River deadpanned then sliced his eyes back to me in a challenge. I knew better at this juncture than to argue with that look, so I didn't. He placed his hands on either side of my body, knuckles to the bar, and leaned so close to me that I felt his breath on my face, and smelled the whiskey on it.

"So let's revisit the part where I walked in to my best friend's club, since I had a babysitter for the night and wanted some drinks with the guys, and find my woman dancing with another man. Another man, who had his hands on that body. My body. And it's not a big deal? Which, Arianna, it is, seeing as I don't share, and I am pretty sure we were both present when I told you that you were mine." He waited, just watching me until I swallowed and answered him.

"River, I know we kissed and what you said. But we haven't even had our first date yet. How can I possibly be your woman? And honestly, I had drinks at the apartment before we got here, on top of the one Rafael made me. It's been a long time since I've had liquor like that, so I'm buzzed and didn't even know that Mickey was behind me." By the look on his face, I failed miserably at trying to explain this. Minutes passed, and I watched his face clear and his eyes smile at me with that look. Shit that look was hot.

"Your outfit, Bird. It's not you. Like the canary yellow color on you though, baby."

"What's wrong with what I'm wearing?" I asked him because I wanted to know.

"It's not about *what* you're wearing. It's about how that *body* wears it. It's on display for more eyes than just mine." Shiver. He felt that and grinned at me. He put his hands in the same position he did when he kiss-attacked me Monday night. This time I was ready. I mentally coached my body not to shiver when he touched the curve where my neck met my shoulders, and I decided to give back a little of what I got.

I stuck my tongue out and swiped my lower lip. He was still close enough to me that he felt my tongue touch his lips. He looked me dead in the eye and said, "I see things differently now. I look forward to seeing you in my space. You put light back into my and my daughter's world as if you were the sun rising every mornin', specifically for us. We're still gettin' to know each other, and I respect that, but, Darlin', I'm goin' to kiss you. Not just now, but whenever I want. 'Cause you see, Arianna, I know you want my mouth on you, and I know how to do it proper like." My world started to refocus into the vivid colors River was painting it.

Leaning in, he kissed me lightly at first with openmouthed kisses, covering every inch of my lips. Then he nipped my bottom lip. I groaned into his mouth, and he caught it between his teeth this time. I took that opportunity to flick my tongue against his top lip. He growled and slid a hand into my hair at the base of my head. I gasped, and he took that instant as a sign to taste and take all he wanted. It was wild, and at that moment, I knew I wanted to kiss him like that any time I wanted to as well.

A bit confused, but aware, I said low, "Holy crow."

"I knew you would go wild." He smirked at me then winked.

"Excuse me? You kiss-attacked me again."

"Clearly you're still drunk. You mauled me." He was smiling full-on and laughing.

"Does this mean you're not mad at me anymore?" I pouted and looked at him through my lashes.

"Fuckin' hell, Bird. You always kiss me like that, you'll never have to worry if I'm still mad or not. I'd prefer if you didn't let Penelope dress you anymore when you go out together. But, no, I'm not mad," River told me, as he slid his thumb back and forth on my cheek.

"So now that we've established that you're my woman, proper first date or not, which is tomorrow anyway, do you want to get out of here or do you want me to show you how it's really done on a dance floor?" he asked me with a raised brow. Shit. He could dance. Someone save me. Speaking of that, where was Penny?

"I will dance with you once you tell me where Penny is," I stipulated.

"Braxton was not happy she was here. He took her home," he so very casually answered me. Hmm. Something was going on there. I needed to find out.

Sighing, I said, "Fine. You ready to show me what you got?"

"Fuck yes, I am."

River had grabbed my hand that time when we walked back out. When we found a spot, he pulled me in front of him. The song that started made me smile huge because it was one of those sexy songs that made you move your hips. It meant I got to experience the hottest guy on the planet, grinding with me to "Ride" by Chase Rice.

So incredibly slowly, he dragged his hands up my sides until they were resting in the spot on either side of my neck. It took a while for me to catch up because the path he had just traveled with those hands, left my body torched.

Looking me dead in the eye, River informed me, "Bird, you have to know, what's about to happen, will turn you on. I dance like I make love."

"And how is that?" My words were out before I even knew why or what I asked.

"Reckless." A smirk graced his face, and his eyes turned liquid metal as mischief settled in his expression.

Before I could get my bearings, I was turned. River was dancing behind me, skimming his hands up and down my arms, raising every hair on my body.

Lightly grazing the sides of my breasts as he traveled to my ass, he gently cupped each cheek, giving just the slightest of squeezes.

Those magic hands then worked back up and found the goose

bumped, bare skin on my shoulders under my crazy curls. He moved to push my hair to the left side of my neck with one hand, while the other stayed tight around my middle so I could feel his erection in my back. With his nose gliding up the right side, and his tongue licking the same route, he stopped at my ear. He grabbed my earlobe in his teeth, sucked on it gently, and then let it go.

So soft, I didn't know if it was meant for me to hear, he said, "You've got a way."

My question came out in a husky tone I didn't think I had ever heard on myself when I asked, "A way with what?"

"You have a way with me." So simple. So honest. So much River; he needed to know it was the same for me.

"You have a way with me too, ya know."

"How's that?" he asked, still in my ear. His breaths bringing out the shiver.

"You make me feel the truth in things, even when it hurts. You make it seem easier to hope." At my words, he growled deep and spun me around. Knowing that we both needed to taste each other, River kissed me soft, sweet, and with tongue in the middle of a crowded dance floor.

It was fun dancing like a lunatic and singing lyrics out loud with no restrictions or cares about who heard me. The music was stuck on country, so we danced through "Blue Jeans" by Jessie James and Martina McBride's "This One's for the Girls" before River took my hand, interlocking our fingers, and drove me home.

He kissed me again after he walked me to the door.

It was hard. It was soft. It was River reminding me that I was his.

I shivered again.

An entire night of foreplay on a dance floor.

He was picking up the speed on things, and I wasn't sure I could stop him.

Chapter 10

Ferris Wheel
River

The left side of my chest felt tight. I was nervous. Thursday night at Reckless was intense, and Arianna was drunk. She must have been in bad shape Friday because she called me to cancel Cady's lesson. My reply was to tell her that she could do a make-up lesson on Saturday before we went out. She argued and said that she didn't think we should go out anymore, but I wouldn't hear her excuses. More than likely she was embarrassed by her behavior at the club, but she had nothing to worry about. I loved every second with her.

But now I was upstairs in my bedroom, listening while she was downstairs with my daughter, and my thoughts were roaming, making me worry that she'd pull away again. I had gone to pick her up, and she was amenable to giving the make-up lesson, but wasn't sure about the night out with me. She was acting off the entire ride to my house. Not exactly the perfect formula to have her not pull away.

Meggie was going to be there at three o'clock to watch Cady while Bird and I went out. I had ten minutes to get my shit together and form a plan of action to ensure Arianna had fun and didn't put me behind her wall again. It was the fair, and she was excited when I asked her, but that seemed like it was weeks ago instead of just days. So much had ignited between us, so I needed to keep stoking the flames.

With some time to spare and all my nervous energy raking through me, I needed to calm down, so I made my way to the stairs. I stopped at the landing after the first section of stairs and sat down. My daughter was in love with Bird. It wasn't hard to see that, and that tight feeling in my chest expanded. Cady was listening intently and watching Arianna's fingers glide across the ivory keys while Ari played and sang "Remedy" by Adele. The lyrics spoke of pain cutting deep and nights keeping you from sleep and how she would be the remedy. Cady just saw the skill Arianna had. I saw, heard, and felt each word down to my marrow. Arianna was totally unaware how much of a remedy she already was to my daughter. Cady had blossomed since she started piano. It was something that I knew only a woman's guidance could have given her.

The song finished and my daughter asked with so much wonderment in her beautiful little face, "Birdie, will I ever play like you?"

"Of course, you will, Princess. You just have to keep practicing." Bird stroked one of Cady's pigtails then gently tugged at it while smiling at her. They both erupted in giggles. The melody and harmony of their combined laughs were the greatest sounds I'd ever heard.

My girls.

Shit. I needed to move my ass and get Bird to give me that beauty every day. I knew she was what I *wanted*. I needed to convince her that my daughter and I were what she *needed*.

I stood up and walked down the rest of the stairs to the entrance of the living room. I leaned against the frame of the arch for a few minutes and just watched Bird and my daughter laugh. Arianna looked at Cady as her laughter dissipated. I watched as that haunted shadow crossed her face and she smiled small, sniffled, and then got up from the piano bench before Cady saw the pain and tears. She stopped and stared at me when she turned and found me watching them.

"I...um...I gave Cady her assignment for the weekend. She should have no problems with it. She's come a long way in the short time I've been teaching her. Do you think we can talk in the kitchen a minute?"

No fucking way is she backing out on me.

"Sure, we can, Darlin'. Just get it out of your head that we aren't going out. I want to take you out on a proper date."

"River. Kitchen. Please?" She practically begged me. I nodded my head in that direction and followed her into the kitchen. Cady had started practicing whatever song Bird had given her to master, so she was fine.

We entered the kitchen and Arianna whirled on me as soon as I cleared the doorway.

"River, I'm not backing out. I'm here already so that would seem a bit pointless. I need you to understand that I was drunk Thursday. Penny has this ridiculous drink that she likes to make before we go out. It's been our thing since college, and I hadn't had much alcohol since… well, since…" Arianna began, but I cut her off.

"I know all of this already, Arianna. We did have a conversation at the club. And, Bird, just to say, I'm happy you aren't backing out. But you've been in a strange mood since I picked you up earlier. If it's about what happened at Reckless, you have nothin' to be ashamed of, baby. Trust me when I say, I enjoyed myself and every inch of you that my hands touched." She had to know how much her body moving under my hands turned me on, and how much I wanted to touch her any damn time I wanted.

"That's just the thing though, River. I liked it, too. Maybe too much. But that's not usually how I act. At least, not in recent years. It was fun, and if I am being honest, it was the freest I've felt since college. But," she moved around the island to the sink and stared out the window, "I felt like I did something wrong when I got up Friday morning. What happened on the dance floor was intense, and I'm having a hard time with it. Training your mind to break that kind of habit will take time but I'm doing the best I can." She sighed and turned around, leaning a hip into the counter while covering her middle with her arms and looking me straight in the eyes.

"You telling me you like my hands on you and feeling free is doing absolutely nothing to curb my dick from getting hard and stopping me from being a Southern gentleman who's about to take you out on a first date. So, for both of our sakes and to not start what we can't finish, let's talk about you feeling like you did something wrong, Darlin'." I tried to change the subject away from her body.

I moved to her. She dropped her hands from around her middle to her sides, and I wrapped my arms around her waist. She refused to reciprocate the gesture, so I just gave her sides a squeeze, took a hand and cupped her jaw, then told her exactly what needed to be said.

"Baby, you aren't doing anything wrong. You had a fun night out with your girl. The only reason you feel it was wrong is because that motherfucker engrained that in you. Let that go, Arianna. With me, as long as you're safe, you'll always be free to be who you really are and have fun doin' it." I brushed her hair away from her face and behind her ear while still cupping her jaw. I felt her shiver and knew we needed to get going.

"I'm hopin' you don't feel that way anymore when it comes to me," I told her as I let her go.

"River, you are completely not what I expected when I arrived in Carson Falls but...." She was cut off by the sound of someone knocking at the door.

"Hold that thought, baby. That's Meggie. Let me get her settled with Cady, and then we can talk more on the way to the square, yeah?"

She sighed, "Fine."

We both headed out to the living room, and I let Meggie in. Cady was so excited to see her. She immediately started in about playing her a song on the piano. Meggie was a good sport and allowed my girl to drag her over to the bench. I walked up to the piano and laid down the routine for Cady so she knew that just because I wasn't there, didn't mean she could have free reign to do whatever she wanted. There were some concessions that she got when it was the weekend, so I told them to Meggie. They seemed to be content at the piano for the moment, so Bird and I said our goodbyes after a very brief introduction between Bird and Meggie. There would be time for them to get to know each other, so we headed out to the truck.

We were just parking outside the firehouse when Arianna turned to me and said, "Do you remember that day at Thelma's when you walked in, and I was talking to Mickey?"

I put the truck in park, shut the ignition off, and turned in my seat to look at her, "Of course. I remember everything that has you in it."

She smiled small, and her face softened.

"Well, what you don't know is that the reason Penny was there was because I had received a call that morning from a detective that my ex was released on bail. I was a mess. He's a very connected, well-known man. He isn't going to be happy that he was in jail. Especially because he was in there because of me," she explained.

"Fucking hell, Arianna. Why didn't you say anything? Monday night when we were talking, you should have said something. Did the detective say he knows where you are?"

"No. But that doesn't mean shit when it comes to him. Like I said, he's connected, and not just in Seattle. I'm probably just being paranoid, but what if he finds me?" Arianna was terrified, and her eyes started to fill with tears.

I reached my hand out to stroke her hair again. I kept doing it and looked over her face and saw pure terror cloud it. That was it. I needed her to understand that I would keep her safe, by any and all means necessary.

"Bird, baby, look at me." I tipped her chin up with my free hand and held the back of her head with the hand that was stroking her hair. Once she opened her eyes, I let go of her chin and used my thumb to wipe her tears away.

"Stop crying. Please. It kills me to see that fear written all over this gorgeous face and have you look so haunted. I will not let him near you. Nothing will happen to you, Arianna. We'll figure out what's going on."

"River, what exactly do you think you can do to stop him?" She wasn't going to like this, but it was happening whether she wanted it or not.

"What I mean is, I also have connections. Sheriff Gaynor for starters. My job pretty much guarantees the authorities having my back and pulling favors. I'll start with him and see what he says." Her eyes dried up and got wide. Here came the sass.

"I don't want to get on his radar if I'm not there already. The authorities snooping around, looking into him, or looking into me will immediately put the spotlight on me. Shit. I knew I shouldn't have said anything until I knew more." She mumbled the last part, but I heard her.

"No, Arianna. That's where you're wrong. If you had kept this from me any longer and something happened, I would never forgive myself for not protecting you the best I could. I'm not leaving this up for discussion. You can argue with me, but you'll be doing it knowing I have your back," I told her.

"This is not a good idea. At all."

"I don't give a fuck. We'll deal with everything as it comes. And I will keep both of my girls safe while we figure it all out." I glided my hand over her hair, stopped at the base of her head, and slid it to her cheek where it came to rest.

Arianna sighed and turned her head into my touch. She closed her eyes again and seemed to shake her mood. Let's hope so. Moving my hand, I slowly brushed her bottom lip with my thumb and watched her lips part ever so slightly. I leaned in and placed the softest kiss to that delicious mouth of hers before she could protest anything. She didn't pull away during or after. She rested her forehead on mine and spoke so softly when she said her next words.

"Okay. I have to tell you, it does make me feel better that you know. And I hope it can explain me being a bitch to you that day."

"Arianna, do not ever keep anything from me, from this point on. If it's something you think I may react to in a way you're scared of, I'll try to check myself before I do that. But please, tell me anyway. I am not opposed to kisses before bad news either," I said with a smirk and watched up close as those beautiful eyes rolled.

"Whatever. Can we go have some fun now? With all this heavy baggage this week, I think we deserve it." I agreed with her, let her go, and moved to let her out of her side of the truck. She waited for me again. My Bird was learning.

Once on the sidewalk in front of the firehouse, I grabbed her hand and interlocked our fingers. We headed straight for the square and to the food tables. There were tents with tables and all kinds of food. They had balloons, streamers, and ribbons in every color all over every surface available. Chili, sausages, hot wings, and even pies filled the air with the most delicious scents. I was pretty surprised when Arianna pulled me in the direction of the hot wings. I didn't take her for a spicy food type of woman. Boy, was I very wrong. She piled more wings on her plate than I thought she could fit in that body of hers, but ate every last crumb. The whole experience of her enjoying all those wings, moaning her appreciation, and licking her fingers was the cue I needed to move her along to the fair before we headed straight to the back seat of my truck.

I teased her, brushed up against her, and generally tried to stay as close as possible to her as we walked the two streets down from the square to the fairgrounds. When we turned the corner, and got the first glimpse of the Ferris wheel turning in the distance, Arianna's face broke out into the biggest smile. She got so excited; it was a nice change from the sadness that I had seen earlier at the house. Bird started dragging me forward toward the entrance with a vice-like grip on my hand, so I yanked on her, not too hard, to get her attention. We needed to buy bracelets to ride the rides for the night.

"Two, please," I said, holding up two fingers in case the attendant didn't hear.

"I want to go on the Cyclone first. Then the swings. After that, straight to the carousel, River." My Bird was practically jumping up and down. I couldn't help but smile. And that tightness in my chest got even tighter.

"All right, Darlin'. Just don't break my hand this time when you drag me there, yeah?"

"Oh crap. I'm sorry. Did I hurt you?"

"No, baby. You didn't. I'm just teasin' you. Come on. Let's get this Cyclone ride over with. I blame you if all the food we just inhaled comes back up." With a wink at her, we started toward the Cyclone.

On our way to this ridiculous ride, we passed a few games. One was a water gun game where you had to shoot the spray of water consistently at the target, which was inside the mouth of a very creepy clown head. The prizes for this game seemed to be tiny versions of the characters from every Disney/Pixar movie available. The second game was where you threw darts at balloons tacked onto the wall to reveal a slip of paper inside the balloon, naming your prize. The prizes here were different sized bags of candies. The last one we passed, was the game where you put a rubbery frog on the end of a catapult-type thing and use a mallet to send it flying to its lily pad. Prizes for this game were more of an incentive. Stuffed animals in every size possible. Unicorns, dogs, and teddy bears hung all around the top of the stand, and from the outside awning, to entice folks to play.

At our destination, I looked at the monstrosity that seemed to be a huge hit if the line was anything to go by. It had eight yellow arms that extended out from the top, each holding spherical passenger vessels. The seats inside the sphere were evenly spread out around a centralized steering wheel. The wheel allowed the riders to spin the vessels as the ride lifted into the air and leaned at an angle as you went around. This was my worst nightmare. Spinning around repeatedly at top speed was not my idea of a good time. But Bird seemed to really want to experience this full force.

Once at the front of the line, after waiting a good twenty minutes, she turned to me and clapped her hands excitedly with a look on her face that I hadn't seen from her yet. It was soft, but it was pure joy. Arianna was...*happy*. I helped give her that. Knowing I did that for her told me I was doing things right.

"Okay, River. Let's go! I can't wait to spin this sucker as fast as it can go. You ready?" Bird asked me, as she hopped into the seat and strapped her safety belts on.

"Like I said. I blame you if I have to taste all that food we ate all over again," I warned, as I did the same with my belts.

The ground under my feet felt like it was a rolling set of waves in the ocean. That was how crazy dizzy I was. Arianna was able to coerce the other two riders in our sphere to help her spin the damn thing as fast as fucking possible. So, they did, and I was now walking like I just drank a bottle of whiskey.

When I finally got somewhat steady on my feet, Arianna went straight to the swings. I needed to sit this one out. My balance was still not all back, and I needed to get my bearings.

"Darlin', go on this one by yourself. I'm goin' to sit on the bench and watch you. My brain is swimmin' from the Cyclone, and I want to enjoy the rest of the night with you. If I go on the swings with you, I won't be able to do that." We were standing at the entrance to the swing ride. She smirked, and I knew the smart-ass comments were about to come.

"Couldn't handle a little ride at the fair, big guy? Is your belly all icky? Do you need a tummy rub?" She joked and teased as she wove through the metal barricades to get to the end of the line and away from me before I could get to her.

"You'll get it for those comments!" I yelled back at her, smiling and shaking my head.

As I sat on the bench watching as Ari got into the swing and began to fly around, arms extended just like a bird, I thought about Cady. I realized that my daughter got to see that same excitement Arianna had on her face this entire night, every day at her piano lessons. The music bonded them together and gave my baby girl new dreams. My ex would never have been able to give that type of hope or love to Cady. Arianna was meant to be a part of our lives. She needed to be there.

After the swings had come to a complete stop, Arianna hopped down and ran to where I was waiting by the exit. As she approached me, I took in all of her again. She wore these tight blue jeans with rips in the knees that perfectly encased her ass. The peach and aqua plaid shirt she had open over a white spaghetti-strapped camisole brought out the aqua color of her eyes. She wasn't sporting makeup like she wore at the club. Today, it was more natural and more her style. Arianna, once again, had on those fucking cowboy boots she wore the day I kissed her. The memory of that kiss made my dick start to get hard. Arianna had broken into my thoughts, and everything else went away.

"Seriously. That felt like I was soaring. I could do that ride all day," she said, before realizing her innuendo in the last sentence.

"That isn't the ride I would opt for," I said with a smirk.

"Whatever. Can we go to the carousel now?"

"Sure, baby. Let's go." I grabbed her hand, and we went in that general direction.

I walked her straight past the carousel, even though she wanted to ride it, and we ended up in front of the Ferris wheel. It was huge for a county fair with its yellow spoke-like arms and red bucket gondola seating. We stood outside the gate to enter the line, and I tugged my hand to bring her closer to me. It worked. She landed with her hands to my chest to brace herself and closed her eyes as I heard her inhale the scent of my cologne. My arms went around her, trapping her hands on my chest. I needed to tell her what I was thinking about and what I wanted to give her.

"Open your eyes and look at me. Really look at me, Arianna. While you were on that swing, I did some thinkin'. Here's what I have come to realize," I said, as I kept her tight to me but progressed in the line as people were let on and off the Ferris wheel.

"River, what are you talking about?"

"Bear with me, Darlin', yeah? I am takin' a risk at maybe ruinin' the night here, but I need to get this out."

"Fine. Go ahead. But just know, you could never ruin this night for me," she said to me with a serious expression.

At this point, we had made it to the front of the line and were shuffled into our very own red gondola. This was good because we could use the privacy. But she sat across from me instead of by my side.

"Let me just start by sayin' that I didn't know the full extent of your story when we met. The only thing I knew for sure was that your ex hurt you." We had started to ascend into the sky.

"Right," she replied, as she brought her feet up onto the seat and hugged her legs to her chest.

"Can you please come over here and sit with me?" I asked, patting the empty spot next to me. She huffed and quickly moved across to the spot beside me. I took this opportunity to put my arm around her shoulder and bring her into my side with a gentle nudge. She snuggled into me, and I released a tense breath. Using my free hand, I grabbed her legs and draped them over my lap. To keep the contact, I rubbed up and down her legs as I began talking and the Ferris wheel began moving again.

"Bird, I'm a man who knows what loss is. Maybe not the same type, but any loss leaves a part of us changed. I know that more than you think. It's up to us how we want that loss to control us. It can take you down the dark alley, which, Darlin', you've already been down. Or, it can teach you what it's meant to, and you can grow and learn from it. I guess my point is that you clawed back to the light. I need you to stay there. Cady needs you to stay there." I squeezed her legs so she would look up at me again. She did, and I could see unshed tears in her eyes.

"Please don't cry, Bird. That is not why I am saying all this."

Her next admission left me reeling.

"I've been thinking about so much too, River," she said so softly, her voice hitched with emotion. She cleared her throat and continued.

"It's crazy, you know. You never know for sure where you'll be when your life truly begins. The last few weeks, especially this one, I felt like I'm home, like I'm truly starting to live. The pain and memories from him are fading every day. But the heartache about my baby is not as easy to forget about."

"Arianna," I started, as I pulled her completely onto my lap so I could hold her.

"We all have scars and carry them with us whether marred on our skin or etched in our soul. You'll always carry your child in your heart. It's a constant battle in your mind and…" I grabbed each side of her head and tried to show her what I was saying was the truth by looking her straight in the eyes while I finished. "I get that. But, the battle is only won once you have allowed those scars time to dim out and can replace the memories associated with them with new memories. And, Bird, I want to be the one you make new memories with."

Watching as the tears spilled over her cheek up close made the spot in my chest burn. I couldn't control her emotions, but I could hold her while she experienced them. And I could be the man who wiped those tears away.

"River, I don't know what to say. That is the most romantic, kindest thing anyone has ever said to me."

"Just say you will let me be that man," I pleaded with her for this.

"You've made me feel things in such a short period of time," she said back to me as the Ferris wheel stopped at the very top, and all of Carson

Falls lay before us. I heard her take in a sharp breath.

"That's the whole town, isn't it?" Arianna asked me, as she looked around, mesmerized.

"It is. Plus, some of the surroundin' ones. The view up here is somethin' that I always look forward to during the fair. But sharin' it with you this year gives it new meanin'." She smiled at me.

"And why is that?" This question, to me, had an obvious answer. But I gave her the only response I had.

"Because I found the moon and sun in your eyes. I don't have to chase after them anymore."

"Kiss me," she whispered.

"It's about time," I whispered back to her as our lips met in a kiss that told me Arianna wanted me to be that man for her.

The Ferris wheel went around a few more times, and we basically held tight to each other and stole kisses while we were in the air. The entirety of the evening was perfect for us. We had fun with each other and sincerely enjoyed the other's company. Bird was becoming easier and easier to talk to. There was nothing that could kill our mood.

We exited the ramp from the Ferris wheel and started to make our way back toward the games. I wanted to win my baby girl, and my Bird, something. The frog game had the best prizes, so I told Ari we needed to stop there. She played the water gun game, the balloon dart game, and even that game where you had to knock down all the old milk jugs from the pedestal they sat on, with beanbags.

Finally, we made it to the frogs. The first three tries, I missed completely. The last two I got two out of the three frogs on targets. But the last two attempts, I won two prizes. A unicorn for Cady and a teddy bear for Bird. Arianna was cute holding the teddy bear to her chest. She did this the entire way back to the truck.

Just as I opened her door to get her in, my phone went off. I looked down at the display and saw 'Penny Calling,' and I rolled my eyes and hit ignore. I got into the truck and started it up. Before I could even get it in reverse, my phone went off again. Penny was calling *again*. I took the call over my Bluetooth earpiece and prayed that she wasn't calling to check up on me.

"Penelope." That was the greeting she got from me. Then I heard her sniffle down the line, and she had my attention.

"River." It was said on a sob.

"What's wrong Pen?"

"The apartment was broken into. I just got home and the door was left open. I thought maybe Arianna stopped home and just didn't close it or something. But I went in, River. It's a mess. I don't know what to do. It's all destroyed," Penny explained through her cries.

"Penny, I need you to stay calm. Call the cops. I'll be there as soon as I can. And Penny, stay in your car with the doors locked until the cops or I get there, yeah?"

"Okay, River."

"See ya soon, Darlin'." I hung up and pulled out of the firehouse lot. Arianna was staring daggers at me, waiting for me to tell her what was going on.

"Baby, you have to stay calm when I tell you this. Promise me." Glancing at her quickly to gauge her reaction, I got what I needed and told her.

"Your apartment has been broken into. Penny said it's a mess. But she's safe and getting to her is all that matters right now. Everything else can be sorted, yeah?"

"Oh my God. NO! Shit, shit, shit! I knew he would find me," Bird said in a hushed tone.

"What was that, baby?" I asked her to repeat.

"He found me," Arianna replied in her haunted, frightened voice.

"What are you talking about? He doesn't know where you are."

"There's something I probably should have told you, River." She turned away, looking out the window but held on to that teddy bear for dear life.

I watched as she regressed back into her shell, re-erecting the wall I thought I had just demolished on the Ferris wheel. I was wrong about our happy mood being killed. Exes with a heavy hand and a lot of money did it superbly.

Chapter 11
Don't Stop
Arianna

"What exactly do you have to tell me?" River asked me angrily, as we pulled down the street heading to the apartment. It took him almost the whole ride here to speak up and ask me.

"Thursday night at the club, when Penny and I first got there, I felt like I was being watched. I even turned around to check, and no one was there. Then, I got hit on by this guy when we were walking through," I looked at him as he growled but went on, "and he immediately made me feel uncomfortable. No one was around," my voice sounded scared, even to me. But I knew I was more scared of River's reaction to me not telling him.

"Is this why you were standoffish earlier today?" River asked me.

"Sort of. There's more. Yesterday, I felt it again when I went into town to get some groceries. When I parked in front of the store, my hair stood on end and a chill settled over me. Both times, no one seemed to be around. That feeling didn't go away until I was back in Penny's apartment," I finished.

"Why didn't you say something when I picked you up for Cady's lesson?" His tone was worried but more so, laced with anger.

"There is more you need to know before things get any more serious. You have to know what you're really getting into. Besides what you already know, anyway," my shaky voice responded.

"If you start in on this 'you don't deserve me' bullshit again, Arianna, I will lose my mind." It was safe to say River meant business.

"It's not. Although, me getting over that way of thinking is going to take some time, River," I said, looking him square in the eyes. My confidence had been building, and he'd helped me more than he could ever know. But years of being told that I didn't deserve to be happy would take some time to undo.

"Fine, then tell me what the hell it is you think I need to know."

"Please don't get annoyed. I'm trying to be honest here. This isn't easy for me." I turned to look at him, as we got closer to Penny's place.

"I'm sorry," he told me, shaking his head as if to clear his mood, and his next words were spoken in a gentler tone.

"Knowing you could be in danger makes every part of my brain spin out of control."

"Knowing the kind of danger my ex can bring makes my head do the same. Now, will you let me tell you what I have to say before you distract me and it's…" I was cut off by the sound of a car horn. As we both turned to find the source, we saw a car heading straight toward us, and it didn't appear to be stopping.

"RIVER!" I screamed, but it didn't do any good. River couldn't stop in time to avoid a collision, so he jerked the steering wheel to the right and we ended up plowing down some bushes and stopping in a ditch.

"Arianna, are you okay? Are you hurt?" I heard him ask, but I was dazed and really not sure what the hell had just happened.

"Yes. I'm fine. Are you hurt anywhere? Did we hit anything?" I countered back. With the sound of my heart racing in my ears, I knew things had just taken a very serious, ugly turn.

"I'm fine. Who the hell was that? Do you know who could have possibly wanted to run us off the road? You need to talk *right the fuck now*. This shit just escalated. What if I had Cady in the truck with us, Arianna?" He was angry and no longer worried.

"Shit. You don't think I've been thinking about her for the last three damn days? What it means for everyone here in Carson Falls? Do you think I'm doing this on purpose? Well, I have thought about it. This is my mess. Not yours. That little girl means everything to me, whether you believe that or not, and I would never forgive myself if something happened to her," I cried. And the tears weren't wiped away this time by the man I'd slowly come to care for.

"Fuck! I don't know what to think right now. What else are you keeping from me?"

"He's a Kelly, River. He has more money than he knows what to do with. His family owns just about every hotel in Seattle. He grew up in money, and he inherited the family business when his father died. But Andrew," another, much meaner growl came from River, "also has cops in his pocket out there because of who his father was. They turned the other way on most of my ex's indiscretions. Including the prostitutes he took home from the clubs. The fact that the cops had no choice but to arrest him when he finally put me in the hospital was a direct hit to his ego and reputation." Telling him this wasn't really taking that pissed off look off his face. It made it worse. Alas, I had to go on. River wanted it; he'd get it.

"My ex truly believes that revenge is profitable, so he's now, more than likely, on a mission. I've seen how he works. Andrew has people do his dirty work for him. But when it came to me, he always took care of me himself. I really don't need to go into how he did that. You've seen the aftereffects."

"Bird, are you telling me that he's here? Is this what you believe is going on?"

"I don't know. If I had to guess, yes. It has all the hallmarks of Andrew. Down to being run off the road," I finished.

"FUCK!" River shouted, and I recoiled back. He noticed.

"Arianna, I won't hurt you, dammit. But I'm fuckin' mad as hell. I don't understand why you didn't tell me about his connections with the cops. I'm furious that you didn't tell me about what's happened the last three days. But most of all, I'm fuckin' livid because your ex is a major dick."

"This is something I already know," I mumbled under my breath.

"Now is not the time to turn on the sass." He started the truck and reversed out of the ditch. We still had to get to Penny.

"Take my phone. Scroll to Braxton's name and hit go. When he answers, tell him what's going on and to get his ass there."

Shit. Penny was going to hate this. There was no other option though. Sighing huge, I took the phone and did as I was told. It rang twice before I heard Braxton speak his rude greeting.

"What the fuck do you want asshole? I'm in the middle of two hot blondes right now." So disgusting.

"Well, shithead, this is Arianna. I have River's phone. Hope you're using protection with the two skanks you've got there. I'm calling because your friend here thinks it may be a good idea to get to Penny's apartment, as soon as you can," I told him with the most attitude I could muster.

"And why the fuck would I do that, sweetheart?" he asked, sounding a bit more gentlemanly than just a minute ago.

"Because our apartment was broken into, and she's pretty shaken up. River and I are almost there. We would have been there already, but we were run off the road by some lunatic." The phone went quiet for a few seconds, and then I heard the sheets rustling, and Braxton as he told the skanks, Sasha and Brielle, they had to go home. There was some whining and pleading, but he stuck to his guns.

"I'll be there in twenty minutes. Thanks for calling me, Arianna."

"Wasn't my idea. Thank River when you see him. And Braxton, you may want to wash the stench of the skanks off you before you come." I hung up before he could get another word in and handed River back his phone.

"You were rude. And you cussed at him." River was shocked, but I'd had all I could take tonight.

"Yes, I did. I don't think it's a good idea to involve him. Penny and Braxton have history. It may be a mysterious one, but it's there all the same. He was an ass when he answered, so he got what he deserved," I snapped, proud of myself for giving River's friend an earful.

During the rest of the trek to the complex, I wandered into this headspace where I just replayed everything since I'd arrived in Carson Falls. Thinking about all that had taken place so far, it seemed as if I'd been there for years already. I snapped back to reality when I swore I heard the words 'moving your ass in' come out of River's mouth as he pulled into the spot next to Penny's car.

"I'm sorry? Can you repeat that? I don't think I heard you correctly." Maybe my hearing was affected when we trampled the bushes.

"You heard me fine, Arianna. Pack whatever you can of your shit. You're staying with me for the foreseeable future. And I'm warning you. Don't fight me on this. You'll lose." All these words flew at me, but I couldn't have been hearing the right conversation. He couldn't be serious.

"You can't be serious?!" I exclaimed as he got out, and I followed suit.

"Deadly." River's face was blank as he looked at me, he could've won the World Series of Poker. Not one tell as to what he was feeling. Bossy, obviously. Protective, maybe. Crazy, definitely.

"This is not happening," again I mumbled so low no one should have heard me. Of course, River also had supersonic hearing, so he did.

"It's happening. Believe that." Shit. This is so not going to end well for anyone.

Ten minutes after we got there and made sure Penny was okay, the sheriff and his deputy showed up to take the report, fingerprint the surfaces around the apartment, and take pictures of every room. We asked the sheriff if I could grab some clothes for the night and some things I would need, but he told me they were all a part of evidence. Until the case was resolved or the evidence was cleared, I couldn't take anything except what I had on my body. No one would be able to get in until whoever was after me, was caught.

Twenty minutes after that news, Braxton showed up. His hair was wet, so I assumed he took my advice. I warned Penny that he was coming, so she wouldn't get a second shock that night, but she was pissed. Penny wanted nothing to do with him, but she didn't have a choice. Braxton made it known that he would be taking her to his house, and Penny tried to run away. She was caught, hauled over his shoulder, and set down, somewhat forcefully, into his truck. He locked her in. Then Braxton turned to River and me, smiling huge, got in, and drove away with my best friend waving her arms and screaming at him. That idiot was going to enjoy the fight he got from Penny.

River looked at me and sternly said, "Let's go."

"Fine, but what am I going to do for clothes?"

"Tonight, you can sleep in a pair of my sweats and a tee. Tomorrow you'll have to go into town and get some things to tide you over. Not sure if those stores are exactly your style though, so you may want to take my truck and go into Gifford. Hit up those fancy shops," he said to me, somewhat snarky.

"What does that mean?" I asked him, as he helped me into the truck again.

"It just means that your clothes seem a little too fancy for the likes of the small town of Carson Falls."

"You never had anything to say about my clothes before. Besides, I couldn't care less if those clothes were incinerated. Every single stitch was paid for with his hush money. They never were my style."

"Look, Arianna. I'm sorry," he let out a huge sigh and continued. "I didn't mean to take a shot at your clothes. Tonight has me all over. We'll figure it all out. Let's just get home to Cady, okay?" he asked, but it wasn't a question that needed an answer. Maybe River didn't mean it how it came out or how I took it, but he said home. As if it belonged to me, too.

Home. Another thing *he* tried to take from me.

That was my thought as we pulled out of the apartment complex and headed to River's house.

This was all a nightmare. It had to be. How could I have found the one man who made me feel worthwhile and brought him and his daughter the kind of trouble that came with my ex? And Penny, too. Because of me, her apartment was ransacked, and she was staying with Braxton, the guy that she'd had a thing for, for years. I, on the other hand, have managed to make myself right at home in River's spare bedroom, where I'd been sleeping since Saturday night's epic return of my living hell.

Saturday was a rollercoaster of a day. It started off shaky, went into the most perfect first date any woman could've imagined, and nosedived into complete and utter shit. I may live with River right now, but that didn't mean things were good between us. He spoke to me, but only when he had to or if Cady was around. I tried to avoid him as much as possible, so I didn't start screaming at him for moving me in. Cady didn't need the details or to see that, so I just stayed quiet. The cordial encounters, with no sign of any kind of affection, told me that I destroyed yet another thing that was good in my life.

The upside of being at River's place was that I could teach Cady from here, I had an actual bed to sleep in, and this custom-made porch couch, which seemed more like a bed, I currently had my ass sunken into, was the perfect spot for reflecting and composing. I spent the better part of the last five days out here until it was time for lessons or dinner. I hadn't been back to work in almost two weeks. Miss Thelma called and said she needed to talk to me about things at the shop, so we set up a lunch date for that upcoming Sunday, since she would be in the square for church. I knew her news wouldn't be good, and I needed to brace myself.

Needing to set up for Cady's lesson, I made my way into the house and to the piano. There was so much going through my head, and I needed to release it. I slid open the cover and slowly brushed my fingers until I was in proper placement and started the opening chords of A Great Big World's "Say Something". As I started to sing the lyrics, I felt all the emotions from the past few days release into my fingers, and I belted out the words like no one was watching. I knew River was watching me, though. I always knew when he was in my general vicinity. His presence didn't cause me to falter. I sang the lyrics to him word for word. I was ready to give up because, at that moment, nothing else felt right, and he had not spoken a word to me.

River approached the piano and stopped directly behind me. His heat radiated into the bare skin of my back that the loose spaghetti-strapped top left exposed. Slowly, his fingers glided up from my elbows, up over my biceps, stopping at the straps. The gentle touch. His careful actions. It was all too much. He stayed there with his fingers barely touching my shoulders as I finished the last chord and lyrics. As soon as the room went quiet again, my emotions got the best of me, and I started to cry. His gentle touch became a firm squeeze on that spot where my neck met my shoulders. My body shook with sobs, but he didn't make a move to comfort me. I raised my hands to cover my face, and I let it rip out of me from somewhere so deep, it seemed impossible that place even existed in a person.

Before I understood what was happening, I was up in his arms and being carried over to the couch. River ended up in the same corner spot he sat the first time I was here and watched movies. That seemed like a lifetime ago too. Being handled like I was delicate was not what I was used to. I had been with other guys before my ex, but he was the longest, and the most recent memories stemmed from him. So, when River cradled me to his chest like I was something precious, it made me relax. River never touched me in a way that was forceful or painful on purpose. I was learning that difference every day. He started to run his hand through my hair, shushing me as he did it. It was calming. It was safe. And it quelled the shakes that raked through my body.

"I know that I've been a massive dick to you the past few days, Arianna. I just needed to make sure the anger was gone. And let me be clear. It wasn't anger toward you, baby, even if it seemed that way," he spoke into my hair, as he continued playing with it and kissing the top of my head.

"River, I'm just so sorry you're even involved in any of this. You've been so sweet to me. And this is the thanks you get." My tears started to silently spill over my cheeks again into his shirt.

River took my head gently, pulled me away from his chest, and stared into my eyes. His intensity terrified me, and I closed my eyes tight, so I didn't have to see the sad look in his eyes. River knew my past. All of it now. He also knew that I would never intentionally do anything to hurt Cady. I loved that kid. As his thumbs wiped away the tears still coming out, his lips gently kissed my cheeks. River peppered me with affection, and it was the most surreal experience. There was never a time my ex comforted me like this, even if he was the one in the wrong. In that moment, River made me realize, finally, that not all men were like *him*.

"Look at me, Bird. Let me see those gorgeous eyes." It was a demand, but it was one I obeyed easily because I wanted to see him.

"Arianna, I am going to kiss you. It will be long. It will be deep. And I promise you; I will try to control myself. But Darlin', I need to taste you. It's been too damn long, and it's time you start gettin' your happy back."

"Don't control yourself. I don't want you to. I want you, River. I want you so bad. I thought you would never touch me again," I panted out to him, already starting to get excited.

"Baby, I can assure you that shit will never be the case. Giving you time to process everything that happened, and giving myself time so I wouldn't fight with you and scare you, was the only reason we've been dancin' around each other this past week or so," he told me in a firm but gentle tone, so that there was no misunderstanding.

I couldn't take much more. His words, my wants, the tension, and all the emotions of the last couple of weeks bubbled up to the surface, and I needed him to touch me. I needed him to take care of me. We needed to take that step because it was important for him, but it was even more important for me to see and feel the difference between what I had with a man that didn't love me like he promised, and a man that I could lose my heart to.

"Kiss me, River. Show me what it's like to be with a man again."

"Are you sayin' what I think you are sayin'?"

I smiled coyly at him and said, "Well, someone had to make the first move here, River."

"Yeah, baby. I just didn't think it would be you."

"I'm stupid scared. And it's been a really long time. With all you know, and all you can't begin to imagine that went down, please don't be mad if I need to stop." He had stopped peppering my face with kisses, and I looked at him. River smirked, and I shivered.

"Bird, I would never make you do anything you didn't want to do. And I would never be mad if you said stop. I need to be gentle with you for a bit. And I'm okay with that," he started to push me down onto the couch but kept on, "but, woman, you best believe there will be times I won't be and trust me, you'll love every second of it."

I shivered, and dammit, he felt it.

"Like that, do you?"

"Oh, shut it. You always do that to me. Besides, you're on top of me. There was no way you wouldn't have felt it. Now, kiss me."

"Is my Bird being bossy?"

"River! We don't have a ton of time, you know! Cady will be home soon," I scolded him because he needed to get on with it already. I was squirming under him, and I wanted him to kiss me like he said he would earlier.

"Shit. How much time we got?" he asked me.

"About forty-five minutes, at most. But you know how excited she is that I am here, so more like thirty-five."

"Fuck. That's not enough time for me to do what I want to do. Will you settle for a make-out and semi-gropin' session now and then we can make arrangements for more to come?" What was a girl to do?

River was wasting precious time by wheeling and dealing with me. I would take what I could get right now. If I knew anything about River Bradshaw, it was that he would make our first time together special. And he would make it romantic. A quickie before his daughter came home from school wasn't what either of us needed right now. Still, I needed something.

I leaned up and kissed him. The kiss started soft, then turned wild in an instant. Tongues collided and swirled around each other. While my hands gripped his hair, River's hands started to roam up my sides. He stopped them right at the underside of my breasts, and brushed the skin there with his fingers lightly, but enough to send the signal directly to my core. He did this maneuver a few times before thrusting into me as if we were naked, using the ever-growing bulge in his jeans to rub me exactly where I needed it.

"You're wet and warm. I can feel it through my jeans. I need to touch you," River groaned out into my mouth.

"Yes," I breathed out, "touch me. Need you to." He kept thrusting into me and hitting the perfect spot. My sentences had started to become mumbles.

He slowly let out a deep groan as his hand traveled further south to the top of my jeans. His fingers found the button and released it. Then he grabbed the zipper and started to pull it down, but stopped. He'd been watching his movement but looked me in the eyes with such a serious expression; I started to think he was changing his mind.

"I need you to tell me again it's okay, Arianna. I don't want you to have any reservations with me. But I need you to give me permission every step of the way," he said with both hunger and hesitation in his voice.

"Yes, River. Don't stop." The hesitation in his eyes vanished. The hunger took over, causing his eyes to turn more liquid and the blue to deepen to an almost royal blue color. He started to shift up on his knees. I let out an aggravated whimper because I lost his thrusts. But what was about to happen would be so much better.

Watching him change right in front of my eyes was the most amazing thing I had ever seen. No man had ever looked at me like that. From the start, River was different. It was something I had always known on the surface. But now, it was more a feeling that my life was planted and rooted. Like there was nothing that could take me away from this place. My safety was no longer a question. Deep down into my heart and soul, I knew I was protected by River. And it was the most serene feeling I had experienced up to that point in my life. So yes, I was ready for him to touch me.

The left side of River's mouth tipped up in a sexy smirk before he lowered my zipper and crashed his mouth down onto mine. He slowly slid one hand inside my jeans but not under my panties. He used the other to push back the loose tendrils of hair in front of my face that had escaped my hair clip when he shifted so he could watch me, free and clear.

"River…" I breathed out as his fingers brushed over my sex.

"Jesus Christ, Arianna. You're drenched," he bit out between clenched teeth. Being the recipient of his touches, kisses, and his words turned me on and made me wetter than I had ever been before. He was losing his hold on his control, and it was taking a stellar effort not to snap. I appreciated him holding on, but I wasn't sure it was what we needed. The past five days contained more tension than anyone ever needed. And this release needed to happen for the both of us, to remind us that what we started at the fair was the beginning of something that could take a lifetime to appreciate.

Chapter 12

Boy Bands
River

Someone once told me that you could be anywhere and with someone you never expected to be with, when you finally realized the path for your life. At that moment, with my Bird so ready and so willing to let me touch her, knowing she trusted me in that way, that sentiment held true. It was a powerful moment, and seeing the future with her by my side, raising Cady along with any babies we made together, taking my name, was more than I could take. Emotions so unfamiliar to me crashed into my heart, and that dull ache that had been there seemed to ignite and spread throughout my body. Staring into Arianna's beautiful face after pushing her hair back, started to unravel me. Not a single woman on this earth could or would ever hold a candle to my Bird. And I would protect what was mine until I took my last breath.

Feeling Arianna squirm under my touch snapped me out of my thoughts, and my focus became her and her pleasure. My world came into plain sight. In the simplest of ways, it became Arianna. I had been an asshole to her and knew I didn't deserve what she offered up to me, but I was a selfish bastard. I would take whatever she gave me.

As I gently tugged her panties to the side and slid my fingers through her wet folds, Ari moaned and wiggled.

"River," she breathed out my name.

"That's right, baby. Just you and me. Feel everything I'm doing. I will take care of you," I reassured her, so she knew she had nothing to be embarrassed or scared of.

"More, River. I need more."

"Tell me what you want, Darlin'."

"I'm not sure. I just need…more." Arianna went after her more by pushing her core down onto my fingers. When she pushed down as far as she could go, the warm heat of her arousal dripping down my hand was my undoing. I began thrusting my fingers in and out of her pussy, picking up the pace, and rolling my thumb over her clit as her moans got louder and she started panting out my name. I knew the more she craved was being satisfied, so I curved my two fingers just right to hit her in the spot that sent her soaring over the edge.

"Oh God! I'm coming," she told me what I already knew.

"Give me that beauty. You are so stunning like this. No one touches you like this but me. No one gives you this beauty but me. I'm the only one who gets to make my Bird soar. Do you understand, Arianna?" My question came off very possessive, but fuck. That was exactly how I meant it. She belonged to me completely and not just in my wildest fantasies anymore. Every. Beautiful. Inch.

Once Arianna caught her breath and landed back on earth, she smiled huge, climbed into my lap without fixing her clothes, and straddled me. I held on tight to her perfectly rounded ass with both hands. She hooked her arms around my neck and started trailing her soft, kiss-swollen lips up my neck, over my jaw, and down the opposite side. She continued to trail kisses over my Adam's apple and down to my collarbone. When she reached the top of my maroon, Carson Falls FD emblazoned t-shirt, she grabbed the hem and pulled it up over my head, in one fluid motion, as I had my hands raised to assist her. When Arianna's hands left my neck, I felt her run them over my chest and sides.

"As much as it pains me to say this, and trust me, my dick hates me right now, I don't think us losing our clothes is a good idea, Arianna.

Cady will be home any minute, and we need to discuss what this means for us. I don't want Cady to have any delusions of what this is if we aren't on the same page," I told her, because I wouldn't risk my daughter getting hurt if Ari wasn't serious about exploring what we could have.

I knew what I wanted pretty much since I laid eyes on her. Arianna had a history that made her doubt her own choices, and that was understandable. Shattering her doubt and any fears she had was a priority. And I needed her to be sure. *God, please. I'm begging you. Let her be sure.* It was so primal with Arianna. I needed her. It wasn't just a want. It was rooted deep inside and not willing to budge. Knowing there was a slight chance that I may not succeed at proving to Arianna that I would cherish and protect her sent me into my own self-doubt.

"Okay. Well, what exactly do you think is going on here?" she asked me in sort of a clipped tone.

"Isn't it obvious, baby?" I asked back, a bit dumbfounded that she hadn't clued in yet.

"I mean. It's obvious that we have a mutual attraction, and I adore your daughter. And I would be lying if I said I don't have feelings for you, River. But…" she started, but I cut her off.

"No buts, Arianna. Those feelings you have for me, we need to explore because, baby, my need for you is overwhelming and overpowering. I have those same feelings. Don't deny me my needs. Please," I begged her and grabbed her head between my hands and made her look me in the eyes again.

"River, I'll mess up and cause you chaos. Look at what I have already thrown at your doorstep. Are you really willing to take that risk to be with me?" she asked me, seriously.

"I have thought about this for the last five days. And even with me being a humongous ass to you, you chose to stay. You could have called Penny to come get you and take you back to Braxton's place, but you didn't. Yes, I'm a thousand percent sure. You're what I want. But more, you are what my daughter and I need."

"I don't really know what to say."

"Say you'll be with me. Say you'll stay and work on building what we've already taken a chance on starting. Tell me you'll keep showing my daughter that she is beauty, just like you are. Let me protect you and keep you safe. But mostly, let me show you how much you deserve this, despite what you think," I pleaded with Arianna. Hoping that she knew I would do everything to make this work. The reward of a life with her far outweighed the risk when it came down to how I felt or any other outside circumstances threatening us.

"You're going to make me cry. I can't promise you forever. I can only promise you right now. I will give all that I have to this, but like I said, I'll mess it up. That's the scariest part for me because mistakes were rectified with bruises. And…before you say anything, I know that isn't you. But if I flinch, or cower, when we're raising our voices, you need to walk me through those moments," Arianna said to me.

"There isn't going to be a moment that you don't feel worshiped. Even when we fight or raise our voices. Disagreements between lovers is passion. It's wildfire. And there's always make-up sex that results from that. So, you see, Bird, there's so much to look forward to."

"Okay, River. Let's see what happens. One day at a time." She leaned forward, after delivering the words that set my hopes floating, and kissed me.

After her attack on my lips, I scooted her off my lap and went to pick up my shirt. I needed to be fully clothed for Cady, but I needed more of her mouth. My cock was still throbbing and straining to get out. He needed to relax because I wouldn't be able to handle him until my Bird started her lesson with Cady. Ice-cold showers had been a regular occurrence in my life since Arianna came into it.

I sat back down and moved Arianna back to where she was. I clasped my hands together behind her back and just looked up at her and smiled. She shook her head at me, smirking, causing the scent of her shampoo to filter through the space. It was a cross between strawberries and mango this time. I moved my hands slowly up her back and into her hair. I let my fingers comb through it and tucked it behind her ears before I rested my hands on her shoulders and brought her mouth back to mine. Slowly I kissed her beautiful lips, teasing them apart with my tongue until she allowed me in.

Our tongues mingled, and the kiss became deeper. It was different.

Maybe it was because Arianna had agreed to see what we could be. There was no doubt in my mind that she would be mine forever. She would see that in time. She was already more of a mother to Cadence than Emma ever was. It was inherently engrained in Arianna. Natural. She was born to be a mother. The child that she lost, as heartbreaking as that was, would not deter her. I wouldn't let that happen. Bird would be the mother of my children. Including Cadence.

There was nothing I want more in this life than to fulfill Arianna's dreams of becoming a mom. Well, except her taking my name. Emma may have been my wife, but the difference between how I felt about her and how I feel about the woman currently in my lap, was worlds apart. When I was with Emma, I thought she was it for me. With a clear and open mind, I can say that she was meant to be with me for that given time to give me my daughter. But she never made me feel that need for her. Not even close to the pull Arianna had on me.

"Hey, Daddy!" I'm jolted out of my thoughts as Cady came bouncing in.

"Hey, Birdie! Why are you in Daddy's lap? Did you get in trouble? Is he giving you a Daddy talk?" My inquisitive child asked in rapid-fire succession.

"No, baby. We were talking, but Bird isn't in trouble. Why don't you come sit over here next to us so we can have a talk?"

"Okay, Daddy, but I behaved today. And Miss Penny was sad, so I gave her my snack. I was really, really good today," she unloaded without prompting.

"I'm so happy to hear you were a good girl today, but that isn't what I want to talk to you about." I patted the couch, and Cady climbed up and snuggled up against us. I wrapped my arm around her and chanced a glance at Bird. She gave me her nod of approval, and we both turned to watch Cady.

"Cadence, Arianna and I are going to spend some time together. We're going to go out places. Sometimes with you, but also sometimes will be without you. You are the most important person in my life, and even if you don't understand what I mean…" I only managed to get out before Cady cut in.

"Are you and Birdie in love, Daddy? Like Cinderella and the Prince? Is that why you were kissing?" My daughter. The most observant five-year-old in existence.

"We aren't in love yet, baby. But we hope to be one day," I said to her but looked Arianna in the eyes. She smiled a shy, knowing, all-for-me smile back.

"THAT'S EXCELLENT NEWS!" she screamed and jumped in place on the couch, clapping her hands like a little lunatic.

"I am so glad you're so excited, Cadence. But let's take it down a notch, please. Now, this is our business. Do you remember what that means?" I asked her. I knew my daughter. She's a little gossip. She'd tell the whole damn school, and then the whole town would know.

"No talking about it at school. When it's time for people to know, they will," she recited back the words I have tried to teach her. My success rate was fifty percent with this one. Once she spoke her first word, she hadn't really stopped talking.

"That's right. I know you're excited and I love that you are, Cady, baby. But, that doesn't mean the rules around here change. Same routines, same rules. Am I understood?"

"Yes, Daddy. Can I just ask one thing?" she asked, raising her little eyebrows up with hope shining bright in her eyes.

"You can ask whatever you want. As for talking about it, as long as we're at home or Arianna and I are with you, okay?"

"Okay. Right. So, I guess it's more for Birdie. If you marry Daddy, does that mean you'll be my momma?" Cadence asked, sending what felt like a punch to my stomach, and causing my heart to pick up its pace. My daughter went right in for the kill. I felt Arianna tense as the words left Cady's mouth, and I squeezed her tighter against my side, where she had moved when Cadence had come in and interrupted our make-out session. Arianna didn't move or speak, so I tried to shake her a bit to snap her out of it. That seemed to work.

"Well, Princess. I can't tell you for sure if I will marry your dad, but I will say that I would be so proud and ridiculously happy if you thought of me that way," Bird told my girl with a calm she didn't have a minute before.

147

"Well, Birdie, will you still be my friend even if you marry Daddy and become my momma?" Cady must really have thought about this before today. It broke my heart that she worried about this, or even had to for that matter.

Damn Emma.

"Princess, I will *always* be your friend. I promised you that, remember?"

"Yeah. I was just scared. I never want to not be your friend. You need me so you aren't scared," Cady let Bird know how it was. I had to stifle a laugh because it was just too much to hear my five-year-old tell a grown woman that she needed her so she wouldn't be scared.

"How about this. To celebrate us still being friends, and maybe one day more," Arianna shot me a quick smile and finished, "we learn a song about friends for today's lesson?"

"YES! I would love that so much!"

"Well, then. Shall we get started? Daddy needs to go shower, so it will be just us girls." Bird told Cady. The more time they spent together, the more my girl fell in love with Arianna. I watched as both my girls walked hand in hand to the piano. I took that as my cue to get out of their hair and do something I haven't done in a long time.

"I'm gonna go for a walk and let y'all do your thing. Then I'll come in and shower," I informed them.

As I approached the weeping willow that had been on my property since I was a kid, an overwhelming sense of nostalgia washed over me. There were so many memories hidden under all those hanging willows. But the best memories were the ones I had with my father. We'd go fishing, and Mom would make us lunch, put it in a cooler, and leave it under the shade of the tree. When we finished fishing, Dad and I would sit and eat whatever Mom had made. Sometimes she threw in extra snacks for me and a beer or two for Dad. No matter what, Dad and I would always sit there and talk for hours. We talked about school, sports, girls when I got older, and even what I wanted to do with my life after college. My father was the easiest person to talk to and one of my very best friends. So, I guess I understand Cady's feelings about being Bird's friend and not wanting to lose that. There wasn't a day that went by that I didn't miss that relationship with my old man.

Making my way back toward the house, I stopped at the stone steps that led down to the lake. The sound of the man-made waterfall trickling into the water lulled me into a hypnotic state. As I stared into the distance, I thought more about my parents and what they would think of Bird. I also thought about the current situation she faced. Not only was her ex a dick of epic proportions, but he also had helpers out here. In the five days that I spent avoiding Arianna, I was able to find out some information about this dickhead and his whereabouts.

Andrew Kelly had not left the state of Washington. He was still in Seattle, but Ari had been right. His money helped him cover up his woman-beating ways and so much more criminal activity; it was a wonder how the FBI or internal affairs hadn't cottoned on to his sorry ass yet. My source in Seattle was an old friend, Rhett Stewart, who had moved there after school to take a job as a Law Consultant to Policy for a major corporation called Marx. He knew exactly who I was asking after when I told him about Arianna. He knew the name and had seen her picture in the newspaper when she still played with the symphony out there. He wasn't sure who Kelly's soldier out here was, but I was determined to find out.

I couldn't imagine who would want to scare or harm a woman like Arianna. She was a kind, strong, big-hearted woman that deserved all the happiness the world could offer her. Rhett and I were going to stay in contact, so we could let each other know about any new developments on either side. He'd let me know if that Kelly asshole left Seattle, and I'd let him know of any more incidents of being run off the road or Arianna feeling like she was being watched.

I must have been gone longer than I planned because I heard girly giggles coming from the house. Then I faintly heard my daughter yammer something to Arianna and then Arianna responding back. And then my descent backward into the 90's and the seventh ring of hell started blaring out from the same spot I heard the small voices. Some 90's boy band. On my fucking stereo system. Hell no. This was not happening right now. Bubble-gum-pop-boy-band music was fiercely forbidden in my house. I needed to rectify this situation immediately. My daughter needed to either stick to that classical stuff she learned in her lessons or the music I liked. Like country. Or rock. Mostly, anything other than the ear-splitting nonsense currently torturing all who could hear it. Yeah, no way I could let it continue, so I walked back to the house.

As I approached, the offending noise got louder and louder, right along with the singing of the two girls I left in there. I walked into the house and stopped dead to watch the scene in front of me. My girls were smiling huge, singing at the top of their lungs, and dancing around the makeshift dance floor they created by moving furniture out of their way. Arianna was twirling Cady and using the remote as a microphone. Cady was bobbing her head and singing the words. My daughter knew the words to this crap. What the hell had Bird done? Even though this was not what I considered music, the sight before me made my heart melt. So, I decided to watch for a bit before interrupting my private concert. Leaning against the frame of the archway, the only thing I could do was smile, laugh, and enjoy that feeling of contentment I got from seeing my baby girl finally get what I wanted her to have. Someone to do girly shit with, even if that meant blasting boy bands.

"Would you be able to bring me into town on Sunday?" Arianna asked me, sitting at the island in the kitchen after we'd eaten the dinner she and Cady had prepared.

"Sure. Any particular reason?" I asked back.

"Miss Thelma called me when we weren't really speaking, and she asked to meet me at the coffee shop to discuss some stuff. I haven't seen her in almost two weeks as it is, and I know that something serious is going on."

"Of course, Darlin'. I'll take you and tag along. I don't want you to be by yourself right now. Even if you're in a public place." She shook her head in agreement, and I raised my eyebrows and stared at her in shock. No attitude. No sass. And absolutely no arguments about me being there. Maybe this was her way of putting even more of her trust in me. Well, whatever it was that was making her so amenable, I would be sure to make a mental note for future reference.

"Honey, I understood what you needed from me when you asked me to let you protect me. I won't argue with that because if I'm honest, I'm tired of living in any sort of fear." She called me honey. It was the first time she used any type of endearment toward me, and it caused that ache to simmer below the surface again. The fact that Arianna really listened to me when I told her to let me be her man, made me want her even more.

Still processing the words Bird said, I finished putting the last of the dishes away; I'd agreed to do the dishes since the girls cooked. When I finished, I sauntered into the living room to check on Cady. I wanted to ensure my Bird and I would have time for a make-out session, so I was relieved to find Cady on the couch, watching that Godforsaken *Frozen* movie again, for like the seven-hundredth time.

Confirmed that my baby girl would be transfixed on the television for the next hour or so, I made my way back to Bird. I walked up behind her and wrapped my arms around her middle. I felt her stiffen, but she quickly relaxed. I knew certain things would still do that to her for a while, so I kept my emotions under control and didn't mouth off about her ex. Arianna rested her hands over the top of mine, and I brushed her loose, blonde, wavy hair away from her neck with my nose and licked a path up to her jaw. Nibbles, licks, and soft, gentle kisses, against her perfect porcelain skin, and I was ready to spread her out on the island and do whatever I wanted to her. Her moaning and grabbing the back of my head to hold me in place so I'd continue kissing her right below her ear only caused my cock to get harder. I pulled away and spun her around on the stool at the island so I could look at her.

"Seems like we've been in this position before, baby," I said to her to see if she remembered our night at Reckless.

151

"You're right, honey. We have been. But, River, there is one very huge difference from the night at the club. Here we have a bed, a lock on the door, and I'm not drunk." The little tease knew how to get me riled.

"Don't tempt me with the promise of you. I want nothing more than to discover the rest of the beautiful body you have to offer. I'm just not sure Cady will allow that to happen tonight."

"Well, let's make it interesting then, shall we?" Wicked woman.

"What exactly did you have in mind?" I eagerly asked her.

"You're only down the hall from me, River. Your daughter is upstairs. What kind of trouble can we get into if, say, I made a midnight visit to your room?"

"The kind of trouble I really, really wouldn't get mad at you over. If you're serious, I'll come to you," I said.

"No, honey. It's about time I came for you, don't you think?" she surprised me by saying. And more 'honey'.

"You'll definitely be coming for me," I told her with confidence. The more I thought about her sneaking into my room, like we were a bunch of teenagers, the harder it was to control the erection trying desperately to escape the confines of my pants. I needed some type of contact with Arianna, so I stepped between her legs and pulled her even further to the edge of the stool. Once her core was settled against my ever-growing dick, I thrust against her.

Arianna's mouth dropped open, her eyes got lazy, it was her tell that she was about to start moaning. That was my hint to take her mouth so we didn't clue Cady in to the scene in the kitchen. It was wet and manic. Desperate to taste each other, we kissed wildly, passionately, and hungrily. There was so much foreplay happening, it was a struggle to remember my daughter was in the next room, and the last thing she needed to see was me groping Ari's perfect tits and ass. I was a man who had needs, but I was also a father who was in no way ready to have that type of talk with his five-year-old.

"Bird, baby. We have to stop, or I'm going to take you on this surface. Let's go watch the rest of the movie with Cady. After that, I'll put her to bed. I expect to see you tonight, Arianna. Don't stand me up." I stepped back and remembered, "and Darlin', there's no need for panties. They'll just be a hindrance to devouring you." With a wink, I walked out of the kitchen and into the living room where my daughter was, indeed, enthralled in that fucking movie. What was it with that movie?

Just as I sat down, Ari came into my line of sight, and she smiled that small, shy smile again that I now claimed as mine. Making her way to my side, she bent down and lifted Cady up, sat down, and placed my girl on her lap. She played with Cady's hair for the rest of the time the movie played, while snuggled up against me. *This is what a family feels like.* I let out a sigh, trying to ease the burn that spread across my entire body.

If I could pinpoint the moment I knew for sure my second chance at happiness truly began, it was most definitely that one.

Chapter 13
I Heard the Lyrics
Arianna

I made my way out of the bed and into the attached bathroom. I looked in the mirror and what I saw kind of shocked me. Nothing really could have prepared me for what stared back at me this time. I tried to avoid mirrors mostly because the last time I looked in one was at Thelma's, and I didn't like what I'd seen reflected back. Now, the exact opposite rang true.

Shining brightly back at me, was hope.

There was no other word to describe it.

There was no mistaking the safety I felt being in River's arms, but seeing that proof come to fruition in my music said so much about how much River and Cady actually meant to me, and what they had done for me in such a short amount of time. It was petrifying and remarkable all rolled into one emotion. The words I wrote in my songs were a truth that I could see now in my eyes as I stared at myself. So much had changed, and I finally felt like maybe, this is something I deserved. Memories of my past might always haunt me but they no longer crippled me because I'd seen what a family was supposed to be and feel like.

Throwing my hair into a messy bun on the top of my head, I reached for the toothbrush and paste. I brushed my teeth, washed my face, and applied some ChapStick before I headed to the shopping bags of clothes I'd purchased since mine were still wrapped up in the investigation. I didn't see the point in full on makeup, but I did want to honor his simple request. So, with only a Tennessee Titans t-shirt on and no trace of panties, I made my way down the hall.

Slowly, I turned the doorknob and made my way inside the very dark bedroom. The only sound I heard as I slid the lock into place was my heavy breaths. I was more nervous than I alluded to when I challenged River earlier in the kitchen. Just as I was going to start making my way to the bed, I tripped over what felt like a boot. Instinctively, I started hopping around clamping my foot in my hand chanting 'Ow' while a low, gravelly laugh came from the direction of the bed.

"It hurts dammit! Stop laughing and help me, River!" I scolded him. He didn't make a move though.

"This isn't sexy and not exactly the way I imagined this starting off," I whined.

"Arianna, you're always sexy to me," River said, as he flipped on the light. When he finally made his way to me, he lifted me up and placed me down on the edge of the bed, out of harm's way.

"Damn that really hurt."

"Let's see if I can make it feel better, yeah?"

Before I could protest, he had my foot in his hands, rubbing my poor toes back to life. He really was good with his hands.

"How's that feel, Darlin'?" he asked with a sexy as sin grin.

"Better, thank you. I'm sorry I'm such a spaz."

"Baby, it wasn't your fault. I should've put my boots away."

"I was hoping that things went a bit smoother, but that's just exactly my luck," I sighed and flopped backward onto the bed as I felt his hands glide up my calves.

River got up on his knees and positioned his torso between my legs. His hands roamed further north to rest on my thighs.

"Baby, sit up and talk to me a minute, yeah?" River asked gently. He knew I was embarrassed by my entrance. I sat up and placed my arms around his shoulders and looked into his eyes. They had gone this incredible dark blue, and his lids were halfway closed in a seductive look that made me swallow hard and breathe deeper. He was only wearing dark colored briefs, and he'd caught me checking out his chest and abs. He licked his deliciously sculpted lips and gave me a half-smile.

"Arianna," River started in a soft, caressing tone, "I don't care what happened before me, when you walked in here, or if you decide you can't do this. Just you taking a chance and coming in here means so much to me. I won't force you to do anything you don't want to do. I know what happened earlier was intense and in the heat of the moment we made promises..."

"River," I cut him off, "I'm scared. But I'm sure. I just wanted this to be perfect. Besides, I've already kept my word. Twice."

"What do you mean twice?" River asked, confused.

"Well, one. I didn't stand you up. And two..." I started to wiggle the t-shirt from under my ass, so I could pull it over my head to show him the other promise I kept. I threw the shirt behind him and watched as he devoured my body with his eyes. Then once it clicked, he watched me lay back on my elbows so I could still see him. His eyes were hooded and hungry, as I lay there waiting for him to devour me completely.

He stood up and climbed over top of me on the bed. He kept his weight off me by using his arms to hover. The veins and muscles in his beautifully sculpted body had me salivating and wishing I could lick every inch of him.

"What do you want, baby?" River bent his head down and brushed a quick soft kiss across my lips.

"I want you, River, any way you want me."

"Arianna, I want you every way you're willing to give yourself to me, whenever you choose to do that. Are you absolutely sure this is what you want?"

"Yes, River. I'm sure. Kiss me. I need you." It came out needy and husky and didn't sound like me. I'd never felt this way before with my ex. This was a need I never knew I possessed. I craved River in this moment like I had no man before. As much as I knew making love to River would mess with me, it was something I had to do, like taking my next breath.

He adjusted us on the bed so we were now in the middle of it, and he knelt between my legs that he'd nudged apart with his. River's mouth crashed down on mine once again. Harder this time but not in a way that made me uncomfortable. His hands slid up my sides while he trailed kisses down my jaw, finding that sensitive spot on my neck that led to right below my ears and ended at the dip where my throat and collarbone met. He licked and kissed his way lower as his hands cupped my breasts, bringing them up to him to explore.

I felt myself getting wetter with every single touch of his mouth. The moment his lips surrounded my nipple, and I felt his tongue flick against it, I moaned out on a shaky breath. My hands grabbed his head and held it tight to me. This only urged River to keep going. He made his way to the other nipple and gave the same attention to that one, making it hard and sensitive to his touch. When he felt me squirm, he looked up to my face.

"Are you okay?" he asked, concern filled his eyes.

"Fine. Need more," I managed to get out. My heart was racing, and I needed him to give me more, so I raised my hips to brush my core against his.

"Tell me what you want, baby."

"Everything. I want everything, River," I whispered to him. Finally admitting out loud that I wanted my dreams back.

"Then everything is what you'll get, baby. But that wasn't what I meant. Tell me where you need me right now," River stated with a small smile on his face.

"I need you inside me," I stated, plain and simple, my hands tracing over every inch of his skin it could reach.

"Arianna, there's nothing I want more than to slide inside of your beautiful body. But I need to make sure you're taken care of first. Your body needs to be ready for me. I don't want to hurt you," he assured me, as his fingers found their way into my wet folds.

River circled my entrance with a finger while his thumb pressed lightly and rubbed my clit. The pressure was just enough to give the first indication that an orgasm was building. I moaned and cried out as he increased his movements. As I moved under him, bucking and raising my hips, attempting to get his fingers to enter me so I could feel any part of him inside me, he slid one long, thick finger inside, and I gasped out with complete pleasure.

River must have thought I was in pain, so he stopped moving, but I gave him my reassurance by starting to move on the finger inside me. Suddenly one finger became two, and my vision started to blur. River thrust his fingers in and out of me, again, hitting that spot deep inside of me, and I felt my body start to shake from the pleasure he was giving me. I had never experienced an orgasm from being fingered. My ex didn't really like foreplay, and most of the time didn't care if I came or not. This was new for me, and my body's reaction scared me. River's thumb kept circling, and I couldn't stop it.

"Look at me, Arianna. Give it to me. I want you to come on my fingers," he said, as my orgasm started to pulse through me in waves and my eyes slammed shut.

"Shit. River, I'm coming!" I exclaimed.

"Open your eyes and look at me. I need you to see that I'm the one who gives this to you," he said, as he stilled his fingers until I opened my eyes and looked at him again.

"Bird, baby, you're the most magnificent when you're soaring from what I do to you. And baby, you're all mine," he said with wonder in his tone.

Once I regained my senses, and my eyes opened, he was still above me, and I reached up to bring his mouth to mine. River's lips turned me on all over again. It was time to show him how much I wanted him. While I deepened the kiss, his length still against my core, harder than any man I'd ever felt, I pushed on his shoulders and managed to flip him over so he was now under me and I was straddling him.

"What are you doing, Arianna?" he growled out at me. I started to grind down on him.

"What does it feel like I'm doing?" I asked him.

"It feels like you haven't had your fill yet. Are you ready for more of me?" he asked, as I started to scoot back so I could release him and his cock from the confines of his boxer briefs and get into position in between his legs. River's cock was much bigger than my ex and that excited me. It took me aback a bit, but I needed to touch him. Wanted to touch him.

I took his length in one of my hands and braced myself on the other one, so I was at the perfect angle to take him with my mouth. I knew that I was at least good at this. *He always told me I had the most fuckable mouth in Seattle.* Slowly, I pumped him. I leaned over and with only my tongue; I licked the tip slowly and circled his head.

"Fuck, baby. That feels so fucking good," he groaned out. His hands came to my hair, and he pulled it back out of my face and held it all in one hand behind my head. The other hand rested at his side, on the bed.

After hearing his approval and knowing that he was enjoying himself, I used both of my hands to brace on his thighs, and I slid my mouth over him. I took him in until he hit the back of my throat. Then I swallowed. He sucked in a breath, and his body jerked.

"Keep that up, Arianna, and this will be over before I even get inside that sweet pussy of yours," he bit out.

That did it. I was drenched. Again. On an upward slide of my mouth, I let him go with a pop. I raised my eyes to his, and he was staring right at me.

"I can't wait any longer, Arianna. My body is telling me to be aggressive with you, but I won't do that, so you have to guide this until I know you're comfortable and believe that I won't hurt you."

"I need you inside me, now, River," I whimpered.

I took his cock in my hand and positioned myself over him. As I slid down on him, he stretched me, and I'd never felt anything so painfully pleasurable in my life. I stayed still to adjust to his incredible invasion. He placed his hands on my hips.

"Baby, I need you to move."

"Give me a minute, River. I need a minute." I breathed out.

After a few brutal seconds, I inhaled a huge breath and started to move my hips in a figure eight on his cock. He moved with me, encouraging and praising me the entire time.

"You are fucking beautiful."

"You already said that."

"I know. But you deserve to hear it, always." River's words were pushing me closer.

I started to move up and down his length, getting closer and closer to my orgasm. I threw my head back and arched myself so that I was able to rest my hands on his thighs. He played with my breasts with one hand and used his thumb to circle my clit as I moved faster and faster. The shaking started again, and I knew I was about to fly.

"I'm going to come again, River."

"I know, Arianna. I can feel you clenching around me. Let go, baby. But eyes on me when you do."

I looked him in his fantastic eyes as I gave him my orgasm.

"Fuck," River bit out, and I felt him come inside me as my body racked with tremors of aftershock.

I slumped down and rested on his warm, hard body. I wasn't ready to lose him yet, so I didn't make any attempts at trying to slide off him. His arm wrapped around my back, and he gently rubbed small circles into my skin. This moment meant so much to me, and I wasn't able to control the tears that slid out of my eyes and landed on his chest. It was an intimacy that I craved and was just beginning to get from River.

"What's wrong, Arianna Did I hurt you?" he asked me, worried.

"I'm fine. You didn't hurt me," I responded.

"Bird, what's going on in your head, baby?"

"I'm not sure. I'm overwhelmed. This was the first time in years I enjoyed sex. And, I guess, I'm just processing everything. And River," I said, lifting my head to look at him and moving so he slid out of me, "we didn't use protection."

"Fuck. You aren't on the pill, are you?"

"I was before I was pregnant. But not since everything happened. I never planned on this. Or on you, so I never really thought to get a prescription," I replied, honestly.

"Well, I get tested every three months for my job, so I'm clean. As for the other, we'll deal with it together, when we need to," he said, so calmly.

"What exactly do you mean, deal with it?" I asked in return. He had to know that if I did wind up pregnant, abortion wouldn't be an option.

"Relax, Arianna. I just meant that we'll cross that bridge when we get there."

"Oh. Okay. Sorry."

"There's nothing to be sorry for. Now, what do you say I go get a washcloth and clean you up, then we can sleep for a bit?"

"I can clean myself up. Let me just…" I tried to move to the bathroom but was stopped by him clamping his arms around me to keep me there.

"No, Bird. I want to do it. Let me take care of you, Darlin'."

"Oh. Okay. Sure."

"Wait here for me, I'll be right back," he said and slid me off him and onto the bed. I grabbed a pillow and brought it to my chest, hugging it to me tight. I was not used to this, and I was a bit embarrassed. Being cleaned was not something I'd ever experienced before. Another first with River.

River gently cleaned me up and returned the washcloth to the bathroom before coming up behind me in the bed, his front to my back. He moved my hair off my shoulder and planted small sweet kisses there, causing goose bumps to grace my skin, and I shivered.

"River Shiver," I said aloud, not meaning to.

"What was that, baby?" he asked me, and I shook my head.

I sighed and was honest with him.

"Well, every time you do or say something that makes me shiver, I say River Shiver in my head. But this time, I said it out loud by mistake. You weren't meant to ever find out about that," I admitted shyly and embarrassed, as I stiffened in his arms. Two seconds later, I relaxed when I felt him shaking behind me.

"I think you're adorable. And you can call it whatever you want, Bird. As long as you always respond to me."

"I'm thinking that won't be a problem."

"Good. Now, baby, let's sleep."

Yawning, I started to protest because Cady could walk in in the morning, but I fell asleep before I could even put up a fight. River thoroughly exhausted me. The next morning, I was up before the alarm went off, and I snuck back to my room without any protest from River.

My life began again that night with River.

I felt the music in my soul again.

I heard the lyrics in my heart.

I had recaptured myself, and couldn't wait to write it down.

The next few days consisted of the same. I would go to River in the middle of the night and make it back to my room before Cady could find us in his bedroom together. I kept my word and delivered the promise of me to River. When he had asked me to let him be the one to do all these wonderful things for me, he had captured me. If it was any other man, I don't think I would have been able to take that step so soon. River was the kind of man you always wished for from the time you understood what having a man in your life was all about.

Now, it was Sunday morning, and I was outside on the porch curled up on the couch bed, writing, before the house woke up and we headed into town. I thought about how much different things with River were. There was no way things would ever be the same for me. I thought about my life then, and how much more I had in my life now.

Feeling a man move inside me for the first time in months made memories of my life before come flooding back in. But the new memories I was creating with River, and even Cady, helped to push any bad thoughts out. The time I was able to spend with the two of them was, by far, the most incredible moments. A few weeks ago, the three of us didn't know the others existed. Now, I couldn't picture them not being in my life.

I was just putting the finishing touches and tweaks on my final verse for the song I'd been writing when Cady barreled out the front door and climbed up on the cushion of the couch.

"Well, good morning, Princess," I said with a big smile.

"Morning, Birdie. Whatcha doin'?" she asked me; squinting to see the notebook I was writing in.

"Writing some music. What're you doing out here? Is your dad awake?" I asked her, curious how she looked ready to go, and her father hadn't even come out here to find me yet.

"Yes. Daddy is awake and fixing breakfast. He's making chocolate chip pancakes. I love them. Do you like pancakes, Birdie?"

"I do, sweetheart. Why don't we go inside and see if he needs help?" I asked her.

"He told me to come out here and to stop bugging him for chocolate chips. So I don't think he wants us in there. But maybe we can play your music you wrote?" Her question was innocent, but the song was nowhere near ready yet.

"Why don't we just go in and practice your song for the week. My song isn't ready yet. I only have words and not the music to go with it." Trying to explain how I didn't think she should hear this was tough, but I think I navigated it all right.

Cady clapped her little hands together in excitement, scooted her little body off the cushion, and darted into the house. I followed her inside, smelling the pancakes as soon as I entered, and I heard Cady yell to her dad that we were going to play music. He just laughed and yelled, "Okay, baby girl."

We sat in front of the piano and Cady started playing. Her progress over the past couple of weeks was seriously astonishing. She was a little savant. Any and every song I gave her, she mastered, no matter the level of difficulty.

We finished playing just as River came in to let us know the pancakes were ready. At the table, we ate like a family. River and I sipped on our coffee, while Cady finished picking out all the chocolate chips from her pancakes. She was too much and always made me smile.

I loved her.

Was that really what I was feeling? Wasn't that too fast to feel that? If I loved her, did that mean I loved River?

No.

I could love him.

Eventually.

Just not yet.

Kids were different and easier to fall in love with.

At least that was what I kept telling myself all morning, in the car to drop Cady at Meggie's, and the ride to meet up with Miss Thelma.

River parked out front of Carla's Coffee Clutch, and we walked in together. As soon as we entered, I saw Miss Thelma sitting with a gorgeous redheaded woman. River told me to go sit with them while he went and grabbed some coffee for us, so I did just that. As I approached, the other woman looked up at me with emerald green eyes rimmed in red and sadness. She'd been crying. I knew this wasn't going to be good. Miss Thelma stood slower than usual, and so did the woman. Miss Thelma grasped my arm and began introductions.

"Arianna, sugar, this is my granddaughter, Jury. She's about the same age as you I believe," she started, then looked at Jury, "and Jury, this is the woman I told you about, Arianna. She has been giving River's daughter the piano lessons at the store. At least until two weeks or so ago."

I stuck out my hand to Jury, "Nice to meet you."

"You as well. My grandmother hasn't stopped talking about you," she informed me with a smile.

"I'm sure not all of what she said is true. But I'm grateful to her for helping me get on my feet," I said back. River approached with the coffees and sat down with us after a quick hello to Thelma's granddaughter. They obviously knew each other from the way they were interacting, and I felt a bit angry because I was so new to River's life and didn't have any kind of history with him. There wasn't anything I could do about that, so I let it go. Besides, I trusted him.

I really did trust him.

Once we were all settled in with our coffees, and we had exchanged pleasantries, Miss Thelma cleared her throat and dove right in.

"Sugar, you have to know how much I've grown to care for you. And please know, I understand how much you have been through. So I need to just rip off the Band-Aid here, alright?" she asked me, as if I had a choice. I braced and grabbed River's hand under the table and squeezed as tight as I could.

"Alright," I shakily whispered, not really okay with anything right now.

"Miss Thelma has the cancer. It's been there a long while, but there's nothing I'm going to do about it. I choose to live my days out the way I want. So, no arguments from anyone, yeah?" she told us, like it was nothing.

"No arguing will change her mind. Trust me, the entire family has tried. She's a stubborn old woman who knows what she wants," Jury said, as we all went quiet.

"I respect your wishes, Miss Thelma. I will collect my belongings from the store as soon as you're able to meet there."

"Now, sugar, did I say that was what I wanted?" she questioned me, angrily.

"No, but I . . ." I started.

"No. Exactly. The store will remain open. Jury will take over for me, and you two will both work there under one condition, Arianna." I felt like I was going to cry from this heartbreaking news, and the fact that she trusted me enough to let me work with her granddaughter.

"What's that?" I asked on a sniffle, my emotions starting to overtake me. River held on to my hand tighter, brushing his thumb gently over my knuckles.

"That you open up the back room to more music students. I know what's going on with your situation because I ran into Penelope and Braxton. You can continue to teach Cadence at home, and then offer lessons from the store as your base. Your gift is too powerful not to share with the world," she said, knocking the wind out of me.

"Bird, I have to agree with her. Beauty. Pure and incredibly powerful. But you know how I feel," River chimed in.

"I can do that," I agreed.

"Wonderful news!" Miss Thelma shouted and clapped her hands together.

"Miss Thelma, can I ask you one thing, though?"

"Sure, sugar. Go on," she said.

"How long do we have with you?"

"God's will, sugar. Couldn't begin to tell you. But my gut says, not much longer." My heart cracked a bit more at that. Thelma had come to mean something to me, and I wasn't sure I was ready to have her torn from me yet.

We sat in Carla's for a while longer, laughing and just enjoying the company. Jury and I set up a day to go shopping for some new items for the store, and I was excited to get to know her a little more. We were the same age, and she had lived here most of her life. For the last few years, Jury was living out in Washington state. Crazy how small the world is. All these people in Washington or Seattle and our paths had never crossed. She had a degree in law with her own practice out there, but gave it all up a few months ago with no explanation, and came home. At least that's what Miss Thelma had told me one day at the store.

After we had said our goodbyes, and I hugged Miss Thelma a little longer than I should have, River quietly escorted us all out to our cars. Thelma got in with Jury, and we stood on the sidewalk, watching them drive away. The sun was shining brightly, and the weather was that perfect temperature that spring always gave. I was inside my head with my thoughts and wasn't ready to go home yet.

"You ready to go home, Arianna?" River asked.

"I don't want to go home just yet. Is Cady expecting us soon?" I asked.

"No, baby. Meggie said to text her when we were on our way to pick her up. Why?"

"Can we just walk around the square a while? I just want to be outside. Feel the sun on my skin."

"Of course, Darlin'. Anything you need."

Anything you need.

That was River. Giving me everything I needed at that moment and not really knowing it.

Chapter 14

Faster Harder
River

It had been a few weeks since that first night Arianna snuck into my bedroom and delivered on the promise of her. It was unlike anything I had ever felt in my life. Even with my ex, Emma, it was never all-consuming like it was and continued to be with Ari. If I hadn't known I was already in love with her, I would have fallen harder than a cowboy being bucked off a bronco. The only problem, with my heart being completely involved, was that Arianna was making me forget to be alert. She saturated every thought I had, but she was hard to read. I had no idea where her head was at, and that gave her the power to devastate Cady, and me. The sneaking out shit in the morning before my daughter woke up had gotten old really fast. I knew that I wanted her with me all the time, and I wanted to wake up to her gorgeous face in my bed every morning. Cady would eventually realize what was going on. She may be five, but she was more like five going on thirty.

After the news that Miss Thelma gave us on that dreaded Sunday afternoon, Arianna started staying with me all night. We talked about it and decided that we both needed the other to sleep better so, little by little, Arianna's stuff made its way into my drawers and closet.

Our relationship was advancing, and being able to provide comfort and safety, while showing Arianna pleasure, made letting her take control for a while worth it. We had tried different things, but I was still uneasy with taking her how I craved. Ari mentioned a few times that she wanted me to lose myself with her. There really wasn't anything I wanted more, but with what she had been through, I hadn't wanted to give her any reason to be scared of me. She hadn't had any more breakdowns or negative reactions to anything since the night she told me everything in my truck, in the parking lot of the coffee shop. Hopefully, she trusted me enough now to talk to me and not push me away.

Jury and Arianna seemed to take to each other fairly quickly, which was a good thing since they would be running Thelma's shop together now. Over the past few weeks, the two of them spent time sipping coffee, shopping for themselves and items for the store, taking Cady out, and giggling themselves stupid with gossip. I think it was good for both of them. Jury was an amazing person, and since Penny had been dealing with the situation between her and Braxton, she had become a staple in Arianna's life. It was good for everyone involved, and I was able to keep my promise to Rhett. But when the three of them got together, they were hell in heels and my worst fucking nightmare. They were some of the most beautiful women this small town had ever seen, so keeping the men at a distance, without getting locked up in the process, proved difficult.

Breakfast was cleaned up, Cady was at school, and I had to go to work. Arianna and I had come to an agreement about me taking her to work in the mornings and Jury dropping her off afterward. Arianna stayed at the store most days until five o'clock, finishing up lessons with the little girl she had taken on as a new student. Most days, she was home by twenty after five, and by five thirty was sitting down with Cady at the piano giving more lessons. Watching the two most important girls in my life play music together was one of the most humbling sights.

We needed to get going, and Arianna was working on a song out on the porch. She seemed to be writing so much these days, whenever she had a free minute to do so. She would never share any of it with me until she had all the lyrics and music written. Her voice was astonishingly beautiful. I hadn't lied when I said she should have been in Nashville recording. Even now, when I heard her sing, my chest tightened, and my dick got hard. On that thought, I walked out to the porch and found Bird asleep on the couch that she had claimed as her special spot.

Quietly, I walked up to her and crouched down. I brushed the long, soft, wavy blonde lock of hair that had fallen forward from behind her ear, away from her face. I leaned in and gently kissed her cheek. She didn't move. It was very unlike her. The slightest caress would usually have her stirring or batting my hands off her. Needing to get her awake and on the move, I tried again, this time placing kisses all over her face. It worked because when I was finished, she had on that smile that was only meant for me, and asked me what the hell I was doing.

"Come on, Darlin'. We got to get going. You have to be at the store, and I have to go to work. You've been out here a while and fell asleep. You never do that. You feeling alright?" I asked her with a concerned look on my face.

"River. I'm fine. Stop worrying so much. I was just tired. I should probably blame that on you. You have this way of keeping me up at night," she answered, shaking her head and rolling her eyes at me.

"Yes, I know what you mean. But, Bird, you always stir in your sleep when I touch you. This time you didn't, so I wanted to be sure you were okay."

"River, you really need to relax. I'm fine. Nothing is wrong. Now, let me up so I can go get my things, and we can leave." I stepped back so she could get up.

The inside of my all black pickup truck tended to get hot very fast, and now that the weather was getting warmer every day, I needed to start the truck and cool it down so that Bird's legs didn't burn on the leather seats. She always had on one of those damn sundresses that made me want to take her wherever we happened to be.

After I had started it up, I walked back to the porch. Before I made it up the stairs back into the house, I saw something out of the corner of my eye reflecting off the sun, under the stairs. I didn't think much about what it was or could be, so I went over to it. Kneeling down, I picked it up and turned it over in my hands. I couldn't place where I'd seen this before. Then, as I read the words written on the card, it came rushing back to me. My blood ran cold and blazed simultaneously. It didn't register that I shouldn't have touched it, but at that moment, my main priority was getting it out of sight so Arianna didn't see it and panic.

Just as I rounded the corner to the porch, Arianna came out of the house. She stopped at the top of the stairs and looked down to me where I stood at the bottom.

"What's going on? Why does your face look like you're ready to kill someone?" My Bird. She knew all my expressions already.

"I was just taking out the trash and found a raccoon had gotten into the bins. That's all. Not exactly fun finding garbage strewn all over because of a critter. Nothing to worry about," I said, lying my ass off.

I know that I'd gotten mad at her for keeping things from me, but this was different. There was no way I would allow her to have a setback when we'd come this far. She'd know what was going on when the time was right. For now, I needed to drop her off at Thelma's, grab the little trinket with the card that I hid behind our trash cans, and take them to the sheriff. I'd call Rhett while I was driving back to the house and fill him in on what I'd found. This was the first incident in weeks since the break-in, and now it was brought to my doorstep. And I was completely clueless. That won't...no...couldn't happen again. Too much was at stake. I would protect what was mine, no matter what.

I helped Arianna into the truck, and we were off toward town. It didn't take us long to get to the store. Jury was sitting outside on the bench in front, the spot I picked Arianna up, that first time to bring her to my house, waiting for her so they could walk in together. This was their routine since they'd started working with each other. If I was honest, I was grateful to Jury for always waiting. She always stayed in the driveway until Arianna was safely inside as well. Must be her training. Either way, it was a safety thing, and it made me relax a bit.

After the door closed and the girls were safely inside, I grabbed my phone and dialed Rhett. He answered on the third ring.

"Yo. What's up, dude?" he greeted me.

"Dude? You seriously need to get your ass back here and find your roots again. Dude should not be a part of your vocabulary," I said.

"Whatever, asshole. Better? Why are you calling? Is she alright?"

"Yeah, man. She's fine. I have an update, though. This morning, while I was waiting for my woman to come out to the truck, I found a bag containing a trinket of a baby and a card half under the steps to my front porch. It looks like someone tried to leave it on the steps but the wind or a critter got to it, and they fell to where I found them. I had to hurry and hide both because I didn't want Arianna to see them," I informed him, getting angrier by the minute as I thought about how close this motherfucker had gotten to my girls.

"River, man. You have to stay calm and levelheaded. You did what you needed to do. Did you handle the bag, other than moving it out of sight?"

"I picked it up and inspected it a bit. But that's all, Rhett. I had no idea it would be this. The card though, it wasn't in an envelope, so it was easy to read. I'm on my way to grab both the figurine and the card and take them to Gaynor's office," I explained to him, while pulling into my driveway.

"Make sure you wear gloves this time. Get them to Gaynor. Let me know what he says. And, River, don't fucking do anything stupid. Arianna and Cady need you with them." I knew that was sound advice, but he needed to know that I was going to do everything in my power to help figure out what the fuck was going on.

"That shit isn't happening. I have people that owe me," I said.

"Not a good idea, man, even if they do owe you," he advised.

"You've known me a long time, Rhett. I've already experienced a loss because I couldn't protect what I claimed as mine. What I feel now, for Arianna, is leaps and bounds beyond that. I will kill whoever this piece of shit is, who's trying to fuck with my woman's sense of safety that she's worked so hard to regain, and the future my daughter deserves."

"Fine. But don't land yourself in jail. It won't do anyone any good, man. Besides, I can't get you out of lock-up being across the damn country. Let Gaynor and his boys handle it. Some boys that owe me are on it, too. But remember what we talked about last week. I've got your back; you better have mine. And you can't have it if you get arrested. Hopefully, I'll get there in a few months and try to fix this mess. Make sure she's good til' then, yeah?"

"Brother, you don't even need to tell me that shit. She's gotten close to my woman and is working at Thelma's. Jury's fine, man. Just get back here as fast as you can."

"Right. I got shit to do. Call me with anything else," he clipped at me and hung up.

Moody bastard.

After I'd retrieved the cellophane bag containing the porcelain figurine of the baby and the card, I went to Sheriff Gaynor's office. He wasn't surprised that the package was delivered to my doorstep undetected. He'd done some digging into Mr. Kelly and his ties. He knew the type of power this scumbag had and how he used it to his advantage. The card was what shocked and confused us all. Especially since Rhett had told me that Andrew hadn't left Seattle. There was no way he could have known about Arianna's connection to the trinket. My anger was fueled as I read it over and over again.

You shouldn't be alive. You couldn't even protect your unborn child. That will be rectified. Not even that man of yours can protect you.

The words were all I could think about since I'd read them. Not even the fire calls I went on could shake them from my mind. I'd just hung up my turnout gear, preparing to leave, when Hank Sr.'s unmistakable voice outside the big bay door traveled inside my office. I grabbed my keys and wallet from my desk and headed out to see if everything was okay with him.

"Harry. Everything alright?" I asked.

"Now, son. It seems I should be asking you that question. So... River, how are things?" This man was worse than a woman with gossip. Retirement must really be boring.

"Jesus. Gaynor has a big mouth. I'm handling it. No need to worry yourself, Harry," I assured him. Sheriff Gaynor and Harry had been staples in this town for as far back as I could remember. Thinking to myself that, although I shouldn't have to, a talk with the sheriff was in order so that all the gossips in town didn't catch wind, and Arianna heard from anyone else what was going on.

"Don't doubt you're going to handle it, boy. You've learned that lesson the hard way. Just know that you have a town of people behind you, cheering you on. We all want to see you get back what you lost, and then some," Harry surprised me by saying. This man didn't show his face often, but when he did, he knew how to make an impact.

"Thanks, Harry. I've got to go pick up Cady. See ya around," I said and shook my head in disbelief as I walked toward my truck. It wasn't that I minded that the man gave advice or his opinion unsolicited, but it was always so profound with him. That could have been attributed to him spending years running a store in a small town. Or, it could just be that he's a good soul.

The ride to pick up Cady from school was quiet. I stewed on those words from the card. I gripped the steering wheel and clenched my teeth so hard, that by the time I'd gotten to the school, the muscles in my arms and jaw were protesting for release.

Pulling up to the school, I looked at where the kids were all lined up with Penelope. One look at Penny and I knew things were not going well at Braxton's. Braxton was my best friend, but he was a complete asshole when it came to Penny. They had this insane history that you would only read about in a romance novel. A chance meeting in New York the end of her freshman year of college and that was it for her. Braxton ran out on her then, because he wasn't ready for Penny or the relationship she deserved.

When she came back home after graduating from New York University, where she transferred her sophomore year, Brax acted like he had a right to say what she did or who she spent time with. Then, there was the weekend Braxton and Penny tried again to hook up. They were both drunk. I still don't know the full details, but it didn't end well. Now, Penny was staying with him, and her face lost that mischievous gleam it always held.

Hopping down from my truck, I closed the door and made my way over to her. She'd been there for me through some of the hardest times, and my friend for as long as I could remember. It wasn't like her to look this way, so I wanted to make sure everything was all right. If Braxton wasn't being good to her, I'd rip his dick off. She deserved the best, even if she was a pain in the ass.

"Hey, Pen. Everything okay?" I asked her, after I made sure no little ears were around.

"Hey, River. Yeah. Everything's good," she responded, lying through her teeth and giving me the fakest smile I'd ever seen.

"Look, if something's going on, and I need to talk to the fool you're stayin' with, you say the word. Your face speaks volumes, even if you don't want to, so I know something is going on."

"Things are complicated. It's my own fault, really. I just need to get the hell out of his apartment and back in my own."

"Have you two talked?" I asked. Knowing Braxton though, I knew he probably hadn't been around much.

"If you mean yelled-at-each-other-until-a-neighbor-knocked-on-the-door-to-see-if-the-cops-were-needed kind of talked, then yes. We sure did."

"Fucking idiot," I mumbled under my breath.

"What's that now?" she barked back, glaring at me.

"Not you, Penelope. Braxton. He's an idiot. I don't get what the fuckin' problem is with him. He says one thing and does another. Hopefully, he'll remove his head from his ass before it's too late."

"It's already too late, River. He brought a woman home from the club this past Saturday night. It's pretty obvious that I'm nothing more than a roommate. Please don't say anything. I don't want to be in the middle of any disagreements between the two of you. I'd better get back inside and finish up tomorrow's lesson plan. He'll be here soon to pick me up. Talk to you later, River."

After I watched Penny walk inside with her head hung down, dejected, I went over to the playground where my daughter and her little friend, Bryce, were sitting side by side on the swings. They didn't see me approach, and I stopped dead in my tracks as I listened to my baby girl tell her friend Bryce how excited she was to have her best friend, Birdie, sleeping over every night. It was cute, and it was Cady's way of gossiping without actually knowing she was doing it. She knew not to discuss certain things, but I couldn't blame her. I may have been even more excited than Cady was to have Bird in my bed every night.

Without scaring them, I approached the kids, grabbed my daughter's hand, and we headed home to the woman that we were both over-the-moon about.

I stirred awake and looked down to find Arianna's mouth wrapped around my dick. This was not something we'd done a ton of yet, because I wasn't sure if I trusted myself not to lose control and totally freak her out. Her initiating sucking me off would most definitely lead to me taking her in a way we hadn't explored yet. It was clear she was at the end of her rope with us only having sex with her on top and was ready to get as well as she gave. This wake-up call was just a surprise. It was a pleasant surprise, but I didn't want her to feel obligated to do anything with me. Plus, we were on the couch in the living room, in full view of anyone who could happen to walk in.

"Arianna," I said in my sleepy voice, and cradled her cheek in my hand and continued, "baby, what are you doing?"

With a pop, she released my dick and looked up at me like I was the dumbest man on the planet. And I just might have been for stopping her in the middle of what could have possibly been the best head I'd ever gotten in my life. But I wanted her to be sure.

"What the hell does it look like, River? I mean it's pretty obvious, no? Unless it wasn't good. Shit. I'm sorry." She started to crawl up my body, but I stopped her.

"Darlin', I didn't say anything about it not being good. I want to make sure you're not doing this because you think this is what I want, yeah?"

"Isn't this what you want, though?"

"Baby, you're mouth on me is like nothing I've ever felt before. But I am not sure I'll be able to control myself."

"I'm ready for you to lose control. You've been treating me like glass since the first night we had sex. I won't break, River. I'm ready for this. If I wasn't, then I would've let you know by now. So, can you please just let me have some fun without all the worry?"

There it was. Just as I had suspected, she was ready to let go and be wild. On that thought, I lay back and watched as she kissed down my torso in a direct line to my dick. Her hand grabbed the base and, like it was in slow motion, I watched her mouth cover me once again. If it were possible, my dick got even harder as she relentlessly pumped me with her fist and sucked with just enough pressure.

"Fuck, that feels good," I moaned groggily, as Arianna's mouth closed tighter around my cock and her hands stopped pumping me and rested on the couch next to my hips on each side.

My hands grabbed her hair and held it away from her face at the back of her head. She looked up at me from under her lashes while her mouth picked up rhythm, sliding up and down my length.

"If you don't stop now, I'm going to come in your mouth, Arianna," I growled out and tried to grab her under her arms to drag her up my body, but she dodged my attempt and kept at me.

Licking, sucking, and the addition of her warm, small hand around me again, made it almost unbearable. I didn't want to come in her mouth. I wanted to come thrusting inside her.

"Arianna," I growled and tugged her hair a little bit harder so that she would get the point and dislodge.

Finally, she let go, and I pulled up my pants. I scooped her up in my arms and carried her back to our bedroom. I didn't want to risk Cady coming downstairs and finding us on the couch fucking like a couple of teenagers.

I slammed the door shut with my foot as I prowled to the bed and basically threw Bird into the middle of it.

"Take off your clothes, Arianna," I demanded as I locked the door.

"But I wasn't really done."

"Oh, you're done. You did what you set out to do. Now, it's my turn to do what I've wanted to do since the first time I saw you."

Watching as she got undressed, I took myself in my hand. Pumping slowly as her beautiful body was exposed to me, inch by inch. Her eyes stayed glued to what I was doing, and she sported a triumphant little smirk on her face. Yes. My Bird knew exactly what she was doing.

Once she climbed naked back onto the bed, I climbed over her, grabbed her legs behind her knees, and spread her wide for me. Slowly, I lined up the head of my dick to her entrance, and in one quick thrust, I powered into her and stilled. I looked down at her to gauge her reaction. I was about to lose myself in her, and even though she wanted this, I needed to be sure she was okay with everything in the process. Her eyes were closed, and her lips were slightly parted. I needed to see her eyes to really get a read on her.

"Bird. Open your eyes and look at me, yeah?"

She opened her eyes and locked them onto mine.

"If at any point I'm hurting you, or you don't feel comfortable with what I'm doing, you say the word, and we stop, yeah?"

"River, honey, I really need you to move," she responded, as she rocked her hips up, trying to gain some friction.

"I will, but I need you to give me the words," I told her as I ground down on her.

"Fine, River. I'll tell you if I need you to stop."

"Thank fuck," I growled out.

As I started to move, my hands glided up her sides, cupping her breasts, and running my thumbs over each nipple, hardening them. Bird's breasts were the best I'd ever seen or felt. Touching her made me start to unravel, and I began pumping into her harder and faster.

"River! Oh my God. Faster. Harder!" she screamed out.

I moved my hands up a bit higher, stopping at her shoulders, so I could use them as leverage to thrust as hard as I could. There was no turning off the beast she unleashed now.

I kept at her like that, for what seemed like hours, until I couldn't hear her breaths coming in pants anymore. She was close; her walls were starting to tighten around me.

"You close, baby?" I asked for confirmation.

"Ye...yesss," she stuttered out. I circled her clit with my thumb.

"Oh God, yes! I'm gonna come, River."

"Come with me, Bird."

Together, we both flew high. It was the hardest orgasm of my life.

Nothing had ever been like that before with anyone. When we both caught our breaths, and the post-sex fog cleared, Arianna's eyes were sleepy.

"Stay right there. I'm going to get a washcloth to clean you up. When I'm done, we sleep," I ordered her gently.

"So sleepy." She yawned huge, and I hurried to the bathroom where I collected a washcloth, ran it under the warm water, and returned to clean up my Bird.

I wiped her legs where I had dripped out of her and down them. Then, gently, because I knew she'd be sensitive there, I cleaned her pussy.

"Not sure how I feel about removing all traces of me from you," I told Ari, as I climbed up next to her in bed, fitting my front to her back, and pulling her into me.

"You didn't remove all traces of you from me," Arianna sleepily told me.

"No?" I questioned, in hopes that she was still awake and would answer me.

"No. You're always with me, my love."

I froze. Arianna wasn't exactly forthcoming with her feelings toward me, so her calling me 'my love' made my entire body lock into place.

"Do you love me, Bird?" I knew I wasn't going to get an answer to that question when I felt Arianna's body go still and her breathing even out. She had fallen asleep.

My Bird loved me.

Good thing, because I was so fucking in love with her.

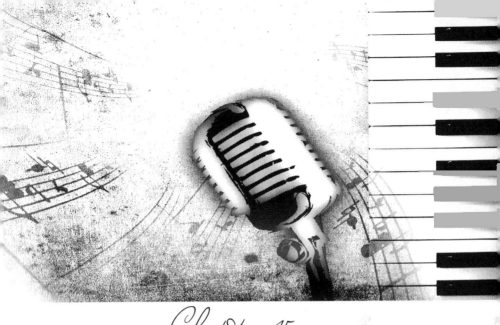

Chapter 15

Mosaic Heart
Arianna

I was in love with River. The truth behind that statement rang true when he took me the way he had last night. My confession wasn't exactly the three words that I knew he wanted to hear. I called him 'my love' when I was right on the cusp of sleep and still incredibly sated from the best orgasm I'd ever had. He seemed to always want to talk when I exposed some emotion or feeling. Right now, I wasn't sure I was ready to admit to him that I was in love with him. It was hard enough to wrap my head around. It wasn't supposed to happen. And it surely wasn't supposed to happen this fast.

The past few days, I hadn't been feeling well. I had an unexplainable feeling in my stomach, and I was always exhausted. I was trying to power through and was hoping this shower would have served two purposes: wake me up and also help me avoid River, so we didn't have to talk about my slip of the tongue last night. But I could already tell that my plan failed and that he knew exactly what I was up to. The man was able to read me better than I could read myself.

Just as I stepped out onto the mat and grabbed a towel to dry myself off, a knock came at the door, followed by a little voice.

"Birdie," Cady called excitedly.

"Daddy said that you need to come to the kitchen and eat breakfast. He said he made us pancakes, and everyone needs to eat breakfast to start their day right!"

"Be there in a few minutes, Princess," I told her and started to wrap up my hair in another towel to keep it off my back. I heard the jingle of the doorknob, and before I was able to cover myself completely, Cady burst into the bathroom. I screamed out in surprise and scrambled to cover myself. I knew I'd failed and got Cady's attention when she tilted her head to the side and looked at me puzzled.

"Birdie, you have big boobies. Will I ever have big boobies like you?"

"Ummm…" was all I got out. How on earth was I supposed to answer that?

"It's okay. I already know I will. I'll have to get a bra soon so I can control them, right?"

"Cadence, where in the world do you learn this stuff?" I asked because, at five years old, she shouldn't be worried about this type of thing.

"Bryce said his sisters talk about things in front of him, so he's an expert on girls. He told me I would need big boobies to find a husband when I grow up."

"Princess, we should go talk to your dad about this. I'm not sure he'll be happy with Bryce filling your head with this kind of misinformation," I told her. She didn't seem too happy with having to go talk to her dad, but I wasn't sure if he would be okay with me addressing it either.

"Wait for me in the hallway, and we'll go to the kitchen together. I just have to finish getting dressed."

"Okay. I didn't mean to be bad, Birdie. I'm sorry," Cady said, as her little lip started to quiver and her eyes welled up with tears.

"Hey, Princess. You didn't do anything wrong. Come here." I opened my arms and knelt down so she could walk into them. I wrapped her up in a tight hug. There were situations that would come up in the future with Cady that dealt with her body, life, love, and boys. My instinct was to tell her all about it the way my aunt had, but I needed to make sure I didn't cross any boundaries here. I loved her like she was mine, but I didn't birth her, so I needed to talk to River.

"Hush, sweet baby. You have no reason to be crying. The problem is, you are wise beyond your years, and your dad just wants you to have all the right information while you grow up. We will talk to him together, yeah?" Oh Lord. I just sounded like River. I guess he was rubbing off on me.

After I had got Cady into the hallway, I finished getting ready. My stomach wasn't happy, and I wound up getting sick. Puking wasn't my favorite thing, but I felt so much better after I did. I brushed my teeth for a second time that morning, dressed in my baby pink sundress with spaghetti straps, and threw my hair up in a messy bun, while it was still wet so that later, it would give the effect of beach waves. Then, I was out the bathroom door and walking toward the chatter coming from the kitchen.

Cady hadn't waited for me. Maybe it was because she heard me getting sick, or maybe because she was five and did what she wanted. Either way, as I walked into the kitchen, River's eyes landed on me and traveled the length of me from top to toe and back again. Then he moved swiftly toward me and grabbed my hand to escort me to the sunken living room to have a chat. There wasn't any time for me to think about what happened last night because he grabbed my cheeks and looked at me with worry etched all over his face.

"Are you okay, Arianna? Cady said she heard you puking when she ran into the kitchen. What's going on? Why didn't you tell me you were sick?"

"River, I must be fighting off a stomach bug is all. I'll be fine. Let's get going. I need to get to the store." My move toward the kitchen to get my phone and purse was halted. River gripped my upper arm as I tried to pass him, and he positioned me so that he was blocking my path. His arms slid around me, and he looked really worried.

"Darlin', I think you should stay home and rest if you're fighting off a bug. I'll call Jury and tell her you won't be in today. Go on back to bed and lie down. I'll bring you in some tea." He kissed my forehead and started to walk away. He was being dramatic about this. I was already feeling much better after upchucking, and there was no reason for me to stay home, so I walked back to the kitchen.

Cady was sitting and eating her pancakes at the island in the center of the kitchen. I walked over to the stool next to her and slid on it. River turned from the stove where he'd been starting to heat the water for my tea. He looked at Cady and saw that she was finished eating and told her to go on upstairs and brush her teeth. He walked over to the other side of the counter and rested his hands on it, knuckles down, looked at me, and shook his head.

"What are you doin', Bird?"

"I'm going to work, River. You're overreacting. I feel much better and will be fine," I informed him with maybe a bit more attitude than was necessary.

"I think you should rest. Jury can handle things for a day by herself."

"I know she can. But that isn't the point. The point is, I feel fine and want to go to work." The unfortunate thing for me was, whenever I gave attitude or tried to sass River, it turned him on. I could tell by his eyes; when they went liquid, he liked it. Not where I needed this to head right now. Also, unfortunately for me, I could tell that this meant something to him. He proved me right when he spoke.

"Look, Arianna. I know you think I'm being irrational or dramatic, but I'm not alright with watching my woman go through what she's going through, has been through, and now sick on top of it all. So please, for my own peace of mind, just stay home and rest. It will do you some good, even if you do feel better," River pleaded with me.

How could I say no when he put it like that? Maybe I could get a good day of writing in. The song I was working on had me hung up on a verse. The time to think and just feel what I wanted to write may be the best thing for me.

"Okay," I agreed.

"Okay? That's it? No protesting or more attitude?" he asked me.

"No, River. I see this means a lot to you, and you're right. I could do with a day of rest and get some writing in."

He just stared at me with this look of pure curiosity, like I was up to something.

"Stop looking at me like I'm some creature from beyond," I snarked out.

River pushed off the counter and rounded it, heading right for me. I didn't move from my position on the stool, so he came up behind me. The straps of my sundress had fallen off my shoulders and my neck was bared, so he took full advantage. Small kisses peppered my neck, shoulders, and all the way up to my ear. Biting gently on my lobe, he let go and started whispering in my ear.

"If you still feel okay tonight, we can go to the fair, just the two of us. Maybe I can take you to one of the best spots in Tennessee to eat too."

I shivered. He felt it and smiled against my neck. I felt that.

"Sounds good to me."

"Alright, well, I'm heading out with Cady, Darlin'. I'll call you a bit later to check on you. If you get worse or need anything, call me," River told me.

"Thanks, River. Did you call Jury?" I asked him.

"Let me do that now," he answered, as he walked out of the room, headed up the stairs to get Cady, and out of my view. I made my way to the bedroom and grabbed my notebook, my lucky pencil, and planted myself in my writing spot on the porch.

About ten minutes after I settled in, Cady and River came barreling out the door and found me in my spot. Cady came up to me, hugged me, and whispered in my ear to feel better. I loved Cady something fierce. The bond we developed in such a short time helped to heal me. It also helped me realize that I still wanted to chase the dreams I'd always had for myself.

"Darlin', I called Jury but didn't get an answer. I sent her a text to let her know you wouldn't be in. No response from her yet. Hopefully, she gets it before she's expecting you and isn't waiting outside the store for you too long," River rushed out.

"Come on, baby girl, you've got to get to school. We're late, again. I'll check on you later, Bird."

"Okay," I giggled out, watching River rush around all disheveled. He came to me and kissed my forehead. Then, he took his girl to school while I smiled and sighed at the thought that I was in love with a man who cared so much about the people in his life.

You forced me to look,
> And really see,
> The light under the dark,
> That suffocated me.

> You gave me new meaning,
> And showed me what I desire,
> Is a love that's more than just love,
> But a lifetime of fire.

That was what I had so far for the lyrics. The music was written. That was the easy part. I'd heard the melody in my head since my first kiss with River. Then I heard all the beats when Cady asked me if she could be my friend. The words were always the hard part for me. It never seemed like anything was ever good enough to convey what I needed it to. And titles. It was hard to sum up lyrics that said so much in a few words. But it was flowing, and I needed to keep going.

There was a certain kind of peace that I found sitting on River's porch, writing. The willow tree didn't show any signs of life as its branches hung low and completely still. Hours must have passed while I just soaked in the serenity of just being still. It opened the creative dam, and it was hard to stop.

This town, this house, and all the people I'd met so far had shown me exactly what I thought I would always have. River had kept so many promises he made to me already. But would he always? I knew I loved him, but I still had a difficult time believing that things could stay this way forever. We hadn't had a knock-down, drag-out fight yet, because I was trying to do everything in my power to avoid that. Sure, River got mad and didn't speak to me for a few days, but that was better than screaming and getting hit.

Time seemed to have gotten away from me. It was just about noon when I realized I hadn't felt sick again. Maybe all I was going to have to deal with was what happened that morning. Puking up the entire contents of your stomach was never fun. Now, I just felt tired. The peace was so relaxing; it must have coaxed me to sleep because I was woken up to kisses along my jaw.

"Bird, baby, wake up." More kisses on my cheeks and neck.

River Shiver.

It never failed.

Every damn time.

I sat up, blinked away the sleepiness, and stretched my arms up over my head. River watched me do this with an amused look on his face.

"What are you doing here? I thought you were going to call me?" I asked him, with a tiny hint of attitude. He just woke me up from a great nap. I wanted to sleep.

"I did call you, Darlin'. Twice. You didn't answer either time," he told me and caressed my hair, smoothing down the wildness I was sure it held from sleeping out here on this thing.

"Geez. I'm sorry. I don't know what's with me. It could be this bug I'm fighting. I haven't felt sick to my stomach at all since this morning, but I feel like I could sleep for days," I started.

"It's fine, Bird. There were no fire callouts, so I left early and came home. If you're feeling better, we can leave in a little bit and get some dinner before the fair, if you want. Cady is all set to be picked up by Bryce's mom after school. They're going to have a sleepover tonight so it can be a date night for us." River seemed tense about something but acted as if he wasn't. He was hiding something from me, but I just couldn't imagine what.

"That sounds like a great plan. Can we not do a fancy place for dinner though? Maybe just grab a burger so I don't have to get changed?" I asked hopefully.

"Anything you want, Darlin'. Let me just make a few phone calls. We'll leave in an hour, yeah?"

"Ok. I'll go get myself sorted while you do that."

River hooked me around the back of my neck and pulled my head to him. He took in a deep breath, inhaling the scent of my hair, kissed my forehead and let me go. I watched his ass as he walked away. It was a really great ass, and the jeans he wore fit snuggly and accentuated every proper part of him. Front and back. It was always a great show. Once out of my line of sight, I turned to collect my notebook and pencil, but stopped and reread what I had written that day. As I did, more came to me.

Bared and raw,
Broken and bent,
Did I tell you yet,
That, baby, you're heaven-sent?

It took me a while to get to the good parts,
The parts where my story takes flight,
You bring me to my knees, torching my heart,
No better ending in sight.

You dimmed out my past,
And now it's a faint memory,
I will be with you forever,
Always and eternity.

In ten minutes, I had written almost the whole song.
Mosaic Heart.
Just like that.
The title came to me as soon as I reread everything in its entirety.
My life was a mosaic.
All the hard, stony pieces coming together, fitting in such a way that it recreated the beauty of what once was, but allowing the cracks to show because they were a big part of who I was and what I'd experienced.
This song was so much about me. It was recognition and healing all in beats and words. From the beginning, I knew this would be different with River and his daughter. He made it well known that he would never

do to me what my ex did, and that he wanted to give me my dreams back. He'd done that and more.

My heart was so full of love at that moment. My eyes filled with tears and they slowly spilled over my cheeks and ran down my face. I audibly sobbed, covered my face with my hands and cried. The tears shed finally weren't those of hurt, pain, or fear. For the first time in years, I cried because I was happy. Because I was truly free. The music was back. My identity was back. My life wasn't what it was, but it was starting its new journey. Just like my song, the cracks were there, but the overall picture was more beautiful than I had thought it could be now.

I gave myself a few more minutes to relish in these feelings then I got up and went to sort myself out for my date with River.

River took me to the diner in Gifford where we encountered Waitress Deb. She was as pleasant as ever. I swear I loved her. I could eat at that diner every day of my life just to watch her interact with the customers. She gave River shit for taking me to a diner for a date. He tried to explain that I had requested a burger and nothing fancy, but she didn't want to hear it.

They went back and forth a bit, and you could tell they'd known each other for a while. The banter never went to insulting, just plain old teasing. Deb winked at me when she got the final word in, and walked away, leaving the check in River's front shirt pocket. She mumbled something that sounded like, "Least, you can do is pay for her, boy." I giggled and kept smiling the whole ride from the diner to the firehouse where we parked to go to the fair.

Hand in hand, we walked into the fair and headed right for the Ferris wheel. The last time we rode it, River rocked my world. He has continued to rock it every day since. I thought it was time for me to do the same for him.

Patiently, we waited in line. I stood in front of him, pressed my back to his front. Instinctively, his arms came around my middle and held me closely to him. He kissed my neck and kept moving us forward.

After about a five-minute wait in line, we made it on a gondola. I didn't sit across from him this time. Instead, I cozied up next to him, laced my arm through his, locked our fingers together, and rested my head on his shoulder.

"I got to say, Bird. I like this go-round on the Ferris wheel much better than the last already," River muttered, as he kissed the top of my head.

"Why?"

"Because, Darlin'. I didn't need to ask you to sit with me or touch me. It's like you finally let me in." Damn River. He was going to steal my thunder if he kept talking. I needed to make sure that didn't happen, but I wanted us to be at the top of the ride before I started to say what I had to say.

I got my wish fairly quickly as we went around and stopped at the highest point. I sighed deeply again at the beauty of the view. It was now or never, so I took a big calming breath and went for it.

"River, do you remember what you said to me the last time we were here?" I asked, in hopes of him remembering.

"I already told you, Arianna. I remember everything that has you in it," he responded, serious as hell.

"Well, that day, you asked me to let you be the man that I create new memories with. What I'm not sure you realize is that you are that man. And as that man, you've given me more good memories than I've ever had bad ones," I began, but he tried to interrupt.

"Arianna…" he started.

"No. Please, River. This is important, and I need to say this."

"Alright, baby."

River Shiver. When he called me baby, instant shiver.

"Well," I started and grabbed his face to turn it toward me, so I had his undivided attention and continued, "you're the most patient, kindest, amazing man I've ever known. You not only made promises to me, but you've kept them. I've never had such a constant or consistent source of protection and love. I feel it down deeper than I have felt anything before."

"What exactly are you trying to say with all those words, Bird?" he asked, seeming confused by what I said. I knew I would screw this up with my rambling.

"I'm in love with you, River. And I'm in love with your daughter. It's a love that I feel so much that if I stopped feeling it, I would break apart at the seams. It's a love that I know if you ever stopped giving to me, which I hope you never do, I wouldn't be able to exist anymore. You and Cadence have given me everything back I thought he had taken from me forever."

"Arianna, you'll never stop feeling my love. You'll always know how I feel, no matter what it is that we are going through," he replied, as he shifted to look me in the eyes and held me close to him in the seat.

"I knew the moment I looked at you that you were different. I may have loved you since then. But when I fell, doesn't matter. What matters is that I'm so fucking in love with you. You are precious to me and my daughter. I told you already, but it's worth repeating. You have a beauty and light that my daughter thrives off of. I've seen it when you two are together. Whether it's playing piano together or dancing around listening to that God-awful noise you call music. It's there, and it's exactly what Cady and I both needed."

I kissed him. No asking. Just doing. He liked when I initiated contact, and I was getting better about it. He outdid me again, but I was finding that to be a common occurrence with River. He always gave me more than I gave him.

We spent the rest of the ride making out. That damn ride was becoming an important spot for even more important moments. Not sure the night River and I confessed our love to each other could ever be topped, though.

We ended up enjoying the fair for a while longer. River won me a cute little stuffed frog, a gigantic teddy bear that he wound up carrying around the rest of the night, and a keychain of a Ferris wheel. I took him on the carousel, which was absolutely hilarious to me. A big, manly guy like River on a carousel horse, holding a huge teddy bear. It was priceless, and I was still laughing as we made our way back to the truck at the firehouse.

Once we were in and pulled out, River's phone went off over the Bluetooth in his truck. He was able to see that it was Jury calling him. He had mentioned in conversation earlier at dinner that he hadn't heard anything back from her yet.

"Jury. Everything okay?" he asked her through the truck.

"River…" her voice broke on his name.

"Fuck," River clipped out.

In a voice that could only be described as shattered, Jury told us that Miss Thelma had passed away. She tried to apologize for not getting back to River, but he told her it wasn't necessary and we were just worried. He saw my face and knew I needed to be with Jury right away, so he told her we'd be right there.

After River disconnected, I cried for my friend's loss, and I cried because Miss Thelma was one of the catalysts to get me on my feet. I would always be grateful to her. The entire time I cried, River drove with my hand in his, and lightly rubbed his thumb back and forth over my knuckles. It was a gesture to let me know that he was there if I needed him, but he was giving me time to feel the loss.

River. Always giving me exactly what I needed.

Chapter 16

Her Little Friend Bryce
River

People always say everyone dealt with grief differently and in their own way. I suppose when you've lost as much as Arianna had, each hit could make you a little bit number to any pain you could feel. Most would harden their hearts and soul. Not my Bird. She felt everything. Every hit she endured, physically and emotionally, made her stronger. There was never a moment I wasn't in awe of that woman and how she gave so much and felt so deeply for those around her.

The drive to Jury's was almost too much for me to bear. I knew I couldn't hold Ari close to me because it wasn't the vibe I was getting from her, so I gave her what I thought she needed, space and a hand to hold on to. It seemed that I'd made the right choice by just letting her get lost in her emotions. Miss Thelma gave Arianna more than I think even Ari realized, so it wasn't a surprise to me that this hit her hard.

The next few days consisted of Arianna writing out her feelings on my porch, helping Jury put the funeral and final arrangements together, and her continued battle fighting off whatever stomach bug had taken up residence in her body. Bird was even more tired than she'd been and nauseous most of the time. She hadn't gotten sick since the morning Thelma passed, but she was definitely not feeling well. Being the fighter that she was, Arianna pushed through to be there for her friend.

Thelma had a living will made up recently, and it read that no fuss be made for her, with the exception of a song performed in her memory by Arianna. It said the song could be an Arianna original or a cover, but it had to mean something. The funeral was basically all taken care of by Thelma. When she knew for sure what her prognosis was, she got her affairs in order, including prepaying for it, so all Jury had to do was finalize everything. She picked her own casket, prayer cards, and even wrote up her own obituary. The whole thought of Thelma knowing that she was dying and doing all of that, tore my heart apart.

Each of the three girls, Penny, Arianna, and Jury, got a handwritten letter from Thelma that was delivered by her attorney but not to be opened until after the funeral. I was bestowed the honor of holding them so that Miss Thelma's wishes were carried out the way she wanted. Jury and Penny were antsy to get their hands on them, but Arianna seemed to be off in her own world.

The night before the funeral, Bird was outside writing. We hadn't spoken much with the whirlwind of activity going on, and if there was any downtime, Arianna was working on what she was going to perform in Thelma's honor. She made the decision the night of Thelma's death to write her own song and play it at the funeral. I knew she would write her own and not cover something. It meant too much, and Bird was a really talented songwriter.

I sat down at the other end of the couch with a beer and just watched her work for a bit. Arianna was so incredibly beautiful and sexy to me. But watching her bite her lip and stick her tongue out the side of her mouth while she wrote, was just another indicator that her heart was all in, when it came to this song. I knew Bird had lost her parents to a car accident when she was younger and was raised by her Aunt Claire. So anyone that showed her kindness, especially when she first arrived here in The Falls, was going to get her full heart and soul.

After what seemed like hours but was, in actuality only a few minutes, she looked up and caught me watching her.

"Hey. I didn't even hear you come out here," she said and smiled at me, but it didn't reach her eyes.

"It's okay, baby. I didn't want to interrupt you while you were in the zone. How's it coming anyway?" I asked her.

"Do you want to read it?"

"I'd be honored," I said and looked her in her eyes so she knew I wasn't lying. She handed me her notebook, and I read.

My throat constricted from the lump forming there. That had to be one of the most beautiful things I had ever read. I looked up at Ari, and now she was watching me. I cleared my throat, but the tears still fell from my eyes, even though I had tried not to let it happen. My job was to be strong for Arianna. But her words grabbed hold of my heartstrings and tugged. I was man enough to know that it was okay to show emotion, so I let the few tears go and didn't hide from her.

"River. I'm sorry. I didn't want you to get upset."

"Why? Because men don't cry?" I snapped back at her. I knew I shouldn't have, but my emotions were going nuts.

"No. Not because men don't cry. You just haven't shown any emotion since it happened. And you've never read anything I've written like this. I didn't mean anything by it," she said, her voice shaking with feeling.

Fuck. I didn't mean to snap at her.

"Come here, Arianna," I demanded. She crawled across the couch and right into my lap.

"Bird, I didn't mean to snap at you. I'm supposed to be the strong one here, but what you wrote captured everything it needed to, and it just hit me harder than I thought. I'm so sorry, baby," I finished.

"I get it, River. I'm sorry, too. I really didn't mean to imply anything. I'm glad that you felt the lyrics, though. That means it's ready. Not sure if I'm ready to perform it, but I can't mess with it anymore. I am drained and need to sleep. Tomorrow is going to suck."

"Alright then, my beautiful songbird. Let's get you to bed," I said to

Arianna as I stood up with her in my arms. I walked us right into the house, kept my hold on her, but had Bird lock the door since her arms and hands were free, and went right to our bedroom. She was giggling, and if I was honest, it was a welcome sound. There weren't many smiles or laughs in the past few days, but it was good to hear Ari wasn't so lost in her grief that she knew there were still things to laugh and smile about. Which, considering all she'd been through, was pretty fucking amazing. Ari had come a long way in a short time, since thinking she didn't deserve any good.

I sat Bird on the edge of the bed and knelt down between her legs. My arms went around her middle, and I tugged her as close to me as possible while her hands rested on my shoulders. I needed her to know what had been going on while she'd been comforting Jury the past few days. We only received one delivery to the house. Whoever was behind sending the baby and the note, had now turned their focus on the store.

The past few days, I drove past to check on things and made sure everything was secured. The first drive past, I must have missed it and just thought it was a note that Jury put on the door letting everyone know the store would be closed. Most folks in town already knew why the store wasn't open because Miss Thelma had lived there her whole life and owned that store for years. It must have been some kind of intuition that told me to stop and just look around the second time I drove past.

"Arianna, there's something I need to discuss with you. The timing couldn't be worse, but you need to know for tomorrow. You'll see some extra officers at the funeral. They'll be there, on my request, for security purposes," I started but stopped when her body went stiff in my arms.

"Why would you need extra officers for security purposes at a funeral?" She asked the question I'd been dreading answering.

"Because, Darlin'. There's been some stuff happening around here that I haven't told you about." Ari opened her mouth to start arguing, but I got there first.

"Hush, Bird. I know you're going to give me that attitude because of how I reacted when you didn't tell me things before, but you need to understand the why behind my choice. The difference with what you did and what I did is that I couldn't bear to see you regress back into the dark. What I'm about to say may hurt you in a way that I never wanted for you again. Please, I'm begging you, please, don't let it drag you back under. Promise me, yeah?"

"River, you're freaking me out. I can't promise anything like that because I don't know what's going on. Tell me everything. I need to know what you've been keeping from me. Shit." A very rare curse word escaped her mouth on an exhale.

"Fine," I bit out but continued on, "but if you think for one second after you know everything that you're going anywhere or try to leave me, I won't let you. You belong to us now. Be mad. Be scared. Hell, don't talk to me for weeks. But do not even think about leaving our home, me, or Cady."

"You need to tell me. Now!" she countered, and her voice was not wobbling with emotions. It was strong and firm and she meant business. It was clear that she was done fucking around. Any emotional wavering she'd been experiencing was now non-existent.

"Alright. Let me start by saying that you have to know I'm so fucking in love with you. and the type of man that I am, what I've been through, I need to protect what is mine. I need to protect those I love from hurting in any way. Part of why I've been giving you space since Thelma passed is because I knew it was what you needed, and for the pain of her loss to not sting as much, you needed to write. So I left you to it," I declared while I looked her straight in the eyes. Her body loosened at my words and that was when I knew we'd be okay after I told her the rest. Reassurance.

That's what she needed. And again, I was able to give her that. The time was right to tell her everything. So, I did.

"A few weeks ago, when we met Jury and Thelma in town, and you asked me why I looked ready to murder someone. I was. I found something tucked under the stairs to the porch with a letter to you. I won't share what was in the letter, so don't ask me to. But I will say that it wasn't kind, and it's now in the hands of the sheriff, along with the item it was attached to. That, I will tell you, was the same or identical to the trinket of a little boy you held in Thelma's store, all those weeks ago."

I heard a sharp intake of breath. I was still staring in her eyes, watching them. They had changed in an instant from strength to pain.

"That trinket was the second thing that made me feel a connection to Miss Thelma. Why would anyone send that to me to hurt me?" she asked me, and my anger started to climb.

Not ever again will you feel the cracking of your heart from your past.

This became my mantra.

"I'm not sure yet, Darlin'. But I promise you; I'm working my ass off to figure it out. Fuck, baby. I hate telling you this shit. But there's more."

"Tell it all to me. I can handle it." Her words betrayed her body at the moment, but the blow she just took rocked her a bit, and it was understandable. Still, deep down, she was stronger now and could handle it.

"Something in my gut told me to check on things at the store, so I drove past. The first time, I missed it, but when I went back the second time, I stopped and went to look around the store. Another note was taped on the door. This one was an apology for the one that was left here. And it was also a declaration of this asshole's love for you. That letter is also with the sheriff. I don't have keys to the store, or I would have checked around inside for more notes. But from the window, I could see the phone hanging on the wall. According to the red digits on the answering machine, I could see there were twenty-three messages," I said.

"You still with me?"

"Yes, River. Keep going."

"Alright. Well, there's a way to check the machine by calling the store's number from an external line. Rhett, my guy in Seattle, told me about it. The sheriff and I did this, and we listened to the messages. Twenty of them were for Jury, people sending their condolences. But those other three were for you," I told her.

Her whole body trembled in my arms as she moved her hands from my shoulders and laced her fingers around the back of my neck tight. She rested her cheek on my shoulder but urged me to continue. My Bird needed me to hold on tight too, and that's just what I did while I finished giving all the information to her.

"Two of those messages were from an unknown number, and as of right now, an unidentified male. The voice sounded eerily familiar when I listened, though. I'm working with the sheriff and the rest of the department to try to find out who the fuck it was on those messages. I swear I know who it is, but I can't put my finger on it. The third message was from Jury. It was from the day you didn't go in because you weren't feeling well. It was basically Jury saying things weren't good with Thelma, and that she wouldn't be in. I'm guessin' she didn't see the texts I sent her until later and assumed you'd be there," I finished.

"You think you know who's sending me stuff and watching me?" she asked me, confused.

"Honestly, I don't know yet. I just know I feel like I know who it is. Wait a minute. Have you still felt like you're being watched?" I asked.

"There were a few times at the store, I guess. Which is crazy, right? I thought it was just me being paranoid. People walk along the storefront and glance inside all the time. I never felt my skin prickle or my hairs stand on end like the other times, if that's what you mean," Arianna told me. I clamped down my response, because at that moment, I didn't have a leg to stand on when it came to keeping stuff from her, even if my intentions were different. Didn't mean I liked it one bit.

"Bird, I need you to tell me every time you feel like someone is watching you or if something out of the ordinary happens. I know we've been here before, but I need to know. It could help the case, yeah?" I asked her to make sure we were on the same page going forward.

"I wasn't the one who kept important information to myself this time, was I?" she asked me with that fucking attitude. My dick twitched in my pants and started to harden. It was seriously inappropriate, but I couldn't help it.

"No, baby. You weren't. I'm sorry, Bird. But if I can shield you from any type of pain or hurt, I will. That's part of my job as your man. And I won't feel bad about it. Just understand it was with the best intentions. I love you, Arianna. I only want you to have beauty and light in your life."

Her hands moved up to where my hair met my neck, and she ran her fingers through my now overgrown mess.

"I understand you're this macho, alpha cowboy, who thinks he knows what's best for me. But, River, I'm the only one who can decide that. Don't take my choices away from me anymore, okay? I've had enough of that to last a lifetime," she retorted. I didn't like her implications, but I understood them.

"Ari...I get it. I do. But I'll always protect you. Always."

"Just tell me the things that affect me, yeah?" She used my word against me, and I smiled at her.

"How could I ever say no to that? I'll be upfront with you from now on. Promise. Are we good?" I asked her because I refused to go to sleep without knowing that things were good between us. My father always told me to never go to sleep with unresolved issues from the day hanging over you.

"Yes, River, we're good. I love you for protecting me. But I love you more for knowing that I can handle this now. You were right to keep it to yourself until tonight. Can we please go to sleep now? I'm exhausted." she said on a yawn.

I didn't answer her. Instead, I just picked her up and crawled to the center of the bed, settled her half on my chest, her arms thrown over my stomach, her face in my neck, her leg hooked over my thigh, and kissed her forehead. Inhaling the scent of her shampoo, I exhaled and felt her do the same. Together, we lay there in silence.

Just when I thought she'd fallen asleep, she said, "You should speak with Cady about how her body is going to change. Her little friend, Bryce, is giving her bad information. She walked in on me a few days ago, before I had gotten sick, as I was getting out of the shower, and she was asking questions. I didn't say anything to her because I wasn't sure of my place with all that. Then everything happened, and I forgot to tell you."

There were two things that needed to be addressed about what just came out of her mouth.

"First off, Bird, *your place* with all that, is simple. She sees you as her best friend. She looks up to you. You can talk to her. Cady is smarter than she should be at her age. But, baby, you will be my wife one day. Make no mistake about that. That makes you her stepmom legally but for her, just her mom since you're the only mom she's ever known. You get what I am saying to you?"

"Yes," Arianna said, breathily.

"What did that little fucker say to my daughter, anyway?" I asked.

On a belly laugh, barely able to get it out, she said, "Bryce told her he's an expert on girls and that for her to get a husband, she'll need big boobs."

"For fuck's sake," I clipped.

"I'll talk to her. Explain things," Bird said, still giggling. It put me at ease. Her girlish giggle was a sound that made the beauty that is her, shine bright.

"Appreciate it, Darlin'. Bryce and I will have a chat as well. Got to teach him to be a gentleman since his own father seems to be doing a bang-up job of it."

"Go easy on him, River. He's five," she told me, and I knew she was smiling when she said it.

"We'll see," was all I said. Arianna shifted a bit and snuggled in deeper to my side. She sighed deep, and before I knew it, she was asleep.

We knew how each other felt now. And she knew everything else that was being kept from her. She still was keeping something from me. But if it was what I thought, no hoped, it was, it would be well worth the wait.

The sun blazed through the window and heated me to the point it woke me. I stretched and went to grab for Arianna, but she wasn't there. The sheets were cold where she'd been, so I knew she'd been awake for a while. I heard the low murmur of voices. It sounded like she was talking to Cady, but I couldn't make out the conversation. I swung my legs over the side of the bed and sat there trying to listen to them. My curiosity won out, and I got up, threw on my basketball shorts and a long-sleeved, navy blue Henley, and walked slowly down the hall in the direction of the voices. I stopped just before they came in to view from where they were on the piano bench in the living room.

Cadence had been questioning why her Birdie was so sad the past few days. I tried to explain to her about Miss Thelma being in heaven like her mama, and that Ari was missing her because Thelma meant something to her. But I'm not sure she really understood. My girl just knew that her Birdie wasn't acting like the same Birdie we saw every day. There was no doubt in my mind that my girls would be okay, and that Arianna would do the best she could to explain things to Cady about Thelma.

Arianna doubted her place with Cady, but she didn't need to. Arianna was so good with my girl. It was a relief to me in a way. Honestly, I wasn't sure if I would have been able to handle any of those hard conversations that daughters need and should get from their mothers. Now, maybe since we are and will be a team, we can guide each other. On the thought of Arianna and I co-parenting Cadence, my chest tightened, and I wondered if there would be more children to parent in our future.

On the same morning that Miss Thelma was to be laid to rest, with their heads together and Arianna's arms around Cady's back, my girls laughed. My breath caught in my throat as I stared at the image in front of me. I thought I heard mention of boobs and Bryce and that snapped me from my trance. The conversation Bird said she would have with my daughter had been had. She made it comfortable for my girl, and they were laughing about it.

I walked into the room and cleared my throat.

"DADDY!" Cady said excitedly and climbed down from her place beside Ari to run to me.

"Good morning, baby girl," I kissed her chubby cheek as I scooped her up into my arms.

"Daddy?"

"Yes?"

"I just wanted to tell you that Birdie told me big boobs won't get me a husband. Bryce doesn't know anything about us women. I will let him know at school tomorrow since I won't be there today," my daughter informed me. And, just like that, my baby girl made this tough day, a little easier. I couldn't help but laugh out loudly at her.

"Go get ready for the service, baby girl. I put the outfit you picked to wear for Miss Thelma in the bathroom," I told her.

"Okay, Daddy. See you soon, Birdie. Then can we practice one more time before we leave?" Cady asked Arianna.

"Yes, Princess. We sure can," Bird told her. My face must have shown my confusion because Arianna explained.

"Cady wanted to help me with Miss Thelma's song so we practiced a short section that she could play. She said she wanted to help me give that honor to Thelma. I couldn't say no, plus Cadence already knows the section after playing it through twice with me."

There was not much that I loved more than my two girls playing music together. It was beauty normally, but today it would be an honor and to show love for a woman who made an impact on the lives of those around her, no matter how long they'd known her. That lesson Arianna was giving my daughter was another thing that made me fall harder for her. On that, I moved to Arianna. When I got to her, I grabbed her by the hips and pulled her into me. Then, as I snaked my arms around her, I kissed up the side of her neck.

"Hey, Darlin'. How you feeling today?"

"My stomach is in knots. I feel like I'm going to vomit, but I can't tell if that's still the stomach bug or the nerves I have about today," she said. *If I got my way, we'd know by the end of the week what kind of "stomach bug" my woman was dealing with.*

"Some may be nerves. But, Bird, I want you to see a doctor after things settle down. You've been sick for days now. I want you taking care of yourself, yeah?" It wasn't an option. Especially if…well, it just wasn't an option.

"Fine. I just need to get through today. Jury was a wreck this morning when I called her. She wouldn't say, but it seemed like something more than Thelma's passing was bothering her," Arianna stated, and I knew that asshole, Rhett, hadn't told Jury he'd be coming to town for this. Seriously, what was with my dumbass friends when it came to women?

"You were up early. Neither of you must have slept much if y'all

201

spoke on the phone already. Look, there are things about Jury that she'll need to tell you. I've known her a while, so I can probably guess what else is bothering her. It's just not my place, Darlin'. She'll tell you when the time is right. But now," I trailed my lips along her jaw and up the other side of her neck to her ear and finished on a whisper, "kiss me and then get ready to go."

"Don't be so bossy, River," she tried to sound stern but that *River Shiver* happened, and I knew she didn't really want me to stop bossing her around. She got off on it. And her reaction to me made me get hard every time.

"We've got to get a move on, Arianna. You're performing, and we need to make sure Cady gets her last practice run in."

"Right."

"And, Bird?" I asked, getting her attention again after I let her go, and she started walking toward the bedroom.

"Yes?" she answered back.

"I love you."

The smile that graced Arianna's face was the one I knew was for me. It was wide but shy. Confident but scared. But whatever it was, it was all mine, just like she was. It was also the sign I had needed that she would be able to handle and make it through what would be an extremely hard, and emotional day.

"I love you too, River."

Just like that, my heart skipped and my world, at that moment, was perfection.

Chapter 17

He's My Husband
Arianna

The truck was so quiet, you could hear a pin drop. Or, if you listened close enough, you might have been able to hear my heart thumping a mile a minute in my chest, from my nerves. My tears were in check at that moment, but I wasn't sure I was ready for this. It may have seemed odd to some of the locals that I was chosen to play in Thelma's honor, or that her death affected me the way it did, but she was more than a boss. She was my friend. Probably the first new friend I'd made here in Carson Falls. Thelma was an angel that walked among us, in my opinion. So I was sad but honored, and completely humbled, to be able to fulfill one of her final wishes.

River held my hand and rubbed his thumb over my knuckles, just like he had the day we got the news about Miss Thelma. It was supportive and gentle but not smothering or overbearing. It was amazing how quickly he learned to read me and my moods. I'd been staring out the window during the ten-minute ride and watched as the funeral home came into view, my mind wandering from memories of working with Thelma, to what she could have possibly put in the letters for the girls and me. I wasn't entirely amped up to read it, but Jury and Penny were.

My gaze landed on all of the sheriff department's men that were crowded around what looked like an old schoolhouse. The small building had white vinyl siding, an old rustic wooden porch with stairs, and a bell tower on top. My heart rate picked up and my stomach turned at seeing all the reinforcements. I yanked my hand from River's grasp and covered my mouth as I gagged. Thankfully, I was able to control myself and didn't upchuck all over River's truck.

"Drink some of that water, Darlin'. Take some deep breaths. This is why I warned you yesterday. Everything will be fine. Just be yourself," River advised me.

"Birdie, are you alright?" Cady asked from her seat in the back. I turned to give her a smile and nodded my head yes.

"You can hold my hand. I won't let go unless you need me to," Cadence added.

"Thank you, Princess. That means so much to me. I love you, sweet girl," I told her and watched as her little lip poked out and started shaking while her eyes got wide and welled up with tears.

"I lo…lo…love you too, Birdie," my poor girl choked out.

As soon as River's truck came to a stop in the parking lot of the funeral home, I whipped off my seatbelt and hopped over and into the back seat, released Cady's seatbelt, and picked her up and held her against my side. No one was going to stop me from getting to Cady. Not even her father.

"Why are you crying, Princess?"

"Because," Cady started and wiped her running nose on the sleeve of her dress, then went on, "I didn't think you loved *me*. Only Daddy."

My heart squeezed at her words. This sweet little girl was loved more than she even knew. Not having a mother around in her short life had already given her such a tough view on being loved. If she would let me, I'd show her how much I loved her.

"That is not and will never be true, baby girl. I love you so much more than I think you will ever know. I loved you the day you asked me to be your friend, after your first lesson in Miss Thelma's store. Don't ever doubt my love for you, yeah?" I told her, using River-speak.

"You're my bestest friend. Even more than Bryce," she told me, her little voice still filled with emotion.

"And you," I leaned in to whisper in her ear, "are mine. Even more than Daddy. But that's our secret, okay?"

River was watching, and I winked at him. A soft look crossed his face, and he returned my wink with an equally soft smile. It was so soft it made his eyes shine. River knew what I had said and he was okay with it. He was seriously the best dad. It made me love him that much more.

"What do you say we dry our tears and go in there," I pointed to the funeral home, "and give Miss Thelma the song she asked for?" Cadence wanted more than anything to play this song for Thelma, so I knew that would do it. She was sad about the reason behind it, but wanted to play for Jury and Thelma. Cady loved Jury and also labeled her a best friend. Not to the extent she did me, but she adored Jury all the same. She was also five, so pretty much anyone that gave her attention was her best friend.

Cady wiped her face. I kissed the top of her pigtailed head, and smiled at her. River took that as his cue to get out and open the door for us. He did this, grabbed Cady's hand, wrapped his arm around my waist, walking us up the stairs and inside. Once inside, I looked around at the almost church-like setup with pews, a long, wide center aisle, and a piano off to the left side. I spotted Jury up front, talking to a man, who I assumed was the minister who would be performing the service. It must be said that the minister was seriously good-looking.

"Let's go up there by Jury," River said to Cady and me.

"Sure," I answered at the same time Cady did. We looked at each other, and I gave her a smile.

As the three of us approached Jury, it became clear to anyone within hearing distance that this wasn't the minister; the exchange was extremely heated between the two of them. We caught the tail end of "...I didn't ask you to come here." And then the man's response, "I don't give a fuck. I'm here. I wasn't staying away." At that, we made it to them, and Jury looked at us and her eyes got wide for the briefest of seconds. Like if you weren't studying her face, as I was at that moment, you would've missed it. She shook her head slightly in a sort of 'not now' motion. Completely understanding her meaning, I nodded at her. She had to know I would NOT be letting that go. However, we needed to get through this first, and Jury had enough on her plate right now. Out of the corner of my eye, I saw River do a chin tip to the man standing with Jury, a small smirk formed on his mouth, and he shook his head. The guy just shrugged his shoulders and smiled.

Hmm.

This man, whoever he was, knew my man. Interesting.

"Jury, where's Penny?" I asked her.

I hadn't seen Penny when we came in. I knew she was having a hard time living with Braxton. It sucked that we couldn't go back to the apartment, not that I would now, but for Penny, it was definitely not fun. Living with a guy you were in love with, since you first laid eyes on him, who didn't return the sentiment and flaunted his manwhoring ways in front of you, had to be the most depressing existence ever. My heart absolutely broke for Penny. She always appeared to have her life under control and knew how to get what she wanted, but her mask wasn't fooling me. Or River, for that matter. He knew her better than I did. He knew something had been off with her since this whole break-in happened and confirmed it when he saw her at school for pick up.

"She's in the bathroom. She's been really upset. Like, even more than me. Maybe we should go check on her?" Jury finished on a question.

"Definitely. Penelope has been having a rough go. Thelma's passing just piled on to that. Let's go." I kissed River and Cady both on the cheek and went into the bathroom with Jury.

As we entered, Penny was sitting on the edge of a chaise in what could only be described as a bathroom lobby. She was wearing an all-black dress that fell to just above her knees with sleeves that went three quarters of the way down her arm, a scoop neck, and black stilettos. Penny was sitting completely still, tears streaming down her face, hands folded in her lap, and staring straight ahead in the huge wall mirror they had, just watching herself cry.

"Penny, honey. What's going on?" I asked, as I sat down next to her, grabbed her hand, and held it in mine. Jury sat on the other side and rubbed her hand up and down Penny's back. It was a few minutes before

Penny answered. But she took a deep breath and started.

"I'm so sorry, Jury. This shouldn't be about me. That's why I was hanging out in here until the service started."

"Stop it, Pen. My gran wouldn't want me to forget my priorities. You're a priority. Tell us what's wrong," Jury told Penny.

In a voice so small, as if someone else spoke because Penny never, ever, sounded so defeated before, she said, "Braxton brought a woman to his place last night. He must have thought I wasn't home or was asleep. Whatever. That doesn't matter. I heard everything. I mean EVERYTHING. How it started, the 'Oh my God' and the 'harders', and even the screams of climax at the end. I know he made it perfectly clear that we were just friends the night he picked me up at the apartment, but he knows how I feel about him. Why would he intentionally hurt me like that?" The sobs she let out brought tears to my eyes. I heard Jury take in a quick breath, and when I looked, she had tears in her eyes, too.

"He's a fucking dick. I'm going to kill him myself, dammit," I said through gritted teeth and a bunch of cussing.

"NO!" Penny screamed. "I didn't tell you so that you would have words with him or even have River confront him. You can't tell River, Arianna. Promise me."

"Pen, he hurt you. I can't let that go. You're my best friend and deserve better than that. He should have more respect for you," I told her.

"I know that. But I need to deal with this. If I have any chance of moving on, I need to process this my own way, on my own time. I didn't think I would react this way, and it's a new emotion for me. That's all. Promise me, Ari, you won't tell River."

"Fine. But know, I don't like it. Maybe River could talk some sense into him."

"I'll handle it," Penny said.

"Right. If I find you like this again, though, I will say something to both Braxton and River," I told her in an 'I mean business' tone.

At that, Penny smiled and laughed. She wasn't used to hearing me take charge of a situation, so I was not surprised she found it amusing. It wasn't an all-out belly laugh, but it was enough to calm her down so we could go back out there.

"Just to say, I'll kick his ass, too," Jury chimed in.

That got us all giggling. We stood up, hugged each other, and gave our faces a once-over in the mirror. As we headed to the door, I thought about the scene with mystery man and Jury before we came in here and stopped dead in my tracks asking, "Speaking of ass kicking, who's the man you were having a verbal sparring match with out there?"

"Can we talk about it later?" Jury pleaded with her eyes to me.

"Sure. As long as we actually talk about it later," I returned. I had gotten pretty close with Jury. She was secretive and knew how to evade certain subjects fairly well. Especially when it came to deeper, more personal topics.

"We will. Promise. Let's get through this first," she added.

"Alright, honey. Let's go honor your gran." I grabbed her hand, squeezed it reassuringly, and we walked back out.

Cady and River had taken their seats in the second pew from the front with Braxton and Jury's mystery man. Jury had reserved them for us because she said we were considered family. I slid in next to Cady, so she was in between River and me, and I glared daggers at Braxton. He didn't seem to notice as his eyes were firmly set on Penny. Braxton stood to let her in to sit, and he watched her intently as she walked to the pew across from him and sat down. To my shock, Braxton clenched his teeth, and a muscle jumped in his jaw. He was pissed Penny ignored him and wasn't sitting with him.

That was seriously not lining up with what Penny said about him just wanting to be friends. I mean, even if he had slept with some skank last night, it didn't add up.

Hmm.

The service began and the minister, the real one, went through some prayers as Miss Thelma's coffin was ushered down the aisle, a bit of background on Thelma, and then turned it over to Jury to give the eulogy. Jury stood up and made her way up to the podium that was in the center of the wide aisle, in front of the pews. She moved the microphone down and cleared her throat. Her eyes were shining with tears. Jury had been pretty held together today, but now, the finality of everything was settling over her, and it was written all over her face. Her eyes scanned the crowd and landed on the mystery man. Watching her take a deep breath, she began reading what she had spent the last two days writing.

"This eulogy is going to be a bit different. She wrote me a letter, so I did the same. I may need to stop every now and then to collect myself, so please bear with me, as this is the hardest thing I have ever had to do…

Dear Gran,

You were my saving grace, my hero, and the only person to ever tell me I was worth anything. My parents, if you want to call them that, never understood the bond you and I shared, but really, how could they when they were either high or drunk almost every day, all day? You were the one that took me out of that and taught me what love was. The gentle, but firm, way you were able to guide me and teach me right versus wrong will be something I use with my own children, if I'm ever lucky enough to have them.

The way your love for PawPaw never faded and continued to grow, until he took his last breath, is how every love should be. There should never be a day that the one you love goes without hearing it, feeling it, and being shown it. True love, unconditional love, and everlasting love are what you have engrained in my soul.

I know I moved away and pursued my dreams. But Gran, you need to know, and I probably should have said this more, it was because of you that I was able to do that. Because of you, I was able to find my place in this world and chase after the dreams I had since the first time you told me I could be or do whatever I wanted to. Thank you so much for that.

Gran, I know you struggled at the end, but I'm so grateful to all the people that came into your life. There is no more pain for you. The only thing for you now is to be with PawPaw and guard the ones you hold closest to you.

You will forever and always be the wind beneath my wings, helping me to soar and go after all this world has to offer me. This town knows who you were to them: the quirky, outspoken old lady that owned a store in town, always up in someone's business or town gossip. But I know you as my Gran. The most beautiful soul and the person I strive to be most like.

Fly free with Paw.

I love you, Gran.

Always and Forever,

Jury

"Thank you, everyone, for coming and honoring my Gran," she finished and started to sob into her hands. Mystery man got up and went to her. He escorted her down to where they were sitting, and he kept his hold on her. Jury didn't fight it, but I assumed she didn't have much fight left in her, at that point.

After she had delivered that closing statement and I was a blubbering mess, the minister asked the congregation if there was anyone else who would like to say anything at this time. A few people got up and spoke. I blocked them out to calm myself down. I had to sing after this section of the service, so I needed to get to the place that would allow me to get through this. My stomach was upset but not giving any indication that I was going to puke, so that was good.

There was this thing I had done when I was in college. Right before a performance, I would think about myself in a recording studio. No one around except me and the music. I visualized the notes, the chords, and just let it wash over me. That was my zone. It was where I'd gone while sitting there, not realizing that the minister announced Cadence and me until River leaned in to me and whispered in my ear, "You're up, Bird."

I stood and grabbed Cady by the hand. We walked together up to the piano and took our seats.

"You ready, Princess?"

"Yes, Birdie!" she whisper-yelled. Her excitement was like a balm to my nerves.

"Here we go," I said, and we positioned our hands and began.

Calling on angels on a regular day,
To come and take my pain away.
Carry me to a different place,

Where I can touch you all with God's grace.

With angel wings, I fly.
With angel wings, I soar.
To a place where there's just love,
And I don't hurt anymore.

Calling on angels on a storming eve,
To give me the strength to fly, to leave.
Soaring fast, take me to the sky,
Where my spirit will live on and never die.

With angel wings, I fly.
With angel wings, I soar.
To a place where there's just love,
And I don't hurt anymore.

Calling on angels on a special night,
To lead me toward the eternal light.
Rest me upon the brightest star.
So I can shine on my loved ones from afar.

I called on the angels and they took my hand.
They led me to that distant land.
I will come to you every now and then,
To show I am not suffering, but happy again.

With angel wings, I fly.
With angel wings, I soar.
To a place where there's just love,
And I don't hurt anymore.

And I don't hurt anymore.

The applause grew as my ears focused in on it, and I came back into myself. Cady was staring up at me with awe in her eyes. Her little hand grabbed mine, and we turned and stood to face the crowd. Everyone was standing. Pride flowed out of me. It wasn't about recognition for myself. It was about Miss Thelma's honor, and how incredible Cadence had done her first time playing for an audience. Her talent was light-years ahead of her age. After such a short time, she was almost on the level I was at when I had been playing for a few years.

We took a bow and returned to our seats. Cadence wasn't going to last much longer sitting still. She was very excited and very hyper. I knew that feeling well. The rush you got, the way the blood flowed and pumped through your veins, was an experience unlike anything I'd ever felt before. Until River. And as I thought that, he stopped me from trying to slide in past him to my seat, grabbing my head on both sides, and lightly touching his lips to mine.

"That was one of the most beautiful things I've ever heard in my life, Darlin'," he spoke low for only me to hear.

I kissed him back and gave him the smile that I reserved for him. He knew it was his. Every time I did it, his eyes got that hungry look in them. He let me go, and we sat down. River seated himself between Cady and me, this time. When we were situated, he grabbed my hand, interlocked our fingers, and placed our joined hands on his thigh, where they stayed for the remainder of the service.

There were some hymns sung, some scripture readings, and the final prayer. The minister asked for the pallbearers to come forward, and with that, Miss Thelma was escorted to the hearse to take her final journey home, to be with her late husband. Everyone else got into their cars and followed to the cemetery. River and I had decided that Cady was still too young for this part of the day, so we headed back to the house to drop her off with Meggie. We planned to go to the cemetery and we had just enough time to drop Cady off.

When we arrived home, Meggie was sitting on the steps. As we all approached her, she stood up and said there was a letter left on the stairs, addressed to me. She went to hand it to me, but River snatched it up and quickly shuffled all of us into the house.

"Gotta make a call," was all River said and moved back outside. That letter was from whoever had been watching me. I needed to know what was happening. But I needed to trust River and his instincts to keep us safe and to remember that he knew people who could help.

So, needless to say, I stayed inside with the girls. I helped Cady get changed and told her how proud I was of her. We had made it down to the kitchen, where Meggie was making a snack when River walked in.

"Ari, baby, we have to go. Jury is expectin' us."

"Okay. Let me just grab a sweater. It's a bit chilly out today," I said. It wasn't really that chilly, but I felt like I needed more covering me. More layers to protect me.

Ten minutes later, we arrived at the cemetery and parked. There were still cars pulling up, and people making their way to where Miss Thelma would be laid to rest. As I waited for River to open my door, I did a scan to locate Penny and Jury. Penny walked with her arms wrapped around her middle but close to Braxton. He walked with his hands in his pants pockets, but again, watched Penny the whole time, teeth clenched and muscles still ticking in his cheek. Jury was under the canopy they had set up for family and close friends to sit under, and was in another heated discussion with mystery man. Trying to decide whom to go to first, I looked at River. He nodded his head in Jury's direction, and he moved towards Braxton and Penny.

Jury was looking up at this man, and her face was set in a way I knew she was pissed.

"Hey. Are you alright, Jury?" I asked her.

"Just peachy. Except I need to go see the groundskeeper about returning someone's money to them," she said, glaring at the man who was still unknown to me.

"Can't that wait?"

"No, it absolutely can NOT wait."

"Woman, I'm telling you right now, if you even think about talking to that man about returning my money, we're going to have problems," mystery man growled out.

"Fuck off! Like we aren't already in the middle of 'having problems?' No one asked you to do that. No one even asked you to be here. I can handle this. I've been handling things on my own for a while now, haven't I? Just go away," Jury shot back at him. She stomped away and headed right to the groundskeeper who was standing close by.

"Fuck me," mystery man barked out and took off after her.

Well, all right then.

The minister approached me and introduced himself as Tom. We chatted a bit about my song and how he wanted to advertise, in the church newsletter, that I gave lessons. It was pretty amazing that he thought so highly of me. He didn't know me, and I didn't attend his worship services on Sunday. As we were chatting, I saw movement out of the corner of my eye. Mickey was approaching us.

"Hey, Arianna. Tom," Mickey greeted us.

"Hi Mickey," we both responded in unison. Tom had to get ready to start, so he walked away leaving Mickey and me alone.

"Where's River? Thought for sure he would be attached to your side," he commented sarcastically, and I immediately became uncomfortable.

"He's here. Went to talk to Penny and Braxton over there," I stated clearly so he knew River was around.

"I see. Well," he began and stepped so close I smelled his rank breath as he continued, "if you ever want a real man, look me up. I'm in the phone book and on Google." That was all he could say before a throat cleared behind us and River stood there with his arms crossed over his chest.

"Let me get this straight, Mickey," River started in a low, lethal tone.

"You, the same person who knocked up some girl, left her, and not once made an attempt to handle your responsibilities to her or your child, are a real man? How on this green earth does the way you treat people, mainly women, or that situation amount to you being a man? In my eyes, that makes you a terrible human being, let alone a 'real' man," River finished.

"Fuck you, River almighty. The sun doesn't shine out of your ass, you know. You aren't perfect, even though you think it."

"No, you're right. I'm not perfect. I make mistakes, but I also take care of *my* responsibilities. More than I can say for you. Now, I won't tell you again. Stay. The. Fuck. Away. From. Arianna. If I have to tell you again, it won't end with words. It'll end with you eating teeth, and a trip to the hospital." River ended this ridiculous and badly-timed confrontation. He grabbed my hand and dragged me away.

"Stay as far away from him as possible, Arianna. I mean it. He's a piece of shit. What I just said doesn't even scrape the surface of Mickey's fucked-up ways."

"Alright, River. But he approached me. Not the other way around."

"I know. I saw him go to you. And I heard the whole conversation. I was trying to talk to Braxton, but his stubborn ass wasn't having any of it, so I came over when Tom left. I just need you to not engage him if I happen not to be around and he is. Find somewhere else to put yourself, yeah?" he asked, but wasn't really asking. More like telling.

"Yeah, honey." What else could I say to that? Nothing. And that's what I did.

Jury, Penny, Braxton, and mystery man had all taken their seats under the canopy, so River and I did the same. Jury was to my left, and I leaned in and whispered, "Are you okay?" She nodded yes, so I left it at that.

This man that was so obviously well-acquainted with Jury had me intrigued.

I was incredibly nosy, so I asked River, "Who's the guy that keeps going round for round with Jury today?"

"Bird, baby. Let it lie."

Hmm. I was even more intrigued now.

Tom said the final prayer, and we all lined up to place our individual flowers that had been handed out earlier, on top of the casket. River was tucked up tight to my back and had an arm wrapped around my waist. I was crying throughout this whole process. Once I placed my flower down, I whispered an 'I love you, Thelma', kissed my index and middle fingers, and placed them to the casket before walking to the spot where Penny and Braxton were waiting for the rest of us, having gone before.

My eyes were trained on Jury to make sure she got through this part. Mystery man was right behind her and bent low to talk to her as she placed her flower. As they both finished, he shook his head in disbelief and walked away, not joining the rest of us.

Jury made it to our group about ten minutes later and asked, "Back to my place?"

There were mumbled 'sures' and 'sounds good,' but I knew she was deflecting. Braxton and River headed toward their trucks. Penny and I looked at each other and flanked Jury on both sides as we walked her to the town car the funeral home provided for her.

"Jury, honey, what's going on?" Penny asked.

"Nothing," she said adamantly.

"It's not nothing. You've been going at that man all day. Who the hell is he anyway?" I added, and asked.

"He's my husband."

Penny and I both sucked in breaths at the same time, and we looked at Jury with wide eyes.

"I'm sorry, come again?" Penny asked, for clarification.

"That's Rhett. He's my husband."

"Well, fuck me. That's what I thought you said. Honey, good fucking choice," Penny gave her approval and sounded more like herself.

"You're married? Why didn't you say something? And Rhett? As in Rhett from Seattle, who is River's friend, Rhett?" I asked.

"One in the same. And I didn't say anything because it's complicated. There are reasons why I'm here, and he wasn't until today. I won't go into specifics, but he's a royal pain in the ass." There was no way she didn't have feelings for him. No one spars with a man like that if they didn't. These friends of mine weren't what met the eye at all. Complex women in interesting positions with the men in their lives.

Well, this was unexpected.

"Will he be meeting us at your house? I'd like to meet him, officially," I asked.

"Unfortunately, yes. He left ahead of everyone to set up the luncheon. The caterers were to arrive before we got there. So he went to meet them and give me some extra time here. Only decent thing he's done since he got here last night," Jury complained.

"Shit. I can't believe you're married," Penny said.

"Neither can I. Trust me. I'll tell you all about it if you get me drunk enough. Whiskey is like my truth serum."

"That's a fucking deal, babe," Penny told her. Once Penny wanted to know something, she'd do whatever it took to get that information from a person. Unless it was Braxton. Jury could count on spilling her secrets tonight if Penny had her way.

We made it to the cars and the guys. We all got in and headed for Jury's house. My phone buzzed in my purse, and I pulled it out. It was a text from Penny.

Penny: Can you believe this shit?

Me: Kind of, actually. The way they were arguing all day, there is definite heat there.

Penny: You are NOT wrong. We are totally getting her shit-faced tonight so she spills. I need something juicier than what I've got going on.

Me: Penny, she just laid her Gran to rest.

Penny: Perfect reason to get shit-faced to me!

Me: SMH.

There was no other response.

Penelope Sloane. Pain in my ass.

Chapter 18

If You Ever Want A Real Man
River

If you ever want a real man.

Mickey's words kept replaying in my head, but I couldn't figure out why. He couldn't be fucking serious. That whole scene at the cemetery with Mickey had me on edge. So much so, it was to the point where I was currently out with Braxton and Rhett grabbing some beer and trying to shoot some pool, but my mood was at 'bite your head off' maximum levels. I knew I was being short whenever they asked a question. I could only assume this was why they stopped the beer, and we advanced to whiskey.

The honky-tonk we wound up at was your run-of-the-mill, clichéd, country bar with wood floors covered in peanut shells, bad lighting, a live country cover band currently belting out some Garth Brooks, and the smell of bad decisions mixed in with cigar and cigarette smoke. This wasn't really my type of place. The boys said I needed to get away for a night. A change of scenery from the regular establishments I frequented might help me clear my head and my attitude.

"River, man, it's your shot," Braxton said.

"Are you sure you're all right, man? I mean Arianna is covered. Her and Jury were going to get the store ready to open back up tomorrow. Jury said Thelma didn't want her to keep it closed longer than they needed and that Jury should get on living life in the fucking letter she wrote her. If it were me; I would've opened the day after the funeral. Keep occupied, ya know? But women are different creatures, I suppose," Rhett told Brax and me.

I knew Arianna was going to go back to the store eventually, but I was uneasy about it. Thing was, I wanted to make sure I was close by when she did, just in case I needed to get to her quickly. Jury had training, due to her background, and I knew she'd try her best to take care of any situation if one came up. They were just carrying out Thelma's wishes, but the more I thought about the deliveries and everything having to do with this crazy fuck going after Bird, the harder it was to focus on enjoying my night out.

That night back at Jury's house, after the funeral, I gave the three girls the letters that Thelma had left for them. Jury and Penny opted to read theirs right then. Arianna didn't want to read hers.

"Not now. I want my memories with her to root themselves inside my heart first before I read what, I can assume by the other girls' letters, was her advice to me for the future," Arianna had said. It was just like her to feel that way. She felt things so much differently than any other woman I had ever met. I gave her a few more opportunities since that night to read it, but the last time I asked her if she wanted it, she kissed me soft, long, and open-mouthed before telling me with a bit more sass than I wanted, that she would ask for the letter when she was ready. And that may not be any time soon, but to keep guard of it for her. So, I locked it up in the safe at home.

"I knew Bird would eventually go back to the store. And we made sure Cady was okay with it, too, for her lessons and such, but she still isn't feeling good, and that whole scene at the cemetery with Mickey is fucking with me. I just keep hearing his words repeatedly in my head," I told my friends as I took my shot and missed. Braxton was filled in on everything on the ride here, seeing as he hadn't been around lately since he'd been dealing with his own situation with Penny. Still not much progress there, but I guess things were cordial now. Rhett knew everything because he needed to know as it was happening.

"What do you think it means, River?" Braxton asked.

"I think it means that he's somehow behind these fucking letters, gifts, if that's what you want to call them, and the voice messages. I knew the voice on those messages sounded familiar to me, I just couldn't place it at the time. I fucking knew it. The thing I can't figure out is how the hell does he know some of what he knows, when I know for a fact that no one involved in this case has said a word about Arianna's full story?" I asked, but I didn't really expect a response.

"We'll get to the bottom of it. This is priority right now for the sheriff's department and me. That's why I decided to stay in The Falls for the immediate future," Rhett informed me, surprisingly.

"Man, you don't have to do that. I know you have shit going on in Seattle. You can't drop everything to do this." I was blown away by his gesture.

"No, River. You're wrong. My *everything* has been in Carson Falls for weeks now. I'm just seeing things clearly for the first time in forever and doing something about it," Rhett said, and I knew exactly what he was talking about. I was the only one, up until the funeral, that knew he was married to Jury. There were crazy reasons behind why they were apart, but it seemed like Rhett was ready to work those reasons out and get his wife back.

"Either way, Rhett, I appreciate your help with this," I told him.

"Wait a fucking minute. You and Jury are fucking married? Where the hell was I when this all surfaced? And why am I always the last to know this shit?" Braxton asked, confused and slightly pissed off.

"Because, asshole. You've had your head stuck up your ass about Penny and been oblivious to what was going on around you. When are you going to admit that you have a serious fucking thing for her and man the hell up and get your girl?" I shot back.

"Shit's complicated. We have history, and I can't seem to ever get it right with her, so I'm leaving it alone. Penelope can do what she wants."

"You say that shit now, until she meets someone. Then what are you going to do? Because trust me, there's nothing like seeing the woman you love with another man." Rhett seemed to reveal some experience in that statement. I didn't know all the reasons he and Jury weren't in a good place, but I think I just got a new look inside their strange situation.

"Like I said, she can do what she wants, and I'll do what I want. That's where it's at. So if you girls are done gossiping, maybe we can finish this game?" Braxton said as he shot his whiskey down. He was agitated, which happened almost every single time Penelope Sloane was discussed in front of him.

"Well, I just hope you both know, it means a lot to know I have your help on this. So, thank you." That was the end of the conversation. We shot some more pool, drank a shit-ton more whiskey, and I forgot, for a little while at least, that my woman was at home without me.

Missing her was not something I was good at. It made my whole body tight and burn with anxiety, and I was still being a moody bastard. With thoughts of my girls playing piano and giggling together, I called a cab to take me home. There was no way I could have stayed away from them for the whole night, especially with all that was going on around us. This was made extra clear to me when I was met at the door with an excited Cady yelling, 'Daddy,' and the way my Bird welcomed me home with her mouth on mine.

I crashed pretty fast, mostly due to the amount of alcohol flowing through me. I hated not being coherent, which was why I didn't really drink to get drunk very often. The gesture from the guys to get my mind off of everything was lost anyway when the conversation veered to the situation with Mickey. I wanted to be with my girls, and there was no fault in that.

The next day, I slept through most of the morning and woke up just before noon. We had lunch and went for a walk down by the willow tree. Cadence was playing with her dolls and walking ahead of Arianna and me. The two of us strolled hand in hand, content and silent to a spot next to the willow. Ari seemed to be feeling okay, but I still wanted her to see a doctor. So, it was time to broach the subject again.

"How are you feeling, Darlin'?"

"I'm doing all right. My stomach has felt good, but I'm still tired all the time."

"You need to see a doctor, Arianna. This has been going on too long now. Please do this for me," I pleaded with her.

"I made an appointment for Wednesday. You're right. It's time," she said.

"Thank you, Darlin'. I love you, Bird, and just want you healthy."

"Believe me, I want to be healthy, too. And I love you, too," Ari replied.

The three of us spent most of the afternoon and early evening by the lake. Just when the sun had started to change the sky from blue to that yellowish-pink it did before it set, Cady was ready for dinner and bed. It was later than usual for her to eat, but she was having fun. Arianna had spent most of the time curled into me on the grass where we'd planted ourselves.

We talked about Jury, Rhett, and Braxton, but mostly Penny. Bird was worried about her. Penny had been in this dark place for a while. Then the day after the funeral, it was like she snapped out of it, but went to the extreme. She was going out every night and, according to Braxton, not coming home some of those nights. That wasn't really Penny's style, but who knew what was going through her head right now? As we walked back to the house, I told Arianna that Rhett decided to stay in Carson Falls to help me nail Mickey's ass for this shit he's been pulling. Of course, that was after I told her about Mickey being the voice I recognized on the voicemail.

Cady had requested that Bird read a new princess story to her tonight. This surprised me. I thought my life would be spent tortured with *Frozen* and *The Snow Queen* forever. Maybe, just maybe, the big man up there was feeling a bit generous and decided I'd had enough. I could do with a little bit of Cinderella or Ariel thrown into my day. Either way, Cady loved her Birdie, and any time Arianna gave her. It hurt my heart a bit that she didn't want her dad, but I understood. My baby girl finally had the mom she craved.

After Cady was down for the count, and the house was cleaned and locked up for the night, Arianna and I made our way to the bedroom. She walked to the bed and pulled down the covers to prepare for us to go to sleep. I took off my boots and put them in the closet.

I wasn't tired.

And I needed to shower.

Arianna in the shower. That would be new for us and hot as fuck.

"Bird, I want to shower before bed," I said, my voice husky. Just watching her walk around what was now our bedroom made my cock hard. Knowing that she was mine, was in love with me, and loved my daughter did it to me. Every. Single. Time.

She turned to me and answered, "That's fine. I'll be here when you're done."

"No, baby. You aren't getting me."

I walked to where she was, grabbed her hips, and pulled her into my body so she could better understand the situation with *my situation* against her stomach, "I want to shower, *with you*, before bed."

Her beautiful eyes got big and went soft as she replied, "Oh."

She gave me my smile, and I felt her shiver. God, I loved how I affected her. She took my hand and led me to the bathroom.

"Lock the door, River," Ari said in a low, sexy voice.

I turned around to click the lock in place and came back to find Arianna starting to slowly take off her clothes. I stuck my hands in my pockets and leaned back against the door so that I could enjoy the show I was being treated to. The confidence exuding from her in that moment made me even harder. It was amazing to watch her get that part of herself back, but it was even better to be the man to reap the rewards of it. Any man dumb enough to do what her ex did and throw this away, deserved to rot in hell.

Slower than my dick wanted, Arianna lifted the pink boy band t-shirt over her head and let it slide off her fingertips to the floor. She didn't go for the clasp on the pink lacy bra she had on next like I thought, but instead, unbuttoned and pulled the zipper down on her jeans. Leaving them hanging open and me panting like an animal seeing the matching lacy pink panties peeking out, she next toed off her shoes. Thank fuck they were flats and didn't require any unbuckling or unzipping, so Ari made quick work of removing them. She made her way back to the jeans and slowly shimmied them over her gorgeously curved hips and bent to follow them to the floor so she could step out of them.

As she stood back up, I grabbed my cock through my jeans. The striptease I was receiving made me feel like I was going to bust right through the denim. Arianna's eyes slid to my hand then back to my eyes. Her lips tipped up in a sexy, knowing smirk. She knew exactly how much she turned me on and was having fun making me slowly lose my mind, which I was. I was teetering on the edge. Ari grabbed her beautiful, long blonde hair and moved it over one shoulder. Seeing her exposed neck where my mouth wanted to be kissing, sucking, and biting, caused the final snap in the hold of my control. When she finally reached her hands to the middle of her back to unclasp her bra, I made my move to her. She hadn't yet managed to undo all four clasps revealing her gorgeous breasts, so I grabbed her wrists together, used one of my hands to move them to her lower back, and held them there.

I leaned in and whispered in her ear, "Keep them there, Bird."

"River." My name left her lips and came out as a moan.

Fuck, I loved her.

My need for her was overpowering, and I knew I didn't need to be so careful with her anymore. I was her man and it had been what felt like years since I sank inside her, even if it was only a week. We hadn't had much time for us since Thelma died, so it was time to get her out of the sexy, pink bra and panty set she still had on. I wanted to get her dirty before taking my time cleaning her up. As her hands stayed clasped behind her back, I made my approach. I put my lips to her neck that she offered up to me, after moving her hair. My hands skimmed up and down her arms while I slowly kissed a scorching path to her jaw, the corner of her mouth, and back up to her ear again.

"Make sure you don't move those hands. It's time this body was explored properly," I told her.

"Oh God. Touch me, River, please," she begged.

I slid my hands inside each cup of her bra. Lightly, I grazed my knuckles over her hard nipples. When I heard Bird moan from just the slightest contact there, I tugged her bra apart. It ripped open, and I left the shreds of the cups and the straps hanging off her. Ari didn't move which told me she was not afraid of what we were doing or of me doing it. The woman before me was who I always thought was inside that scared, hurt woman I first met. I would never take for granted everything she has put in my hands to trust, love, and protect.

Arianna was beautiful, and I took that time to really look at her. There was a small smirk on her lips, a sexy, yet new, gleam in her eyes, and she absolutely, without any doubt, had regained the power that motherfucker took from her. Arianna's skin was sun-kissed, with the beginnings of what would surely end up being a fantastic tan, from being outside so much with Cady over the past few days. It made my mouth water, and my fingers itched to touch her. The idea of worshipping her tonight and taking my time, made my dick jump. Ari made me crazy and tortured me with her beautiful body every day. If I hadn't known it up to that point, I knew now that I was the luckiest bastard on the fucking planet.

There were way too many articles of clothing still on me, and my erection was getting painful being held captive in my jeans. Quick work was made of my t-shirt. My impatience at removing the belt I had chosen to wear made Arianna giggle. Once that annoying as fuck belt was gone, my jeans were down my legs, and my poor dick had freedom to fly, I moved my attention back to the beautiful woman in front of me.

Now her panties needed to go.

My hands cupped her full breasts. Arianna's breasts were always sensitive, but they seemed more so at that moment, and I was going to take advantage of it. Leaning in, I captured one nipple in my mouth and sucked. My tongue flicked at the tip, and my Bird started to squirm. I switched to the other nipple and repeated the motion then started to slide my hands slowly down Ari's sides, over her hips, and inside her panties. My fist gathered the material on one side, and I brought my other hand around. Just like with the bra, the panties didn't stand a chance. Not with the amount of need coursing through me. I tore the panties on one side, then the other. The pink lace was shredded and hung down in front and back of her, exposing her to me completely. Quickly, I removed the destroyed garment and threw it aside.

Ari's hands had left their position behind her back, and she grabbed my hair and held me tight against her breast, urging me to keep going. I bit her nipple roughly before I released it. Arianna yanked my head back so our eyes met. Our breathing was heavy, and we both needed release.

"River. Please, honey. I need you inside me," she said with a groan.

"Not yet. You moved your hands. Where did I tell you to keep them?"

"Behind my back but, River, I need to feel your warm skin. I want to feel the push and pull of your muscles as you touch me. I'm not scared, but I just need this tonight," she pleaded. "I feel like I could come just from you sucking on my nipples. It's never been that way before. River, I need you, please." Her begging me didn't do a damn thing to calm me down.

"Hold on to me, Bird. Put your arms around my neck, and wrap your legs around my waist," I instructed her.

She did as I asked, wrapped herself around me, and I guided her down onto my hard-as-steel cock. My Bird was ready for me. She was so wet when I slid into her. I had to still all movement once I was balls deep inside her, as I stood with her tangled around me.

"I want this to last, but, Bird, it more than likely won't since it's been a week since I've felt your heat wrapped around my cock," I warned her.

"River, I don't care. But you better start moving, or I will."

"Well, aren't you bossy when you're turned on?" I teased her.

"Shut up and move!" Demanding little thing, too, but I totally understood. I'd been there. Hell, I was right there with her.

I started to move her up and down my shaft. Slow and steady was not going to please my woman tonight. We had both worked each other up with Ari's striptease, and it was time to give my woman what she wanted. She would always get what she wanted, within reason. But right then, she wanted to soar, and I was happy to be the one to make her fly.

With her still on my dick and her limbs still tight around me, I planted her sweet ass on the counter. The change in positions happened fast, and I brought her to the edge of the counter so that she could drop her legs and take what I was going to give her.

"Bring your knees to your chest, and grab the edge of the counter to hold on, yeah?" I commanded her.

"Who's bossy now?" Arianna asked but still did what I told her to do, because she knew I would make it good for her.

Every man says that when they sink deep into the woman they love, it's heaven. Arianna wasn't heaven. She was whatever that thing was beyond heaven. And in all honesty, I just wanted to keep going there.

My hips rolled and adjusted to the new angle. I started to thrust in and out of her tight, warm, and totally soaked pussy at a steady pace. My hands found her heavy breasts, and I pulled and pinched her nipples, causing Ari to arch her back in pleasure and open her pussy to me even more. With every outward glide, her eyes, which were staring straight into mine, would roll back in pleasure. Her heartbeat pulsed faster in that spot on her neck. The very thought of not having this for the rest of my life made me manic, and I started to pound into her, giving her all my fears that I'd kept bottled inside me.

"Christ. You feel so fucking amazing, Arianna."

"Oh my God, River. I'm so close. Harder. Please," she whimpered out between moans. I loved watching her come.

"Fly, Bird," I told her, as I really picked up the pace. We were going to come together, and I felt her get tighter around me.

"Fuck. I'm there. You with me?" I asked her.

"Yes! SHIT! YES!" she screamed out in pleasure.

"Shit. Fuck!" I barked out through my release.

After we caught our breaths, Arianna's legs slipped down and were dangling off the counter, my cock slipped out, and we both felt the loss when she grabbed and pulled me to her.

"My God, River. I don't know what came over me," Ari whispered in my ear, her hold on me getting tighter and her heart rate starting to settle.

"Whatever it was, Darlin', I'm not complaining," I said into her hair. I cupped her face and brought her head to me to kiss. Then, I pulled away from her body and stepped out from between her legs. I moved to the shower and turned the water on to a comfortable temperature.

"Ready to let me clean you up, dirty Bird?" I asked and teased her at the same time.

"Yes," she said, as she hopped down off the counter. I reached my hand out to her so she wouldn't lose her footing. Before moving to step into the shower, she cupped herself between her legs and looked at her hands, kind of in shock.

"What's wrong? Did I hurt you?" My heart started pounding inside my chest because I was really rough with her.

"Nothing's wrong, River. Your cum is leaking out of me. It's not something I can say I've ever really experienced before you. It feels strange when it starts to come out. Stop worrying so much," she explained, easing my mind.

Did she really just tell me that?

Seriously, that was one of the fucking hottest things I'd ever heard a woman say to me. Ever. Arianna's mouth seemed to only get dirty when we had sex, which if I am honest, turns me on even more because it's not something that I am used to hearing.

"Christ. You're definitely something else. Let's clean you up, yeah?" I asked her. With her nod of agreement, I pulled her into the shower. While I washed her hair, we talked. When I tried to start washing her body, Arianna got turned on again. I gave flight to my Bird's second and third orgasms of the night.

The second was with my tongue and fingers.

The third came when I took her from behind under a steady stream of water.

I came with her on her third.

Then I had to wash her again.

After we finally cleaned and dried ourselves, we went to bed completely sated and tangled in each other's limbs.

Bird fell asleep before me.

Just as my breathing evened out, Mickey's words once again played in my head. I had forgotten the shit storm going on in our lives for a little while.

If you ever want a real man.

Motherfucker.

He'd know the true definition of real man when my fist met his face, and I watched the sheriff lock his ass up.

The next day started like every other day had since Arianna Morgan came into my life and my home. The alarm was set for seven, but I was always up before it went off. Mornings always set the mood for my day, and it was instilled in me since I was a boy to get a jump on the day. It was mid-May now in the Falls, which equated to the perfect mix of rainy and sunny days. Ari slept in while I got my daughter breakfast and ready for school. When I came back home, Bird was up and on the porch writing before she needed to go to work. She wasn't feeling well that morning, and it showed in her face. But, just like Arianna, she had me take her to the store anyway to work her shift.

My father always told me two things, repeatedly, while I was growing up, about life in the South. The first was, when you're arguing with a Southern girl and she breaks out the 'sweetheart,' shit's about to get real. The second was, that you could always tell danger loomed if you heard a rooster crowing after daybreak.

If I had known the series of events that were going to happen that day, I would have taken a little longer looking at the woman I loved, in my bed, sleeping peacefully on her side with her hands together, tucked between her chin and the pillow.

If I had known the series of events that were going to happen that day, I would have hugged my baby girl a bit tighter and a bit longer when I dropped her off at school before watching her walk off with her friend, Bryce.

If I had known the series of events that were going to happen that day, I would have paid more attention when I pulled into the firehouse and heard that fucking rooster long after day had broken.

Chapter 19

Mickey
Arianna

Most days at the store were spent just dusting all the inventory and shelves, or playing around with melodies running through my head. Generally, it was boring. The past week or so, my meddle-meter was at an all-time high since Rhett had come barreling into town, trying to win his wife back. His wife. Seriously. If anyone besides Jury would have told me that she and Rhett were married, I may not have believed it.

There was no denying the chemistry and the overwhelming sexual tension that radiated off them when they were in the same vicinity of one another. But there were secrets that hid behind all of that, too, and I'd not yet been able to figure out what they were. I let Jury know over the past week that I was curious about the mystery behind why she was living across the country from her husband, in hopes that she would tell me. No such luck yet. But whatever Rhett had just said over the phone to her, set Jury off on a rant.

"He's driving me crazy, Arianna," Jury started from the aisle where she'd taken the call on her cell and been pricing some new items. She continued, "After my gran's funeral, it's like he won't go away. He's been constantly showing up where I am, calling me every hour on the hour, and texting me like twenty times a day. I ignore most of the phone stuff, but when he shows up while I'm eating lunch at the square or getting coffee in the mornings, I seriously want to punch him in his throat. He looks so pleased with himself. And another thing, that fight you heard us having at the cemetery about paying for the funeral? Well, he transferred the money that I paid for the funeral with back into my account. Isn't that just crazy?" Jury asked me. If it were up to me, I would've told her no. It's not crazy because he's her husband. Jury was not ready to hear that, so I bit my tongue and just shook my head in agreement with her.

Jury was in such a state and going on and on about Rhett and not paying attention to me, I snuck my way back into the storeroom to get some playing in before Cady got out of school and came for her lesson. The song I was currently working on was inspired by Jury and Rhett. It was about need. The lyrics were complete but I needed a melody to go with them, so it was the perfect time to lock myself away and just feel the notes come to me.

It was still fairly early when I'd made my way to the back room and got completely caught up in what I was doing. I hadn't realized how much time had passed when Jury came in and told me that she was going to grab lunch, at a little past one in the afternoon. She told me she was going to order from the diner in Gifford, and she asked me what I wanted. Seeing as I'd been feeling better the past few days, I ordered some chicken fingers with fries. Not very healthy or smart since I hadn't eaten that heavily in a long time, but it was what I wanted, so I treated myself.

When she arrived back about thirty minutes later, we locked up the store and went to the gazebo to eat. It wasn't raining for a change, and it was warm, so we sat on the bench where I first met River and Cady. As we ate, Jury and I avoided the Rhett topic and discussed how we felt about Braxton and Penny's situation. Penny was avoiding Braxton at all costs. When he was home, she wasn't. River actually told me that Braxton said that Penny could do what she wanted, but he knew Brax was lying. Especially when Rhett told him he'd feel differently when another man put his hands on Penny.

"Do you think Braxton will ever see Penny the way she sees him? I mean he tries to put on this facade, and has this playboy air about him, but it doesn't really fool anyone that truly looks, you know?" Jury asked me. It was interesting that she was able to pick up on that in someone else's relationship but didn't see what we all saw in her own.

"Their history is complicated. From what I was told from River, they met in New York City when Penny and I were in college. It was a series of unfortunate events and misunderstandings. Penny has never really explained the whole mysterious night to me. She says the only thing she got that night was a hangover. I hope she starts to see he isn't the guy he wants us to believe he is," I said, explaining what I knew to Jury as I finished up the delicious chicken and fries. The sweet tea she picked up finished off the meal, and it completely satisfied me.

"I think there is more to it than Penny and Braxton are letting on, but that's just my opinion." Jury wasn't wrong. It would be interesting to see how both she and Penny navigate through their own situations.

When we finished eating, Jury and I went for a walk around the square. The warm, late spring breeze was picking up, and my hair was whipping all over the place. I had worn it down that day with an off-white sundress and my brown cowboy boots. I had some extra time to straighten it that morning, so I did.

We made it to the far side of the square, and in the clearing between the swaying trees, I saw the top of the Ferris wheel at the fair. That damn ride had housed some pretty monumental moments between River and me. I stopped walking and just stared up at it. My mind took me back to when River asked me to take a chance on him and to when he told me he loved me. I was so scared when he asked me to let him be the man I made new memories with. Making memories with him seemed to be the best thing I ever decided to do. So much had happened and so fast, but I wasn't scared anymore; I just wanted to keep things moving forward. I loved River and Cady more than anything in this world. When I watched them together, it made my heart race and my lady parts tingle.

"Arianna," Jury said, as she nudged my shoulder to bring me out of my daydream.

"Sorry. Just got lost in a memory for a minute there. You ready to go back?" I asked her.

"Yeah. I hate to be inside on this gorgeous day, but it seems we have a store to run."

"You're right. We should get back. It won't be long before Cady gets there," I replied back.

As we rounded the gazebo in the center of the square from the far side, Mickey appeared and stopped both, Jury and me, in our tracks.

"Well, if it isn't two of the biggest bitches in town," he sneered at us.

"What's your problem, Mickey? I've barely said a handful of words to you since I've been back, and Arianna has done not one thing to you, but that's how you greet us?" Jury asked him.

"Don't pay him any attention, Jury. Let's just go," I said, so we could get the hell out of there. I had a bad feeling. Mickey looked strung out and dirty like he was on something and hadn't washed in three days. He had on ripped, dirty-looking jeans, and a dark blue t-shirt with holes all over it. His eyes were shifty and constantly moving. He wasn't the same guy from the store that I'd met so many weeks ago or even the guy from the cemetery. There was a total change in his demeanor. He was no longer cocky. He was dangerous, and if there was anything I knew, it was how to tell when a man's eyes turned cold and dangerous.

Jury and I started walking away from him. He grabbed me by the upper arm as I tried to go around him.

"Don't fucking walk away from me. I got something to say to you, bitch," he snarled, and it sounded like he was right by my ear.

"Let go. You're hurting me, Mickey," I demanded and tried to shrug out of his grip. He let go but stayed in my space and started speaking in my ear again, but low enough so that Jury didn't hear him.

"I'm coming for you. Soon. We'll be together very soon." His breath smelled awful and every hair on my body raised. Fear was coursing through me, but I'd been knocked down and around by a man before, and that was never going to happen again.

"That will never happen. River is and will always be the only man for me. Now, if you'll excuse me," I told him and quickly went around him and was almost running back to the store when Jury caught up to me.

"What did he say to you that has you so freaked out?" she asked.

"It doesn't matter. Mickey is just a jerk. And he seriously needs a toothbrush and a shower." I didn't know why I hadn't just told Jury what he said. I probably should have, but no man was ever going to threaten me or scare me again. I had my quota of that. Things in my life were at a place where I didn't ever want to go back there, for any reason, and I knew what having confidence in my strength was like now.

"If he threatened you, I need to know. More, River needs to know," she advised me.

"Look, he's gone now. Let's just get back to the store."

"Well, he's gone, but if he's a danger to himself or others, you need to say something." It felt like Jury was scolding me like a child. It wasn't that I didn't remember what happened the last time I didn't speak up about stuff; it was just that I was in a different headspace and could handle some strung-out junkie like Mickey. What did he mean when he said he was coming for me? Maybe I *should* call River. But if I did, then I'd just be giving another man control, right?

Ultimately, I decided not to call River or tell Jury what was said.

I should have.

Hindsight was always twenty-twenty.

"Birdie! Birdie!" I heard being yelled from the front of the store as Cady came barreling inside. She was always so excited to see her dad. But she was now excited to see me, too. Cady's innocence and purity of heart made me love her that much more. My heart was so full, and it made me all melty when she called me Birdie.

"In the back room, Princess," I yelled out to her in response, through a smile. Cadence was a natural-born piano player; I was still amazed at how much more skill she had than some people who'd been studying it for much longer.

"Birdieeee!" Cady dragged out the end of her nickname for me in unbridled joy. She was clearly very happy to see me today.

Smiling down at her I asked her, "What has you so excited today, my girl?"

"Well, it's Friday. And Daddy said I can have a sleepover tonight at Fiona's house. I have always wanted to go to one of her sleepovers, and she finally asked me. Daddy had to talk to her parents, though, to make sure everything was okay. He said it was, so tomorrow night I get to go to Fiona's sleepover. It's my first ever, Birdie!" It was like that child didn't even take a breath. Her excitement was contagious, and I giggled at her. A girl's first sleepover was a big deal. At least until it turned into a sleepover with a boy. And if I knew her father, that wasn't happening until she was married.

"Well, since you have so much to do, let's get started with your lesson, yeah?"

"Okay, Birdie," Cady said.

I slid off the piano bench so that Cady could slide on. Out in the front of the store, I could hear Jury clanking around, organizing, and rearranging stuff, so I walked to the door and closed it. The door handle sometimes locked on its own so I double-checked to make sure it hadn't gotten stuck before I walked to the chair in the corner. You could still hear noises from outside the room and in the main section of the store when the door was closed, but it did suppress it so that Cady could focus.

When I sat, Cady started her scales, which we always did to warm her up. As she made her way through the last one, every hair on my body stood on end, just like it had earlier that day. My stomach turned, and I got a bad feeling. My intuition told me that something was wrong outside the protection of the room River's daughter and I were currently in. My heart picked up speed. So much so, that I had to talk myself out of a panic attack.

Just as my heart rate and breathing evened out, I heard a crash, and it picked right back up again. Cady heard it, too, and stopped in the middle of the song she had moved onto after her scales and just gazed at the door with confusion. I waited for what felt like hours, but was only minutes, before I headed to the door. I tried turning the knob, but it didn't move. It was stuck. I held my ear to the door to try to see if I could decipher what the noise was out there.

That was when I heard *him* talking to Jury.

Mickey.

All I heard was Jury whimpering, and Mickey taunting her and asking her if she could handle him now. He was hitting her. I heard the unmistakable sound of bones crunching and cracking when a fist or foot connected with a body. I knew that sound like the back of my hand. *Shit.* Jury was tough, and there was no way she would have allowed him to get those kinds of hits in on her. Mickey must have bound her so she had no use of her arms and legs.

There was no more whimpering and everything had gone silent for what seemed like forever. I was shaking all over and tried my hardest to control it. Cady was with me, and I needed to make sure she didn't see that I was afraid. She needed to know everything would be okay. I walked over to her and knelt down by her side. I grabbed her beautiful face in my hands and held steady.

I told her, "Cady, baby, go hide behind the chair in the corner. Don't come out until I tell you to and don't make any noise, okay?"

"Birdie, I'm s . . . s . . . scared," Cady choked out, and tears started to fall down her cheeks.

"I know you are, baby girl. I promise everything will be okay. Just do as I said, yeah?"

"All right, Birdie," she said and ran to the corner where the chair was and tucked herself down low behind it. She was barely visible.

Once I knew she was calmer and not openly crying and sniffling, I walked back to the door and again put my ear up to it to see if I could hear anything.

That was when I smelled it.

Gasoline.

No, no, no. Shit. This can't be happening.

Bang! Bang! Bang!

"I know you're in there. Open the fucking door, Arianna," he snarled.

"I can't, Mickey," I lied.

"What do you mean you fucking can't?" he asked back

"I mean I can't. The door is stuck. Why do I smell gasoline, Mickey? Is everything okay out there?" I wanted to throw him off and at least try to convey to him that I wasn't freaking out. I had River's daughter. The little girl I'd grown to love and adore, with me. If something happened to her, I'd never forgive myself. Not ever.

"Don't you worry. We're going to get that asshole here so he can watch me get the fucking girl for a change."

"Mickey, Cady is in here with me. Please don't do anything that could hurt her." It came out as a plea.

"Fuck. Why is she here, Arianna? It's supposed to be just you and me." He was agitated, and it was evident that he wasn't prepared for Cady to be here. He should have known she would be. He knew why we brought the piano in.

"She has lessons with me every day. You knew that though, didn't you?" I asked, because I didn't know what the hell I was supposed to do here. I wanted to yell and curse and instigate but it wouldn't help the situation at all.

"I'm sorry, sweetheart. It has to be this way. I hadn't planned for the kid, but it won't matter. It'll just be another child you weren't able to save when all is said and done. Isn't that right, Ari?" The use of any endearment from him immediately caused bile to rise in my throat. But what caused that bile out and onto the floor next to where I stood at the door was the 'not being able to save another child' comment. It rocked me, and felt like Andrew hitting me all over again.

Cady started sobbing.

"Hush, baby. I'm okay. Nothing is going to happen to you. I promise," I calmly told her even though she just witnessed me getting sick. That sweet little girl just shook her head and kept on crying.

The realization dawned on her, and it was clear that Mickey was there to hurt me. And because she was doing the thing she loved, Cady was in danger of becoming an innocent casualty of whatever his infatuation was with me.

No. No. No.

The silence screamed.

It was the loudest when the fate of a child rested in your hands.

Then I heard the striking of the match.

"MICKEY, NO!" I screamed at the top of my lungs. Cady ran to me, screaming and crying harder than I had ever seen her do. She was terrified, and I couldn't blame her. The feeling was shared.

"Not a day goes by that I don't fantasize about having River Bradshaw's life. Always getting everything he wanted. Down to a second chance with a beautiful woman and having a family. I never got that second chance. He made it that way when he started dating Emma. Emma belonged to me. Did he tell you about Emma, Arianna?" he asked in a fairly sweet tone that totally contradicted the circumstances. I sighed some relief when I heard him blow out the match.

"Yes, Mickey. He told me about Emma. We don't have secrets."

Lie. I didn't tell River about the encounter with Mick earlier.

"Well, then you're dumber than you look. River knew Emma and I had something special. He had to have. He just swooped in and fucking took her from me. But no one knew that Emma was mine. Not even the almighty River. So now it's time to return the favor." He was manic now, and I was shocked that Emma had anything to do with Mickey, but everyone had a past. I'm proof of that.

"Mickey, please don't do this. If River didn't know Emma and you had a thing, how can you blame him?"

"Because instead of fucking asking me about the neighborhood lore, he chose to believe what everyone else said. Emma was the girl River was talking about at the cemetery. Emma was going to have my baby," he started. I could hear him pacing back and forth in front of the closed door, and he went on, "River was wrong though. I did make an attempt to right my wrongs with her. It was just that by the time I got to her house, two days after she told me she was pregnant, she had already had an abortion. Two fucking days. I waited too long, and it all went to shit from there. So you see, Arianna, River has not one fucking clue what happened, so he has no right to say dick about me or my past."

"Mickey," I whispered, and put my hand up to the door as if reaching out to him to comfort him. Tears ran down my face, and my heart ached for him. As crazy as it was, I knew what losing a child that you wanted did to you. Mickey let it bring him to the dark, and he stayed there. I found my way because of River and Cady.

"NO! It's too fucking late for your sweet whispers. I don't want your sympathy. You're just as bad as Emma. You didn't protect that baby you carried." He was back to being mean, and dammit if his words didn't hit me again like a punch to the gut.

"That's not fair. If you knew I was pregnant, then you know how I lost my baby. I tried everything in my power to protect my stomach from the abusive man I was with. The case is public record. It's all in the police report," I tried to explain, so he saw the difference.

"I know that, bitch. The Internet is a fabulous tool for information gathering. Now shut the fuck up." He was done with the small chitchat.

He lit another match. His footsteps stopped, and I heard him quietly say to no one in particular that he was sorry. Then, the bell over the door sounded, and I heard the whoosh of the flames igniting with so much force due to the gasoline he'd poured throughout the room.

I ran to Cady.

The crackles and pops of the spreading flames were louder than you could have imagined. Cady was shaking and crying, and I just hugged her tight to me and rocked her. Smoke had started to filter in under the door, and I knew our chances of making it out of there alive had just drastically decreased. Still rocking this precious little girl, I started to sing to her. Martina McBride's "In My Daughter's Eyes" was what came to me. I needed to be Cady's protector now.

There was no way to block the smoke from coming into the room. We didn't have towels or extra clothes that could have been put against the door to stop the flow. There were loud crashes in the main store area of items falling and, what I could only assume was, some of the structure starting to fall down.

BANG.

Time was running out quickly. Whatever came crashing down out there compromised the old wood of the door enough to split and crack the upper panel and smoke was now billowing in fast and furiously.

The noises caused me to jump with Cady in my arms, and I stopped singing. I felt her pulse speed up under my hand that was resting on her neck and cradling her into my chest. Her lip was quivering, and she looked up at me with terror in her beautiful blue-gray eyes. Cady needed assurance, and it was my job to give it to her. River dealt with fires every day with his job, and he would rescue us. Cady needed to know that, too.

"Shh, Princess. Your dad is going to come for us. He will get us out before anything happens. I just need you to be brave for me, yeah?"

"B . . . B . . . But we can't get out, Birr . . . Birr . . . Birdie," she sobbed.

"I know, baby girl. Daddy is on his way. Remember when you asked me to be your friend so I wasn't scared?" I asked her because I needed her to focus on something else.

"Yes."

"Well, remember that now and be the best friend you can be, and listen closely. Keep your eyes closed tight and," my voice broke with emotion and panic as I struggled but managed to rip a piece of my dress to hold over Cady's mouth to prevent her from inhaling, "hold this over your mouth and nose so you don't breathe in this bad stuff, okay?"

"Okay, Birdie."

My eyes couldn't see through the smoke now. The temperature had risen exponentially, and I was sweating profusely. Cady was still in my arms, but her breathing changed and was slower. The smoke was getting thicker and thicker. My eyes closed briefly until the door crashed in, and they opened again. The flames flicked into the room, and I could barely see the orange glow from them through the smoke. It was blacker, heavier, and completely suffocating.

Cady was still breathing, and that was what mattered the most at that point. The piece of my dress was acting as a filter, but the smoke was just too thick for it to work for very long. Her body and lungs were so tiny that there wasn't much time before that stopped working.

River would be here soon.

He had to be.

My breaths had gotten shallow. I heard Cady in my ear.

"Birdie, please don't leave me!"

Before I could tell her that I didn't want to leave her and that I was so sorry for not protecting her, another child in my care. I closed my eyes.

Chapter 20
My Girls
River

I sat at my desk way past the time I usually stayed in the evenings, to finish up some paperwork I had slacked on. I had just finished detailing the last call report I had to fill out when my radio chirped, and the control operator's somewhat disembodied voice came across with the call.

"Control to Carson Falls, Ladder 1, trucks two and three. We have reports of a 10-70 in progress at the southern section of the town square. Address given was building six Main Street. Requesting all available personnel and units on scene. Emergency and sheriffs' units have been notified for immediate response as well. 10-4."

Six Main Street. That was Thelma's store.

10-70. That was a structure fire.

I fell to my knees.

No, no, no. This could not be happening.

My girls.

Before I knew what was going on, everyone around me started moving. Garett Chandler, who was new to the firehouse but an excellent firefighter, came over to me.

"Don't worry, Chief. We'll get to them."

"Yeah," I said as he helped me up. He knew what that address was and who was there.

"There isn't any other option but getting to them," I told him.

Garett got on his radio and just said, "This is Firefighter Chandler to control."

"10-4. Go ahead, Firefighter Chandler."

"Carson Falls, Ladder 1, truck two, en route to 10-70 at building six Main Street. Please be advised there is possible in house. Battalion Chief's wife and daughter," he finished telling the control operator while I geared up. I didn't correct him about the wife part. She'd be my wife.

Unless she was dead.

"10-4," control said.

All geared up, we hopped on the back of the truck and took off. My stomach churned over and over again, and my heart pounded against my chest. Tears filled my eyes. The reality was that a structure fire in an old building like Thelma's store would be catastrophic. The beams were too old and the metal would never hold up, especially attached to adjoining businesses.

"They're going to be okay, Chief," Garett said in reassurance. I just tipped my chin up at him.

We turned the corner, and I saw Gifford's and some other surrounding town's fire trucks there already. They were hosing it, and it looked like the back end of the building, where the music room was, was not engulfed yet. Smoke, really thick, black smoke was seeping out from everywhere, but I knew that my girls were in the music room, so I directed Garett to pull the truck around the block so that we ended up at the back.

There were no flames that I could see, but the smoke was making it almost impossible to gauge if there was a safe entry point. Garett parked, and we both flew into action. Garett grabbed the ax, and I grabbed the sledgehammer. Nothing was going to stop me from saving my girls. And nothing was going to take my future away from me or my daughter again.

As the water from the hoses out front poured over the store, I started to hammer away at the weakest point of the wood, while Garett chopped through it. It didn't take long for it to crack enough to where we could make a decent enough sized hole to climb inside.

I knew better than to go rogue at a fire site, but I needed to get to my girls, no matter the rules I was breaking or the outcome. Fuck. I couldn't think like that. They were alive, and we'd all be fine. It couldn't be any other way. I couldn't lose them. My body was trembling, and I felt sick to my stomach. Instinct to follow protocol and to save my daughter and woman battled inside me, but instinct to save my family won out.

No one was going to stop me from going in through that hole to get the two most precious things in my life. Quickly, I removed my fire jacket so I could access the entry point easier than with it on. Carefully, I maneuvered my body through that fucking hole, while Garett called for the paramedics to be on standby. Just as I was about to clear the entrance we made, a beam came crashing down across my back and the nail sticking out from it scraped a path in its wake.

"FUCK!" I bit out. For me to have felt that through the adrenaline flooding through me, I knew that nail must have dug in deep.

"Chief, you all right?" Garett called back.

"I'm fine. Just a loose board." Like I said, nothing was going to stop me.

Inside the music room, visibility was nonexistent. There was a faint sound that I could barely make out in the distance. I tried to zero in on where it was coming from, but it was so low that I could only hear my own heart pounding in my chest. Guessing which way to head in from where we broke through the wall outside and knowing the room from being in it, I headed to the right. That was the way to the piano.

I heard the sound again but before I had a chance to chase it, there was a loud crash from a falling section of the ceiling, and I saw the glow of orange coming from the flames that were trying to invade the music room. Time was running out. I knew that. The smoke was too thick to keep inhaling. Even with my mask on, it was thick. The temperature was rising by the second. And the smell of gasoline told me that I needed to think, yet act fast because we were going to be engulfed very soon.

"Birdie, please. Wake up. Please don't leave me!" It was Cady's voice.

It sounded gritty and shallow. Every emotion I wanted to feel had to be tamped down so that we could get out alive. If I lost my shit, no one would get out of this.

"Cadence! Baby girl, it's Daddy!" My face gear was making it harder to scream for her.

"Daddy?!? Help, Daddy!" My princess tried so hard to scream, but her little body was being annihilated by smoke and heat. She was loud enough that I could follow her voice.

"I'm coming, baby girl. Keep talking so Daddy can find you."

"Birdie is sleeping. She left me all alone. I'm so scared, Daddy. She won't wake up. I tried," she kept talking. In between each sentence, she tried to breathe deeply, but it was a struggle.

"Is she near you, Cady?" I asked to keep her talking just a bit more, and so I knew if I needed to redirect myself after getting my daughter.

"She is. We hid behind the chair, Daddy. But she won't move," she told me. She was crying, and it was breaking my heart. I knew Arianna was in trouble, and if I didn't get her out of there fast, my world would come crumbling down.

Just as I went to ask Cady if she was still with me, my leg banged into what could only be the chair, and I knew I had made it to them. I grabbed the chair without thinking of telling my girl that I was going to move it and tossed it to the left, which I knew was not in her or Arianna's direction. I grabbed Cady and pulled her to me tight. She screamed out.

"It's me, baby girl. I got you. I'm gonna get you and Birdie out of here, okay?" I said as I held on for just a few seconds.

"Okay, Cadence. I'm going to put you down so I can carry Arianna out with us. I need you to listen to exactly what I say, yeah?"

"Yes, Daddy. Hurry. I don't like it in here, and this smoke tastes yucky," she told me. My daughter. So brave.

"All right. I'm going to need you to walk out, but I have to go in front so I can keep the way clear. Hang on to Daddy's work pants as tight as you can when I place your hand there. Once I have Birdie, we'll walk toward the hole I made. Then Daddy's work friends are going to get you safe, okay?"

"Okay, Daddy."

I put her down and grabbed her little hand. She was holding on to something that felt like a handkerchief. We didn't have time to get into what it was so I just put her hand on the back of my leg and bunched my fire pants up so she could grab there and hang on.

"No matter what, don't let go, baby girl," I told her.

"Okay," she answered back.

I felt her grip get tighter, and I made my move to get Bird. Bending down, I had to use my hands to feel my way down to where she had lost consciousness on the floor. Getting my hands under her body to scoop her up in a bridal hold was a challenge. There were flames starting to overtake the room by the door. This was the only chance we had, so I got my hands in position and raised her up to my chest. Once I had my hold on her, and I felt Cady still hanging on to me, I started walking us back the way I had come in, toward the hole.

Weaving around pieces of what once was the music room in the back of Thelma's store, we approached our only exit. My mouth opened to call out to Garett so I could pass off Arianna to him and then grab Cady when what must have been the piano succumbed to the flames. And that meant the fire was closing in on us. I needed to get my girls out of here.

"Garett! I need you, man. Come over to the opening," I commanded.

"I'm here, Chief." He'd been waiting for me.

"I'm gonna pass Arianna through the opening. Get her to an ambulance immediately. She lost consciousness. And Garett?"

"Yeah, River?" he questioned back.

"Tell the paramedic that she may be pregnant."

"Shit. Pass her through." We both leaned into each other for the transfer, and when I knew he had a good hold on her, I moved my arms back. Then I turned and picked up Cady.

"Almost out, Cadence," I reassured her, and made my way through the hole with my daughter cradled tightly to me.

I saw tons of people everywhere once I was able clear the smoke coming out toward us. I saw Garett running with Ari to the stretcher. He hadn't gotten there yet, so I ran his way to catch the paramedics. I took the oxygen tank and mask from one of the paramedics not working on

Arianna, and held it on Cady's mouth and nose, but kept moving toward the stretcher Ari lay on. As I glanced left, I saw Penny and Braxton, but no Jury or Rhett. Penny was standing watching with her arms hugging her middle, Braxton's arm around her. When she saw me, she took off in my direction.

I skipped the pleasantries. Not to be a dick, but because my daughter and my woman needed to get to the hospital.

"No time, Penny. Meet us at the hospital. Have Braxton take you," I said harshly, but we needed to get a move on.

I turned just as they were strapping Bird to the gurney. As they lifted her, I climbed in the back of the ambulance transporting Arianna, with Cady still in my arms, and told them right before they shut the doors, "We need to go. If she's pregnant, we've already lost a shit-ton of time."

I looked back through the window and saw Penelope's eyes get big as the shock of what she had just overheard settled in. Braxton guided her away and moved toward his truck. The town was small, so it wasn't surprising that Penny and Braxton had heard what had been happening and came over. But where were Jury and Rhett?

The paramedics tried to explain the possibility of Arianna having carbon monoxide and cyanide poisoning due to severe smoke inhalation. She was still unconscious and the longer she stayed that way, the lower the chances of survival for a baby. There was not much they could do besides give her oxygen in the ambulance, and we would just have to wait until a doctor gave a definitive answer.

Like a rocket, we shot away from the burning store, toward the hospital. My heart cracked a little bit more as each sound from the sirens blasted into the air. I looked down at my daughter and saw she still was holding on to some type of fabric. It wasn't a handkerchief as I first thought.

"What's that in your hand, baby girl?" I moved the mask away so she could answer me.

"Birdie ripped her pretty dress so that I could hold this over my face when the smoke started coming after us," she told me. I put the mask back on her.

Even in the chaos, Arianna put my daughter's safety at the forefront.

Protecting her the only way she could in that type of situation. My chest tightened, thinking about what my daughter said, and what she must have seen and felt inside that inferno. The tightness almost suffocated me when I thought about the fact that Arianna could be carrying our child. I know she didn't quite understand, but Cady and I could lose them both.

When we finally arrived at the hospital, the ambulance backed into the emergency bay, the doors flung open, and everything else happened so fast, it was a blur. Nurses and doctors swarmed us as I tried to get out of the rig, and a woman nurse yanked Cady from my arms and carried her into the hospital to a room already prepped for our arrival.

Not wanting to leave Arianna as they wheeled her into an exam room to determine her injuries, I didn't have a choice. My daughter needed me. When anyone ever said the expression about their heart being torn in two when they had a child, I never really understood that. Now, not only was it understood, it was what my nightmares would consist of. That feeling of complete helplessness for someone you loved was not something I wished upon anyone.

It felt like we had been in this room forever without a word about Arianna. Cady was doing so much better. The oxygen was helping her. That piece of dress more than likely saved her life.

"Sir, the back of your shirt is covered in blood. We're going to have to take a look at your back. We can examine it in here, so you don't have to leave your daughter," Nurse Layla, according to her name tag, said.

"The woman brought in with me, are there any updates on her? She was possibly pregnant with my baby," my voice was gruff with held back emotion when I asked her. I needed to stay composed. There were too many people counting on me to lose my shit right then.

"I'm not sure right now, but let's get your back checked out and cleaned up, then we'll see what we can do about getting you an update, all right?" Nurse Layla calmly bargained with me. The other nurse, Pam, who had finished taking Cady's vitals, didn't seem at all concerned about any serious effects from the smoke.

"Sweetheart, how are you feeling?" Nurse Pam asked Cadence as she removed the oxygen mask and hit the button on the reclined hospital bed to bring it up to a sitting position.

"I feel fine," she answered Pam then turned to me. "Can we go get Birdie now and go home?"

"Baby girl, we can't leave just yet."

"Your back is fine. Just seems to be surface lacerations," Nurse Layla informed me.

The curtain shielding us in the exam room was thrown open, and Penelope was there with Braxton. Penny flew in and wrapped Cady in the biggest hug. Braxton walked to me and clasped me on the shoulder. Low, so Penny wouldn't hear, he asked, "Any word on Arianna yet?"

Just as low I replied, "No. No one knows anything yet. Man, I need to know. It absolutely killed me to have to leave her."

"River, don't do that to yourself, man. Your daughter needed you. Penny and I will go see what we can find out."

"Thanks, Jenks."

"It'd be the same," he said on a squeeze of my shoulder. I knew what he meant, and it was the truth. I would do the same for him because he was a brother. Not of blood, but one all the same.

Cady and I had both been cleared. The doctor that came in to check her about ten minutes after Penny and Braxton had left, and the nurses that had finished up said, considering the firsthand reports of the fire, we were very lucky. But no one said a word about Arianna.

Discharge papers in one hand, Cady's hand in my other, we walked toward the waiting room. Rhett was there sitting with his head aimed at the floor, his hands hanging over his knees. He looked up as we approached. Cady let go of my hand and raced over to Penny. Penny scooped her up and sat with her, rocking and twirling the hair of one of her pigtails. Before I could make it to Rhett to find out why he looked like he'd been in a street fight, Braxton stopped me with a hand to my bicep. Our eyes met, he shook his head no, then motioned with his chin to go outside.

"Pen, you good to hang with Cady?"

"Go. She'll be fine. Do what you need to do. We aren't leaving until we know Arianna is okay," she said softly.

"Thanks, Penelope," I told her as I patted her head, so she knew I appreciated her staying with my girl.

Then I bent and kissed my daughter's cheek and told her there, "I love you, my sweet Cadence. I'll be back."

"I love you too, Daddy," she said. The sweetest words ever spoken to me.

Then Braxton and I headed to the other side of the waiting room, away from everyone.

"Look, we got word on Arianna. She was still unconscious, and they were treating her for mild carbon monoxide poisoning. There was no cyanide poisoning, which is good news. They said they needed to give her oxygen treatments because of hypoxia, or the lack of oxygen due to the fire consuming it. They ordered tests, including a mandatory pregnancy blood test, to be sure," Braxton explained.

There was no way to communicate what I felt inside. How the hell had this all happened? I needed answers. But I needed to get to Arianna more.

"They aren't allowing anyone up to see her yet. And the only reason we got this information was because Penny said she was Ari's sister. They said a doctor would come out to get us when we're allowed to go up. But River, there's more. And you need to hear this," Braxton said in a tone that told me he was serious.

"Tell me everything. Give it all to me because I need to have my shit together when I get into that room with my Bird."

"Rhett saw Mickey leave the store from across the street. The bastard is in love with his wife and was buying her flowers. But Mickey didn't leave the store alone. He had Jury with him. Mickey had assaulted her, and she was out cold. Mickey dropped Jury to the ground and took off. Rhett got him quickly. They wrestled around a bit, and Mickey got some hits in, but I think Rhett did that on purpose. Rhett had to be pulled off him by four men that ran over to them. But Jury is here too, River. Mickey broke two of her ribs, her arm when he dropped her, dislocated her jaw that had to be wired shut to correct, and gave her a black eye," Brax told me.

"Is Jury going to be okay?"

"Yes. She had the oral surgeon wire her mouth already, and she'll be here a few days, but she'll make a full recovery."

"And you're sure they got Mickey?"

"I am. I saw Gaynor put him in the back of the car myself," Braxton reassured me. I took in and released a deep breath. So many lives uprooted by one crazy motherfucker. The sheriff better charge his ass with every possible thing. From stalking to attempted murder.

Braxton also told me Rhett had been there for a while. It took two paramedics and three doctors to hold him back from entering the room where they evaluated Jury. He wanted to be with his wife, and I didn't blame him. Rhett was an intense guy where Jury was concerned. Even when we spoke on the phone while he was still in Seattle, it was obvious he wanted to do everything in his power to keep her safe. Mickey was lucky he was in jail. If Rhett had his way, he'd go back out after him.

Braxton and I made our way back to where the rest of our group was waiting. I took a seat on one side of Penny and a sleeping Cadence. My daughter was one of the bravest little girls in the world. The piece of Arianna's dress was still in Cady's hand, and she had it resting against her face near her eye, while she sucked on her thumb. It didn't matter what anyone else said. I was inside that fucking building while the fire raged. It was a miracle no one was dead. *Well, that we knew of.* Braxton sat on the other side of her and stretched his arm out behind Penny.

He didn't know it, but I saw him take a lock of her hair and twirl it.

"River. River, wake up, man." I felt my body being shaken and heard my name. I blinked my eyes open and lifted my head off the back of the most uncomfortable waiting room chair. You'd think since so much time was spent waiting, they would allow you to do so comfortably. Not on these old blue, thinly-cushioned, metal torture devices.

"I'm up," I said to whoever had woken me and saw the doctor standing near the nurses' station.

"The doctor is here, River." That was Penny.

I jumped up and went to him.

"Are you River Bradshaw?" the doctor asked.

"Yes, sir, I am."

"Please come with me," was all that he said.

I followed him around the corner and through the gray double doors that led into the examination area. We walked straight through to an elevator. We got on when the doors opened, we heard the ding, and the doctor pushed the button that took us to the eleventh floor. There were some people already on board, but they made room for us. As I watched the numbers of the floors get higher, all I could think about was Arianna. How scared she must have been in that fire. But worse, how scared she must be right now. *If she's awake.*

That was the longest ride I had ever taken in an elevator.

When we got to the eleventh floor, the elevator pinged and the doors opened. I waited for the doctor, whose name I still didn't know, to guide me off the elevator after the other staff and visitors got off. The hallway before us was your typical hospital hallway; long, white, and had that sterile hospital aroma to it. The rooms along the way all had the same look to them with the exception of the patients inside them. The doors were all the same, light wooden brown with a spot for charts on each one. Each door I passed that was open, I saw folks crying over injured or sick family members, families praying, and even some enjoying laughs together.

We had made it to the end of the hallway and stopped at the door that held my answers. The doctor began to speak.

"River, my name is Dr. Crane. I wanted to get you up here before I told you anything, so we had some privacy. Arianna is under my care. We treated her for smoke inhalation, resulting in mild carbon monoxide poisoning. We needed to use hyperbaric treatments to increase the amount of oxygen dissolved in the blood since she lost so much in the fire, as well as keep her on oxygen. I ordered some blood tests, which always includes a pregnancy test when a female patient is admitted through emergency, to rule out any other issues. We understand that it was unknown if she was pregnant or not. Is that correct?"

"Yes, it is. She told me she made an appointment to get checked because she had been sick on and off for a while. She was supposed to go this coming Wednesday," I answered him.

He replied back, "Well, there won't be a need for that appointment any longer."

Chapter 21
Our Family
Arianna

My chest hurt, and it was crazy hard to take deep breaths. There was oxygen being administered to me through my nose in a steady flow. I felt like an eighteen-wheeler had parked on my chest after running over my head. My hospital gown was hanging down low on my chest, exposing all those circular EKG leads stuck to me, and there was some sort of meter on my finger monitoring what I could only assume were my oxygen levels.

My eyes were closed when the door opened, and I heard two sets of footsteps approach my bed. I wasn't exactly thrilled to have to see River right now. There was a little girl that I failed to protect. The nurses told me she was fine, but the words I heard right before I went out, keep replaying in my head over and over again. My failures almost cost him his daughter. And now, he was here to tell me that when I got out of here, we were done, and he was sending me on my way. I just knew it.

So with that heartbreak settling inside my already heavy chest, I kept my eyes closed as River pulled the chair up to the side of my bed. I kept them closed as he grabbed my hand in his and ran his thumb across my knuckles to soothe me. And I kept my eyes closed as he whispered his nickname for me with such warmth and gentleness, begging me to open them and look at him. The last thing I wanted was to lose these two incredible people, but I knew if I opened my eyes and looked at him, he was going to see failure.

"Bird, Dr. Crane told me you woke up. I know you can hear me. Please look at me," he begged. I shook my head and turned away from River.

"Her throat might still be hoarse from everything. She can have water to try to help with that, but she should rest her voice," the doctor chimed in.

River grabbed my chin with his thumb and forefinger and brought my head back to him, and his lips whispered across mine briefly as he rested his forehead on mine.

"God, Arianna. I never thought I'd be able to kiss those lips again," he spoke against my mouth.

"River, I…" I trailed off. My emotions overcame me, and I started to sob.

"Don't cry, Bird. Everything is all right, and everyone is going to be fine. We need to talk to the doctor, baby. You have to calm down," he said.

Why did *we* need to talk to the doctor?

I agreed and saw Dr. Crane step forward and grab my chart from the end of the bed, while I elevated it to sit upright. I held River's hand tighter as the doctor flipped through some of the paperwork, until he found what he was looking for.

"Ah. Here we go. All right, Arianna. River and I spoke briefly before we came in here. He told me you've been feeling sick on and off for a while now. Is this true?" he asked me, and I shook my head yes.

"And you were supposed to go to an appointment to find out what was going on this coming week?"

Again, I shook my head yes.

"Well, you won't need to keep that appointment. As you know, we had to run some tests when you arrived, as standard protocol. The state of Tennessee requires mandatory pregnancy tests to be included in that blood work. Ms. Morgan, Mr. Bradshaw, it seems congratulations are in order. You're going to be parents," the doctor finished.

Did he just say what I think he said?

I croaked out, "Come again?"

"We believe you're anywhere from six to eight weeks along, but we'll need to see an image of the fetus to know for sure. I wanted to have you both present to tell you the news. But also, we need to get that ultrasound done. Due to the reason you were brought in, and the amount of oxygen you lost, we'd like to take you up now. We have the technician on standby. River, you can accompany Arianna, if you like," he said. This was all too much. He had to be mistaken.

"I wouldn't have it any other way," River said softly. I looked at him, and he was watching me, a small smile playing on his lips. Shocked at how calm he was being, I looked at Dr. Crane and agreed to the ultrasound.

About five minutes later, with River by my side, we went for an ultrasound to see how far along in my pregnancy I was.

We were waiting in the hallway to be brought back to the ultrasound room. There was someone in there who was finishing setting up the machines. River was still holding my hand. I felt his eyes on me, but the surprise of this took over, and my mind wandered.

Me. Pregnant. I just almost lost Cadence. There was no way we were all ready for a baby. How did I not even think that all that was going on with me was because I was pregnant?

Because your life has been a whirlwind and you didn't think you'd ever get a second chance to carry a baby.

Just as I thought that, River squeezed my hand and said, "Don't even think it, Bird. If it wasn't for you and your quick thinking, Cady might have suffered major injuries or worse, not have made it altogether."

"What?" I croaked in complete astonishment.

"We'll talk about it later. Let's make sure this," he placed his big hand on my belly and finished, "little one is okay. I'm sure Cady wants to see you. After we get done, and you're back in the room, I'll go down and get her. I want my girls with me."

I nodded in agreement.

Then, we were whisked into the room to check on our baby.

Our baby.

Our family.

It wasn't clear if I was dreaming or not at that point, but there was no way I wanted to wake up.

Cady

Two days later…

Daddy and Birdie talked to me a bunch over the last two days. They told me I was going to be a big sister, and I was so happy. I wanted a little sister so we could play dolls. But then Daddy and Birdie told me there were two babies in Birdie's belly. So I told them I wanted a brother and a sister. One of each so we could be best friends. It was going to be so much fun, and I might even let Bryce be in the best friend group with us. As long as Daddy wasn't mad at him anymore for talking about boobs.

It was always just me and Daddy, but now it was going to be *our family.*

We also talked about Birdie saving me. She didn't think she did because she couldn't wake up and left me alone, but she put me behind the chair and ripped her pretty dress for me. My dad said we just had to keep telling her that she was silly and that the truth hurts. I don't know what the truth hurting had to do with it, or even what that means, so I just kept telling Birdie I'm her best friend, she did save me, and that I loved her.

I kept that piece of her dress because it made me feel better. Birdie and Daddy let me sleep with it, so I don't think about that day, but sometimes I do. Jury was still in the hospital and Uncle Rhett was there every day with her. When I think about that, I think about what happened. The good news about that was, though, Jury was getting out of the hospital tomorrow. Uncle Rhett was going to bring her to our house so we can visit. They weren't staying long because Jury needed to get home and rest, but it made me happy that I was going to see her.

Daddy and I were on our way to pick up the present we'd gotten Birdie. It was the last thing we talked about, but it was just him and me.

Birdie couldn't know about this. I helped Daddy pick it out, and he said I would be a big help when he gave it to her tonight at the fair. Birdie was feeling much better so we were all going, and it was going to be so much fun.

River

Later that evening...

I kept thinking about what I had up my sleeve. Cady was in on the secret, and after all that had happened, I wanted this more than anything in this world. We were going back to the one place that held every single pivotal moment in our relationship, so it was fitting that it happened there. But more, it was everything to have both my girls with me. I just hoped this worked.

Our family.

We sure were in for the ride of our lives. It was difficult taking care of Cadence when she was a baby, but now everything would be times two. The biggest difference this time around was that the woman giving me those babies was the strongest woman I knew, and would stick with it no matter how hard it got. We had each other, and we'd make it work.

As we pulled into the firehouse lot, I looked over at Arianna. She was turned to the back seat talking girly stuff with Cady. Like I said, I didn't know about glitter, dresses, or anything else considered "girl territory," as Bird called it. I smiled at their back and forth banter and the excitement in both their voices. Arianna was slowly coming around to the fact that she saved Cady and hadn't failed her. She'd get there. It had only been two days.

I didn't interrupt their discussion to let them know we had arrived. Instead, I thought about two days ago. But the good parts, not the bad ones.

Arianna and I held each other tightly when the ultrasound technician showed us the screen with the two babies. When we heard Baby A's heartbeat, then Baby B's, the noise that filled the room brought tears to my eyes. Memories of Cady's flooded my mind. Each baby had a strong heartbeat. This made Ari sob into my neck and repeat over and over,

"Thank you. Thank you. Thank you."

Ari stayed overnight for observation. Dr. Crane was amazed and very pleased that she had bounced back so fast and let her go the next morning. Her throat was still a bit scratchy, and her voice was still a tiny bit hoarse, but other than that, you'd never know she'd been trapped inside a burning building only two days ago.

"River, sweetheart. Are you okay?" Bird's voice pulled me back to the moment.

"I'm good, Darlin'. Promise. Are we ready to do this?" I asked my girls.

"YES!" they both shouted their excitement at me.

"Then let's go!" I said as we all piled out of my truck, and headed to the fair.

Arianna
Thirty minutes later...

River was up to something. We'd been around each other enough for me to pick up on it. Cady and I were enjoying ourselves and were perusing the fair games when he grabbed us both by our hands and basically dragged us to the Ferris wheel. He said we were going to miss the sun setting and everyone knew sunset was best experienced at the top.

I felt like I was being stared at. It was uncomfortable, but I dealt with it for Cady's sake. The line wasn't long, but there were some folks watching and whispering. News of what happened and Mickey's involvement had been spread countywide.

The police report was public record now so everyone knew about Emma and Mickey. What Mickey shared with me in Thelma's store about the whole thing was explained to River when Sheriff Gaynor stopped by the hospital room that night to check on Cady, River, Jury, and me. The sheriff needed to ask River some questions, then told him how Mickey admitted to everything and explained why he did what he did.

River's eyes seemed haunted as he listened to the story being rehashed. When everything was said and done, River looked at me and said, "When Emma told me she was pregnant, her eyes flashed with something that I knew was wrong and should have been a red flag. Now, I know what she had been going through and feeling was hurt, regret, and fear. And it had absolutely nothing to do with my daughter or me. Her demons were her own. I stopped trying to slay them a long time ago because she didn't want them to die. Not my burden to bear anymore."

Cady pulled me out of my head when she tugged my dress so we could board the red gondola. Once inside with the door closed, Cady sat across from her dad and me. She was turned around watching the scenery as we started to go around and head to the top. Her excitement was always contagious, and in that moment, it was no exception.

"Bird. Look at me," River said, and I looked at him. I waited for him to say something else but he just stared at me. My heart picked up at the warmth, desire, and love directed my way. After a few more seconds, I smiled his smile at him. His lips tipped up, and he leaned in to kiss me. That kiss was hard, wet, and it made me feel like my world was yet again altered.

"Stop it, Daddy. It's time," Cady said strangely, as we pulled apart and the Ferris wheel stopped at the top, The Falls in clear view below.

"Okay, baby girl. You ready?" River asked her, and I looked toward Cady. She scooted to the edge of her seat, leaned left, and reached into her right pocket for something. Whatever it was she had it in her fist when she pulled her hand out. Then she stood before her dad and me.

"Birdie?" she asked.

"Yes, Princess?" I answered her, and she opened her fist to me. In it was the most beautiful, antique, emerald cut engagement ring with smaller square diamonds circling the entire band. My mouth dropped open, and my eyes welled up with tears.

"Daddy loves you, I love you, and the babies love you. We know you love us because you say it a lot. But will you marry us? Will you be my mommy for real and be Daddy's wife?"

My heart melted, and I was now crying like a maniac. I grabbed Cady and hugged her to me. I whispered in her ear through my sobs, "I would love nothing more than to be your mom, Princess. I love you so much."

"YAY! But wait. Do you want to be Daddy's wife, too?" she asked, confused.

"Yes, Arianna Morgan. Will you be my wife?" I heard River from beside me. He was on his knee with the ring, holding it out to me. I laughed a nervous laugh and held my face in my hands, sobbing harder.

"I'm going to need an answer, Bird," he demanded as he pulled my hands away from my face.

"Yes! Yes, of course, I'll be your wife," I told him.

"You had this planned, didn't you?" I asked him.

"Arianna, this was my plan since the first time I saw you. It didn't matter to me why you were brought here, just that you were. So, yes. You could definitely say that I had this planned."

"I've belonged to the two of you since that day in the square, haven't I?" I asked.

"Pretty much. You're stuck with us now since you said yes. Right, baby girl?" he asked Cady.

"YES, DADDY!" our daughter shouted excitedly.

Our daughter.

"That's right," River started, slid the ring on my finger, then finished, "and we'll all have the same last name in *our family.*"

River held me against him in the seat on one side and Cady on the other, arms around us both tight, once we started moving again. I sighed and stared at my ring, thinking about where I was when I arrived in Carson Falls and where I was at now.

This Ferris wheel was so much more than a ride at a fair to me. It's like River's love for me. It made me get past the fear of my past and really enjoy the view of what was right in front of me.

Epilogue

Arianna

Three and a half months later…

"Oh, you've got to be kidding me. Seriously, Penny? At my wedding reception?" I asked my maid of honor and best friend as she straightened her strapless, floor-length, bridesmaid dress as she walked out of the men's bathroom.

"What? I wasn't the one that got married. Hot, slutty, wedding sex is my given right. Besides, I have no attachments and no one to answer to," Penny said.

"You are such a pain in my ass, Penelope Sloane." I turned and stormed off toward my husband, who was waiting for me in the banquet hall. Just as I grabbed the handle to the large, stained wood door, I heard Penny say, "It doesn't mean shit, Braxton. You were a means to an end. Sound familiar?" as she walked away on her stilettos.

Braxton growled out in frustration, "We'll see about that."

You'd think that me being pregnant with twins, and it being my wedding day and all, I wouldn't have to deal with the fact that these two idiots still hadn't figured out their issues, but I did. And of course, they would be the two to get caught having sex. I didn't want to deal with this. All I wanted was to dance with my husband and eat some damn wedding cake.

Penny had had her eye on Garett Chandler, River's firefighter friend, for weeks now. I don't understand why she wound up bringing him as her date if she was just going to go off and have sex with Braxton. Garett was a good guy and would be really good for Penny, but she was playing games. I knew she was hurt by Braxton when he did what he did months ago when Miss Thelma passed, but collateral damage, just to get back at someone, was never okay in my book.

Whatever. I'd deal with my best friend another day. It was time for cake and my surprise for my husband.

My wedding was everything I had ever hoped it would be. Small and intimate with the people I loved the most surrounding me. Penny and Jury were my maid and matron of honor, respectively, while Cadence doubled as flower girl and what she called 'my best girl.' It made sense to her, and I wanted her up there with me, so it worked.

My dress was every bit the princess gown, thanks to my daughter. It was custom-made due to my ever-growing midsection, and complete perfection. It had a strapless, sweetheart neckline embellished with pearls that went to an empire waist, with a satin, floor-length, ball gown skirt, and a three-foot train. My silk tulle veil was chapel-length and edged with satin piping. It was gorgeous, and I wore it with a tiara made of pearls and sparkling rhinestones.

River stood up with Braxton and Rhett by his side. Every single one of them looked like they walked off a wedding magazine shoot. Each was dressed in a classic black tuxedo and cowboy boots. Apparently, in Tennessee, you wore cowboy boots with tuxedos. I didn't care, as long as River had something that made him stand out from Rhett and Braxton. While Rhett and Braxton had the classic black bowties, River went with a deep teal color to match the colors we went with for the girls' dresses. Again, it was perfection.

Now River and I were on the dance floor dancing to our wedding song, "Amazed" by Lonestar, after we cut our three-tiered, vanilla and buttercream cake. Each tier of the cake was white fondant with edible silver pearls placed where each layer met the next. And cascading down and around from the top, were flowers alternating in teal and white. We opted to replace the couple on top with the word love because this day was filled with so much of it.

As the next song, "I Won't Let Go" by Rascal Flatts began; we stayed in our spot on the dance floor. I had my hands wrapped around my husband's neck, and he held me close with his hands around my waist. I sang a bit of the song in his ear, and it was time to give him his surprise.

I knew it didn't matter to him as long as everyone was happy and healthy but he had mentioned a son a time or two.

"River?" I asked him.

"Yeah, Darlin'?" he answered.

"I want to give you your wedding gift now."

"You didn't need to do that. You and our family is gift enough."

"Well, it has something to do with that," I told him, and grabbed his hand and walked him over to our table. I had Penny bring in the envelopes and leave them on my seat when we went to dance.

"Here," I handed it to him. He undid the clasps and took out the images.

The first picture was Baby A. Or our daughter.

The second picture was Baby B. Or our son.

We were having one of each.

Tears welled in his eyes, and he looked up from the pictures at me and said, "A baby boy and another baby girl. Do you have any idea how happy you've made me?"

"I think probably about as happy as you've made me," I said, as I wrapped my arms around him and went in to kiss him. The kiss started sweet, with just closed mouths. Then River's tongue slid along mine, I opened to him, and we started making out like teenagers. I didn't want to, but I pulled away from him because my surprise wasn't done. There were still two more things.

"I'm not done with your gift, honey. Turn the pictures over. You said as long as the three of us were happy and healthy you didn't care what we had. But during that conversation we had that day, you also told me I could name them," I explained.

Then I watched him flip over the picture of our daughter or Baby A.

Lyric Bradshaw.

The smile that graced his face told me it was perfect.

And then the picture of our son or Baby B.

Ryland Bradshaw.

The smile got huge.

He didn't say anything. So I did, after I handed him the second envelope.

"Inside this one, is the final step to completing our family. We all have the same name, and now, I legally have three children. In my heart, I've been Cadence's mom since everything started with us, but now, it's on paper. Thank you for allowing me to adopt her."

"Fuck me," he replied. He didn't know what to say. Which was fine because I didn't need him to say anything else. I did need him to kiss me.

"Kiss me, River."

"Gladly," he said, and we were once again making out.

There was a crash that caused us both to jump, and we looked in the direction it came from.

"Keep your fucking hands off of her, asshole!" Braxton growled out at Garett as he lay on the ground, holding the side of his face where Braxton had just punched him.

River and I looked at each other; he let me go and ran over to where Rhett was holding Braxton back. I followed and stood next to Jury, who had made her way over, too. River helped Garett up.

"What the fuck happened, Braxton?"

"Your fire buddy had his filthy hands on Penelope," he said, chest heaving.

"They were dancing, dickhead," Rhett said.

"Yeah, and his hands were on her," Braxton explained.

"That usually happens when people dance, brother," River said.

"Okay. So answer me this, if Ari or Jury were dancing with another man, when you knew you had just been inside her not thirty fucking minutes ago, would you allow another man to dance and touch either of them?"

Rhett and River both said, "Fuck no."

Jury looked at Rhett and said, "Go to hell, Rhett. You lost that right a long time ago," then stormed off.

Penny walked up to Braxton, slapped him across the face then she stormed off.

I kept saying to myself that I loved all these crazy people over and over, so I didn't lose my mind. It didn't work.

"Y'all are a pain in my ass!" I shouted. I couldn't handle this and went to my seat. It was my wedding for crying out loud. I shouldn't be dealing with this bullshit. I had enough to worry about in the months to come, with having to head back to Seattle for Andrew's trial. Today should have been about moving forward and love, not drama.

I ate more cake, and that helped a bit. Cady had seen the drama and came to sit next to me.

"Momma Birdie, it'll be okay. Uncle Rhett and Uncle Braxton will make it better."

Momma Birdie is what Cady decided to call me, and if I was honest, it was also perfect. She always made things seem so simple and easy.

"They better, Princess. It's time everyone found their happiness and grew up," I said.

"I agree. If everyone were happy like us, they wouldn't fight. They need to love each other," Cady, my now six-year-old, said.

"Sweetheart, you are so right," I replied.

So, while my husband stood in the middle of the dance floor at our wedding reception, trying to talk his friends down from going after the women that stormed off, I sat with my daughter, ate cake, and thought about how a six-year-old knew more than all of my adult friends.

I wouldn't have had it any other way.

It was heaven on earth.

No, that isn't right.

It was a place far beyond whatever heaven was.

THE END

ABOUT THE AUTHOR

Paisleigh Aumack was born in Red Bank, New Jersey. She grew up in a small barrier island town and has lived there all her life. She has always loved music, going as far as being a trained musician. Her tastes in music range all over the board, but currently, her heart belongs to country music.

Paisleigh is engaged to the love of her life and lives a fairly quiet, peaceful existence. When she isn't working, she is writing or she is reading. Or singing at the top of her lungs. Paisleigh began writing a short time ago because she had a story to tell

You can reach Paisleigh at:

www.authorpaisleighaumack.com

Made in the USA
Middletown, DE
04 September 2017